# Wastralls
## A Novel

*by*

C. A. Dawson-Scott

Double 9
BOOKS

**Wastralls**
**A Novel**
**by C. A. Dawson-Scott**

Copyright © 2024

All Rights reserved.

ISBN: 978-93-58595-08-6

Published by

**DOUBLE 9 BOOKS**
2/13-B, Ansari Road
Daryaganj, New Delhi – 110002
info@double9books.com
www.double9books.com
Tel. 011-40042856

This book is under public domain

# ABOUT THE AUTHOR

Catherine Amy Dawson Scott (1865-1934) was a British writer, playwright, and poet. She gained recognition as a co-founder of International PEN, a global association of writers, and played a significant role in promoting literature and defending its place in society. Born in England, she began her writing career while working as a secretary. Dawson Scott published several novels and poetry collections, often under pen names. She was known for her diverse literary output, tackling various genres and themes, including romance, mystery, and social commentary. During World War I, she created the Women's Defence Relief Corps to support the war effort and provide opportunities for women. After the war, she founded the To-Morrow Club, a gathering of aspiring writers mentored by established authors. This club eventually evolved into the International PEN Club. Dawson Scott's literary contributions and her efforts to foster a community of writers continue to be celebrated. She left a lasting impact on the literary landscape of her time.

# CONTENTS

# CHAPTER I

Trevorrick River was but a little stream to have fretted so deep a cleft between the hills as that which sloped from the main road of Tregols parish to the sea. From the source to the engulfing sands was barely a mile, and the twinkling waters, if full and fierce in winter, showed a summer fear of their own broad stepping-stones. Nevertheless the sharp declivities, the juttings of rock, even the shelves and crags and walls of Dark Head, had been formed by the gnawing of this tiny but persistent flow.

The valley ran east and west. The sun, rising beyond St. Cadic Mill, poured its noon warmth over Hember and sank behind the sheltered plateau on which stood the old home of the Rosevears. The dying beams, however, could not reach the deep-set windows of Wastralls, for the crest of Dark Head reared itself between the farmstead and the harsh threat of the Atlantic. The house lay in a fold of land, hidden equally from those who moved upon the face of the waters, and those who might be said, though their habitations were at a distance, to neighbour it. As a refuge in troublous times, the position had its value, and there were indications that this shelf of rock had been, many centuries ago, the nest of some wild brood.

Upon their heels had followed as descendants or conquerors—the script is too nearly obliterated to be read—men who in their own strong person represented the law. The gate-posts of Wastralls were crowned with the egg-shaped stones which indicated that it was a manor-house, and that its owner had the right to dispense justice. Within the house, and occupying a space from wall to wall, was the ancient Justice Room; but its stately uses had long been abated, its irrevocable decisions had lost their force, in the autumn of its days it had become a lumber-room and more lately a bedchamber.

A century ago, from the mill at the head of the valley to the Wreckers' Hut on the foreshore, Trevorrick had been the property of one man. Of peasant stock, how Freathy Rosevear came by land and money was matter of surmise. 'He had gone out one morning a poor man, and had come home rich.' Little need, however, to invent tales of hidden treasure, witchcraft, divination, when the caves in Morwen Cove made so safe a store-house: when the Wreckers' Hut stood behind the teeth of the Mad Rip: when the lanes that converged upon the towns—the towns in which queer commodities could always be sold—were so deep and secret. Whatever the sources of his income, as fortunes went, in that remote district, Freathy Rosevear was accounted wealthy. He was also a man to take the eye. Big, florid, fair, he might have stepped out of a Holbein canvas, and tales of his unusual strength were told and retold of a winter's evening in the cottages. Did his wife complain the store of wreck was running low? Forthwith he had gone out, caught the first of the homing donkeys, and carried it, load and all, into her presence, with "A fardel for my Lady"—so the story.

The man was as Saul to a kingless folk, a head and shoulders above the multitude. Like the last of the Tudor monarchs he brought the people among whom he lived material well-being, and, like other outstanding personalities, stamped his impress on the current coin. Before he died he was "Old Squire" and, as such, he lived in the long memory of the countryside. Not that to them his death was the final exit from the stage of his influence and activities. Though they followed him to his burying, though they saw the sods falling earth to earth, they could not believe that abundant, penetrating, imperial vitality could be resolved into its elements. Recognizing that neither heaven nor hell was the fitting place for it, they showed their faith in the life after death by a hardy belief that Old Squire, though rendered invisible, was still among them.

When this man's grip upon Trevorrick relaxed, the land fell to his three legitimate sons: for his other children, and he had done his part in peopling the neighbourhood, he had provided during his life. The legitimate sons, Freathy, Constantine, and Tom, were good farmers all, but cast in an ordinary mould. They lived, they replenished the earth and, in the fullness of time, went back to it, dust to dust. A younger Constantine now owned the mill, a younger Tom tilled the fat slopes of Hember, and Wastralls, the cradle of the race, was become the property of Freathy's only child, his daughter Sabina. Every rood of land in the valley was still Rosevear property, and the cousins, shut in by their hill boundaries, formed a community conscious at once of its kinship and its isolation.

Of the three farms, Wastralls was the largest and most important. Across the valley were wide commons—the wastralls—once bare, blown sand, but now converted by spire grass into turf for the fattening of red-brown bullocks. On the heavy land between the house and the little stream were orchards and cornfields, while behind the cliffs, tethered in pairs to prevent them being blown over the edge, a flock of sheep nibbled the short grass. The manor itself was a low two-storied oblong of country stone and, with its courts and outhouses, seemed as much an excrescence of the rocky ground as more solid outcroppings. A grey irregularity by day, it sank, when twilight fell, into its surroundings. At dawn St. Cadic Mill was a black tower against the saffron; at dusk Hember windows flamed with reflections of the west; but both at dawn and dusk Wastralls was more a presumption than a fact. The house was older than Hember, older than the mill, and its obscurity suggested that the forgotten builder had hoped the Storm-god might take Wastralls in his stride, that Death might fail, among so many grey swells and hummocks, to distinguish it.

The place had been built to house two families. A dividing wall cut the fine chambers on the western front from the low-pitched rooms that looked across the yard. A green door, stout and with a heavy lock, was set in the dividing wall to allow of communication between the old-time lord of the manor and the bailiff who tilled his fields; but the families, living back to back, having different modes of egress and ingress, the one taking the field path, the other the road, preserved each its privacy. When Old Squire brought a wife to Wastralls, she, preferring the homeliness of the farmstead, had made it their dwelling-place. From thenceforward the life of the house centred in the roomy, whitewashed kitchen; and the fine chambers, swept and shuttered, were only used on ceremonial occasions. Old Squire had no use for state or trappings and when his son Freathy reigned in his stead, the lesser man asked no greater luxury than had satisfied his sire.

This second Freathy married a woman so indistinct that it was a wonder he had seen her sufficiently well to fall in love. She ruled Wastralls with a boneless hand, and used her knees for praying rather than scrubbing. Of this vague, colourless creature was born the vital bright-haired Sabina. Her father welcomed her as a beginning, "first a maid and then a child," but his wife's effort left her exhausted. The tonic air of the valley made it difficult for her to die, but she failed a little, month by month, until, unnoticed, she was able to slip into her grave. Freathy's thought was "must marry again, try to get a boy; 'twon't do to let a maid be heir of the land." But he was comfortable as a widower, more comfortable than he had been during Dusha's pious, slatternly existence and, Time, the inexorable, drew the daisy quilt about his neck, while he yet procrastinated.

For lack of a son Freathy had taken his daughter with him about the farm. His thoughts being of the cattle-market, of soils and crops, it was of such matters that he spoke; and Sabina picked up the lore of the seasons as naturally as another child learns to sew and cook. Her father was a man who drank, not continuously, but at intervals which, like a perspective of posts, showed diminishing interspaces. The child accepted his habits as she accepted rain and shine and, when he was under the influence of liquor, did her young best to grapple with his duties. By the time he died—from the effects of a night spent inadvertently in the open—she had gathered a little store of experience, had indeed been farming Wastralls for over a year.

Freathy, intending to remarry and leave hearty sons, had not troubled to make a will and the girl of one-and-twenty succeeded to an unencumbered freehold of five hundred acres, the manor-house and what remained of Old Squire's savings.

Offers of help came from both Hember and St. Cadic. Each was willing to work Wastralls with his own land, each hoped Sabina might listen to a cousinly tale of love. She, however, having inherited the robust confidence of her grandfather, was determined to undertake on her own account the adventure of farming. Nor were Tom and Constantine Rosevear altogether surprised. They had not played with her as children without recognizing her quality; and if they wondered 'what hand she'd make of it,' it was as those whose hearts prophesy unto them.

The brothers who had inherited Hember and St. Cadic had died young, but each had left a son. Tom, the owner of Hember, thought that as its fields marched with those of Wastralls, he ought to marry his cousin; while Constantine sought her because the glint of her bright hair had dazzled him. A fine maid was Sabina, blue eyes flush with rounded cheeks, not the passionate eyes of Old Squire, but the blue of ice-depths when the sun is shining in a clear sky; and when it was a question of marriage she found the straight sticks who offered themselves for weapon and support were of a too familiar wood. She would go a little farther into the forest.

> Ar ise up, Maid, all in your gown of green
> For summer is a-come into day;
> You are as fine a lady as wait upon the queen
> In the merry morning of May.
> Arise up, Maid, out of your bed
> For summer is a-come into day;
> Your chamber shall be strewed with the white rose and the red
> In the merry morning of May [*]

[*] Padstow Hobby-horse song.

The green waves of the Atlantic roll strange flotsam into the sandy bays of that bitter coast; and the sea, hungry though it be, can give up more than the dead. One summer on the bosom of a forgotten sunset, a boat had drifted into Morwen Cove, to strand, when the tide turned, amid the weed and rubbish of the foreshore. In it, swollen with cold, unconscious, nearly dead, lay a waif, the survivor of some obscure wreck. Leadville Byron, a hind who with his childless wife lived over the disused fish-cellars at Wastralls, chanced upon the boat. Its contents stirred the father in him and, as he carried home the bit of human waste, his anxiety was lest it might be reclaimed; indeed he never quite lost his fear that what the sea had given the land, that unknown of towns and country beyond the hills, might take. If inquiries were made, however, they did not reach Trevorrick and the child, a lusty, black-browed youngster, grew to manhood, without further change in his surroundings.

His native tongue had been unintelligible to the villagers and he could not give himself a name. His foster-parents, therefore, felt themselves justified in calling him Leadville. If his name were ever discovered he could return to it, meanwhile he was buttressed against the curiosity of strangers. As was only natural the Byrons bred him to work on the land; and at eighteen, Wastralls—the delectable hillside, the edge of cliff, the tumuli of the ancient folk—were all he knew; indeed, it required a cataclysm to prove to him that he was not a clod of Wastralls earth.

In outward seeming the lad was not unlike the people among whom he lived. A little more swarthy, with a more sombre expression in his dark eyes, a broader chest than was often seen, he might have passed for a Cornishman. The difference was one of temperament and it was a difference so great, that never to the end of his life was he to be other to them than a 'foreigner.'

One autumn, after a rainy, reedy summer, a summer of losses, Mr. Rosevear was forced to believe he could work the farm with fewer labourers; and young Byron, being the last to join the little band of hinds, must be the first to go. The lad took his dismissal hardly. By dewing the land with his sweat he had made it his and, against his will, a deep and narrow will, he could not be disinherited. He considered himself as much part of Wastralls as a bush of tamarisk in the hedge. As, however, he must go, he listened to his foster-father's suggestion and returned temporarily to the great waters which had spewed him up. He went, but in every ship's wake, in the reek of foreign cities, in the wind that blew from home, he saw visions of those few fields which to him were the world. He had the inward eye of the dreamer and, as the year turned, saw spring drawing her green skirts over the hillside and hanging the orchard with her gossamers. He saw the dandelions starring the thick grass by the river, the lush dark grass in which he had rolled himself moved by the ecstasy of life; and to him the salt sea was barren and unprofitable, a desert upon which he must go to and fro until the days of his pilgrimage were accomplished. The death of old Byron brought the wanderer back to Hindoo Cottage—as the fish-cellars were called—only to find that the wife had followed her man; and that he—Leadville the younger—was again without even the semblance of a human tie. He had not loved the old couple, love did not at any time come easily to him and all the emotion of which he was capable had long been concentrated upon Wastralls; but he was anxious to secure his foster-father's berth as teamster. To the outpourings of the neighbours he listened unheeding and presently took his way to the farmhouse, there to learn that Rosevear had been laid in a neater ditch than that of his inadvertent choice and that Sabina—big, ripe, fair, a woman who might have stepped out of the Elizabethan age—reigned in his stead.

The opportunity was self-evident and Byron, back in his place and once more happy, soon realized that his heart's desire was within reach. It was not Sabina that he wanted but Wastralls; and that, again, not for ambition's sake, but because his late experience had taught him the value of security. Asking no more of life than permission to spend his youth, his strength, his passion on the land, he found consent in Sabina's awakening interest. She had disdained the easy-kindled fires of Tom, of Constantine, and of the Tregols lads, but the sombre glow in Byron's eyes was disturbing. It moved her as something unknown and full of a strange promise, that promise which is in the rising sap and germinating seed. The neighbours expressed a kindly apprehension, for though marriage between persons of different race may be eugenically sound, it seldom brings happiness to the individual; but Sabina was beyond reason, for in the stranger she had found her mate.

Within a month the banns were called and a little later the oddly assorted couple pushed off into matrimony. Whereas, however, Byron believed himself to be marrying Wastralls—the good farm and the waste lands by the sea—making it for ever flesh of his flesh, his in indissoluble union, Sabina did not intend to endow her lover with her worldly goods. She held the land by right of inheritance and by a worthier right, that of the farmer who deals understandingly with her fields. Although she cultivated the farm in the way that had brought prosperity to the family, her stock was pedigree and realized good prices, her seed was the best procurable and she was always ready to try new manures and dressings. She was not a woman of ideas, neither was she reactionary but a fold of Old Squire's mantle hung from her shoulders and, as the neighbours said, "to give the maid her due, her's a first-rate farmer." She loved her farm, but as a sportsman loves a good dog. She exacted from it the utmost it could give and was its considerate master, but she could have no conception of Leadville's attitude. If it had been explained to her that he loved the land as a man loves a woman, she would have doubted her informant, and if convinced have thought her husband a fool for his pains. As it was, when he attempted to assert his new rights, as he did immediately after their marriage, she stared in surprise.

"'Oo told you to give the orders to the 'inds when I've got a tongue of me own?"

"I thought I was savin' of 'ee a lot of trouble."

"I don't want yer to do my work for me. I can do it meself."

"I should think you got enough to do indoors without goin' outdoors workin'. I don't see what a woman want to be out in all weathers for."

Sabina laughed good-humouredly. "My dear feller, I always bin outdoor. Rain or fine don't make any difference to me."

"Well, my dear, you'll lose all they good looks o' yours. I don't like to see women all burned up. You'll be an old woman before you'm a young one."

"I don't care what I be, and I don't believe a word you say is true. Ony'ow I shall chance it."

"Well, 'tis the man's place to teel the land."

"A fine mess you'd make of it, too. Look at the Mill fields! If Con turned the ditches out they wouldn't be so wet; even Tom don't keep 'is fields so clean as mine."

"I don't care 'bout that, 'bain't a woman's work."

"Aw, git away. 'Tidn't all women that want to farm; but those that do, let'm 'av it. 'Tis just whether they can farm or can't."

"Well, I think it's my business as I'm yer 'usband. You ought to let me 'av it."

"What's the good to let you 'av it, you dunno nothing about farmin'. You bin to sea most all yer life. 'Tis years an' years since you ploughed a bit o' ground."

A dark colour came into the bridegroom's cheek. "'Ow can you say that when I was brought up on the land. I knaw all about farm work. 'Aving married you, to 'av the farm's my due."

Sabina sat very straight in her chair. "Now once for all," said she, "let's settle this matter. Wastralls is mine, and I dare you to so much as lay a finger on it. If you want to farm so much as all that, Higher Polnevas is to let, and its fields are joinin' ours. Why don't you go over and take that? I'll let you 'av the money for that, but you won't 'av Wastralls."

Byron had not expected opposition. Sabina, being a woman, would naturally be glad to have the outdoor work taken off her hands. His surprise at her attitude was so intense that he stared at her in a helpless silence, until she clinched the matter by exclaiming in her hearty, fresh-air voice, "'Tis no good for 'ee to think anything about it."

This phrase opened the flood-gates. Usually somewhat silent, he had moods when the words tumbled over each other in a multitude beyond counting. Perceiving he had miscalculated he set to work to retrieve his error and, during the course of the evening, learnt many things but not how to make Sabina change her mind. The poor man, desperately afraid, did all he knew. He entreated and she smiled, he blustered and she laughed, he cajoled and she warmed to him but, though she warmed, she did not weaken. Her first word was her last: "'Tis no good for 'ee to think anything about it."

Byron was helpless. He could not win her to his will, neither could he break her. She was capable, as she let him see, of separating from him. If he appealed to the hinds, they would side with her. Her cousins at Hember and St. Cadic, the neighbours in the adjacent valleys, would take her part.

Turning the matter over, however, he perceived that time, by giving Sabina fresh interests, fresh cares, might prove his friend. Nurslings tie the mother to the house and when the babies came his wife would have her hands full. She must let go what she could not hold; and he would be ready to pick up, bit by bit, what she let fall.

In this hope he settled to his new life. It was unthinkable that he should attempt to farm Higher Polnevas, when his mind was filled with Wastralls. Of a brooding nature, through which at times flames of emotion broke, he was content to spend his days thinking out and dwelling on the changes he would make when his opportunity came. Sabina's farming, cautious and well-considered, chafed him. He wanted the land to bring forth a hundredfold where she now gave a mere return. He was her lover asking of her all that she could give, eager only to have the exploiting of her possibilities. To make her fruitful was to be his work. He saw the seed swell in her bosom, the silent marvel of growth, the harvest that should reward his husbandry; and, because out of the heart the mouth speaketh, when he talked it was of intensive farming, of the money that lay in sugar-beet, strawberries, asparagus, of market-gardening and the use of glass. Thereby he damaged his cause; for Sabina, listening, came to the conclusion that she had married an unpractical dreamer. If he believed in his theories why did he not rent land and prove them? That he only talked, satisfied her that she had been right in her refusal to let him farm Wastralls and her grip on the land tightened. The kindly fields deserved better of her than that she should put them at the mercy of a dreamer.

Whether or no the man's life that she led did her disservice, it is certain that no children came to modify the situation. In the loft, the carved wooden cradle lay with only the wind to set it a-rock; below, the rooms were as empty of new life as is a whispering conch. The bustle of the farm was like the swish of water about a rock islet, that little spot of sterility and stagnation at the heart of multitudinous life. Sabina, who had natural instincts, who had mothered a bibulous father and many a bit of life from the fields and hedges, was disappointed; but her feeling was mild compared with that of her husband. His children were to have delivered Wastralls into his hand, assuaged at last the long ache of his passion; but the years turned on their axes, going as they had come. At first Byron bore himself with a good courage. After the unprofitable days of his seafaring it was enough to watch the tamarisk stems warming into red life, to spend the daylight wandering over the well-known ground, to return at night to the grey house on its shelf of rock. If, after a while, these delights palled, it was because they led nowhither.

Meanwhile, under Sabina's judicious management, the farm prospered. Neither cared to spend, the one because she had no wants, the other because what he desired could not be bought. With every year the bank stocking grew heavier, also the man's heart; and every year found his thoughts fixed more bitterly upon his disappointment. Sabina saw but without understanding. Her man was moody, foolish too with his perpetual harping on his rights, but she was not thereby alienated, for, wise or unreasonable, he was her man. Though she envied Tom his houseful of daughters and Constantine his big sons, her own lack left her the more leisure to care for her husband's comfort. The standard of living at Wastralls was higher than that of the surrounding farms. Byron ate according to his fancy and lay soft; was given indeed those things to which he was indifferent, and denied that after which he hungered.

"I'm kep' like a prize bullock," he said morosely, "when what I want is to be workin' and doin' for meself."

"Well, my dear, 'oo told you not to work? There's plenty to do, there's that four-acre field, why don't yer go and plough up that, 'stead of in 'ere mumpin' about?"

"As though I was yer 'ind?"

"What, still wantin' to be maister?"

"Iss, an' shall be till I die."

"Now look 'ere. If you want money to buy Polnevas you can 'av it, but Wastralls you will never 'av."

"Well, if I can't 'av Wastralls I won't 'av nothing; but you mark my words"—he bent towards her and brought one hand with a thump into the palm of the other—"if I can't 'av it by 'itch, I will by crook."

"Not so long as I live then, any'ow."

Byron was slightly underhung, a formation which gives the face a look of strength and purpose. "We shall see, some day, which of us is the strongest of the two."

The woman, happy in her work and with her main affection satisfied, could answer with reasonable good-humour: "Well, my dear feller, 'tis my land and I must do my duty by it. 'Tis I'm responsible, not you, to the folks up yonder," and a movement of her bright head indicated the burial-ground at Church Town. "I'm sorry you're disappointed, but I can't 'elp it."

"Oh, hang it—sorry?"

"Well, I be sorry. I'd like for 'ee to 'av everything to make yer 'appy; but Wastralls I can't give." She smiled at him in her friendly fashion, a sweet inviting smile. "I do my best to make it up to yer in other ways and that you know."

"Iss, I want bread and you do give me a stone." He turned away, leaving her, as ever, uncomprehending. It was impossible for her to think of him as other than a child, who for his own sake must be denied and prevented, who was hers to care for and, in ways that could not harm him, to indulge. The truth to her, as to so many of us, would have been unbelievable.

The break-up of the situation was due to an accident. Sabina had driven a young horse to the fair at St. Columb Major and this animal, excited by the unwonted traffic, the smells and the noise, became unmanageable.

Plunging down the hill, he came into collision with a heavy van. The prancing feet slipped and he fell, shooting his driver over the shafts. Though clear of horse and cart, she was flung with considerable violence against the front wheel of the van. This startled the van horses and the heavy lumbersome creatures, with a prodigious clatter, started up the street. Sabina, rendered unconscious by the blow she had received, had fallen between the wheels and the van, lurching forward, passed over her.

It was thought at first that she was killed but the crushed woman who, later that afternoon, was admitted to the little hospital at Stowe, was still breathing. As the case seemed hopeless, the husband was sent for, and Byron, in a ferment of excitement, came pounding in on the heels of the messenger. His horse was in a lather when he checked him at the hospital gate. "Poor Sabina, poor old girl, it was a terrible thing for her to die as she lived; away from home like that. No doubt 'er 'ead was full of the farmin', never once thought of dyin', but the Lorrd would be merciful."

"If she's goin' to die, don't 'ee keep it from me," he said to Dr. Derek, who was in charge of the case. "I'd rather knaw the worst."

"And," as he explained to the neighbours, on his return home, after being allowed to glance at the unconscious face on the pillow, "the poor doctor 'ee couldn't give me no encouragement."

# CHAPTER II

The sight of Sabina, her florid face grey against the white bandages, her pale lips open to facilitate the drawing of difficult breath, had convinced her husband that she could not possibly recover. That evening he called the hinds together, told them what had happened, and for the first time gave them their orders. As he went back into the house, old George Biddick, who had been many years on the farm, and was of a noticing disposition, drew the attention of a new-come labourer to the receding figure.

"Speaks as though 'e'd been maister all the time, don't 'e? An' carries 'isself pretty straight, too, considerin' as 'e'm bowed wi' grief."

"I don't s'pose 'e realize things yet," said Jim, a Rosevear from across the hills. "Must 'av been tarr'ble shock for'n."

The other man glanced sideways out of small brown eyes, and gave a non-committal grunt. He was queerly shaped, with a high-shouldered short body and long legs and, being related to most of the cottagers, was known generally as "Uncle George!"

"Dunno so much about that. Missus is so strong as a dunkey," he said, as he returned to his work of bedding down the horses, "an' she may chate the crows yet."

But Jim Rosevear was not listening, his thoughts had run before him up the road, to where, at the stone stile, a maid would be waiting. The rest of the world might be concerned with death; but he was young and his concern was with life, more life.

When, on the following day, Byron rode over to the hospital, he was told that his wife still breathed; but that an operation had become necessary, an operation which it was scarcely possible she could survive. He found it difficult to understand why it must be.

"Why punish 'er so? Wouldn't it be better to let 'er die quiet than to 'ack 'er about?"

The wheel of the van had gone over both legs, crushing together bone and flesh and the surgeon proposed to amputate. The limbs were injured beyond hope of saving; and it was explained that their removal might give the patient a chance.

"Do you think then, sir," said the anxious husband, "that she'll be better if she 'av the operation?"

"She may. The condition is critical and unless the operation is performed she might at any moment take a turn for the worse." He was afraid blood-poisoning might set in.

"I shouldn't 'av thought she'd be strong enough to bear it."

Dr. Derek's opinion was that Sabina would probably die on the operating-table and this, without putting it into so many words, he managed to convey. As soon as Byron understood, although the idea of the amputation was curiously repugnant to him, he gave leave for it to be attempted. Sabina had to die, poor soul, and it was hard on her that the doctors should think it necessary to try their experiments on her, should not be able to leave her in possession of her limbs. Still ... theirs the responsibility.

Byron was allowed to remain in the hospital till the result of the operation was known. He sat in an austerely furnished waiting-room and, through his mind, coursed dim memories of Sabina, handsome and active, Sabina vaulting the gates and climbing like a boy, Sabina with her free gait and her hearty open-air voice. From the other side of the picture, the Sabina whose mangled limbs were at that moment being cut from her body, he sedulously turned his gaze. That she should be thus mutilated was abhorrent to him.

Dr. Derek, his spick-and-span brightness a little dimmed and his eyes tired, came in at last. "She's still alive, Byron."

"I didn't think she would be, sir."

The doctor hummed and hawed. The operation had been long and delicate and he was weary; but he could not let the man take away with him an illusory hope.

"We have to reckon," he said gravely, "with the shock to the system."

"You don't think," returned Byron in his deep rumbling bass, "as there's much chance for 'er then, sir?"

"The condition is very serious."

"I shall be lost without 'er, even as 'tis—" he stared before him out of the window and the melancholy of his rough, unkempt appearance impressed the other man.

"Are you alone at Wastralls?" he asked, contrasting in a mind as neat as his body, his trim, small house on the main street of Stowe, with the grey homestead and irregular outbuildings of the lonely farm.

"I've a woman that do the housework but she go 'ome by night."

"Sounds a bit dreary." Dr. Derek was essentially a town bird. The noise of footsteps on the pavement, of voices in the street, was music to him.

"Well, it's what we'm accustomed to," said Byron carefully, "an' after all we'm pretty and busy. O' course I got the farm to see to as Missus is 'ere.'

"Yes, yes, of course."

"I was wonderin', sir, if you could send out and let me knaw 'ow she's gettin' on. Course, I should be delighted to set by 'er if she knawed me; but, seein' as poor sawl's gone past that, and I've so much to do, I'm better off 'ome—till I'm wanted."

"I've no doubt it could be arranged. I'll speak to Matron about it."

"Thank you, sir; an', of course, anything she want she can 'av, only send in and let me knaw. Money's no object when it's 'er life."

"You can trust me, Byron. Everything possible will be done for her," said the other gravely, "only, I'm afraid..."

The first bulletin that reached Wastralls told Byron to prepare for the worst. His wife was still alive but sinking.

That day he went about the farm in a ferment of emotion. Poor Sabina, poor soul, but if she had to die, better now when he was in his prime. She had had a good time and now it was his turn. He trod the fields as blessed souls may walk in Paradise. The dear land, the land he loved deep as Dozmare, was his and he had got it fairly; he had not pushed his wife out of it. Accident had befriended him—oh, happy accident!

When he came in from his work, he took down a well-thumbed list and wrote an order for glass, for frames, for certain much-advertised manures and for young plants. The season was advanced and, if he hoped for a speedy result, he must not lose time. The next bulletin, dropping on his happy absorption, gave but little hope that Sabina would see another dawn. She was alive and no more.

Byron, who was at breakfast, found his hunger easily satisfied. The letter had been meat and drink. Thoughts, indeed, of a day spent striding over the Cornish moors, of a night in the sacred, haunted solitudes of Rowtor passed through his mind; but, while he was considering them, his glance fell upon the honeysuckle of the porch. Long the pride of Sabina's heart, its untidy growth had been to him an eyesore. Here then was the outlet for his passionate elation, an outlet, too, symbolic of his mood. With his own hands he pulled it up, digging out the roots so that nothing remained from which a fresh shoot might spring. Jealousy, an old jealousy, the jealousy of the brooding years was in the action.

Wastralls, which had been Sabina's, was to affront him with no memories of a past humiliation. The new Wastralls was always to have been his.

At the end of the week he was surprised to learn that Sabina still hovered between life and death. Riding into Stowe, he sought out Dr. Derek and was reassured to find he took a pessimistic view of the case. Though acknowledging that Mrs. Byron showed great vitality the surgeon did not think she would outlive the week. He condoled with the farmer and Byron, satisfied that all was well, went back to his work.

A wagon, drawn by three great brown horses, had brought from Wadebridge the various articles which the farmer, lavish for the first time in his life, had ordered. Having Sabina's savings upon which eventually to draw he had commanded glass, manures, plants, in abundance. The little band of labourers, accustomed to Mrs. Byron's caution, looked on with the stolid disapproval of men averse to change. The delicate processes of market-gardening were new to them and they did not think the new scheme should have been inaugurated while she lay on her death-bed. The farmer found them irritatingly slow, but did not realize that this seeming stupidity was the cautious expression of their unwillingness. If the mistress died this man would be their employer, therefore their wisest course was to be outwardly docile but a little hard to teach. They talked among themselves, however, and, what is more, spread the tale of Byron's doings over the countryside.

Wind of it had already been wafted up the valley. At Hember and St. Cadic the cousins, after trying the one for Sabina's land, the other for her love, had long since settled to a second choice. Tom Rosevear, indeed, had gone back to an earlier fancy, a girl with whom both he and Sabina had been at school. Isolda Raby was the daughter of a fishseller and her marriage with the prosperous farmer had been for her a rise in life. Since the time they had sat on the same school bench, she had been Sabina's most intimate crony — the only interruption to their friendship being caused by the frailty, the land-hunger of man! But Tom, after some plain speaking on Sabina's part, had returned to his Isolda and the friendship had not only been revived, but placed on a wider, more satisfactory basis.

When Sabina met with her accident Mrs. Tom's heart was wrung. An imaginative, tender-hearted woman, she felt an anxious desire to be a stay and a comfort, to do something, however small, to mitigate her friends sufferings. There was at first little that she could do beyond keeping an eye on poor Sabina's household and seeing that Leadville did not lack food or service. After the first anxious days, however, she was allowed into the hospital and from that time, her eldest daughter being able to 'tend house' in her stead, she spent as many hours at her friend's bedside as the rules of the place permitted. At first Sabina was for long periods unconscious. She took nourishment, she drowsed, she suffered many and various discomforts; but it seemed to her that whenever she came to the surface her glance fell on the comforting vision of Isolda, the same pretty matronly Isolda, who with kind talk and kinder offices had for so long pervaded her daily life. Sabina was so badly injured, in such incessant pain, so low in herself, that she took little interest in her surroundings. To hear the familiar click of the knitting-needles, to open her weary eyes on that understanding smile, was, however, some sort of pleasure.

When Mrs. Tom heard that Byron was busy with carpenters and masons, putting up glass-houses and introducing a new system of tillage, she was not so much surprised as indignant. She had not gone in and out of Wastralls every day for so many years without becoming aware of the husband's disappointment and impatience. She understood that he, like her own Tom, had loved the land not the woman. He, however, had not been able to adapt himself and his life was a daily weariness. Though she allowed that the result was a judgment on him, she found it in her kind heart to wish that he could have had his way. The mad impatience which made him inaugurate far-reaching changes in anticipation of his wife's death, met, however, with scant sympathy from Mrs. Tom. A woman of moderate councils, whose very civility sprang from a sincere kindliness, the fact that Byron went so far as to tear up Sabina's honeysuckle while she yet breathed, put him beyond the pale.

When the talk reached Mrs. Tom's ears, Sabina was still undecided whether to attempt the weary climb back to health or slip quietly away. The loss of her limbs inclined her to the latter course. She could not bear to contemplate life as a cripple. The thought of the fields over which she had ridden, of the market-place in which she had bought and sold, of the whole familiar countryside, was unbearable. Better lie quiet up at Church Town than go limping where she had once leaped and run. Mrs. Tom, coming into the ward at a moment when Sabina, with "I don't want any o' that old traäde," was refusing good nourishment, decided that the truth might be as good for her as a tonic.

"How be 'ee to-day, S'bina, how be gettin' on?"

The injured woman looked at her with weary bloodshot eyes. "I dunno. I don't feel very special."

Isolda seated herself on a cane chair facing the patient and took out her knitting. As she made not only her husband's stockings but those of her five daughters, she had always one on hand. "What do 'ee feel like?"

"My dear life, I suffer like a Turk. I'd soon be dead as livin'."

Mrs. Tom's face expressed her sympathy. "'Av 'ee got much pain?"

"Yes, I ache something awful—in my legs."

The other stared in surprise. "In yer legs? But you 'aven't got any."

"Well, seem like I 'av them."

Mrs. Rosevear laughed. "If that doesn't beat everything!"

The sufferer moved restlessly on her pillow. "I'd rather be out on Gool-land,[*] than like I be now."

[*] Gulland, a barren islet off the north coast of Cornwall.

Looking at the hollows of the face once so apple-round, Isolda's heart misgave her.

"I feel," continued Mrs. Byron in a dragging voice, "that I can't stand much more of this."

"Nonsense, you'll cheat the crows yet."

"Don't care whether I do or no. What is there for a woman like me? I've neither chick nor chield."

"Well, there's Leadville to think about."

Sabina sighed. "He'd cut a poor shine without me; but there—I dunno..." her voice trailed away into silence.

Mrs. Tom's heart began to beat more quickly. "Well," she ventured, "he's workin' pretty and 'ard now."

"He's got to keep the thing going," assented the wife.

"He's doin' more'n that."

Sabina's voice was still languid, but she showed a little interest. "What's ah doin' then?"

"A cart come over from Wadebridge o' Thursday piled up wi' boxes and bags. Now just let me turn this heel."

"Boxes and bags?" murmured the wife. "Good gracious! What's ah going to do with that?"

After a few seconds given to her work, Mrs. Tom looked up. "He's teelin' the li'l medder wi' sugar-beet."

The other's mind, dulled by suffering and loss of blood, took time to grasp the significance of this statement. "Sugar-beet?" she said, slowly, "but I'm goin' to 'ave the li'l medder teeled wi' dredge-corn."

"You bain't there to give the orders."

Sabina's lips took a firmer line. "I won't 'av it teeled wi' that new-fangled traäde. You tell'n so."

"Better tell'n yourself; I reckon—" She glanced shrewdly at her friend, for Sabina's unexpected illness had put new thoughts into Mrs. Tom's head. She was not greedy, but the most self-effacing creature will scheme a little for its young. "I reckon he'd do far different if you wasn't 'ere."

"You think so?" Sabina shut her eyes the better to realize the situation. The news had been stimulating, and when she spoke again her voice was stronger. "I don't think as I'm goin' round land this time, Isolda."

"I do hope an' pray as you aren't, my dear soul."

"What else is ah doin'?"

"Tom went down to see'n last night, thought as 'ee might be lonely in that big 'ouse all by 'imself; and Leadville was tellin' 'im he didn't believe in the way missis was farmin'. He'd like to try and see what the land'd grow best. He said—terbacca."

"Terbacca? I should think he was maäze. Never heard tell of such a thing. Whatever next is he gwine grow?"

"He think the land would grow vegetables as 'tis the right sort o' soil and that 'tis wasted in corn."

Sabina gave a feeble snort. "What do 'ee know about soils—a sailor!" She shook her head. "As long as I live he'll never have nothing to do with Wastralls."

Mrs. Rosevear's needles clicked in agreement. "As long as you do live, S'bina."

"Iss, why not me livin'? I 'ent older than he is, and there's no reason I should turn up my trotters first; at least I don't see why I should."

"We'll all live till we die, sure enough; but it's been touch and go lately with you."

"I'll live in spite of'n," said Mrs. Byron.

"I hope you will, my dear, but sposin' you don't?" Mrs. Byron returned her friend's glance with a startled look. "Ah, iss, sposin'." She saw at last what her death would have meant both to her husband and her kinsfolk. "Well, I make no promises, but I do see now where I'm to. Iss, I can see through a very small hole, and I'm not too old to learn."

Sabina had been effectually roused. Possessions that are menaced increase in value and as long as Leadville was making changes at Wastralls she would not want to die.

"There's things as you can't alter," she said, thinking Sabina should be prepared for what could not now be helped.

"What can't I alter?"

"He've pulled up the honeysuckle by the porch."

A fugitive colour dyed the wan cheeks. "Have 'ee now, the old villain? Whatever for? The honeysuckle as my poor old mother planted."

Sabina's thoughts were finally diverted from her own trials and, lame or not, she was now only too anxious to stop this meddling with what was hers.

"He's always after something new." Leadville could not have known that she treasured the climber. She was sure he would not knowingly have hurt her feelings. Whenever he did anything that to her was incomprehensible, Sabina put it down, not to design, but want of thought. She was of those who cannot see into the heart of a matter.

"I like the old things best," she continued, and her eyes, those impersonal eyes, which were the blue of a December sky, shone with new purpose. "We'll have no more of they doin's. Where's that traäde Nurse wanted for me to take? I feel I could drink some now."

Byron, busy putting his plans into execution, nearly forgot on what their success hung. He had thrown himself into the work with the eagerness of a man in all ways extreme. He was living his dream and he was happy. After one or two non-committal post cards from Dr. Derek, however, came the news that, though her husband would be wise not to build on it, Mrs. Byron was holding her own. By this time some of the glass-houses were up, and the land below the house, which should have been in dredge-corn, was planted with sugar-beet. For the first time Byron felt a qualm of anxiety. He had not imagined it possible Sabina could survive the amputation of her legs. In giving leave for the operation to be performed, he had believed that he was hastening—with the doctor's kind assistance—the inevitable end. With a sinking heart he now began to wonder whether he had underestimated her vitality. What if, after all, she should recover? She was a sound, harmonious being, whom exposure and a simple strenuous life had only toughened. If any one could survive so terrible an accident, it would be she.

That day he did his work in perturbation of spirit. He had no illusions as to what Sabina would think of the changes he was making. She would be stubbornly opposed to every one of them and Sabina's stubbornness was the force with which for so long he had had to reckon. A gleam of hope came with the thought that even if she recovered she would no longer be able to manage the farm. A poor cripple could not get about the fields, especially such up-and-down fields as those of Wastralls. She would be obliged to appoint a deputy and who so suitable as the man she had married?

He cursed the impatience which had led him astray. If he had waited, the matter would have arranged itself in accordance with his wishes. Now, if Sabina recovered, it was only too likely that she would make it difficult for him to carry out his schemes. He tried to imagine what form her opposition would take, but though he had lived beside her for so long, the writing on the wall was in characters he could not interpret.

To add to his anxieties the man was finding himself short of money. One of his counts against Sabina was that when they married she had refused to have her banking account put in their joint names. "Tedn' a woman's business to sign cheques," he had told her in a futile attempt to bring her to his way of thinking.

She smiled as at a good joke. "I don't think you ever signed a cheque in your life."

"I didn' marry yer for yer money," he assured her hastily.

"Don't bother yerself about it, then. I done business for my old dad all the time you was to sea; and I'd be a pretty malkin if I didn' knaw more about signin' cheques than you do."

"I'm told I ought to be able to draw cheques on your account."

"Shouldn't listen to all you 'ear. If you want money, go and work for't. I'll lend 'ee any to start with."

"There never ought to be two purses between man and wife. They should share alike."

"When you got something," she assured him, "we will."

In spite of her words she had not been niggardly. As much as Byron asked for he received and, believing that all was rightly his, he had taken as much as he wanted. He had seen, however, no reason to save; and now found himself unable to pay for what he had ordered. Sabina was too ill to be approached, and when he took the tale of his difficulties to Hember he found Tom Rosevear civil, as usual, but evasive. He did not say much, but it was evident the 'improvements' did not meet with his approval; that he could not understand Byron's initiating them while his wife lay at death's door. The trifling loan which the farmer succeeded in raising did not do more than pay the wages of the extra workmen, the carpenters and masons he was employing; and, as time passed, and his agent at Wadebridge began to press for the money owing, Byron found himself awkwardly placed. Money he must have, but when he tried to raise it on his expectations he discovered that the security was not considered good. The obvious course was to tell Liddicoat to send the bills in to Sabina; but this, as he well knew, would entail on him unpleasant consequences. Meanwhile the injured woman was slowly gaining ground. Isolda's tale had roused in her, not only the will to live, but the will to overcome, as far as might be, the disabilities of her condition. In the days when she was accounted handsome she had been without self-consciousness; and she did not develop it now that she knew herself to be "a poor remnant." What were looks when the heart was beating warmly and the mind was clear? Her mutilation being the result of accident, it did not occur to her that any one—any one to whom she looked for love and tenderness—might find her repulsive.

After the operation was performed Byron had inquired after her welfare, but had not come to see her. Although so happily occupied he felt at times a little uneasy. Sabina's attraction for him had been her flawless health and the amputation aroused in him, not pity, but a faint stirring of repugnance. He sent her a message that he "must be on the spot to see to things," and, undemonstrative herself and not yet instructed as to the nature of the "things," she had accepted his excuse. A day came, however, when he felt that he must overcome his unwillingness to see for himself the difference in her which the operation had made. Liddicoat was pressing for payment, and he had other liabilities. He rode into Stowe, therefore, rode at his usual breakneck pace and, having stabled his horse, called at the hospital.

Although his visit was unexpected, Sabina had had the long leisure of a slow convalescence in which to arrange her thoughts and make plans for the future. Leadville had tried to take advantage of her being ill. He had thought that when she recovered she would accept the changes he had introduced. He had acted like a child without thought of the consequences. The foolish fellow! Sabina was not angered. She had always been an indulgent wife, and she could overlook this attempt to steal a march on her, as she had overlooked his many efforts to get the management of the farm into his hands.

Looking neither to the right nor to the left, Byron dragged his reluctant feet up the ward. Sabina, who disliked sewing, and did not care to read, had been lying back on her pillows, her hands folded on the white sheet. As she caught sight of the well-known figure; a little flush of surprised pleasure spread over her pale cheeks. She was very glad to see him. In her eyes his breadth and heaviness, the strong growth of his black hair, the jut of his square chin, were so many attractions. She had always admired his strength; and the evidences of it in deep chest and hairy skin were to her taste. She could have wished, however, that he would look up, would answer her ready smile, instead of staring before him like a bull who is not quite certain whether the people he is encountering are friend or foe. She had no suspicion that every step her husband took was more unwilling than the last.

The moment came when he must look at her. His furtive glance swept in one unhappy second the bed and its occupant, then he bent forward and gave her a clumsy kiss. The truth was not as bad as he had feared. By some deft arrangement of the clothes the bed gave a false impression. As far as appearances went the woman in it might have been in possession of her limbs. Byron, escaping the shock he had expected, experienced, however, one of a different kind. The face he touched was indeed that of his wife, but it was changed. Sabina's red-gold hair, which had been rippling and abundant, the very symbol of her gay vitality, had lost its colour. When he last saw her a bandage had concealed it, now, white as that bandage, it framed a face lined and haggard.

"Why—my dear life—" he stammered, staring, "'ow your 'air 'av altered."

She put a hand to her head. "Yer didn't know? Well, can't be 'elped."

"Yer 'air was awful pretty." The change troubled him vaguely; he was not pleased to find that his wife, who had kept her looks beyond the average, should have aged.

"I reckon I'm as God made me, but I was never one to trouble about my looks." She sought for words to express her thought. "Red 'air or white, I'm the same."

"Iss," he said and continued to look at her thoughtfully.

She might be the same woman, but her effect upon others, and in particular on himself, would be different. "'Ow be 'ee?"

"I've 'ad a prettily and draggin' time, but now I'm doin' grand."

He uttered a rough sound of no meaning, but she took it to be congratulatory.

"I shall be up afore long."

"Up?" he murmured, glancing sideways at the bed.

"I shall get Raby Gregor to make me a little trolly so that I can get about."

He pushed his chair farther away. In spite of appearances she was not a woman, but the distorted remnant of one. A shiver ran down his spine. "You bain't thinkin' of—of tryin' to get about?"

"Me not gettin' about? Iss. You've never seen me settin' down wi' me 'ands folded."

"But you'll find things'll be different now," he stammered. He thought of the trolly as some sort of wheel-chair. He had no conception of his wife's inventiveness or of her indifference to comment. "You've been a strong woman, but you can't look to be that again."

The resolute look he knew so well came into Sabina's eyes, and for a moment he doubted whether after all she would not conquer her disabilities. "I bain't strong now," she said, "but a month or two'll make all the difference. I'll soon be up and about again."

The momentary doubt passed. "I wouldn't make too sure of that, then," he told her. The fact that Wastralls had not so much flat land as would make a football field was reassuring. No wheel-chair, whatever the power of its directing will, could climb up and down those fields.

"I'm hopin'," said Sabina obstinately, "to teel Wastralls as I 'av before."

"We must see 'ow you do frame."

"Bain't a matter of gettin' about," she continued, guessing his thoughts. "I know Wastralls like the palm of my hand, every 'itch and stitch of it, and the 'inds'll carry out my orders. I can trust old George Biddick to see as the others do their work. I've planned it all."

"And me?" asked Leadville grimly.

"My dear feller, you don't like farmin', you wouldn't make no 'and at it, you an' your old rigmaroles."

"I c'd teel Wastralls so as it brought in double what you get now."

She shook her head. "You bain't goin' to try."

It was as well for her peace of mind that eyes cannot speak. That this mutilated trunk of a woman should still be in a position to withstand him! His great chest heaved with bitter emotion, but he did not answer.

"Come," said Sabina peaceably. "Tell me how things is going."

He stared out of the window until he had mastered himself sufficiently to speak. "I came to ask mun for what you aw Liddicoat."

"Aw Liddicoat?" A smiling light came into her eyes. "How much do I aw'n?"

"Couldn't tell 'ee for a pound or two; but if you was to draw out a cheque for me I could full'n soon as I get 'ome."

"You send me in the bill and I'll pay'n after I've checked'n."

Byron's face darkened. He would not be able to hide from her much longer the changes he had attempted. What did it matter? She could only be angry. He thought he would be glad if she were. "There's the men's money—three weeks 'awin'."

"I give'n Isolda yesterday. I expect she's paid'n by now."

"You ought to 'ave give it to me and I could 'av paid'n."

"So I should 'av," she answered peaceably, "if you'd been in to see me. But I give it to Isolda instead."

He was not to be placated. "Looks mighty queer you don't trust me with the money. I've to keep the place goin' and if I don't pay the 'inds who's to know I'm maister?"

"There's no need, for you bain't maister. You may blate morning till night, you won't 'av Wastralls, no never for, come to that, I don't trust 'ee."

"S'bina!"

She held up her hand. "You do take too much on your own 'ead."

He knew then that the tale of his imprudent labours had run before him and that she was expressing her disapproval. She was not angry with him; a mother is not angry when she sequestrates a forbidden toy. "I always thought," he stammered, making no further mystery of the matter, "that we should grow sugar-beet."

"An' you was welcome to try it—at Polnevas. Now come, it bain't too late to put the li'l medder in dredge-corn. You'd better see to't at once, or I'll 'av Tom do't."

He cried out at that last humiliation and it was still the same cry, the cry his wife thought so unreasonable. "You'd put Tom Rosevear over me? You'd take away what belong to me?"

"'Long to you? I should like to know 'ow it come yours."

"You give it me, you give it me when we married."

"Never."

In his disappointment and rage he stumbled over his words. "You'll see, you'll see! Iss, you'll see whether I won't 'av it or no."

"'Tis mazedness of 'ee to think so," she answered. "Come, be sensible. I'll pay for these old fads of yours and you can pile'n away where you mind to. I'll pay this once, but 'twas a fulish game for 'ee to play and maybe you'll see that before you'm done."

# CHAPTER III

Near St. Cadic Mill, at the head of the valley, a hamlet had gathered, a few deep-set cottages built of cliff stone and planted irregularly about a smithy. Sheltered by a rise in the land from sea winds their gardens were rich with produce. A green broadened from their little gates and in the wall of the smithy had been set a scarlet post-box, a flaring touch of the official in a land sufficient unto itself.

In these, houses, which were known far and wide as 'Cottages,' dwelt a cobbler, who was also the barber of the community: Mrs. Bate, the Stripper; her friend Aunt Louisa Blewett, the seamstress: one or two independent labourers, and an old sailor. Here, too, was the Dolphin, where could be obtained a little muddy cider and some home-brewed; also, the village shop. The self-respecting and thrifty community was like a family which, having grown up and married, had continued to live in a group, separated only by the walls of their homes and gardens. Ties, acknowledged and unacknowledged, linked them, linked them also with the farmer folk; and, as all respected the axiom that you must not 'step on a Cornishman's tail,' the hamlet was to the outward eye an abode of peace.

Mrs. Byron's accident had caught the imagination of her humble neighbours. For years they had watched her riding about, a wholesome hearty woman with a ripe cheek and a commanding eye. Not one of them, but had had experience of her vigour and capacity. She was now reduced to a helplessness greater than that of child or dotard and to her helplessness was added the mystery of mutilation.

During the long light weeks the cottagers sat at their doors of an evening and, while Charley Brenton trimmed hair in the front garden, discussed the inopportune event.

"I was almost sure there was ill luck comin'," said Mrs. Bate, the woman who was Stripper, or Nurse for the hamlet, that is to say who laid out the dead.

The man upon whom the barber was operating was a Brenton from the neighbouring valley of Polscore. The gossip was new to him.

"'Ow d'yer think so?" he asked.

"I b'lieve she was ill-wished. Never mind 'ow I think so, you wait an' see. My belief, there's they 'av got an evil eye on 'er."

Aunt Louisa Blewett looked up from her sewing. She was a peculiarly neat and clean old woman, who spent her time going from one house to another, mending and making for the long families. She did not speak, but her toothless mouth worked as if over a choice morsel.

"I thought the witches were all gone years ago," remarked the stranger Brenton.

"Well, there is witches, only they don't come out in their true colour," asserted Mrs. Bate, whose mother was said to have been the last in Tregols.

"Besides," urged old Hawken, the sailor, who was sitting on a stone awaiting his turn at Charley Brenton's hands, "who's goin' to do Mrs. Byron any 'arm? A nicer woman never lived. She's noted for 'er kindness at Christmas time or any other time."

"Iss, iss, we knaw she's well liked," said Mrs. Bate non-committally. Unlike Aunt Louisa she had still an occasional milestone of tooth. The old women were handsome now, and what must they have been when they were the village belles? "Still, I b'lieve there's one that bear 'er a grudge. I don't mention any names but you can think 'oo you like."

"Go along, you don't think as 'e'd do 'er a mischief do yer?"

"Hush!"

For some time the sound of approaching hoofs had been carried to them on the still air of the evening; and the voices died into silence as Leadville Byron, on his black stallion, clattered by. The animal was as usual flecked with foam, the master stained with the mud of the road. Returning from his humiliating interview with Sabina, he had found in the hard gallop up hill and down, an outlet for his rage and disappointment. What did he care if he lamed the horse? Whirling through the hamlet he noticed the curious cottagers no more than the birds in the hedges.

"'Ow 'e do ride," said old Hawken, as the furious figure melted into the growing dusk and only the beat of the hoofs reached the listeners, a beat which in turn was merged in the distant sound of the tide. "One of these days 'e'll break 'is neck."

"'Tis like 'e's tearin' away from something," said Aunt Louisa suddenly.

"Do 'ee think," said Mrs. Bate, lowering her voice, "do 'ee think th' Old Squire knaw what's happenin' above ground?"

"If 'e do," said Hawken, "'e must find it terr'ble 'ard for that feller to be in 'is place."

"And alterin' things," said Aunt Louisa.

"Old Squire," said Mrs. Bate mysteriously, "can look after's own. You mark my words, thiccy feller 'ont 'av all 'is own way."

Willie Brenton took the towel from his neck and handed it to the sailor. "Your turn, Mr. 'Awken."

The old man got up painfully. "My feet's terr'ble knucklin' to-day and my poor laigs is stiff with the rheumatism; but still they'm better'n no laigs. I wonder 'ow poor Mrs. Byron'll manage?"

This was a matter of interest to the cottagers. They supposed that, for the cooking and cleaning, Mrs. Byron would employ one of themselves. Mrs. Bate, who had not been married, had yet grandchildren old enough to go out to service.

"We've all worked there in an' out," she said, "but now the poor thing'll 'av to 'av some one there altogether. She'll be so helpless as a baby."

"I bet she won't," said Aunt Louisa, folding together a patched garment and preparing to go indoors for the night. "Mrs. Byron'll frighten us all yet for what she can do."

"I reckon she 'ont 'av the 'eaft to go about the work as she used to. My mind tell me she's done for," said Hawken.

Aunt Louisa nodded her trim grey head in the direction of Church Town. "Not till she's laid alongside the Old Squire," she said and, going in, shut her door with the precision of touch characteristic of her every movement.

At Wastralls, the following morning, Byron went as usual into the yard. Two breeding sows, black as a cave's mouth, were wandering about and, on a heap of straw in the sun, lay an old sheep-dog. The dog wagged its tail but, unfortunately, did not rise and the man's sore heart registered its laziness as an affront.

"Shep's gone past for work," he said to George Biddick, who was standing by waiting for orders.

"Iss, I b'lieve 'e is. Gettin' blind."

"Better give'm a dose. You come to me at twelve and I'll 'av it ready for 'ee." He cast a vindictive look at the old dog. "And, Biddick..."

"Iss, sir?"

"I've changed my mind about the li'l medder. I'm afraid 'tis too late for sugar-beet this year, I'll 'av it teeled in dredge-corn."

He went back to the kitchen, a roomy whitewashed place, the rafters of which were dark above the blue flagstones, stones which had been worn smooth by feet, trampling for a little to and fro, then going as they had come. In a wall-cupboard to the right of the slab-range, the farmer kept such matters as ammunition, packets of seed, medicaments for the stock. Crossing the kitchen, with a step which was light for so large-framed a man, he stood for a moment contemplating the medley of articles—bluestone, cattle-salts, turpentine, oak-marbles which had been through the coffee grinder, bottles of Red Drink—which confronted him. By the last named stood a small blue bottle with an orange label. He had bought it some time ago, he had used it on old and useless animals. He would pour out a little now and give it to Biddick for the sheep-dog; but the rest he would put by again. He felt that to rid the place of Shep would be a satisfaction. If only other things which stood in his way, which refused to recognize his authority, could be got rid of as easily.

Sabina's interview with her husband had made her realize how necessary she was to him. She thought of him as a foolish child who, the moment it was left to its own devices, got into mischief. The conviction that she stood between Leadville and disaster was soothing. It increased her wish to live and was as good as a tonic. Not that tonics were necessary, for once she had turned the first difficult corner she made good progress and, when Raby Gregor came to discuss with her the trolly she had designed, he was agreeably surprised to find her as cheerful as of old.

This trolly was for long the wonder of those who saw it. On a three-wheeled stand, a cone of cushioned basket-work, itself strengthened by iron stays, had been set upright. Into this wicker receptacle Sabina, who had strong arms, presently learnt to swing herself and, once in place, the cushions supported her in comfort. The front wheel of the trolly had a guiding handle and she was thus enabled, as long as the ground was flat, to go where she would.

"I want to be on a level with other people," she said, "so don't make the stand too low. I can't bear to be down; 'av to look up to everybody as I'm speaking to'm."

The little contrivance, when finished, proved admirably suited to her needs. The nurses, proud of her as a case, helped her over the first difficulties; and, as the figure she cut did not trouble her, she soon learnt to swing herself in and out. Before long she was able to steer herself about the ward and Mrs. Tom, coming in one afternoon with eggs for the patients and saffron cake for the nurses' tea, found her pushing herself about as contentedly as a child.

"I shall be comin' 'ome next week," she said happily, "so Leadville can send in the cart for me."

"I shall be pretty and glad for 'ee to come 'ome again, but why must 'e send the old cart?"

"Why, to bring this 'ome in." She put her hands to the sides of the trolly and sat erect, a smiling cheerful woman. Her face, though pale from the long confinement, had lost its lines, was indeed showing a tendency to over-fullness and she looked older, but she was herself again. "If I didn't I should 'av to lie down an' I don't want to do that. I want to sit up and see all there is to be seen. Besides I want for the people to see I'm able to get about again, if I be a cripple."

Mrs. Tom perceived that Sabina meant to celebrate her recovery by a triumphal return. "Well, my dear, I'll tell Leadville to send in the cart for 'ee."

"This 'ere thing do run so smooth as a die," said Sabina, returning to her happy absorption in the trolly. "You'd never believe 'ow easy I can get about in it," and she began, with her strong, illness-whitened hands, to turn the wheels.

"Will it go uphill?" said the other, after observing with interest the paces of this new steed.

Sabina's face fell. "Lorrd bless me, I never thought o' that!"

"'Owever will you manage?" Only the shelf on which Wastralls—house, yard and garden—stood, was flat.

"I..." Sabina hesitated. The brightness had died cut of her face. "I don't know if Leadville will carry out my wishes or no."

"Well, you can 'ardly expect 'un to."

"I dun't see why 'e shouldn't. 'Tis my land, why shouldn't 'e do as I want for'n to do?"

"'Cos 'e's so obstinate in 'is way as you are in yours."

"My dear life, I bain't obstinate. 'Ow can 'ee say so? I only do same as my father and granfer did. I'm sure they wouldn't like for me to alter it."

"No, I don't 'spose they would," said Mrs. Tom, "still..."

Sabina was troubled, but not on account of Isolda's mistaken view of her character. That she had already forgotten. "Well, I've got th' old George Biddick. I'm sure 'e'll do what I want for'n to do, if Leadville won't."

"Still that isn't like seein' for yerself."

"I shall 'av to take the chance of that," but she did not seem happy about it. She mused with knit brow for some seconds, then changed the subject. "Isolda, I'd like for Mrs. Bate to put my bed up in the big room."

This—the old Justice Room—occupied one end of the house. For many years it had been used as a storeroom, but underneath dust and litter lay evidence, in painted panelling and marble mantelpiece, of former state.

"'Tis a proper old lumber-shop," said Mrs. Tom, "but that doesn't matter."

"You see," explained Sabina, "I can't go overstairs."

"I wonder 'ow Leadville'll like sleepin' on the ground floor?"

"Well, he must like it or lump it." She spoke with the confidence of one whose marriage had been a success. "We'll get the room to rights for yer."

"And Isolda, I don't want to keep on Mrs. Bate, nor I don't want her Jenifer nor her Janey."

"'Ow'll 'ee manage then?"

"I want some one of my own flesh and blood. I should love to 'av one of your li'l maids. Why couldn't I 'av Gray? We've always 'greed like chickens."

"Well, I don't know I'm sure." Mrs. Tom had been expecting this, she had even schemed for it. She had five daughters, pretty maidens all of them, and Gray was the eldest. What more suitable than that she should fill a daughter's place at Wastralls? Nevertheless it would not be wise to jump at the offer. "She's young to go from 'ome."

"Wastralls is only next door and she'll be all right with me."

"An' 'as you've none of yer own," agreed Mrs. Tom, "Gray's the nearest."

Whatever Sabina's intentions, however, she would not promise to make the girl her heir. "'Twill be for the maid's good," she said vaguely.

"I'll see what Tom got to say about it." Gray was eighteen and, with Richbell coming on, could well be spared. No doubt Mrs. Constantine Rosevear would think Wastralls ought eventually to go to one of her sons; but, in this world, a hen scratched up what she could for her own chicks.

"Gray think more 'bout 'ome than Richbell," Sabina said thoughtfully. "She's not after the chaps so much."

The mother's pride was touched. "Whenever she go up round the parish, there's always three or four pairs of eyes lookin' at Gray. She can always 'av a chap if she like, but she don't trouble whether she do or no."

"Is there any special young man, do 'ee think?"

"Well now, I don't care to say..."

Sabina's curiosity was aroused. "Now Isolda, there's somethin' gone on since I come in 'ere. Who is it?"

Mrs. Rosevear had spent some of the happiest hours of her life, discussing her children with this trusty friend. "No stranger," she said smilingly.

"Who then?"

"One of your 'inds."

The other opened her eyes. "My dear life, didn't she ought to be lookin' for some one better off?"

"She don't think anything of money."

"They don't at that age, we got to do that for'm. Who is it then?"

"Why, Jim Rosevear, the yard-man."

Mrs. Byron knitted her brows in an endeavour to recall the young man's face. "Jim Rosevear? He come just before my accident. I can't think who 'ee is."

"Why, iss you do. You know, Jack Rosevear of Treketh's son."

"Jack Rosevear—th' old chap who's so contrary?"

"That's of'm. When he get in a temper, you know, 'ee take off 'is 'at, swing'n around, and fling'n down and stamp on it."

"Oh iss, I know, I remember." She meditated. "That 'edn't as bad after all."

"No, 'tedn't bad, though 'ee've quarrelled with's father. But Mrs. Andrews over to Gentle Jane is 'is auntie and, as she's nobody of 'er own and 'er man's dead, there's a farm there and Jim's nothing to do but go in and 'ang up 'is 'at."

"Then what's ah doin' at Wastralls?"

Isolda smiled, that secret smile of the mother. "Well, you needn't ask me that. Ed'n Wastralls next door to Hember?"

"So that's it, is it?"

"There was heaps o' maidens after 'im, for 'e's a pretty boy and, at Christmas Tree last New Year, 'e ad some mistletoe in's cap and they all astin' for't; but Gray was the one 'e gived it to. And that's 'ow 'e come to you as yard-man."

"And do she think anything 'bout 'im?"

"I believe she do, but she don't go round and tell everybody what she's doin'. She's so meek as a mouse."

"Then tedn't known?"

"You're the first I've told anything to about it."

Sabina nodded. "Then if Gray comes to me, it'll hurry matters up?"

"Well, I'm very 'greeable for 'er to 'av 'im, 'cos I think 'e's a nice boy."

"And Gentle Jane is a nice farm and you've four other maidens? Well, I dunno as I shall want to lose 'er as soon as I get 'er, still we can settle that by and by."

# CHAPTER IV

A few days, spent in trundling herself about the ward, and Mrs. Byron was ready for the long journey, over Big Hill and down to the sea. Leadville, who saw in her return the extinction of his last hope, had not the heart to come for her.

"Pretty pickle I should look," he said to Mrs. Tom, "drivin' missus 'ome sittin' up in that trolly, showin' 'erself off like that. Better fit she should 'av Mr. Brenton's covered cart and cover 'erself up. Any one'd think she'd want to 'ide 'er affliction."

"You fancy S'bina 'idin' of it?" said Mrs. Tom, who had suggested his going. "She'll be quite proud for people to see 'er goin' about with 'er poor old stumps. Leavin' out 'er laigs, you knaw, she's as strong as ever."

When he frowned Byron's black brows came together in an ominous line. "Strong as ever?" he said, "that's different from what Dr. Derek told me. He give me no encouragement as she'll make old bones."

"I wouldn't give much for that, then. She'll be like a barley weed, always dyin' and never dead." She had been cleaning the house in readiness for Mrs. Byron's return; and now, her labours ended, was drinking a cup of tea with the master of it. "They old Rosevears was long-livin' and they do say, she's more like Old Squire than either Tom or Constantine be. 'Oo be 'ee gwine send in for 'er?"

"Jim can go in for 'er; there is two or three things wanted into Shoppe" — this was another hamlet in the widespread parish — "and 'e can bring 'em 'ome."

"I'm sorry you bain't goin'. You're the one ought to fetch 'er."

"I've got a very poor 'eart for that sort of thing and this'll be worse than Hobby-horse goin' to Traytor."

"Iss," nodded Mrs. Tom. "I bet everybody'll turn out to give S'bina a welcome 'ome. After all, your ways bain't like our ways."

Leadville could not let that pass. "I might 'a 'bin born down east o' Truro, still I can't tell you whether I was or no. But I feel in my bones an' veins that I'm no 'foreigner.' Couldn't fancy this place as I do if it wadn't so."

"'Tis your misfortune," said Mrs. Tom, taking her cloak from the door-peg, "as you fancy it so. If you was one of we, you'd act different."

Mrs. Byron had a bright day for her journey, a day with but one cloud. The staff of the hospital had gathered to see her start and when, on her trolly, and followed by her luggage and a certain long wooden box, oddly suggestive of a shortened coffin, she rolled herself down the hall and into the roadway, they broke into a cheer. The gallant bearing of this mutilated creature had drawn from them an emotional response. The beauty of it, the poignancy, touched them. Men pressed forward to offer their help and tears stood in the eyes of the women. That was the spirit, this elemental courage, this defiance of unhappy fate. Yes, Sabina was indeed true descendant of Old Squire—he to whom men for so long had given their respect.

In the road, drawn up and waiting, stood the farm wagon. Jim Rosevear, with a proper sense of the ceremonial nature of the occasion, had plaited the horses' manes and tails with coloured worsteds. The brass harness twinkled in the sun and the cart-horses had been groomed until their coats were nearly as bright. Sabina, occupied with her trolly, which was showing a tendency to turn a little to the left, was not immediately aware that the driver was not her husband. Not indeed until the trolly had been lifted to its place on the floor of the wagon and secured by ropes, was she at liberty to look about.

When she saw who was come for her she leaned forward in the cone. "Where's the maister to?" she asked.

Jim, who was getting ready to start, looked over his shoulder. "He's gone fishin'."

"Fishin'?" She had thought he might have gone on business down one of the many crooked streets of the little town, business from which he would return in time to drive her home.

"Fishin' for bass on the Head."

"Whatever took'n in the 'ead to do that to-day?" she said and dwelt for a moment on the incomprehensible nature of man. Strange that Leadville should not want to share her triumph, the triumph of the woman who belonged to him, who was flesh of his flesh; to share this triumph which was, in part, his. She had been in excellent spirits, but his absence dashed them. It required the manifested goodwill of the people in the streets to restore her equanimity.

In spite of this drawback, however, her progress was, in its way, royal. Throned in the wagon she passed slowly along the main road. Placed thus high and with trunk and head emerging from the wicker cone like an amazing flower, she was undoubtedly a queer figure; but the people who came running up the lanes and out of the houses along the route, to give her the blessing of their good wishes, missed the queerness. They had known her all the forty years of her life. She was part of the setting in which they played their humble parts. A little prejudiced in her favour through long association, this display of primitive courage moved them. They welcomed it as in keeping with the family tradition, as something worthy, and they offered it the kind encouragement of hearty handshakes and good words.

"I be pretty an' glad to see yer come 'ome again, ma'am. Terrible, terrible accident, you must 'av 'ad; still you don't seem to make much of't. Mary Elizabeth's brought 'ee a few lilies."

"That trolly be a clever thought of yours, Mrs. Byron. I never see nothing like it before."

"I reckon you've 'ad a draggin' time, ma'am. We'm all glad to 'av 'ee back again."

"Do 'ee take and drink up this cup of milk and eat a bit of yeller cake or 'ee'll be faintin' before 'ee come to Trevorrick," said a farmer's wife.

"If 'ee'd like a glass of wine now, you've only to say the word, and you can 'av it," interposed the landlord of the Dolphin; "I'd be proud to serve 'ee."

"I be come 'ome," said Sabina to her charioteer as they jogged on and her voice had a contented ring. She had forgotten the disappointment of Leadville's absence. She was come back to her own people and her own place and she was welcome.

The young man lifted a smiling face and she remembered that this was the 'pretty boy' who was courting her niece. She looked at him with interest. He was certainly good-looking, definitely so, a tall slim youth with a fine profile, deeply-set dark-blue eyes, black hair and a small tawny moustache. She wondered how the courtship was progressing. Gray, with cloudy hair about a wind-flower face, would make a charming bride. Sabina's thoughts ran nimbly forward. She saw the young couple housed at Wastralls, Rosevear working the farm under her direction and the old cradle once more in use. The prospect promised her an autumn happiness. Wonderful indeed, the way in which the wind is tempered to the shorn!

When the farm cart turned off the highway by St. Cadic Mill, Sabina found Constantine Rosevear and his wife waiting by the roadside. The big florid man, though he had wife and three grown sons, had never been able to forget that Sabina was the woman he should have married. His Betsey was all right but, about Sabina, lingered the glamour of romance.

"I been in terrible fear," he told her simply, "and I'm 'avin' holiday to-day. If you don't mind I'll walk down to Wastralls with you. You don't know 'ow glad I be to see ye 'ome again and lookin' so well too."

Sabina's heart beat irregularly for a moment. If only Leadville would talk to her like this! She comforted herself with the thought that his being undemonstrative did not mean he was unfeeling. Words did not come easily to him, but still waters run deep.

The cottagers about the smithy threw more flowers into the cart. "Might be May Day," as Sabina said, with her happy smile. At Hember, Tom Rosevear was waiting with four of his daughters. "Mother's down to Wastralls wi' Gray," he said and the blooming girls, the so-called nieces, raised their young voices in affectionate greeting. 'Aunt S'bina' had been the fairy godmother of the family, always willing to abet them in any piece of innocent fun. They were sincerely glad to have her back.

The drive had been long for one just out of hospital, but the kindliness of friends and neighbours had proved a stimulant. When the wagon turned into the yard of Wastralls, however, Sabina was almost too tired to note the changes that had been made. The absence of the honeysuckle caused the porch to look bare, the old sheepdog was no longer lying in the sun; but Leadville had come back from the fishing and was ready to lift her down. At sight of him the tired face brightened. "I'm glad to come 'ome again," she said.

The man had been standing idly by the door. Having drawn nothing out of the sea he had come back in a mood which was not uninfluenced by his lack of success. Everything had gone wrong, his hopes were dashed, his plans had miscarried and he searched the landscape in vain for any hope of change. Sabina was well again, she had already asserted her will with regard to the farm and before him lay a future as dreary as the past.

He lifted his eyes as the beflowered cortège rolled into the yard. He had expected a sort of chair and the trolly with its basket-work cone was an unpleasant surprise; while the sight of his wife, in brightly coloured gown and pink sunbonnet, swelling out of it like a monstrous fruit, completed his dismay. She was a figure of fun, a queer oddity, repellent as something out of nature. The bravery that faced the sunshine as simply as in the days of its strength did not appeal to him, he was only conscious of the deformity. His heart contracted, emptied itself of good-will, then slowly filled again—but not with kindliness.

The business of unloading occupied the men for some minutes and Mrs. Rosevear, taking the parcels, handed them to her daughter.

"What a lovely lot o' flowers. I should think every garden for miles round will be bare."

"Take care o' that box," cried Sabina, suddenly, as they lifted out the case that was suggestive of a coffin. "I value that."

"Where be 'ee gwine put it, auntie?"

"In the cupboard in the big parlour."

"What 'av 'ee got in it?"

"Ah, my dear, ask me no questions and I tell 'ee no lies."

"'Ere, I'll take that," said Mrs. Tom, intervening, "I know where it got to be put. 'Tis what you told me of, S'bina?"

Mrs. Byron nodded. "Iss, I've brought it back wi' me. Doctor said I was maäze to do it; but I said I would, an' I 'av."

A meal was ready on the kitchen table, a piece of stout wood which had weathered the use and elbow-grease of more than a century. This room had been for three generations the gathering-place of the family. Innumerable savoury meals had been cooked on the slab range; hams in a succession longer than that of the Kings of England had been lifted from the rafter hooks and, after the buffetings of winter and the scorch of summer, men had taken their ease on the bench while women made and mended. Old tales had been told and retold by deep voices, tales of witches, of wreckers, of people 'pisky-led'n'; and the sound of them lingered in the dim corners. They were waiting for the new generation which should utter once more the familiar words and keep alive the traditions.

"I never thought I should ever be back 'ere any more," said Sabina, contentedly, as she ran her trolly up to the table and, by a contrivance similar to that on a dentist's chair, reduced her height to a sitting level. "It do seem good to be 'ome. Everything look so natural."

"Well, 'twould be funny if it didn't," said Mrs. Rosevear, helping the meat.

"Don't seem as if I'd been all that time away."

"I expect it do to Leadville."

His wife turned to him. "What do 'ee think of my invention?"

"I can't abide it," said the man, with the emphasis of sincere feeling.

The others looked at him in surprise. "I'll always be thinking of what you was," he added hastily.

Sabina's face clouded, but only for a moment. "Let's make the best of things," she said. "I'm goin' to forget about them times, I'm goin' to live for the moment."

"I'm not one as forgets," said Leadville heavily.

Revived by food and rest Sabina was soon impatient to begin a further progress. She trundled herself into the linhay to inspect the milk and butter; then into the two seldom-used rooms known as the Big and Little Parlour. Beyond them lay the wide shallow stairs, the door into the front part of the house and the long Justice Room.

Mrs. Tom threw open the door of this and Sabina, pushing the trolly in, uttered an exclamation of pleasure. The litter of agricultural implements, broken harness, bags and boxes, had been cleared away, the grates had been blacked and the panelled wall painted a shadowy grey. Between the two fireplaces stood a large bed, the posts of which were carved with corn, fruit and other emblems of fertility. On it lay a patchwork quilt, the work of Sabina's grandmother. Drift-wood fires flamed under the white marble mantelpieces and the coverlet shone with the glistening silks of other days. The spacious room with its white-hung bed and its white curtains, smelt of the sea and Sabina turned and smiled at her husband.

"'Av you moved your clothes down?" she asked.

"Not that I know of."

"Well, you better make 'aste an' do't."

Looking past her into the beautiful room he thought dimly that it was too large. "I shent like it down 'ere," he said and something ancestral moved in him, assuring him that the upper parts of a house, the upper branches, were secure from the marauding enemy, the terror by night. "Never slept on the ground-floor."

Laying a hand affectionately on his shoulder, the woman looked into his face with a touch of softening and appeal. Surely he would not leave her to sleep there alone?

To the man, this light touch was illuminating. "Oh, leave'n go," he muttered.

In the bedroom, Gray Rosevear was moving deftly to and fro, unpacking Sabina's clothes and laying them in the drawers of the tall-boy. The man's eyes followed her light figure, at first unconsciously, but before long with a strange quickening of emotion. If it had been this girl who was asking him, he would have given up his eyrie with an eager willingness. He did not understand himself. What was Gray to him?

His wife's voice when she spoke again, seemed a whisper from far away. "I can't go overstairs," she said pleadingly.

Byron turned his eyes deliberately from Gray's wildflower grace to the thick shortened figure in the trolly and his incipient repugnance grew. Sleep with this deformity? He could not bring himself to it. To live in the same house with her would be difficult; at least he would shut her out of his nights. Already he knew instinctively what those nights, moon-silvered, star-set, nights not of bitter brooding but of dreams, would be to him.

"I can't sleep 'ere."

Sabina sighed. The people had given her the froth of sweet words but this was reality. "Well, my dear, I can't 'elp it," she said resignedly. "I can't do much nowadays."

"Ah now, if 'ee'd only reckernize that."

The touch of opposition was a spur. "Still there's a lot as I can do. This trolly now, 'll 'elp me a lot."

He eyed it with distaste. "Oogly thing, can't think why 'ee do want to be runnin' round like a toad on a red-'ot shovel. Seein' 'ow you be, 'twould be more to your credit if you was to die down and be quiet, 'stead o goin' about on an old thing like that. You'll be the laughing-stock of the parish."

"Nothin' 'ud get done."

"Oh, fiddlesticks, 'ow won't the things be done? Can't I do't for yer?" For the moment Gray was forgotten and he was back at the old gnawing bitterness.

"Whiles my 'ead's above ground, I'll look after the place myself," said Sabina who, being tired, was a little captious. She was disappointed that her welcome home had been so commonplace. She had expected, she knew not what, but something culminating.

"A pretty mess 'ee'll make of it," muttered Leadville and, turning about, walked off with himself. When he and Sabina differed, which was not often—their differences being fundamental, trifles took the subsidiary place so seldom granted them—he invariably ended the discussion by going out of the house. With all the open from which to choose it was easy for him to get away from a woman's tiresomeness, to get back to his own quiet company and his thoughts.

Sabina looked after the husband whom she had long ago decided was difficult, but probably not more so than other men, and her heart sank. She had so wanted Leadville to rejoice with her over her recovery, to be proud of her. Though she carried herself gallantly there were periods when her poor heart acknowledged a weakness, a lowness. She had longed sometimes to stay it on a greater strength.

"Where's Gray goin' to sleep?" asked Mrs. Rosevear who, standing quietly in the background, had been a shrewd spectator.

"Gray?" said she, and a feeling seldom hitherto experienced, awoke in her. If she had been as young as Gray, soft-eyed as she, would it have made a difference?

"Twill be a bit lonely for 'er upstairs," said the mother thoughtfully. "Though, of course, Leadville'll be near."

But it was envy, not jealousy, that had been awakened in Mrs. Byron. "Let her come in wi' me. We'll 'av a little bed put up, there's plenty of room for 'er."

When Leadville came back, and he must in time grow accustomed to the idea of sleeping on the ground-floor, a fresh arrangement could be made. Meanwhile the maid would be company. Sabina felt that the place was peopled with the judges and judged of long ago and, to her Celtic mind, the shadows moved. In the dark hours it would be comforting to hear the movements, the breathing, of some one still this side the grave.

From an upper chamber they brought the small bedstead which, when Mrs. Byron was a girl, had been hers; also a chest of drawers.

"Where's your traäde to?" asked the mother.

"Jim's bringin' it down. I believe he's out in the kitchen now. I'll go and see."

As she went from the room Mrs. Rosevear sank into the nearest chair. "I'm glad you'm back, S'bina. I bin so whisht without 'ee. Not a soul to speak to besides Tom and you can't tell a man very much."

"No, they don't understand." Her thoughts wandered for a moment. Leadville had been strange in his manner but of course it was only that he did not understand.

"Now you've seen Jim," continued Mrs. Rosevear, "what do you think of him?"

Sabina roused herself. "I call 'ee a proper chap," she said smilingly. "Lovely curly 'air he 'as."

"Yes," confided the mother, "and Gray's as maäze as a rattle about 'im.'"

Mrs. Tom's confidences made Sabina feel as if she had a share in the other's happy motherhood. They sat gossiping until the shadows began to fill the valley. Jim was a long time on his way with Gray's box—but to every man and woman their hour!

Leadville, on leaving the house, had turned his face towards the cliff. Beyond its dark wall was space and light. He took the little path that led over the head, passed the deep curves of what in prehistoric times had been the earthworks of a stockaded hold and came out upon a broad shelf of rock. The tide was in, large green waves were rolling, with a break like gunfire, into the caves below, and, facing him, was one of the strange sunsets often seen on that coast. The western sky was scarlet and across the light was a trail of black clouds.

"A red sky at night, is the shepherd's delight," muttered the man, flinging himself down above the booming uproar of the water. Below, the shags were nesting on inaccessible ledges and a solitary seal was diving through the crests of the green rollers. Byron felt unusually, inexplicably cheerful. The glories of the sunset were in keeping with his mood, a mood, as he realized, of the incoming tide. On his shelf of rock he lay in a happy dream. Hitherto he had loved nothing but a few acres of land; he had hungered after fields and rocks, had dragged out a dark existence of craving and disappointment. Now his tormented spirit was at peace. The wide expanse of heaven changed from scarlet to poppy-red, the raven clouds grew more numerous and Leadville looked on with happy eyes. In his breast was a ferment, like the unresting ferment of the sea, but neither cold nor lifeless. A wind was blowing steadily from the west, but he did not feel it for he was warm. His spirit, with its capacity for intense feeling, had crossed a boundary line, beyond which was neither heat nor cold, hunger nor thirst. He had loved Wastralls, now he was in the power of a force stronger than that love, of a force the strongest in the world.

# CHAPTER V

Mrs. Byron, wheeling her trolly through the "houses and courts" of Wastralls, along the garden paths and down the neglected drive, found that her creation had a feeling for rises in the ground that was almost uncanny. "Thus far shalt thou go," said the trolly and Jim Rosevear spent many a half-hour levelling surfaces which Mrs. Byron had hitherto believed to be as flat as the yard pond. On the whole she got about as much as she had expected to; and far more than her husband or even the hinds had believed possible.

The latter had served her well, partly because she, being a good master, it was difficult for them to do otherwise; but also because, being raised above them, a woman and unfamiliar, she was in some dim way that Golden Helen of all male dreams. For her part she understood them as she understood the animals on the farm, their idiosyncrasies, their capacity. She worked them as she worked her horses, as kindly, with as much consideration; but without feeling that they were nearer to her in the scale of creation.

On her return to Wastralls she found that her long absence and Leadville's slack rule, hard work one day, off shooting the next, had demoralized the little band. They gave their employer a hearty welcome, vicariously, proud of one who, though desperately injured, had refused to give up the struggle which is life; but it soon became evident that they believed her accident and subsequent mutilation had changed her into something weak and strange. Her orders were questioned. Unconsciously the men were testing the power that for so long had kept them subservient.

"George," said she to Biddick, one bright June morning, "you'd better cut that 'ay in Cross Parks to-day."

"I think I should leave it a day or two longer, missis. I b'lieve we're goin' to 'av some rain," returned the old fellow who, at the moment, had a job more to his liking.

Sabina's voice rang out. "Never mind about that. You get the men and 'av it done at once. It'll be done before the rain come then."

She had a sense of weather so keen that she had been known to predict it for months, even seasons, ahead and Biddick looked at her uneasily. When some days later, he came for his week's money, she spoke to him sharply.

"If you'm too old for yer work, better jack it up and I'll hire a younger man."

"I thought missis, as we was in for a lot of rain."

"I'm missis and I'll 'av things done my way."

As she once said, "Don't meet fear half-way, go all the way and you'll crush 'un in the egg!"

But although Sabina asserted herself with promptitude and decision, it was not in the old effortless way. Her health was far from satisfactory. She held her own, reduced her team to an obedience which for them was happiness, but paid for her victory in restless nights, in pain and weariness. She thought sometimes that it would be impossible for her to carry on.

"I do ache so bad," she told her faithful crony, "that I feel I shall 'av to give up and be a bed-lier."

"My dear life," said Mrs Tom, pursuing her old tactics, "'tis just what Leadville'd like for 'ee to be."

"D'yer think 'e would?"

"Iss, I'm sure 'e would, 'e'd wait on yer 'and and foot."

"I should like to see 'un then."

"I can't fancy you being a bed-lier," said Mrs. Tom comfortably. "Did Gray tell 'ee there's a piece of hedge down in the li'l medder?"

"No, she didn't." Sabina was interested. "An' I thinking to 'av the sheep turned into the lower field! I'll send Jim down this afternoon to mend'n. 'E's a good boy."

"Farmer's son and got farmin' in's veins."

"I like to see the way he wait on Gray. I should be glad for'm to live 'ere after they'm married. The way he's goin' he'll do fine. Biddick's gettin' old and Jim shall be foreman and teel Wastralls for me. He got an eye for the stock and he's a good-working li'l feller. Oh iss, Gray's a lucky maid."

Mrs. Tom did not think the suggested arrangement would prove satisfactory; but the young couple were not yet married, were not even engaged and, if Sabina could not see what was going on, it was not for others to point it out to her.

"Jim'll be agreeable," she said non-committally, "'tis all the same to him whether he go to his auntie at Gentle Jane or whether he stay 'ere. All 'e think about is Gray. Ah, my dear, I should like for 'ee to get as far as Hember and see they two sittin' together wi' us. 'Tis so good as a picture."

Sabina nodded. "Leadville was only sayin' yesterday he never seen a maid so fond of 'er 'ome as Gray. Soon ever 'er work's done she's off 'ome like a bird."

"I 'ope she don't leave 'ee too much by yerself?"

"No, no, my dear, if she'd been my own daughter she couldn't do more for me," and she sighed, feeling that if Gray had been the child whose place she filled, Leadville would have been able to rest his heart content. She could see that the pseudo-relationship in which the young girl stood to him was unsatisfactory and she understood, though too vaguely to put it into words, that for people to share a home they should be bound by blood or sex.

"Well, I must do so well as I can," she added, reverting to the main topic of their wandering talk. "'Tis live from day to day and though I don't feel very special, I must be surely stronger than I was."

"Iss," said Mrs. Tom encouragingly, "I can see as each month make a difference to 'ee."

Sabina might talk of becoming a 'bed-lier,' but only the slightest spur was required to nerve her to fresh effort; and by living, as she had said, from day to day and leaning on the young strength of Gray, she won through the summer. Indeed the glooms of autumn were brightened for her by the conviction that she would live usefully and might live long. Leadville on the other hand saw his last hope fading. Dr. Derek had declared that she could not stand the shock to her system; that, if she survived, it would be as an invalid. Sabina however had the will to live and the trolly—a contrivance which Leadville both detested and contemned carried her from kitchen to linhay and from barn to byre. Her husband looked on with growing exasperation, opposing to her good-will a sulky silence. At meal-times he sat with eyes fixed on his plate or lifted them for a quick glance at Gray. When he went out, he took his gun, the gun that hung on thongs over the kitchen door and which, as he had inherited it from old Leadville Byron, was the one possession he did not owe his wife. When he came back it was to sit in Old Squire's big chair and spend his time cleaning and oiling it. Whither he went, Sabina did not know. She sighed over his withdrawal of himself, his dull hostility, but did not lose heart. In the end Leadville, seeing that the struggle was hopeless, must return to her. What else could he do? He, too, was middle-aged and except for her was alone in the world.

Although Mrs. Byron felt sure of the ultimate issue, she had not missed the import of those quick glances when Leadville, she and Gray sat at table together. He would answer when the girl spoke and, if she were likely to be making butter or plucking chickens, would hang about and offer his help. When he brought in fish or birds it was to Gray that he took them and, in the evening, laying the gun across his knees, he would lean forward and stare at her. The wife looked on, not indulgently but with her usual robust common sense. Middle-aged men were often transiently attracted by young relatives—nieces or cousins—but the girls went to homes of their own, the old fellows forgot and no harm was done. In a better-managed world, the generations would be sharply defined and each would be sufficient unto itself. Sabina could not wonder that Leadville should prefer the delicacy of tint, the soft dewy eyes of the maid to her own stale and faded charms. She looked at herself in the glass, at her white hair, the loose skin of her neck, the fixed colour in her cheeks. She had been handsome and she had not cared. Now that wrinkles had come about her eyes she thought longingly of the pale smooth lids between which she had so contentedly surveyed her world. The mood, the regret, were new to her, an outcome of her illness and she returned before long to the old comfortable indifference. If she were in the forties so was Leadville. His figure was heavy, his face lined and weatherbeaten. Gray comparing him with Jim Rosevear could not fail to mark the contrast.

"Aunt S'bina, you been in the house all day," the girl said one evening as they sat at tea.

"Well, my dear," returned Mrs. Byron easily, "I've been busy; I had the baking to do and this afternoon I've cleaned out the rubbish your mammy put in the stair-cupboard and after that"—she smiled and looked hopefully at her husband—"I mended yer uncle's socks."

Leadville, who was cutting himself a slice of ham, threw the knife into the dish with a clatter. Why did she meddle with his clothes? He'd rather wear them all holes than have her mend them. 'Your uncle,' too! He wasn't Gray's uncle, he wasn't even her cousin. No, but—and he drifted out upon the wave that was for ever lapping about his feet.

"Do you think you can spare me? I should like to go home after tea," pursued the girl.

"Iss, my dear, I can spare yer."

"Why can't you come too, Aunt S'bina?"

"Me go up that hill? Why, you know trolly won't take the least rise in the ground."

"Well, I'll push behind."

"Don't believe you'm strong enough."

"Why not Uncle Leadville push it then?"

Byron returned from his dream to sweep a lowering glance over the little platform of shivered wood. "I'd like to see myself pushin' that thing."

"'Twould do Aunt Sabina good to have a craik with mammy."

As this was to him a matter of indifference he made no answer and Gray turned to Mrs. Byron. "Anyhow, auntie, you'll come as far as the gate with me, won't you?"

"Why, of course I will. I did last night and the night before, didn't I?" said the other innocently. From the yard gate the road was in sight as far as Hember.

"Yes and I like for you to be there. It's company till I get home."

"I'll give you my company," said Leadville abruptly, "without you askin' me for't."

Gray turned a face, from which all expression had been banished, on the speaker. "I think you better stay with Aunt S'bina."

"Oh, she don't want me," he answered, a touch of pleading in his manner.

"Iss, Leadville," said the wife tranquilly, "I'm glad for 'ee to stay in wi' me. Let the young ones go, they don't want we old 'uns followin' of them up. We've 'ad our day."

The man turned on her quickly. "Me old?" he cried with manifest irritation. "I'll tell yer about old. I bain't old."

"You'm in yer prime; but that seem old to a young maid."

"Do I seem old to you, Gray?" demanded he, and his eyes were both pleading and threatening, eyes so hungry that the girl had some ado to give him an unmoved reply. Not that she felt any sympathy with him in what she looked on as a tiresome aberration, but that under the quiet surface she was a little stirred and a little afraid. "You'm older than dad," she said at last.

"I'm ten times the man your father is!" He stretched his arms and expanded his deep chest. He was desperately anxious to prove to her his unabated virility, while she, timid, and on the threshold of awakening sensation, would have avoided the thought of it. His strength, present with her, and always desirous, was a subtle menace to the young happiness which her bosom shrined. "There isn't a feller for miles round can wrestle me or box me. You know I can carry four hundredweight on my shoulders where other chaps take two. I hain't old."

The girl, moved by her longing to escape, had risen and drawn nearer to her aunt. Here was, at least, protection, protection from all but that dim admission of her own heart that Leadville Byron was indeed all he claimed to be and more. For he was not only strong he was persistent, he was forcible. "Don't make no difference to me," she said, in a voice she tried to render careless, "whether you're old or not." And she spoke the truth. It was not his age that mattered.

When she came to Wastralls she had been prepared to find Leadville devoted to his wife's interests and deeply thankful she had been spared to him. By degrees it dawned on her simplicity that his thoughts were otherwise busy, that Sabina was a matter of indifference to him, or worse, that he was living a dream life of which she, Gray, was the centre. An unhappy little centre! She had had her share of attention from the young men of the scattered community, a little sighing, a soft pursuit, a hot word and the end. But Leadville was a stranger and his pursuit was not soft but fierce. He did not sigh but she could not be in the room with him without feeling that his brawny chest, his strong arms were aching with the longing to lay hold of her. She could not touch him accidentally without feeling the thrill of his desire. She was enveloped by his thoughts; and she struggled, resenting this emotion which threatened to overwhelm her and the bright prospects of her youth. For Gray was in need, not of a conflagration, but of a little fire upon the hearth.

With the man, matters were gradually coming to a head. He had not loved the old couple who had adopted him, he had been only mildly attracted by his wife, but he had in him a fund of passion which, through the fallow years, had been growing in concentration and of which the fuse had at length been lighted. His love for Gray was as overwhelming to himself as it might prove to its object. He had not known what a furnace was smouldering at the heart of him and, when the flame broke forth, to resist was impossible. He did not attempt it. On the contrary he gave himself up to these new sensations that ran through him, wave after wave, like a burning but not scarifying fire. His new passion pushed Wastralls for the time being into the background. He could not contain more than one absorbing emotion. He had been the persistent, passionate lover of the land, so but with more fever, did he love Gray. Wonderful as to him were these new feelings, he found them almost too poignant. When she entered a room in which he sat his throat went dry, he could hardly speak and the brief contacts of skirt or hand proved unendurably sweet. He turned from these moments of a troubling ecstasy to the languorous long intervals when she was absent and he, recalling her face, could dwell on it and imagine the fulfilling, tender, fiery, wonderful, of his every hope.

During the first months that Gray was living at Wastralls, Byron spent much of his time on Dark Head; but in the end he woke to a desire for more than dreams could give, a desire which grew in intensity after the manner of Jack the Giant-killer's bean. He began to haunt the young girl's steps and her honest attempts to discourage him passed with him for a sort of tantalizing encouragement. He could not believe that the object of a feeling so intense could be unresponsive, that these troubling sensations were not mutual; and when Gray avoided him, escaped from him, even, when protected by Sabina, flouted him with a little angry ruffling, he smiled with the conviction that his hour was at hand.

Steady untiring pursuit is apt to demoralize the victim and while Sabina thought the summer heats had washed the colour out of Gray's cheek, Mrs. Tom, uneasy as a hen when hawks are hovering, went to the root of the matter.

"Do 'ee like being to Wastralls, Gray?" she asked that evening when, having left Sabina stationed at the yard gate, the girl had run up the road, to arrive breathless and panting.

"Oh yes, mammy, I do dearly love Aunt S'bina."

"Why was you runnin' so just now?"

Gray hesitated. Very few girls confide such matters to a mother's ear. Experience shall not teach. Each generation will make its own mistakes and gather its handful of treasures and keep its secrets. Gray was however very doubtful and unhappy and, having no girl of her own age to consult, she turned to her mother.

"It's Uncle Leadville. He's always wanting to come with me and I don't want'n. I dunno—" she paused.

"Iss?" said Mrs. Tom quietly.

"I dunno as Jim'll be agreeable."

"My dear, why don't you wear the ring that 'e give you?"

"I don't know, I don't like to. I"—she smiled anxiously, yet with a glimmering of humour—"I don't believe Uncle Leadville would like to see me wearin' a ring."

Having said so much, Gray was willing to make further admissions. "I feel afraid of Unde Leadville, he's always after me and his eyes seem to be watching me as if they was coming out of his sockets. I can't sleep by night, mammy, I—I'm always thinking about him and," she looked shyly away, unable in this moment of revelation to meet her mother's understanding eye, "I don't want to, I'm—" her voice sank, "I'm afraid."

"'Tis a shame," said Mrs. Tom warmly. She knew how compelling are strength and intensity but thought it wisest not to let her knowledge appear. The susceptibilities of young people are easily ruffled.

"I think it's wicked of him, mammy." She was righteously indignant that he should be making life so difficult, "and auntie is so good to him."

"Iss," sighed the matron, "but men's so, they can't help theirselves—poor old villains. Why don't you come 'ome with me for a bit and leave Richbell go down with your auntie?"

Gray's face brightened hopefully, then she shook her head. "I don't think Aunt S'bina would like it."

"Well, I'll talk to yer auntie about it an' tell 'er what I think."

"Don't you say nothing about what I've told you," cried youth, anxious as to the discretion of gossiping middle-age.

"You can trust me," and Gray, looking into the kind shrewd face, felt that she might.

"You know she see Uncle Leadville's tiresome but she don't think he mean anything."

"Poor sawl, no she wouldn't, of course, bein' 'is wife. He'll say one thing to she an' another thing to you."

Gray nodded. That was the way of it.

"And she'll believe what 'e say."

"He'd tell her I was making a fuss about nothing. Yes, he would."

"There's Jim comin' up the road," said Mrs. Tom, who was sitting by the window; "I wonder 'e and Leadville get on."

"They don't see but very little of each other. If I was to be with Jim when Uncle Leadville come, I believe they'd fight; and the fear of that keeps me on pins and needles when I'm with Jim. It's all horrid."

"Well, dearie, I'll see what I can do with yer auntie. 'Twould be better if you could say as you was engaged to Jim, but I suppose you can't?"

"I daren't, mammy." Her large eyes, softly black, filled with tears. Courting-time is April weather but Gray felt that more showers than sunshine were falling to her share. "I'm frightened of Uncle Leadville and his old gun. We often say we'll do things but we don't after all; I got an idea he would."

Mrs. Tom took from behind the door a purple knitted bonnet and a cloak. The evenings were dark and the wind from the sea cold. She did not stay to take off her apron but went as she was, in her dark gown and with her kind face bright between the flaps of the woollen bonnet.

Sabina, lonely, because the husband who should have been sitting opposite to her at the end of the day was gone out, gave her a warmer greeting than was her wont. She was tired and the peace and good-fellowship to which she was looking forward seemed long in coming. She, also, would be glad of a chat.

# CHAPTER VI

"She've a whisht 'eart, poor Gray 'as," said the mother in deprecation of Mrs. Byron's stout advice that the maid should wear her ring openly and tell Leadville to go hang.

"Whatever is she 'fraid of?"

"Oh, I dunno, maids is like that sometimes."

"She needn't be afraid of Leadville, 'e 'edn't goin' do nothing."

"I don't say 'e 'av so far," was the cautious reply.

The wife laughed. "You don't think I've lived with'n all these years an' don't know 'e's all blow?"

But Mrs. Tom knew just how much justification there was for Gray's alarm. "Well, you know, Gray's easily frightened," she said thoughtfully. "I don't believe she'd come down the lane at night for all the gold in Tregols."

"Well, I never. Whatever is there to be afraid of?"

"You know she 'ad a bit of a shock one night."

"She didn't say a word about it to me, then."

"Well no, I s'pose she didn't like to."

"Whatever was it, then?"

"I don't think she 'ud like for me to say anything about it."

Mrs. Tom had successfully aroused her friend's curiosity and Sabina clapped her arm impatiently. "I'm sure Gray wouldn't mind you tellin' me of't."

"No, p'raps she wouldn't, still 'tis a awkward thing to say to 'ee."

"Never mind for that. I reckon I can listen to what you can say."

"Well, my dear." Mrs. Tom hitched her chair nearer to the trolly and lowered her voice. "Jim 'ad gone over to Treketh to see his mother and the maid was to home and she wouldn't leave 'er father see 'er back 'ere, said she'd be all right by 'erself. An' as she was comin' along, something rustled in the 'edge. 'Twas one of they dark nights and she couldn't see, but she thought 'twas a bullock."

"Iss?" Sabina's mind, by now ready for it, leaped to the natural conclusion. Leadville was trying to meet Gray on the quiet.

"And some one springed out and catched 'old of er and just about pulled the clothes off 'er back, they did," was Mrs. Tom's startling end to the story.

"My dear life! You don't mean to say so?" This was worse than she had feared; presented her, indeed, with a new and surprising view of her husband.

"I dunno 'owever she got away from 'im."

"Isolda!" and the fixed colour of her cheeks was a dull red patch on the pallor, "you don't mean to say that 'twas really 'im? You can't mean 'twas?"

"Oh, my dear, don't 'e ask me."

"I can't 'ardly believe," said the wife miserably, "that 'e'd do such a thing. 'E's always been a good-livin' feller, 'e don't drink and 'e never seemed to be after the maidens. Can't think," she said, surrendering the point as proven, "whatever ail the man."

The fact that Leadville was capable of using violence to gain his ends had sunk into Mrs. Tom's mind. She was like an old hen when a hawk is in the blue. "I don't want to keep Gray 'ome," she said uneasily, "but if Leadville worry the life out of 'er..."

Mrs. Byron had rallied from her consternation. At the bottom of her heart she preserved a little doubt. The story was perhaps substantially true, true enough to show in which direction the wind was blowing; but Gray, being a timid maid, the tale had not lost in the telling.

"'Tis a pack o' tommy-rot," she said at last, anger beginning to colour her unhappy amazement, "a man of his years runnin' after young maidens; but once Gray's married 'e won't think no more about it. 'Tis disgraceful of him; and, what's more, 'tis madness for'm to think she's goin' to 'av anything to do wi' an old man like 'e. Isolda, I do think 'tis time Gray was married."

"Iss, my dear, so do I."

"Well—why don't they?"

"It mean a good bit o' money to get married, you know," said Mrs. Tom who, in spite of her alert mind, was not capable of quick decisions, "and one thing more, marrying isn't horse-jocking."

"Why don't they put the banns in and get married on the quiet?"

The other went off on a side issue. "You know," she said, uttering her thoughts aloud, "Leadville's bound to know one day."

"If Gray was to walk in one morning and say 'I'm married,'" continued Mrs. Byron, "what could 'e do then? 'E'd 'av to 'old 'is tongue."

The thought of Gray doing anything so bold brought a smile to the mother's lips. "I'm sure she wouldn't do that, S'bina."

"Well, p'raps she wouldn't." Mrs. Byron had realized that her friend, in revealing the incident of the lane, had meant to convey a warning. The aunt did not wish to have Gray replaced by the handsome more noisy Richbell and yet... "I feel I belong to speak to Leadville about it," she said reluctantly. "But I don't want for'n to think I'm always watchin' 'im." The little doubt as to his having been as guilty as Isolda would have her think, had grown. She could not believe his jumping out of the hedge had been more than a trick, a practical joke. Gray, in her alarm, must have magnified it. These inexperienced girls were as easily frightened as a sheep! A way out of the difficulty occurred to her. "My dear, 'ow would it be if Leonora was to come and stay for a few days?"

Mrs. Tom thought that Sabina was only postponing the reckoning which in the long run she would be bound to make, but aloud she gave consent.

"Well, Leonora can come for a bit and see 'ow they get on, but she'd 'av to sleep 'ome. She'd better come down early in the mornin', for 'tis breakfast-time, when you'm in bed, that Leadville torment Gray."

"Every month," said Sabina hopefully, "I feel I shall soon be able to get up early in the mornin's; by spring, I'm sure I shall be able to."

"I hope by that time, please God," said Mrs. Tom, getting up to go, "the maid will be married."

She felt it would be as well for Gray to have the protection of a man, in love with her and constantly at her side and, as she went uphill between the November hedges, she considered what she should tell her husband. Tom was a peaceable and cautious man, but his blood was hot. The wife wondered whether he would be willing for Gray to be married quietly? A good deal depended on the girl. Since the time, as a little child, that she had fallen into the pail of boiling pig's meal and they had nearly lost her, she had been her father's pet. If he understood that she was unhappy and that Leadville was the cause, he would be certain to make himself unpleasant. Mrs. Tom did not wish to stir up strife.

Leonora, when told she was to spend her days at Auntie Sabina's, shook back her curls and declared herself delighted. One of a big household she knew the stint of comparatively narrow means and a change would be welcome. Before Gray was out of her aunt's room the following morning, impatient fingers were rattling at the handle of the porch; and Leadville, stealing down as usual in his stockinged feet, heard with surprise a sound of voices in the kitchen. He stared when Leonora came from the linhay carrying hog's pudding and a frying-pan.

"I've come to breakfast," she said, smiling up at him with bright and friendly eyes, "and I be comin' every morning. I like comin' 'ere. Aunt S'bina says I shall be company for Gray and I dearly love 'og's puddin', Uncle Leadville, don't you?"

Leadville's tortured spirit was in the gaze he turned from the busy child to her sister. Was he to lose the hour with Gray which had been the solace of lonely night and empty day, the one hour out of the twenty-four that was his? He did not answer Leonora but looked his anxious question. Was Gray at the bottom of this? But no, she could not be. It was a scheme of Sabina's, of Mrs. Tom's, or simple accident.

Drawing Old Squire's big elbow-chair up to the table he took his customary seat. Leonora chattered of school, of the little pigs that had had to be killed because they had worms, such dear little pigs, all black; and Gray served the breakfast. Leadville, sitting opposite to her, drank in her morning freshness and looked forward to the time when this flower should be blooming for him.

A voice called from the Justice Room and Leonora jumped up. "I'll see what auntie wants."

"No, dear, I'll go."

"Leave 'er go," rumbled Leadville in his compelling bass and she was off on the wings of happy service. He stared resentfully after the flying figure. "What's she doin' 'ere?"

Gray's heart was aflutter. "I miss the children so."

His eyes grew tender. "You do want a nest of your own, my bird. I can see you in it, a li'l place away from 'ere."

She shook her head, repudiating the idea with courage born of her sister's nearness. "I don't want never to leave Trevorrick and mammy, and any of them."

"You'd 'av so much of your own things to think about," he murmured, his mind full of the nest he would build for her, "you wouldn't 'av time to think upon 'ome."

Before she could answer, Leonora was back. "'Tis you auntie want, Gray."

Suspicion flamed in Leadville's eye. "If they're schemin' to come between us," he said angrily, "they'd better look out. Don't you go, Gray."

But the girl, running on light feet down the long dark passage, was glad to escape. When Uncle Leadville looked at her like that, she had ever a fluttered feeling that she must run away, or something, she knew not what, but something terrible, would happen. Instinct was warning her, instinct that is wiser even than experience and Leadville might sit on in the kitchen, waiting and waiting, but until he was gone, Gray would not return.

# CHAPTER VII

The year ran mildly down to Christmas, but the wind with its tang of cold did not fling a rose into Gray's cheek or buffet her into keener life and, when again the friends met in council, it was to discuss changes which both saw to be necessary.

"Jim's taking the cart into Stowe, week before Christmas," said Mrs. Byron when they had talked the matter over, "to bring 'ome some coals and flour. P'raps that day'll suit Gray?"

"Well, I'll talk to 'er and see what she got to say."

"Very well then, Friday before Christmas."

"And you'll 'av Richbell till you see 'ow things turn out?"

"Iss. She growin' to a fine maid. They'm all pretty but Richbell's got the best colour. 'Tis lovely an' I don't wonder the boys is maäze about 'er. Still," she sighed, "give me Gray."

"We all know Gray's the favourite here," smiled Mrs. Tom, sticking her needles into the stocking she was knitting and looking round for her cloak. "Well, I think we'm doing the best we can, seein' Leadville's so teasy."

"He'll settle down right enough now. 'Tedn't as if 'e was a young man. When 'e do realize 'e's out of the running, 'e'll take it quiet and we'll be all comfortable again."

"Well, my dear, I hope we shall. It 'as been a draggin' time for 'ee since you was laid up."

"'Tis funny," said Sabina, "'ow you think 'Now that's over and done with,' but 'tedn't. I thought 'Once I'm out of 'ospital I'll soon put things to rights,' but I 'aven't done it yet."

"Takes time, my dear."

"Iss, and time's life."

Leadville had become so remote and unapproachable that Sabina did not find an opportunity to tell him the wagon would be going into Stowe the Friday before Christmas and that Gray would be taking fowls, cream and butter, to the market. Not even when the day dawned did he realize that anything unusual was afoot. He had come down to breakfast, stared with sullen aversion at Leonora, as the cheerful child ran to and fro between kitchen and linhay; and sought in his uninventive mind for expedients which should leave him alone with her sister for a blessed few minutes. He did this morning after morning, sometimes successfully; but generally, as Gray wished to keep the child near her, without its making much difference. On this particular day Leonora, chattering of Christmas festivities, the tree they were to have at the chapel on New Year's Eve, the tea the following day, was eventually seen off to school and Gray, turning a deaf ear to Leadville's plea that she would linger, went candle in hand, for the sun was still below the eastern hill, to Sabina's room. Her mind was brimful of the practicalities of the day in Stowe. She had no time for Byron, had forgotten even the fear with which his hungry presence was wont to inspire her, was only conscious of the many things to be done before she could change her workaday raiment for clothes befitting the occasion.

To Leadville all seemed as usual, though Gray was perhaps unusually full of domestic business but, as Christmas was the following week, that was to be expected. He heard her low singing voice in the Justice Room as she flitted about, tidying the place, putting what Sabina needed ready to her hand; and he decided to smoke his morning pipe in the yard. He enjoyed looking on critically while the men worked. He told himself that if he had been master they would have done as much again. He had said so to Sabina more than once and she had smiled, thinking that she knew better.

As he watched them that morning, idly content with the fine weather and with his heart momentarily at rest, he called to mind that on the previous day he had seen a seal sporting in the surf beyond Morwen Cove. The end of an Atlantic gale had been lashing the cliff-face and a procession of monstrous waves had been rolling in out of the grey distance. In that welter of far-sounding sea, the living atom had been at play; and Byron, detecting the springing shadow in the curl of a wave, the dark speck in the racing tide of the Mad Rip, had reflected that the last bottle of seal-oil had been sold. Remembering this, he had thought the opportunity good and, returning to the kitchen, had lifted his gun from the leathern thong above the door. The room still lay in obscurity, the only light being that of the frugal banked-up fire. Long handling, however, had given the gun-butt a bright dark polish which reflected the faint glow, and Leadville's hand had gone out instinctively. Crossing the kitchen to the wall-cupboard on the right of the slab range he took out the ammunition of which he stood in need. Some empty bottles, not over-clean, stood on the top shelf, bottles which were to hold the fresh supply of seal-oil, a medicine for stock with which he did a trade among the farmers of the neighbouring valleys. Already Treherne

Gaskis had sent once to ask for a pint. As Byron slipped the pouch into his pocket, a sound broke the stillness which lay like dust over the rooms.

"When the wind is off the hill
Flows the water to the mill..."

sang a voice in the linhay and, though West-country birds sing sweetly, they cannot compare for music with West-country maidens. This voice, though without much volume, had a tender, joyous note as of one singing out of a full heart and Leadville hardly recognized it as Gray's. A narrow gleam of candle-light, edged the dark oblong of the door and, from beyond, came the brisk slap-smack of a beater upon newly made butter.

As the man stood to listen, a look, human, eager, almost happy, broke like a shining over his swarthy face. The seal-hunt was forgotten, for the voice singing of the rain had a thrill in it, the thrill of a love-call and the man's wild heart was assured the call was for him.

For a moment, the habit of years reasserting itself, he glanced at the door on the other side of the kitchen. At the end of the long dark passage his wife still lay abed, or so he hoped. The swift glance had been unintentional, the drag of a chain from which he was about to free himself. He threw back his head, the brooding night of his deep-set eyes quickened by emotion and, laying the gun on the table among the breakfast crocks, pushed farther open the door of the linhay.

This room, at once the scullery, larder and dairy of the house, was high and narrow, with a sloping roof. A pump stood by the outer door, and the place was lighted from above; but, as the dawn had not broken, Gray was butter-making by the light of a candle. The living jewel of flame illumined faintly the high and shadowy place, was reflected from the tiny surfaces of the wet butter and, outlining Gray's figure of a young and happy maid, shone on her absorbed face. The butter had "come" quickly. She struck it with the heavy beater until the milk ran soundingly into the pail below and, as she worked, she sang in that voice of infinite allure,

"When the wind is off the land
It brings the weed on to the sand."

For some time Leadville, aware that his self-control was limited, had been trying to get Gray to himself. Like a wisp of blossomy tamarisk swaying in the bright upper air, however, she remained tantalizingly out of reach. He spent himself in the attempt to lay hands on her, to force her to hear his suit; but Sabina's presence was for ever being thrust between him and his objective, until between fury with his wife and baulked desire, the man was in a dangerous mood. His highly strung temperament prevented his being able to seize opportunity by the forelock; but so often had he met with disappointment, grasping shadows in place of a woman that, when he realized Gray was alone and ignorant of his proximity, he obeyed for once a natural prompting. Stepping quickly across the linhay, he threw his arms round the busy girl and sought her lips.

To his almost incredulous joy, Gray did not offer any resistance. He had come up behind, had taken her strongly in his arms and the soft young body yielded as if his coming had been in answer to her own unexpressed desire. Though the month was December, spring was in the air and with an unmistakable murmur of content, Gray abandoned herself. He bent to hers a transfigured face and then, but not till then, did she realize she was in Leadville Byron's arms.

Her body stiffened suddenly and, uttering a cry of horror, she began to struggle. "You!" she cried and made a frantic effort to escape. So surprised was he by this change of front that, with his mood in the balance between love and rage, he let her go.

"My little umuntz," he cried, "don't 'ee play with me." A moment before she had yielded herself, her voice had been liquid with invitation, he had heard in it the mating note. Now she stared at him from a safe distance with a spark in her soft eye.

"If you don't leave me alone," she said angrily, "I shall go home and never put foot inside this door no more, whiles you're here."

Byron stood with his head bent. He too was angry. He felt defrauded. Only a moment since she had lain in his embrace, thrilled by his touch, a warm and palpitating woman. Now she spoke as if her heart were virgin.

"Don't 'ee play with me," he said again. "I couldn't bear it, I've 'ad as much as I can stand. 'Ee knaw I love 'ee."

"I—I don't—I don't want to."

"Don't want to? Don't want to know that night after night I can't sleep for thinking of 'ee?" He struck his chest with a strong blunt-fingered hand. "Here's your place, love, and my arm'll ache till I 'old 'ee again."

Hot colour dyed her face. To think that she should have lain in his arms! On that day, too, of all the days in the year, of all the days in a lifetime! "'Tis all a mistake."

"The day'll come when you'll worship the ground I tread on."

"No—never."

"I'll make 'ee love me. I loved 'ee from the first day you come 'ere. I've never wanted nobody but you and I've wanted 'ee ever since I did see your 'andsome face about Wastralls and heard you singin', 'appy as a greybird. Wastralls an' you, they go together in my mind. I love 'ee, Gray, and you know what that means to a man like me, what cares for nobody and nothing. I'm eaten up with the love of you. I'd do anything to get 'ee. I must 'av 'ee and I will 'av 'ee." He came a step nearer, but she drew back.

"Leave me alone, leave me alone."

"Leave 'ee alone? I want to be kissin' of 'ee all the day."

The girl was trembling. She leant one arm upon the stone slab behind her, and the shock of its coldness was a steadying influence. "I bain't gwine let you kiss me. I'd rather slap yer face for yer. What d'yer think then?"

He coaxed her tenderly. "Bain't I worth 'avin' then?"

"I bain't gwine 'av nothing to do with 'ee. I wouldn't 'ave 'ee for the world." Taking up one of the butter pats she began mechanically shaping the mass.

"What's the matter with me that you won't 'av nothing to do with me?" Straightening himself, he opened out unusually broad shoulders and the candlelight revealed a face of black shadows and strong saliences. How strong, how ruthless, how confident he looked! Gray felt her old fear returning, she could not believe that this strange man would be held in check by any of the received standards.

"You'm married and old enough to be my father."

She clinched the matter: "You'm married to Aunt S'bina."

He laughed contemptuously. "Ah, but you would 'av me, if I was a widower, a widower wi' Wastralls for my own."

Putting down the pat, Gray turned at that in a sudden ruffle of indignation.

"Take an' 'old your tongue," she commanded. "I'm ashamed of 'ee to talk like that."

"Well," he persisted, only anxious for her to realize that he meant to make her mistress of all he hoped for in life—Wastralls. "I may be before long. I don't believe the missis'll live very long."

"I hate that kind of talk!"

Her anger, a spark in the dark eye, a flush on the soft cheek, became her and he stared admiringly. Her wrath was like the peck of a captive bird and, whatever she might say, from henceforth she would know that his pursuing love was no light matter. "I do love 'ee so," he pleaded, his voice dropping to an intimate compelling whisper. "I tremble when you come into the room. But I can't set 'ere and not touch 'ee; I 'ave to go out on cliff 'till I've walked it down. Seems sometimes at night as if you was near me and I put out my 'and—ah, if you was there I should die of joy. You'm mine and I've waited so long. I can't bear it. I can't eat or drink or sleep. I'm in a fever and I ache with longing for 'ee till I feel as if I should go mad——"

Gray caught her breath in a sob, as a soft trundling sound came from the next room. Unable to speak she pointed shakily at the door.

Leadville also heard the sound, a scrooping noise as of rubber-tyred wheels being turned about. Sabina was in the kitchen, could hear every word, would probably, in another minute, roll herself in at the linhay door. His face grew savage and rage rose in a black flood about his heart. Was it to be always like this, was this poor remnant of humanity, feeble, distorted, ageing, always to come between him and Gray? His mind grew blurry with a wild spindrift of menace. Green withes or new ropes, fools to think he could be bound by either law or convention, he whom only the lustreless black hair of one woman might hold. Love had come late, but it had come in overwhelming force and he would break every convention, every law that stood in his way! Laws?

As he stood, stricken dumb by his wife's nearness, but on the edge of passionate revolt he became conscious of a peculiar change in his surroundings. Silence fell, a thick silence like a wall, a silence that shut out the cackle of a hen in the yard and the distant baa-ing that came irregularly from the hillside. The man was alone behind this wall of soundlessness, shut away by it from the homely noises of the indoor and the out. When it had lasted for a bewildering second, it was succeeded by a faint far-off sound. The sound came out of a red distance and grew rapidly louder, resolving itself at last into the regular tap-tap of a hammer which is being used for knocking in nails. This hammering was to Byron a familiar sound. It had been heard by him at other times of stress and strain, at other moments when raging passions seemed about to drive him over some dark verge. The sound was arresting. It went as he well knew with flashes of vision, during which he would see a piece of light wood and the glint of brass-headed tacks. As the wood appeared out of the white mist which surrounded him, Byron passed into another state of consciousness. His mind, abruptly disconnected, was filled with a queer eagerness and curiosity. His wife, Gray, Wastralls, everything, were momentarily forgotten. What was it, this knocking? No carpenter was at work in the houses and courts; and the wood too, a full curve narrowing to an angle, was a curious shape. He stared about him, seeking an explanation and his eye fell on the girl at her work.

"Did you 'ear?" he said, turning on her a face from which the tide of emotion had ebbed.

Gray, thankful for the respite which had followed her aunt's entry, had seized the pats and, with feverish industry was cutting pounds and half pounds off the mass of butter.

"I heard Aunt S'bina in the kitchen," she answered coldly.

"I wasn't speaking of 'er. I meant the knockin'."

"What knocking?"

"I didn't know as the mason was comin' to-day to put up the new pigs' 'ouse?"

"He isn't coming till after Christmas."

"Well, I'm sure I 'eard some one 'ammerin' in nails."

She shook her head. "I didn't hear it."

The noise of dishes being piled together on the breakfast table caught Byron's attention. He glanced at Gray and the sight of youth, with a blush on the hot cheek, a suggestion of tears on the long lashes, was to him as the opening of a door. He came out of his preoccupation and the knocking either died away or was forgotten. Forgotten, too, were his rage and disappointment.

"What's she doin' out o' bed so early for?"

"I'm going into Stowe with the butter and there's a lot to do."

"'Oo yer gwine with?" asked Byron, instantly on the alert.

"With Jim."

"You needn't go." He was reluctant to have her out of his reach, even for a morning. He wanted her at home under his eye. He was going to renew his pleading as soon as the moment was auspicious. "Rosevear can take that in."

"I want to go to-day."

His mind examined the statement with that ever-ready fear of the lover who is uncertain of his standing. "What you want to go for?"

"Shopping!" said she and, with a smile that was faintly malicious, enumerated the items, groceries, liniment for her aunt, pitchers, cloam pans.

"Shopping?" But what he saw was that five-mile drive over Big Hill into Stowe. He saw her beside Jim, driving away from Wastralls, from him. "I'll drive 'ee in!"

Gray's heart sank and she remained silent.

"Would 'ee like me to?"

If she said 'No,' he would be all the more eager. "Once I'm in Stowe I shall be that busy you wouldn't see anything of me."

He laughed. "I'd take care of that. All right then, 'tis I as'll drive 'ee into Stowe and not the lad. I'll not trust Rosevear to drive 'ee, I'll do it myself." He looked back at her from the door, his dark face alight. "My God, if I caught 'ee with one of they, I'd—I'd break his neck."

The door banged to behind him, and Gray putting down the printer laid her head on her arms. If Aunt Sabina should not be able to prevent him!

But Aunt Sabina was a tower of strength.

# CHAPTER VIII

In order that Gray might start for the market in good time, Mrs. Byron had swung herself out of bed that morning as soon as she had swallowed her simple breakfast of tea and buttered split. But though she had brush, comb, garments, in fact all toilet necessaries at hand, and could therefore dress expeditiously, she found when she reached the kitchen that day was breaking. A red sun, having topped the south-easterly slopes of Brown Willy and Rowtor, was smiling in at the many-paned window and winning an answering brightness from surfaces of steel, of yellow glaze and of glass. Mrs. Byron's eye as she pushed the trolly into the room took in the homely details. To the right of the range yawned a cloam oven and, before long, Jim Rosevear would be bringing faggots of tamarisk wood with which to fill it. Before the fire in a deep pan the dough was 'plumping' under a linen cloth, and nothing makes a house so homely as dough on a low chair 'plumping' in kitchen warmth and stillness. As she gathered the breakfast crocks together, preparatory to cleansing them, she smiled to herself well-pleased. Her plans were working smoothly and although the past year had been one of change and discomfort, she could believe that the disturbance, like yeast in flour, would bring good results. Mrs. Byron's movements were still quick and deft. She set the remains of the fry aside, poured hot water into the wooden tub for washing up and stood the knives, blade down, in a pot. The trolly, being of cane and shivered wood, ran lightly over the blue flags; but as she turned from putting the refilled kettle on the fire she heard voices in the linhay, the deep bass murmur that was her husband's and a clearer sound, the voice of some one young and troubled, of some one angered, but also afraid.

The smile died off Mrs. Byron's lips and for some minutes she stared unseeingly at the steaming water in the round wooden bowl. So he was at his tricks, the old villain! She had taken the matter lightly as a vagary, a passing fancy: but as the sound of his voice fell upon her ears she experienced a doubt, the first real doubt that she had known. In these tones there was a passion wholly new to her. It shook the wife's heart with fear, the fear of ultimate irremediable loss; with such fear, that for the moment she went sick and faint and leaned perilously forward in the cone of her trolly.

In the linhay, the voices dropped into silence and, when they began again, they were pitched in a more commonplace key. Sabina, sitting by the table, stunned by a late realization of what had happened, heard a well-known step, a pause and the utterance in quick, fierce tones, of some threatening phrase. Upon that, Leadville came quickly into the kitchen.

"S'bina," he said and she noticed with a fresh pang that his face wore a warm and eager look, a look of happy anticipation, "I want the money for they veares."

The year's pigs had been made into hams and bacon and Mrs. Byron, discussing the matter with old George, had decided not to buy young animals—veares or slips—until the New Year. She could not understand why Leadville should want to restock the empty sties. What was it to do with him?

"Pigs," she said non-committally, "'ull be cheaper after Christmas."

"They won't go down again."

"I know they will. You can get good-sized slips after Christmas for less money than you'll give for veares now."

He thrust his hands into empty pockets and tried to think of another way in which he could procure money. How could he take Gray into Stowe if he had none? He wanted to give her pretty things, to spend on her, to impress her: but he could not ask the one woman for money to throw away on the other. "Ah," said he, "but I can go to-day and get them and after Christmas I shan't be able to."

Only then did Mrs. Byron remember the errand upon which Gray was bound, the errand which was taking her into Stowe. She smiled and a tinge of malice crept into her thoughts.

"It bain't often as you're so keen to do things for us," she said, "and I didn't know as you'd time to spare."

"Iss, I can spend the day in buyin' they veares for 'ee and welcome."

"There's things as I want more'n veares. Wi' the wind off the land there'll be a pretty lot of oreweed in the bay. You might give a hand to that."

"I been down and there 'edn't a bit in."

She knew that he had not been farther than the yard that morning. "I don't say 'no' to a fair offer," she said, her upper lip lifting a little over the still white and regular teeth. "They turmits want bringin' in from the Willows Field, else the rabbits will eat'n all."

"I 'eard Biddick say as 'e was goin' after'm to-day." He had a habit of shifting his weight from one foot to the other, as he stood, and it gave him an appearance of restlessness, as if at any moment he might start off on some errand. "I don't want to bother with oreweed or turmits. I'm going into Stowe and I thought you might like for me to get the pigs. Come, leave me 'av some money."

"I don't want they veares." She rested her strong hands on the sides of the cone and looked at him with understanding. He must be made to realize that this was folly and that it must come to an end. "An' you don't want to buy them. All you want is to go with Gray."

Leadville, as always when his subterfuges were detected, fell back on the truth.

"Well?" he said. "An' s'posin' if I did?"

Sabina was startled. Had matters gone so far that he no longer had the decency to deny his feelings? "Isolda's goin' wi' Gray," she said, with a shrug of her plump shoulders.

"Isolda?" he said and his disappointment, bubbling up from the depths, showed as anger. Among them they took good care of Gray; but if they thought their scheming and underhauling would prevent his reaching her, he would very soon show them they were mistaken. "Fine thing you," he cried wrathfully, "to be jealous over a feller."

Mrs. Byron had grown stouter since her long illness. She filled the wicker cone to overflowing, a big rosy woman with abundance of white hair above a face the strength of which time had made plain. Her husband's thrust was shrewd, so shrewd that she gave way before it. "You'm wishin' me daid, I s'pose?" she said bitterly and waited to hear him deny the accusation.

Leadville shifted from one foot to the other but did not speak. People say terrible things when they are angry, but silence can be more terrible than speech.

"I shen't die any quicker," cried poor Mrs. Byron, "for you wishin' of it."

For months the man had concealed his feelings behind down-dropped lids and avoidance; but now the repugnance with which she filled him rose to his eyes, eyes no longer moody and dull, but suddenly, revealingly, alive. Hitherto the secrecy which was natural to him had seemed the only possible plan; now, driven by jealousy, by anger, by a mounting hatred, he suddenly discarded it. Raising his lids he stared at Sabina for some seconds and his soul showed her its loathing and threatened her and condemned her; and — like a rabbit held by lanthorn light — she stared back.

The truth was riding nakedly through the street of life. It spoke with a clear note of warning and Sabina — for a moment — both saw and heard.

# CHAPTER IX

"You'm lookin' whisht this mornin', missis, what's the matter with 'ee?"

Jim Rosevear had brought two faggots of tamarisk wood for the cloam oven. His shy glance, taking in every corner of the now brightening kitchen, had assured him that Gray was not present; and, putting that main preoccupation momentarily aside, he had leisure to note that Mrs. Byron's face was haggard, that she looked older, more worn, than he had thought. It followed that she must be ill and for illness he had always a solicitous word.

After that revealing look Leadville had walked quietly past his wife out of the house. His dark thoughts, his secret hopes had risen to the surface. He had held them in for months but, in the end, they had escaped from him in a glance.

His footsteps died away on the hard mud of the yard, the warm silence fell again over the kitchen and, in the midst of it, a modern Lot's wife, Mrs. Byron sat strangely still. The steam died off the surface of the water, the sun crept a little farther into the room and the untidy pile of breakfast crocks gave back a glint here and a dazzle there. Mrs. Byron was undeniably shaken. Her poor hands were trembling and now and again a quiver passed over the rubicund cheeks. It was as if the woman would have wept, as if only a summer rain could have dissolved the ice at her heart, but as if the source of tears had for too long been dry.

At the sound of the yard-man's voice she raised eyes which, though tearless, were dim. Jim seemed a long way off but kind and human. She was old enough to be his mother and, like a mother who has secret sorrows, she answered him.

"I'm down in the dumps to-day, terr'bly. 'Aven't got any 'eart for nothing."

"Can I do anything for 'ee, missis?"

Being the eldest of a 'long tail,' he was used to doing odd jobs for a woman; and, at Treketh, his mother, dependent now on the unsatisfactory help of younger boys, sent him daily a regretful thought. Jim had been so handy, so good-natured.

Rousing herself, Mrs. Byron looked about. "You might light up the fire in the cloam oven for me, Jim, there's a good sawl."

Breaking a faggot apart he filled the oven with bushes and set a light to them. The smoke curled up the black chimney and little flames ran along the brittle wood. When the earthenware sides were sparkling hot the oven would be ready for the tins of bread, the cakes and pasties which were to feed the household during the ensuing week.

"Anything else I can do for 'ee while oven's hettin'?"

Mrs. Byron's eyes were the brave frozen blue of the seafarer and wistfulness was not possible to them, nevertheless Jim was conscious of that quality in their gaze. The son of a cross-grained father, words were not needed to tell him that the Byrons had had a difference. He moved deftly about, emptying the cool water and replacing it with hot, setting out the array of loaf tins and filling a scuttle. He was glad to be of use. It made him think of happy evenings with his mother, made him wonder which of the elder boys, Sidney or Charley, was carrying coal and water for her and what hand they made of it.

"Anything else, missis?"

She had watched him unseeingly, but with a growing sense of comfort. "I'm in better 'eart now you've helped me so." She would have this young man at hand to help her in all her future difficulties and the thought was reassuring. "'Tis near time for 'ee to be goin' into Stowe. Gray's all but ready."

As if she had been called, the girl opened the door of the linhay. At sight of Jim, a sight by no means unexpected, her pale-tinted face bloomed like an opening rose.

"Good mornin', Jim. You're late." If only he had come one little half-hour sooner!

He was looking spruce in clean shirt and new tie, a fresh smooth-skinned youngster. "Well, my dear," he said awkwardly, "I 'ad a lot to do this mornin' before I could come away."

"Jim 'ad to put 'is best bib and tucker on," said Mrs. Byron. Her interest in these opening lives helped her to push her anxieties into the background. Never one to nurse a grief, she smiled at the boy and girl, glad to be looking at a morning face.

"I'd thought," said Gray, and in her voice was a regret he could not fathom, "you'd be earlier, so as to take the chickens and eggs."

"Well, to tell 'ee the truth," the young man threw himself on her mercy, "I went down in the orchard to see if I could find a few vi'lets for yer. I want yer to look vitty to-day." He stepped back into the porch, returning with a little posy. In the West, flowers bloom the year round, and these were scented violets.

"Oh, Jim," said the girl, taking them—and could say no more. The violets were a charming thought; but if he had only known what hung on his keeping to the arrangement he had made with her the previous day, to come to the linhay after breakfast!

"Your uncle wants to go in with yer," said Mrs. Byron, making an effort to speak of the matter with her customary cheerfulness, "but I bain't goin' to let'n go." She was rewarded by a grateful glance from Gray, a glance which laid for all time the incipient doubts of a natural jealousy. "Now Jim, by the time you've tackled up Lady, Gray'll be ready. My dear," she turned to the girl, standing dreamily by the table, the violets in her hand, "'av you finished the butter?"

In the warm air of the kitchen the flowers were giving forth their scent. "Yes, and packed it," said Gray, raising the posy to her face. It had been dearly bought.

"Couldn't find your dress anywhere this mornin'. What 'av 'ee done with it?"

"Aunt Louisa carried it to ma's, and ma said I'd better come up there and dress."

Mrs. Byron looked disappointed. "P'raps 'tis best," she said, common sense triumphing as was usual with her, over the longing for a little personal gratification, "still I should like to 'av seen the costume."

"Well, I'll wear it down to-morrow for you to see."

"Iss, my dear, do."

The girl looked affectionately at the older woman, conscious for a moment of her disabilities and her still young heart. "I wish you could come, auntie."

"You don't wish it more'n I do." She shook her head, but in her eyes the old smile was relit. She had resigned herself and with her, when a decision was reached, the natural thing was to turn from it to the next item on the programme of life. "Now, my dear, you must make haste and clear off," she said, beginning to roll up the sleeves of her blue cotton gown. The day promised to be busy and it was high time the young people were on their way. She did not even wait until Gray was out of the room before reaching down for the 'springing' dough. The oven was nearly ready, but she was all behindhand. That would never do.

The atmosphere which Mrs. Byron diffused was so practical, so reassuring that it had soothed her young cousin's natural distress. As the girl walked quickly away to the room they shared, though she could not altogether forget the scene with Leadville, she remembered that she was about to escape from his importunities; and, though an occasional shudder still shook her, she encouraged herself to think of other, happier things and in particular of the errand upon which she and Jim were bound. Gray was bidding good-bye to Wastralls, at least for a time; and the green box she had brought with her had been packed ready for him to fetch away. For immediate necessities however she was taking with her a brown leathern bag, which had been given her by her aunt and which bore the initials G.R., initials Gray was never to change.

In an otherwise empty drawer lay a little pile of garments of superfine quality and workmanship; and for these, after cleansing herself from the stains of butter-making and household work, the girl exchanged her everyday clothes. Jim had made her a moleskin cap and necklet and in the latter, she pinned the little bunch of violets.

"It don't seem hardly possible!" she said dreamily, on her return to the kitchen, where Mrs. Byron was kneading the dough.

Memory carried the older woman back to a like day in her own life. "Well, my dear," she said, from the other side of Time's river, "you'll know all about'n by to-morrow." She contemplated the blushing girl for a moment then turned to practical matters. "Did you think about bringin' out the list for groceries?"

"Never thought nothing about it." She ran off, returning with a blue-lined page, torn from a penny account book.

"Whatever you do, don't 'ee forget yer uncle's pipe."

No man shall instruct deaf ears or open the eyes of the blind. Already Sabina's optimism was reasserting itself. She had exaggerated the import of her husband's look. Leadville, poor chap, had been disappointed and had shown it. No need for her to make 'the worst of a bad bargain.'

Christmas is a time of good-will and Christmas was coming. She had noticed he was in need of a new pipe and who knew whether such an offering might not prove a milestone on the difficult road to reconciliation?

"No, I won't forget," said Gray, who saw the commission as yet another instance of nobility exercised towards the entirely undeserving. She kissed her aunt warmly. "You are a darlin'," she said. "I feel awful to leave you to do all this work," she glanced from the dough to the bread-tins, "I can't bear going."

"Well, my dear," Sabina felt the pleasantness of this young and partisan affection, "'tis only for a little while. Richbell will do so well as she can."

"Richbell'll never think to make your cocoa of a night or to get your hot-bottle and make you comfortable."

"Please God, I'll 'av you back again soon. Now you go on and be 'appy and don't you think about me. I shall be all right. There—" she glanced through the diamond panes of the window, "the mare's being tackled up, make haste."

A slight frost had hardened the mud of the yard and above St. Cadic Mill the December sun had risen into a sky of little far-off clouds. Between the shafts of the wagon stood Lady, the young mare, glad to exchange the warm dark stable for the adventure of the public road. Jim Rosevear, in well-brushed clothes and with a tie that matched the blue of his eyes, was fastening the last buckle as Gray came out, with a basket of eggs and butter in one hand and her bag in the other. A larger basket, containing poultry, was already in place and, beside it, lay a piece of broken mechanism which was to be left at the smithy. As the girlish figure stepped out of the dark house Leadville, who, with frowning brow, had been watching the preparations, came forward. Gray had a momentary qualm; but saw with relief that he had not made any change in his dress. In old clothes and without a collar even Leadville, though he set many conventions at defiance, would not think of going to Stowe.

"Hullo!" said he, "what be yer gwine do wi' that bag?"

"I'm going to stay home to-night."

"'Ome? This is yer 'ome 'ere."

"Well, I'm going to stay to mammy's for a change," she spoke lightly, willing to placate him and hasten her escape.

"I think you ought to 'av ask me if you can stay 'ome or no." He had stepped between her and the wagon; and his eyes had the smouldering light which she had learnt to dread.

With her heart fluttering, she controlled her voice to a pleasant, "Well, what is there to hinder me?"

Her docility appeased him. After all she was only going to the butter market.

"Well, can I? Can I stay to mammy's?" asked the singing voice with its rising inflexion on the last word.

"I s'pose you can," he said reluctantly. "You can go if you'm a good maid and bring me back something."

"I'll bring you back something that'll surprise you," promised Gray, her eyes soft and smiling, but an edge of malice under her tongue.

He towered over her, ardent and dominating. "There's only one thing I want and that you know."

She knew and was both angered and afraid. In vain she tried to think of Leadville as wicked, for her he was worse than that, he was terrifying. She did not know what he might do, whether there was any limit.

Jim having finished harnessing the mare, came up on the other side of the wagon. Gray, glancing aside from her tormentor, saw his courageous eyes and took heart of grace. She had a protector and this was the last time, the very last, that she would be at Leadville's mercy.

"Come now, Uncle Leadville," she said and her young voice, carrying across the wagon, dissipated an incipient jealousy, "I want to be gone."

He drew back as if he had received a blow and, in a moment, the girl was climbing nimbly to her place on a bag of chaff which Jim had placed ready. As she turned, a little anxious as to the effect of her words, but glad on any terms to have got away, she was met by a black scowl of wrath. "Mind I never 'ear yer call me that again."

With a graceful swing, Jim sprang on to the rail of the wagon and the mare, fresh from her oats, began to move. Gray, secure at last, looked down on Byron with an air of innocent inquiry and the lad beside her smiled. For some time he had had a suspicion that the other was more attentive to her than became a married man; and this suspicion had stimulated a wooing which might otherwise have seemed too tame.

As the wagon wheels turned, Leadville perforce gave way, but unwillingly, for in his heart was suspicion, a fear of all men, a shaking terror lest one should have been before him. The memory of her supple yielding form yet thrilled him with its promise. For a moment she had abandoned herself and though she had drawn away at once the yielding had betrayed her. Gray was no longer a chrysalis of cool dim life and unfolded wings. Emotion was quick in her, she was ready for full experiences, the blue sun-warmed air and the flight. Instinct, teaching Leadville she was no unawakened maid, was brought up short by the word she had flung at him. Uncle? What did it mean? Had some younger man dared to approach her? Had she listened, listened because he was the first and young love is sweet? Was there some light fancy that must be extinguished before she could be wholly his? Surely not. Surely she had meant to mark the gulf between herself and Sabina's husband, to point out to him that he was married. The theory explained her momentary yielding, her quick withdrawal, her words. He smiled to himself. If Gray imagined that, because long ago he had gone through a form of words with another woman, they were to bind him now that for the first time in his life he loved with passion, she should learn that she was mistaken. As soon as she returned to Wastralls, he would show her in what estimation he held the worn unwelcome bond.

From the low window of the kitchen Mrs. Byron had watched the scene. Jim's handsome head had been bent over the mare's shiny coat as he thrust the tongues of the buckles through the brass. He moved easily and well, for life had not yet taken advantage of his strength and she saw him as a proper lad. When Gray came out, Mrs. Byron felt a motherly pride in the little rounded figure, the soft fair face between the furs of cap and necklet. "An' she've pinned they vi'lets on, trust her for that."

Leadville's appearance cast a shadow on the scene. In the bright winter sunshine he loomed up, a threatening unhappy figure, the incarnation of a desire which might not be gratified. The light fell on his uncovered head with its thick black hair, on his muscular figure, growing heavy with years but still a wonder for its strength, on his eager face. Sabina, in a reaction from the blow she had received, felt that the time was come for her to assert herself. Anxious not to drive him farther away she had played a gentle self-obliterating part and she felt that in doing so she had made a mistake. She would grasp her nettle more firmly, let him know that Gray was bespoken. Conscious, as she went, of envy, she began to push herself towards the porch. What a thing it was to have an old body, a body that had 'gone abroad' and a young heart! Jim and Leadville hung about Gray with the same hope. Sabina, for all her vitality and strength, had no longer anything to give. She was old and done, while Gray, to them and every man, was incarnate promise.

The wagon was turning out of the gate as Mrs. Byron reached her husband's side and the off-wheel rose over a stone. The body of the cart swayed and lurched and Gray, with a little cry, caught at Jim Rosevear's arm.

Byron swore fiercely. "If anything 'appen to her I'll wring his neck."

"You needn' fear. He'll take care of she."

The man turned and stared at the distorted figure in the cone of basket-work. He had not heard her come up but his mind was too deeply occupied with other matters for him to be startled. "Why?"

"Because they'm courtin'."

She had thought it would be difficult to tell him but the words sprang out of her resentment at the way in which she, struggling with difficulties, she who should have met with consideration from her husband, had been treated.

"Courtin'?" repeated Leadville and his swarthy skin turned a dull grey. The wagon was rattling up the road at a good pace, the cheery sound of hoofs and wheels and voices growing fainter as it turned towards Hember. The man stared after it and about him was the falling of dream castles, of built-up theories, false hopes. He had heard the truth and could not turn his back on it, could not refuse it credence. He knew, now, that Gray's response that morning had been to Jim Rosevear and not to himself. The pieces of the puzzle fitted. He was momentarily stunned by the revelation. Only when he realized that they were driving away together did he come to himself. The vision of their propinquity was intolerable and he started to run towards the gate.

"I won't let'n go with 'er."

Sabina raised her voice. "'Bain't a bit of good for 'ee to interfere. They'm to 'Ember by this time."

From the gate he could see the wagon had been stopped and that Tom Rosevear was lifting down his daughter. The family had gathered in the road and the younger girls were talking to Jim, doubtless giving him Christmas commissions. A little air of festivity pervaded the group, an air which as Leadville did not understand it, he found ominous. He wanted to rush up the road and seize and carry Gray off from among them, carry her away from Trevorrick, out of the complications of life there and, above everything, carry her away from Jim. For a desperate situation, desperate remedies. He did not mean to sit down under misfortune, to accept tamely the blows of destiny. All things come—not to those who wait, but to those who fight; and he who cannot fight for his mate is no man.

"They've been courtin' for months," said Sabina. "Anybody but you would have seen it, but you're never 'ome. You can't expect to know things when you'm out mumpin' around the cliffs like an old dog."

Gray had gone into the house, the big bold house on the hillside, with her mother; and Leadville turned back from the yard gate.

"I'll send 'un off neck and crop," he cried, ragingly. "He shall go to-night. He shall never stay 'ere on the place another night." His words came stammeringly, like liquid out of a bottle that is too sharply tilted. "I'll send'n goin' neck an' crop out of this, then we shall see."

"Iss, my dear," returned Sabina bitterly, "then we shall see. They'm courtin' and before long they'll be married—then we shall see; and when they'm married they'll live 'ere along with we, then we shall see."

But the unhappy man, unable to endure her words, had rushed blindly away.

# CHAPTER X

Beyond Wastralls rose a line of black cliffs culminating in the high ground of Dark Head and, towards them, Leadville turned. No roads crossed these solitudes. Sheep cropped the fine herbage, sea-gulls built on the inaccessible ledges, tumuli and earthworks showed that man too had once sheltered here. Far inland an occasional grey homestead, in its nest of farm-buildings, could be discerned, while in clear weather the daymark was visible on Stepper Point. Otherwise the eye was given only the wide spaces of sky and sea and earth.

On the storm which had strewn the coast with wreckage had followed a land wind; and this had brought in the weed with which the coast-dwellers manure their sandy fields. The sea, in big unquiet rollers, fell heavily against the walls and islands of rock. It was dark with the slippery oreweed and, when the tide went out, the coves and bays would be ankle-deep in shining olive-brown masses. In that treeless wind-swept land however, the people look to the sea-harvest for more than weed. To the beaches drift beams that can be split into gate shivers; hatches, which put together, make a reasonable pig's house; chests and spars and miscellaneous wreckage. From cottage and hamlet the folks converge upon the coast and, at any other time, Byron would have stopped above the nearest sandy cove to shout down an offer for some of the piles of wood. Now he strode by, unconscious of the tiny carts being filled with planks and boxes, of the little figures intent on their grim work of salvage. The man was fleeing from the intolerable revelation that had been thrust upon him. He was closing his ears, his mind, his heart, seeking to delay the inevitable moment when he must give heed; yet with him, in the depths of his being, was carrying that from which he fled.

So obsessed was he with the desire to get away, to put space between him and that terrible prophetic voice, that he did not realize his solitudes had been invaded. He pressed on, crossing cliff-faces and climbing steeps. The crags, the wide prospect, the sea-unrest were familiar to him, this waif and foreigner who had come up out of the deep and could claim no place as home, no human being as of his blood. He was as safe among the crags as if he had been born to wings. The people, labouring far below, saw the grey figure on the heights and craned their necks to watch his perilous progress; and the salving of a good ship's bones went on more slowly because Leadville Byron, on a ledge six inches wide and cut away underneath, a ledge of black and crumbling slate, was risking a possession dear to no one but himself.

The man was coming to Dark Head as a hurt child rushes blindly to its mother. Hither had he fled after every difference with Sabina and here had he found a vastness, a changelessness, an impersonal peace upon which he could rest his little and tortured soul. His trouble was greater now. He was in the grip of powers which, if he could not escape from them, might break him. By climbing peaks on which cormorants had nested in a confidence hitherto secure, by ploughing through deep sands and up the slippery shale, by crazy leaps and a wild expenditure of force, he tried to exhaust himself. By so doing he might avoid, not only knowledge, but the sinister possibilities of his nature.

Dark Head is a narrow peninsula of rock which stands knee-deep in water. A green mane of turf ripples to the black edge and Leadville, scourged across the waste, came at last to a softness of thick untrodden grass. This was the world's end and behind lay the amazing cruelty of life. The great spaces were clean and they were sweet. The man strode to the sloping edge but, because he was not yet ready to surrender his atom of consciousness, drew back. For a moment he stood, looking vacantly across the breathing sea, then turned and flung himself upon the bed the ages had prepared. The grass, wind-swept and deep, yielded a little, closing about his heavy figure like the displaced water of a pool.

On a rock below, an oyster-catcher chattered disapproval but the gulls and shyer cormorants came back to their resting-places. The man was harmless and after the storm they must make the most of the sunshine. They stood about, preening themselves in the red light and above the southern hills but near them, the sun made the half-circle of the sky.

In moments of overwhelming emotion Byron, when the strain grew too intense, had hitherto passed into another state of consciousness. The sound of hammering had as it were, opened a door, beyond which was a bewildering peace. Forgetfulness had fallen on him like a garment and when he came back it was, always, to begin afresh. Sabina's words however, though they roused him to a frenzy of feeling, had not had the usual effect. He had not been able to escape.

Drowned in an agony that was elemental he lay on the cliff-top, supine and motionless; Sabina's bitter revelation had been like the pouring of vitriol over his heart. Loving for the first time in his life, loving with the passion of a highly emotional temperament, the hopelessness of his love had been thrust suddenly upon him. A disappointment so elemental, so profound, put him beside himself. His instinct was, somehow, to escape the ultimate pangs. He had fled before the flood, fled from himself, scrambled and sobbed himself across the cliffs until he came to rest, deep in the deep grass of the headland.

His exhaustion was so great that for some time he lay supine as the wreckage on the sands below. As the moments passed, however, consciousness began to return and with it, through the darkness of his mind flitted unhappy thought, a greyness here and there, a vague suspicion. By degrees Sabina's face detached itself from the background. He saw it resentful and defiant and, tired as he was, his gorge rose. The woman was for ever in his road. She had withheld Wastralls from him, now she would come between him and Gray. He saw again the strong lined face, the unlovely trunk; saw them with a dislike which had for some time been growing in intensity. Since her accident Sabina had been to him a death's-head, a creature which, without the power to enjoy, yet clung to its possessions; which, though its grave was yawning, persisted in dragging a repulsive mortality about the earth. A person with any decency of feeling, would have lain her down under the turf and slept the good sleep; but Sabina was neither dead nor alive. That trolly! He cursed it for the hideous thing it was and for the unseemly activity of which it was the symbol. He would have liked to break it in pieces. He would have enjoyed the wrecking and scattering.

Circumstances had put Sabina in opposition to him and had given her the upper hand; but if it came to a struggle he did not fear the issue.

Sitting up on his bed of grass he stared out to sea and, on the horizon, the ships went along and along, far off blacknesses, dim trails of smoke. He did not see them, was indeed unconscious of his material surroundings, but his mind was beginning to work. Behind Sabina's denying face he sensed the opposition of Gray's mother. Hitherto he had regarded Mrs. Tom as a friendly circumstance; but he knew she was shrewd and, in a small way, ambitious. Jim Rosevear of Treketh would be a satisfactory match. He had the promise of a good farm and was a steady chap. And Gray? Would she take her mother's penny shrewdness for wisdom, marry a young man for his youth, do the commonplace thing?

For the first time since the blow had fallen, Byron allowed himself to think of Gray driving away from him with Jim Rosevear. Suffocating with rage, he fell forward again upon the grass.

Such passion as that of Leadville Byron is the creative force at its human strongest and the man who feels it, recognizes in it something of the divine. He cannot doubt that he will be able to inspire in its object an equal flame; and he seeks, with a persistence worthy of its sacred object, for his opportunity. Byron had the most precious thing in the world to offer Gray and nothing, not her mother, not the hampering circumstance of a wife, not even her girlish preference for another man, would be allowed to stand in his way.

Noon found him by the yard gate of Wastralls. He had drifted back across the waste because the way was familiar to his wandering feet; and he reached the farm as the kitchen clock began to strike. The familiar sound, hoarse and creaking as the voice of an old person, carried across the sunshiny yard and the man stood to count the strokes. Twelve o'clock! Where had the morning gone? He rubbed his eyes like one waking out of sleep and, as he did so, became aware that a horse had been tethered to the staple and that beyond the horse, was a gig. The varnish of this threw off a hundred cheerful reflections while the buckles and bosses of the harness were of a highly polished brass. The glitter and hard cheeriness of the whole were like the sharp gleams of frost on a sunshiny winter morning. Byron recognized the gig as belonging to Dr. Derek of Stowe. Whenever other business brought him into the parish, the doctor was apt to drop in for a chat with his late patient. He liked her, but he had also a professional reason for coming. Her recovery had surprised him, for such vitality is unusual; and he meant to keep an eye on the case.

The farmer hesitated for a moment. He was not in a mood for talk. Nevertheless the force which had already set his feet upon a hidden road drove him forward and he took his accustomed way across the now slushy yard, straight to the porch. Clean blue flagstones ran by the hedge-gripe, turning at right angles along the side of the house; but, as Byron had once contemptuously said, "They were all right for cats and women, he wasn't afraid of a little mud."

As he opened the door the appetizing smell of new bread rushed out. Sabina had been baking and, on the side-table, stood a row of crusty loaves flanked by lightly piled splits while behind was enough white cake and saffron cake to carry the household over Christmas.

Byron stood for a moment, his bloodshot eyes scanning the place. The kitchen being a dark room, a new-comer required time to forget the sun. As his pupils widened, however, he perceived ensconced in Old Squire's big chair, a little man, rosy-gilled and grey-haired. This man was eating, with an air of pleasant enjoyment, a thunder-and-lightning split and, beside him on a stool, stood a cup of tea. Though Dr. Derek had been out all night he looked as if fresh from his bath; and no one could have supposed that this snack of new bread was in place of the breakfast he had missed. Opposite him, her unwieldy bulk seeming about to overflow the wicker cone of the trolley, sat Mrs. Byron, a quiet somewhat distrait figure. The contrivance had been made when she was a comparatively normal shape. Since then she had grown stouter, 'gone abroad'; and a new and roomier cone was becoming imperative. She looked tired after her morning's bread-making and her face had lost its jovial look. Over it a breath had passed, dulling the gaiety, wiping away even content, and the breath was one to which all of us, unhappily, can fit a name.

Dr. Derek looked up at the farmer's entrance. "Just come from Curvithick," said he, "and thought I'd look in on my way home."

Curvithick Farm, the mistress of which had been cheerfully expecting her thirteenth child, lay on the other side of the main road at the head of the valley. The land marched with that of Constantine Rosevear. "Maggie Martin 'av got a baker's dozen now then," said Mrs. Byron but she spoke without her usual interest in her neighbour's concerns.

"She's done better than that," and Dr. Derek helped himself to another split. "She's got twins!"

"Twins? My dear sawl and body, whatever they gwine do now with so many childer?"

"Twelve last night and fourteen this morning!" Dr. Derek looked pleased. He held that a declining birth-rate meant the opportunity of his country's enemies and was himself the father of five sons and four daughters. He was wont to declare blandly that he lived in the West because the women there had, on the whole, a sense of their duty to the empire.

"Boy and cheeld?" pursued Mrs. Byron.

"Yes, one of each kind, a pigeon pair." He beamed at her through round glasses, the rims of which had a yellow gleam, and passed his cup for more tea. "Your splitters are excellent, Mrs. Byron—but you," he shook his head, "what have you been doing with yourself?"

Sabina glanced at her husband who, after greeting the doctor, had seated himself heavily on the window-bench. The family physician has slipped gradually into the place of the family confessor and, if Byron had not been present, she might have taken Dr. Derek to a small extent into her confidence. As it was, she acknowledged her state without offering to explain it. "I don't feel very special. I be all any'ow to-day."

Not having seen her for some time Dr. Derek did not suspect that her wan looks and cheerless air were what a day had brought forth. Remembering the keen hearty cross-country woman of former days and contrasting her with this dulled stay-at-home, he found support for his theory that the amazing rally after her accident had been the last flicker of a strong vitality. She had gone downhill since he saw her last.

"You've been doing more than you should," and a glance at the array of loaves emphasized his words. "That heart of yours won't stand much, Mrs. Byron. A little extra strain, you know, and you'll find yourself in Queer Street."

Leadville who had been staring down at the gun which still lay across the table, turned his heavy eyes on the doctor. "'Tis no good tellin' 'er to stop, for she will carry on as long as she mind to. I tell 'er I'll do the out-o'-door work for 'er, but 'er won't listen, so 'tis so well I leave it drop."

The little bright doctor glanced from wife to husband and back again. With neat compact theories about everything, he held that Sabina's childlessness was the key to the situation. "Here's a man ready and willing to take the work off your shoulders! Why not make use of him? He'd save you all sorts of worries."

"I reckon he would," and Sabina covered bitterness with a smile. "He'd never say nothing about 'em. He'd keep 'em all to 'isself."

"Considering," retorted the doctor crisply, "that you have by no means regained your strength, surely that would be a good thing?"

Sabina shook her head. He did not understand and she could not explain. "I'd rather ride my own 'obby-'arse," she said vaguely.

"Don't overtax your strength then or you'll be sorry for it." After all, whether she should wear herself out quickly or rot by the chimney corner, was her affair.

Leadville withdrew his fascinated gaze from the gun. "Didn't I 'ear you say, last time you was 'ere, she ought to 'ave a operation?"

"I did, it wouldn't be a serious one, a matter of a week or so in hospital. What do you think, Mrs. Byron? To have it done would make you much more comfortable. Stronger too, I fancy."

But Sabina's recollection of the days after her accident, those days of pain and discomfort when she had hung conscious and half consenting on the edge of the void, was still clear. She wondered why Leadville should be showing this sudden interest on her concerns. Did he wish to get her out of the way again, so that he might be up to his tricks? Or did he think he still had a chance with Gray? She could smile to herself over his infatuation. It would not be long now before he realized its hopelessness.

"I don't like that old knife business," she said. "I'll live as long as I can and then I must die."

"This is hardly worth calling an operation."

"Thank you, doctor, I'll stay where I'm to."

"A wilful woman!" he said, rising. "Well, then, I must send you a tonic and Byron'll see that you take it."

"He's likely to," she said.

"Now come, Mrs. Byron, can't have you saying things like that. The person who is really interested in your getting better is your husband. You don't know what he was like when you were in hospital."

"I think," said she, with a little twitch of the lips, "as I can make a guess. But thank 'ee all the same, doctor."

Picking up his gun, Byron followed the doctor out of the house. The farmer might prefer to strike a path for himself but Dr. Derek had a feline dislike of dirt and wet. His patent-leather boots, small and pointed, twinkled in the sunshine as he stepped along the blue flagstones, and through his bright round glasses, his steel-blue eye shot an inquiring gleam at the man, padding heavily at his side.

Against that neat personality, Leadville's big frame showed rough and heavy. He was the hulking unshaven countryman, powerful as a bear and with a bear's light but ungainly walk. He did not attempt to accommodate his stride to the other's city gait but lounged along somewhere in his neighbourhood.

"The missis 'aven't been 'erself lately," Byron volunteered as they came up to the gate, "an' I wish you could make her do as you say. P'raps, next time you come, you'll try and persuade 'er?"

With his plans not yet matured, one way out of his difficulties was as good as another. If Sabina could be persuaded to return to the hospital for a time, he would only have to deal with Mrs. Tom.

The doctor climbed into the gig. "'Tis no good, Byron. When she says 'No' there's no moving her."

The farmer's vague gaze was fixed on the glittering harness but his heart sank. "I should like to have everything done that can be done," he growled in his deep voice.

"I know, my good fellow," comforted the other. "Well, don't let her do more than you can help and keep her diet as light as possible. Not too much pork, you know, and no heavy suppers."

"She won't be said by me," returned Byron.

"Well, well, one does the best one can and there's no more to be said. Wonderful case! Never thought she'd turn that first corner; yet, there she is, doing a day's work. It's a pity she's growing so stout. When I think of what she was!" With his small well-kept hands, the polished nails of which scattered tiny reflections of the light, he made a gesture of pity and regret. "The strength of a man, and now — —"

Byron stepped back from the gig. "And now," he said grimly as the cob began to move, "now, she's a proper wreck."

# CHAPTER XI

An hour later Byron came into the kitchen carrying a small dead seal. Climbing down by a little treacherous path, he had seen it lying at the mouth of a cave and for some minutes had stood to watch it. By means of an inner membrane it was clearing first one nostril of sea-water and then the other; and he had shot it while it was still unaware of him.

"What's become o' the furnace?" he asked. "I told George to leav'n by the hedge-gripe."

Sabina, though a farmer, preserved some feminine traits and in particular a love of tidiness. She was as clean as a cat and to see her yard churned up by the hoofs of the cattle, and the farm implements at the mercy of the weather, troubled her. The rusty furnace, an outdoor stove used for farm purposes and, in particular, to try out seal-oil, had been an eyesore and she had had it removed.

"'Tis out in the bullocks' house."

Leadville 'damned 'er up in the 'eaps for interferin' with 'is things'; but he spoke, not harshly so much as absent-mindedly.

"I'll 'av the place as I've a mind to," returned Sabina placidly. Her husband had often raged against the equable good nature which suffered without malice, as a mother surfers the unreasonableness of her child. Now he only muttered vaguely as he set the gun in its thongs over the door.

"Where's Dick to?"

"Drayin' oreweed." Sabina, who had manoeuvred the trolly close to the fender, had been nodding in the agreeable warmth. An indoor life had made her susceptible to cold and this afternoon she felt tired and ill. The emotions rather than the work of the day had exhausted her, and she had thought to snatch a few minutes' rest before Mrs. Tom, whom she was expecting to call on the way back from Stowe, should arrive.

"You'll catch afire one of these days if you keep on gruddlin' so," said Byron, with a fathering wish. Sabina could not follow his thought, in fact she mistook it for solicitude. It was long since he had shown any interest in her welfare. Could the doctor's visit, revealing that she was in a poor way, have brought her husband to a better mind? Like the rest of us she could not believe that it takes all sorts to make a world and, in the eyes of others, saw consequently only the reflection of herself. She looked hopefully at Leadville and at once he turned away, hanging his big head and balancing from one foot to the other. His mind was stirring, as the sand crawls under an army of ants. He felt the movement, was perhaps vaguely conscious of the direction in which he was going, but could not see the end; not yet.

A cart laden with glistening weed, wet and olive-brown, had come up from the beach. As Leadville lounged out of the porch he saw that Dick Bennett was the driver. The weed had been left by the receding tide, left ankle-deep in every sandy bay, strewn over the black rocks; a generous provision, enough for every potato-patch in the parish. Nor did the glossy slippery weed constitute the whole of the sea-harvest. Manure for the fields, wood for the kitchen fires and, what that wood had held—oranges and shelled walnuts, crates and bags and boxes—had floated in during the night. The sea had been good to the lonely dwellers on her coasts; and she had offered, in her own gruesome fashion, a Christmas gift.

"The furnace, maister? I knaw where 'tis to. Leave me empt up this and I'll get it for yer."

When the stove, red with rust, had been reinstated in the shelter of the hedge, Byron took up the limp body and began to prepare it.

"That's every bit of coal we got, till Jim bring 'ome some from Stowe," said Bennett as he poured a shovelful of round knobs, which had been salvaged from the sea, on to the furze bushes, and set them alight.

"There's plenty of wood there," grunted the other, "so we must burn that."

"I should think 'twas time Jim 'ud be back." The hind was a little mournful man with a grievance. He had seen Jim drive off that morning, in his Sunday suit, with a pretty girl for company; and he had felt that he himself, older in service, should have been sent. "But these young chaps, when they go an errand, they take good care they don't come 'ome very quick. Course," he added grudgingly, "'e can spend the day in Stowe without any trouble."

"Oh, shut yer mouth," cried the other savagely. The man's grumbling chatter had obliged him to remember that Jim Rosevear was with Gray. Till then, he had succeeded in keeping the thought of their proximity at the back of his mind. It had been difficult, but he had done it. Dick had made it no longer possible and the day in Stowe unrolled itself before his jealous eyes—the drive in, a drive of five good Cornish miles, the drive behind Lady who, though a good mare, was slow: the stall in the market where Rosevear would set up the trestles, help the girl arrange to the best advantage the eggs, the poultry, the pounds and half pounds of butter: the meeting after market on the Quay where, the wagon being loaded with coal and flour, they would leave Lady by the warehouse while they hurried from shop to shop, she buying and he carrying the parcels: finally the long drive home in the windy dusk. Leadville tortured himself with the thought of that drive, of Gray's softness and nearness, of the little face between the fur of cap and necklet, the little smiling face....

He had been skinning the seal. Much as less powerful men skin a rabbit, he had been tearing the coat, grey and damp, from the smooth pale body. A stone wall, five foot broad at the base and crowned with tamarisk bushes, is what in Cornwall is called a hedge. It is at least a shelter from the wind, and Dick Bennett had been careful to set the furnace in a lew corner. The furze bushes burnt with a crackle and above them the sea-coal smouldered slowly in large red lumps. The air in the yard was fresh but still, and through it, a warm reek, rose the smell of blood. It rose to Byron's nostrils, affecting him as it affects the children of the wild, rousing in him that primitive, long-forgotten, but deathless passion which claims survival as its right and, battling before the hosts that wait to be called across the threshold, stakes its life. Between his hands hung the limp body and he wrenched at the skin in a growing fury of impatience. His blunt dark-skinned fingers were foul and, as the sealskin slipped he noticed that a trickle of thickening blood had run down his palm on to the wrist. He stared at this from between narrowed eyelids for a second, then, stooping his big head, licked it away. The taste of it, salt on his tongue, further affected an equilibrium already unstable; and the beast which slumbers behind the arras of our civilization, which stirs with a faint growl at every shaking of that decent cover, that savage incalculable beast of the long past, awoke. The blood-lust rose in him. He forgot the presence of the bullock-man, the time, the place, everything but a sudden overmastering need. Something, he could not remember what, had defied him and it was of paramount necessity that this something should be done away with, destroyed, ground into the earth. To rend and crush had become obligatory, the vindication of his claim to live. The poor body of the seal was gone and in its place was an enemy who had been given into his hands. He caught up the carcass, seeing not it, but all he hated, all he was burning to destroy and the dismemberment degenerated from honest butchery into an orgy. Dick Bennett stood aghast. In the master's eye was a wildness which made the hind thankful he was even more inconspicuous than small. For once his querulousness was hushed. "The old devil pulled and dragged and 'acked as though 'e was mad," was his description afterwards of the scene. "'E fetched 'is spite out on the poor creature. It made me fairly sick to see 'im."

Bit by bit the crushed fragments of bloody flesh were cast into the cauldron; but as long as bone or sinew held together, Byron tore at the body with unabated passion. The last lump was flung in with the same fury of effort as the first; but as soon as his hands were empty, the mood passed. The sweat was on his forehead, his knees were knocking together and he was trembling, but he seemed unconscious of his condition. For some minutes he stood by the furnace staring vacantly into the bubbling depths but by degrees his breath came more evenly, and the suavity of successful effort began to wash over his tortured mind.

Daunted by his master's incomprehensible ferocity, the hind waited in the background; and, behind him again, the chickens picked and scratched and on the lichened roof the pigeons balanced in the sun. Byron was watching the formation of a large iridescent bubble. His eye dwelt languidly on the red and green transparence, on the smaller bubbles hurrying to its side; but as the film burst and disappeared he pushed the stirring-stick into the labourer's hand with a deep, "Mind you don't leave'n burn," and swung away. He was come fully to himself, a weary and a hungry self and he remembered that the dinner hour was long past.

The outer door of the linhay opened on to a paved drying-yard and, as he passed through, he stooped his head under a sagging cord with the practical man's comment that a new prop was needed. Trifles, common-place and wholesome, were distracting his mind. He felt cold, noticed that what little wind there was had gone round to the north, noticed too that above Dark Head the sky was flaming with a sunset of good augury. The short December day being so near its close, the linhay was dark; but the hungry man knew where to lay his hand on a rabbit pasty. He had shot the rabbits and brought them in—to Gray; and now Gray was—where? Behind him lay the old house with its many chambers and not one of them harboured her. For the first time he realized that without Gray, Wastralls was but an empty shell.

In a row on the shelf stood the loaves and, beside them, on a big white dish lay the pasties. Sabina had added onion and bacon to make them appetizing, parsley to give flavour, freshly dug potatoes to hold the gravy; and all was folded in a responsible crust. Her pasties were renowned; but Byron, satisfying his hunger, did not notice the quality of the food. He was still obsessed by his vision of the empty house. The barren years, when he had paced the friendly fields as a captive paces his cage, unable either to take action or to escape, had done their work. He had supported life on a meagre hope; but he was older now, less patient, had a shorter time left him in which to enjoy. The young Samson can afford to ask riddles and play tricks, it is the ageing man who, grown desperate, brings destruction upon the people. Standing by the shelf, eating hungrily but absent-mindedly, Byron presently became conscious of voices in the kitchen. For a moment his heart beat in swift anticipation. Was Gray back? He stopped eating to listen, but the voice which had suggested that of the young girl was older and had lost some of its West-country music. He recognized it disappointedly as that of the girl's mother.

Filling himself a mug from the pitcher of milk that stood on the flags, Byron drank. If Mrs. Tom were in the kitchen the little party must have returned from Stowe, and the thought was, in a way, reassuring. Gray would be at Hember now and Rosevear would have come on to Wastralls with the mare and cart. At least they were no longer together.

Byron's thoughts dwelt fleetingly on Rosevear. Should he go back, find the fellow and send him packing? He hated the sight of that womanishly smooth face. Some day he would send his fist crashing into it, put the weight of his shoulder into the blow. If he could fell a bullock it would be child's play to spoil Rosevear's beauty, to make him so as the chap's own mother wouldn't recognize him. When Gray saw what he made of her fine sweetheart, there would be no more hesitation—Leadville could not believe it to be more than hesitation. She would turn to the man who had proved in primal fashion his right to her.

In the kitchen the women's voices rose and fell, lifting at the end in the Cornish way. Phrases and half words reached the man's ears and brought him to a distrustful consideration of them. These women, with their 'under-hauling,' their scheming, the way they 'held for each other'—what were they discussing? Him and his affairs? He fell to again on the pasty, biting into its hard crust with unnecessary force, biting indeed into more than crust and meat.

Mrs. Tom, having brought in the Christmas groceries and stacked the tins and parcels on the side-table, had settled down for a chat. The bond between the women, which like themselves was stout and workaday, had been embroidered by the years with a pattern of memories; and what can be pleasanter at the end of a winter day than to sit by a bright fire with a friend who has been tried by time? Sabina talked of her husband, of the farm, of the future.

"Ah!" said Mrs. Rosevear cheerfully, "and now the time 'as come for 'ee to make a fresh start. When Leadville knaw about Gray, 'e will 'av to rest 'is 'eart content."

Sabina stirred her tea in a meditative fashion. With a simple faith in good and evil, reward and punishment, it was puzzling to her that she who was a 'member and had gone to prayer meeting and chapel all right and been a good livin' woman,' should have had so much trouble. "I think it's a awful thing for 'e to be running after Gray, when 'e got a wife of's own?" she said. "Too bad, I do call it."

"Well, there 'tis, my dear, I 'spose 'e can't 'elp it. Men are like that, bain't they, poor old dragons? Best thing to do is to keep temptation out of's way."

"Do 'ee think so? Now I'd rather show'm as 'e can't 'av what 'e wants."

The more clear-sighted woman did not dispute the matter. Even if Sabina wanted Gray and Jim to live at Wastralls, the decision would not rest with her. Gray would not care so long as she was with Jim, but he, though good-natured and easygoing, knew his own mind. Not long since, he had been over to Gentle Jane where his aunt, receiving him warmly, had been urgent that he should live with her. He had not given a definite answer, but Mrs. Tom knew he was considering the matter.

"Better for Leadville if 'e 'ad something to take up 'is time," she said. "E's always mumpin' around the cliffs like a wandering Jew."

The wife's happy-go-lucky faith in Leadville's harmlessness did not commend itself to Mrs. Tom. She remembered the zest with which he had torn up the honeysuckle, the indifference he had shown as to whether Sabina lived or died, his moroseness since her return. They might yet have trouble with him.

"Well, 'tis 'is choice, 'e could work if 'e like; there's plenty to do, but 'e's not that way inclined."

"'E 'as got fever of lurk,
Two minds to eat and none to work,"

quoted Mrs. Tom as she helped herself to a slice of yeast-cake. "If a man got nothin' else to think about, 'e sure to get into mischief. Can't you find something for'm to do? Why don't yer let'n go to town for 'ee in an' out, and work a team sometimes?"

"'Av yer forgotten the trick 'e served me when I was in the 'ospital? 'Twouldn't do at all. 'E's one o' they sort, if you give'n a inch 'e'll take a nail."

"Well, you'm Job's comforter, but all I can say is you're both gettin' upstairs and, after a bit, you'll settle down all right again. Of course Gray'll stay 'ome now, until we see what's to be done. The young folks must please their own minds, then they can't blame nobody."

Sabina agreed, though with some reluctance. "Whatever be I to do without 'er?"

"You needn't trouble yerself about that. Richbell shall come down in the mornin' and light yer fire and get the breakfast. Iss, and while I think of't, Tom say you must sure to come up to Hember to spend Christmas. He'll fetch yer 'isself. The Constantines are comin', and we shall be all together; and by then, please God, I 'ope Leadville'll be settled down."

"I should like that very much." Her face brightened at the thought of the welcoming faces and the cheer. "I'm sure 'tis good of 'ee to think about it and I'll bring up something with me. 'Tis years since we've spent Christmas together."

"My dear, 'tis more'n ten years ago. Now, 'av you told Leadville about Gray?"

"I said to'n 'They're courtin' an'll be married very soon an' I expect they'll come 'ere to live.'"

"What did he say about it, then?"

"'E give a nasty grunt-like, 'e did; still 'e'll get over that. To-morrow I'll tell'n of 't; but I don't feel I could bear any more to-day."

"Well, to-morrow'll do."

As she spoke, Byron opened the linhay door. The dancing flames illumined the low-browed room sufficiently, for him to see the two women seated one on each side of the hearth; and with a short mutter of greeting he walked over to the window-bench. "Who brought they groceries back?"

"I did," said Mrs. Tom.

"Is Gray come back then?"

"Gray? She idn't comin' back. Me and S'bina 've made arrangements for Richbell to come in 'er place."

He had suspected the women were plotting against him. He had been conscious of their intangible opposition and a spasm of hatred took him by the throat. He shook in the grip of it. "Why?"

Mrs. Tom was resolved that there should be no ill-blood between Hember and Wastralls and her reply was non-committal. "She do dearly love 'er Aunt S'bina but she want to be 'ome."

"She'll soon be back 'ere," asserted Byron.

"She's very grateful for all your kindness but she'd rather live 'ome with me for a bit."

"I don't like changes and I won't 'av them."

"Dear me," said Mrs. Tom placidly, "won't is a big word!" She turned to the figure in the wicker cone as if, having disposed of one matter, she were ready for another. "Shall I put they groceries in the cupboard for 'ee, S'bina?"

Leadville had risen from his seat. They had taken Gray from him and they meant to keep her away. Would she be a consenting party to their scheme? He feared she might, yet if she only knew! Mrs. Tom, tranquil, occupied with household thoughts, seemed to the angry man to possess a tremendous, terrifying power. She could make Gray inaccessible and she would.

"We want 'er 'ere," and his harsh voice shook so that Mrs. Tom, aware of him out of the corner of an eye, could not but pity him.

"I knaw 'tis very good of 'ee to make so much fuss of her," she returned, pushing back her chair, "but just now she'd rather be 'ome."

Through the turmoil of his fears and hopes Leadville heard his wife's easy, "You can put they things away if you like, Isolda; but leave out the tin of boot-polish for I know we want one."

They could talk of groceries and boot-polish! He was astounded at their lack of understanding. A man might be suffering the pains of hell and they would still be occupied with trifles. With an effort which set the blood drumming in his ears he forced himself to sit down. Behind him in the thickness of the wall was the bench and above it the many-paned window, with a geranium on the inner ledge. The kitchen table stood against this bench and, as Leadville sank back he gripped the stout edge, putting into the clutch the passion or his disappointment, his revolt. The women moved about, pouring sugar and currants into jars, filling the bin with flour, folding up bags and paper. The murmur of their casual talk filled the air—their talk of the markets and the shops, of prices and of people! Murmur of women's voices is the breeze in the tree-tops; murmur of men's, the sea on the beaches, the sea at night! Leadville heard as one a great way off hears a familiar sound. He heard and gradually the gale of his impatience ceased to blow. He was no longer occupied with the soft movements of the women, no longer exasperated by their intangible opposition. He had turned from the latter as from a thing of little moment, and in the depths of his spirit had found enlightenment.

Take Gray from him, would they?

He understood at last that Mrs. Rosevear and Jim were not his chief enemies. The person who stood between him and the realization of his dreams was Sabina. She had withheld Wastralls; now, by merely living, she blocked his path to Gray.

# CHAPTER XII

"I've asked Gray to get Raby Gregor to come down and alter trolly a bit. I've thrived a bit since I lost me laigs."

"Good sign that."

"Shows I'm in better 'ealth, still I don't like bein' so fat. I've 'ad to 'av Aunt Louisa alter all my clothes and if Raby Gregor takes a long time to make trolly bigger, I shan't be able to get about for goodness knows 'ow long."

"Well, I should think Mrs. Bate 'ud come in for a day or two to 'elp yer. I shouldn't 'av trolly done till after Christmas, if you do you won't be able to come up to our place."

Leadville, sitting engrossed in secret thought, had had a withering effect upon the women's talk. It lost spontaneity, it grew spasmodic and, as soon as the last tin was on the shelf, Mrs. Tom said she must go home.

"I'll go out as far as the gate with yer," Sabina had answered eagerly. After the hot kitchen it would be pleasant to have a breath of air from the sea, pleasant also to finish their chat. The flags being level it was an easy run but the gate marked the end of the journey. From it the ground fell away to the sandy commons covered with grey spire-grass, which had given the place its name. The Wastralls had been bare blown sand, but the stiff spire held the ridges from shifting and on its heels had come bright lady's-fingers and silver-weed, coarse herbage and, in depressions, the thick yellow moss. Sabina found it rested her, after the dark confinement, the depressing influence of the house, to look across the commons. The sand was piled in fantastic bulwarks but between these wind-formed bastions and ditches glimmered a white unrest of tides.

The short winter's day was drawing to a close. The sun had sunk below Dark Head and the black shadow of the cliff had fallen on Wastralls. Grey in the dip of the grey land, it lay like a rock; but unlike a rock it was hollow and the many chambers were full of echoes from the past. Above the eastern hills a vague brightness gave promise of the moon and the women, pausing by the egg-crowned gateposts, looked up the road to where Hember windows were aglow. Their thoughts had run before them and they fancied they could hear faint sounds of voices and laughter.

"They will keep it up to-night," said Mrs. Tom and with a kiss bundled off down the lane. She was returning, full of pleasant anticipations to a merry circle—a circle which on her appearance would make her affectionately welcome. With the five girls it was always 'Mother!' with Tom too.

She had not taken many steps before the contrast between what she was leaving and that to which she was hastening, brought her to a standstill. Her heart misgave her.

"S'bina!" she called to the lonely figure, motionless by the gate. "S'bina!"

"Well, what is it?"

"Would you like for Richbell to come down to-night?"

In the kitchen Leadville could hear the high-pitched question and reply.

"Spoil 'er evenin'? My dear life, I wouldn't think of it. Don't you worry. I shall get on all right."

"I don't like to feel that you are all alone." She knew Sabina would not have welcomed a reference to her helplessness.

"Now don't 'ee think about me, go and enjoy yourself."

Mrs. Tom hesitated for a moment. At the few merrymakings of the countryside Sabina, jovial and buxom, had been a welcome guest; but, since her accident, the difficulty of getting about had kept her at home. Mrs. Tom decided she must be persuaded to go out more, that a pony must be got for her and the trolly adapted. That Leadville would be violently opposed to such a proceeding, that he would object to his wife's making a 'laughing-stock of herself,' did not weigh with Mrs. Tom.

More than once that evening when the young people, singing the old hymns to the old tunes were gathered about the harmonium, the good woman's thoughts returned to the friend of her youth. What a fine woman Sabina had been, putting them all in the shade yet unaware of it and what happy times they had had. She remembered childhood's days and how often she had waited at the cross-roads for Sabina, so that they might walk the length of the way together. The fish-seller's daughter would bring a pasty for her school dinner and there being nine at home, it was generally more pastry than meat; but Sabina had supplemented it with red apples and cold sausages and other delectable foods. Sabina had also supplemented the other's wardrobe, perhaps even her prospects.

Mrs. Tom, thinking of the lonely figure at the gate, was glad her own days were passed at Hember, in rooms that led out of each other and were crowded with children. Wastralls, silent and old, depressed her. Not all the fires Sabina lighted could warm its bones and do away with the faint but pervading smell of mould. Life that had been thinned to ghostliness, drifted through the passages; and the rooms lay in a brooding hush. She thought of the place with a dim prevision, too dim for her to grasp, a prevision of calamity.

"Somebody digging my grave!" she said and drew nearer to the fire.

The wind which blew in gusts, dropping now and again into a deceitful lull, sent a cold breath up the valley and Sabina, lingering by the gate, drew the shawl closer about her shoulders. The shadow that rested on Wastralls, a shadow to which she was as a rule wholesomely indifferent, had grown a little, grown till it included her. Though her perceptive faculty was slight, she was in no hurry to leave the clean sanity, the freshness of the night.

Above the black oblong of the mill the rim of the moon was showing golden, that wonderful West-country moon, which hangs, a clear lamp of light, far above cloud and mist. The beams falling across the yard, across the ricks, had not yet reached Wastralls. The house stood withdrawn below the hills and, for the first time, Sabina felt her home to be remote from the warm friendliness of the world. She saw it that night approximately as it appeared to others, a place cut off by its situation. The valley being far from the main highway, strangers were unaware of it. The road through, led to nothing but the teeth of the devouring sea and, as the hamlet of Cottages was the most cheerful spot in Trevorrick, so Wastralls was the most lonely and the most lost. Hember windows were always aglow. The sun found them by day and the moon by night. They glowed from within, from the fires of driftwood and sea-coal, from lamps swinging under the dark rafters, from the fires of life. Sabina, reluctantly returning to the house, could not but contrast the light and music of Hember, its continual coming and going, with the dark desolation, the stagnant peace of Wastralls. Never had it been otherwise. Her earliest recollections were of long hours when, her father being at the Dolphin, the servant would take advantage and be 'walking out.' The child, given the run of the empty rooms and left to her own devices, had peopled the place with imaginary figures. Even at this distance of time she could recall their 'names and attributes — Tinkle Minkle who was black and made of sugar, Creekuk and Clokuk the eiderdown men, and Tinkle Farg who, still more absurd, had been 'shy with a buffalo!' Naturally social she had liked to imagine a face at every window, children playing under the 'grubby elms' of the avenue and among the animals in the yard. She had looked forward to the time when she should be grown up and married. "One child is a misfortune," she had told her father at the ripe age of ten, "I'm going to 'ave lots when I marry. I'm going to full the rooms."

The sound of a harmonium came to her through the stillness, but so faint was it she could hardly distinguish the tune. At Hember they were singing the familiar hymns in which all could join. The sound drew the listening woman. How often when weary of imaginary companions had she run up the lane and joined her cousins at their play! Hember had been a bright spot in her life. All that she knew of sewing and housewifery, her aunt had taught her; and Tom had wanted to marry her, yes—Tom and Constantine. Poor old Constantine, he had tried his best. But Tom, the rascal, Tom had been looking two ways at once. She sighed, the gusty sigh of a stout middle-aged woman who wishes the hot cake of youthful joys, with its plums and its citron and its spice, was once more whole in her hand.

A puff of wind, increasing the volume of sound, enabled Sabina to recognize the hymn. She could almost see the happy group, Isolda knitting in her chair by the range, Tom opposite to her and, about the harmonium, the bright heads and smiling faces of the girls. Ah, if only one of them had been born to herself! She, who had been going to 'full the rooms,' had had neither the full quiver nor the faithful mate; she had had, as she realized at last, nothing in all her life but hope; and from her, time had stolen, even that which she had.

In the kitchen, absorbed in brooding thought, Byron, a thicker shadow in the growing gloom, was awaiting her return. Her mind, from wandering far afield, circled to the present, to the slight repugnance she felt at entering the house. She was not a 'nervy' woman, indeed, in a countryside peculiarly susceptible to the so-called supernatural, had been known to declare, "Out at all times, night and day, and never see nothing worse than myself." Her unwillingness to go back, an unwillingness which, in truth, was but another of the warnings which had been tolling like death-bells all the day, seemed to her foolish.

"'Tis owin' that we've been bad friends for so long," she said. "I'm feelin' awkward as tho' 'e'd been a stranger. The sooner I take an' go in the better."

The door of the glass porch stood wide in a yawn of blackness, a blackness so thick that Mrs. Byron felt as if she were pushing her way in against a resistance intangible and, on the whole, yielding but which could yet be felt. Afraid of what might be lurking in the depths of that gloom she forced herself to move noisily and, making a greater effort, to break the silence.

"'Tis darker 'ere than 'tis in the yard," she said, thinking of the moon, and the pale flood it was pouring over meadow and common, over the nestling farms, over every place but the dark corner in which her home lay hid; contrasting the black and silver of the night with this brooding hush.

She put her hand on the shelf to find the matches. Once the lamp was lighted, once its cheery beams had driven out the dark, she would be more at ease. In a hurry to finish her work, Gray however, had forgotten to fill the brass receptacle with oil and Mrs. Byron was faced with a domestic problem. To manoeuvre the trolly sufficiently close to the wall would be difficult. Nevertheless it did not occur to her to ask Leadville's help and he, sitting motionless by the window, did not offer it.

"Strange 'ow I feel I must keep on craikin'," she thought, as, at last successful, she trundled off to the linhay. "'Tis just like Leadville 'ad now comed in and I must talk to'n. I dunno when I felt so whisht."

"We 'aven't got very much paraffin left," she said aloud as she returned with the lamp. "Jim didn't bring any. I dare say we got enough for to-night though, we don't burn much."

"Where's Jim to?" asked Leadville suddenly.

"Couldn't get a bit of coal," said Mrs. Byron, hanging the lamp in its bracket and trying to conceal the fact that his unexpected utterance had jarred her unruly nerves. "'Awken 'adn't a bit, but the boat is expected in to-night so Jim'll 'av to go in to-morrow and fetch it."

"Where's 'e to?" persisted Leadville.

Sabina held that if no fuel were thrown upon a fire, that fire must die. "'Ow d'yer think I knaw?"

"Is 'e to 'Ember?"

"Well, where else should 'e be, seein'..."

The man's deep chest lifted and fell. "Seein'," he interrupted fiercely, "as Tom wish for'm to be there, seein' as 'is wife wish it..."

"'Is—'is wife?" stammered Sabina.

"Don't Isolda wish it? You know she do; but my li'l bird don't wish it. I don't believe she do."

The blood, which had drained out of the woman's face, returned with a rush. She opened her lips but found herself voiceless and gasping. "Don't say like that, Leadville," she whispered at last. "Don't 'ee, don't 'ee say it— not to me."

The man threw back his head and, as if unable in any other way to express his feelings, broke into a laugh. "You!" he said. "You!"

Sabina turned the trolly handle, pushing it blindly out of the room. She was running away as a man runs from licking, climbing flames. She could not yield, could not knuckle under, but she could retreat until strong enough to resume the struggle. The tears were running down her face as she turned into the linhay, but they were tears forced from her by pain. Like the child in the story she could have said, "It is my eyes that's cryin', not me."

For behind the wall of her tired and suffering body was her indomitable spirit.

# CHAPTER XIII

Sabina's mental attitude towards events and persons was often one of surprise and protest. It was now.

"What 'av I done that 'e should treat me like this?" she thought. Her right-doing was the outstanding thing in her life and could not be missed. It was like a bonfire on a hill. If the wages of sin were death, the reward of righteousness which she deserved, should be love and faith. Laying claim to this reward, her poor mind, groped in a long bewilderment. For love and faith had been withheld.

Leaning for support on the stone shelf, gathering the dark and quiet and coolness of the linhay into her soul, her tears gradually dried up and as gradually her personal feeling, her bitterness and resentment, gave place. She had asserted a claim, had protested as a wife against the outrage of Leadville's words, had protested as a child against that flourishing of the wicked as a green bay-tree; but the habit of her mind was impersonal and very kind. Dispirited, sad, almost despairing, she yet could not do other than return to it.

"Poor chap's that worried, 'e dunno what 'e's sayin'," she told herself. Her lack of children was an oversight she had done her best to remedy. She made for Leadville the blind tender excuses of her maternal heart. "I knaw 'e don't mean it.' Ye'll be all right in a day or two's time. Always been a good-livin' feller and I'm sure 'e wouldn't 'urt a flea. I don't belong to mind..." a quivering nerve gave her the lie.... "But I do, I do mind," she said piteously, "'e's all I got. No, and tedn't that. 'Tis I do love'n."

Drawing water she bathed her eyes. The burst of emotion had left her drained of strength but supper was yet to get. "I did mean to fry for 'is supper," she said, the word covering as many varieties of appetizing food as can be cooked in a frying-pan, "but I don't think I will, I feel so tired and weary, I think us'll have to manage with what we've got." She glanced along the shelf. "That bit of cold meat'll do. 'E do dearly love a bit of fat pork."

Although her tears, easing the strain on her nerves, had left her less apprehensive, the kitchen still loomed disquieting. "'Tis because I made a fool of myself," she said, bracing herself for further effort.

Leadville was in his old place by the window. He neither moved nor spoke, seemed indeed too much absorbed in thought to be aware of her. Sabina felt relieved. She told herself she had had enough of his tantrums for one day: let them have the meal in peace and get off to bed. Putting the meat on a clean dish she began to lay the cloth but, as she moved about, a dim suspicion flitted through her mind that she was being watched. She dismissed it hurriedly and went on with her work, but it returned. Though Leadville appeared lost in thought, no sooner did she turn her back than his heavy lids lifted and his eyes followed her with a furtive question. She felt them on her, felt in his glance a quality which made her uneasy. What did he want to know? Why couldn't he put his question into words? Why should his following and thoughtful glance remind her of the way a cat, crouching, watches a bird? She was sure he was watching, yet not quite sure. Turning sharply she fixed brave blue eyes on his face, but immediately he looked away. He was not watching her, he was occupied with his own dark and brooding fancies.

The blank unconsciousness of his gaze was reassuring. She had been mistaken, fanciful. How foolish of her! Well, she was tired, she could not help it if she did fancy things. She had been through a lot that day and it had shaken her. Perhaps too the lamp had something to say to her fancies. It was not burning well and, while a good light cheered and encouraged, a jumping insufficient one bred more than shadows. Mrs. Byron went into the linhay for scalded cream, for syrup and the cocoa-jug, but as she passed her husband she felt that if he did not quite look at her, she was yet the centre of his thoughts. And he was looking. Her back was towards him, her unprotected back, and his glances were like arrows. The hair crisped on the woman's head. What did this furtive watching mean? This down-dropping look which, when unobserved, followed and considered? Leadville was sitting back in the corner, his head resting against the wall and, though his heavy features wore the expression habitual to them, his eyes were no longer filmed with inward brooding. Sabina, wandering over the moors had once stooped to look along a deserted mine-shaft and, in the darkness, had seen two round eyes, eyes of green fire, eyes which though distant had been full of a wild menace. They had stared out at her, threatening her advance and, so inimical were they, that she had left the mine-shaft unexplored. Leadville's eyes reminded her of the savage daunting thing from which she had retreated. "I wish 'e wouldn't watch me like that," she said, lingering over her errand, "it makes me feel any'ow; I wish—" her thoughts flew to Hember, Hember which, whenever she had been in a difficulty hitherto, had come to the rescue—"I wish I'd let Richbell come down."

A candle stood on the furnace and, by its light, Mrs. Byron searched the upper shelf for a jug of which she stood in need. During her long convalescence she had suffered from sleeplessness but, as her health improved, so had her nights. She put the latter down, however, to the fact that she had formed the habit of drinking a cup of hot cocoa as soon as she was in bed. A warm drink at night, a nourishing, non-stimulating drink which needed care in preparation was, she had felt, more likely to bring a return to normal conditions than patient waiting on the mysterious processes of nature. The cocoa-jug, brown, high-waisted, girdled by a gold line, stood a little behind the other pitchers. In her haste that morning, Gray had pushed it back and, the shelf being high, her aunt had some difficulty in recovering it. The effort to reach it distracted her mind and, when she returned to the kitchen, she was thinking more of the healing effects of cocoa than of the tiresome ways of husbands.

On one side of the range hung a small square mirror, such as can be bought of any gipsy pedlar for a shilling; and as she leaned forward to put on the kettle she caught sight of her face. Used to rubicund cheeks below bright eyes, she was surprised to see that, though her colour was fixed, it had lost its warm tone and that her lips were a bluish grey.

"I bin frightened," she told herself, "I knaw 'tis fulishness of me but I can't 'elp it. Pretty mawkin I be, fancyin' things like that." The eyes in the mirror were strong and encouraging, the grey lips smiled at her. Here was a tried comrade who knew what she had to endure and who sympathized— who sympathized as no one else could! Sabina was captain of her soul and could rely on it for strength and for support; yet with her reviving courage came a hint of the old discomfort. On returning from the linhay she had found Byron staring at his knees. Now that her back was turned to him she felt—and the feeling sent a quick shudder through her—she felt that he was at his trick of watching. She felt it, then suddenly she knew, for in the depths of the mirror was another face, a face which had fixed narrowing eyes on her; and these eyes travelled over her, considering her, asking a strange inhuman question.

She swung the trolly round in an access of nervous fear but that inimical glance had slipped away and Leadville was once more staring blankly at his knees. Mrs. Byron remained for a moment waiting, but he neither stirred nor looked. He had been on the verge of making the discovery he sought and her sudden movement, scattering his thoughts, had angered him. If she would go on with her work, the thing that was eluding him, would creep back and this time he would grasp it. He sat like one in a trance, focusing his mind on a dimly seen spot, a spot of dreadful knowledge.

Sabina manoeuvred the car so that she no longer had her back turned to the dark figure on the bench. To make the cocoa while in a sideways position was awkward, but the defenceless attitude had become impossible. She must know what was happening on the other side of the room. Profoundly disturbed, she yet measured the spoonfuls of cocoa with a steady hand. As Gray would not share the beneficial draught that night her aunt was mechanically careful to make only half the usual quantity. The lavish hand does not pile up a balance at the bank.

As Mrs. Byron set the jug of cocoa on the stove, in order that it might be kept hot till she was ready for it, Leadville broke the silence. He did not speak, but once more he laughed, and this time his was the satisfied laugh of a man who after long endeavour has found that of which he is in search.

His wife stared. "'Ow you made me jump," she said, a little breathlessly. A quality in the laugh, a certain sinister satisfaction, had made her flesh creep. What was it that had pleased him, that by his secret watching he had discovered? She tried to shake off the conviction of his strangeness. "Dunno what's come over me. I spose 'e can laugh at 'is own thoughts; but it's a funny thing, it makes me all goosey flesh."

Conquering an inclination to go out of the room, to leave Leadville to his secret satisfactions, she rolled herself to the table. "I should think you was feeling so leary as a grey'ound by this time," she said and, by speaking of the commonplace, would have relieved the tension. The queerness of Leadville's behaviour might after all be due to hunger for, as far as she knew, he had not had any food since morning.

The man cleared his throat. "There's no butter on the table," he said, looking past her at something on the other side of the room.

"Gray's taken every bit to market." His habit being to eat without comment what was set before him, Sabina felt a dim surprise that he should have asked for butter.

"She 'aven't. I see some on the shelf."

To ask him to fetch it did not occur to her. Turning the handle of the little car she went back to the linhay. It was possible that Gray, thoughtful for others, had put some aside.

As the trolly disappeared behind the door it was as it a hand swept from Byron's features the mask which hitherto had shrouded his resolve. Obscure, unrecognized, it had lain for many a day behind his everyday thoughts. The general upheaval had thrust it forward until it shone naked in a dreadful candour. So long had it been familiar that it came tame to the man's seeking hand. He knew at last what he must do. Sabina making the cocoa had shown it him.

Getting up from the bench and treading carefully—he whose step was always light—he tiptoed over to the wall cupboard. It yawned before him, a darkness hollowed in the solid masonry and with unerring certainty, as if his hand had gone that way in dreams, it fell on that which it sought, a little ribbed blue phial, with an orange label. The last occasion on which he had used it, had been when he adjudged Shep to be old and useless. The bottle was only a quarter full, and he felt sorry that he had wasted any of the precious contents on the dog. Would the quarter be sufficient for his purpose? For a moment he hung uncertain, but the passions which were riding him to destruction forced him to take the risk. He heard Sabina crossing the floor of the linhay and the repugnance with which she inspired him rose like nausea in his throat. He went blind with hatred, the hatred so long repressed, that primitive hatred of the under-dog. As one pressed for time, he uncorked the bottle and held it to the jug of cocoa. The colourless fluid gurgled as it flowed over the blue rim and the sound, striking through the man's absorption, woke in him the beginnings of fear. Even now, she might be able to come between him and success, this necessary, intolerably-longed-for success. He stared with wild eyes at the linhay door. If she had heard, if she came in and in her high brave way faced him and accused him, he was done. To use violence to Sabina was not in him. He could only work against her in secret, get her at a disadvantage, strike from behind. If she found him out, he would not dare any more, he would be beaten and it would break him. His spirit acknowledged that there was a limit.

He listened but Sabina was still moving from shelf to shelf on her fruitless errand. He grew conscious that the sweat was running into his eyes. Raising a hand, a hand foul with seal's blood, to wipe it from his forehead, he left a brown smear in its place.

The drops fell hissing on the red-hot coals and, out of his other hand, Byron dropped that ominous blue phial into the fire. A splutter and crackle of flame, louder than any of the man's furtive movements, spat out at him. Terrified he turned to the box beside the hearth, a strong old box which had come in from the sea and was now used to hold driftwood. From it he snatched thick pieces and thin queer-shaped bits of old dead ships, of their gear and their furniture, and piled them on the tell-tale bottle. When Mrs. Byron returned from her unsuccessful search, he was holding his trembling hands before the blaze and the flames were leaping over the heap of sea-rimed fuel.

"Mercy!" cried she, at the sight of what seemed to her careful mind a waste of good wreck, "you'll catch the chimbly afire. Us don't want a big fire, 'tis near bedtime, now."

She rolled forward as if to remove a log but Leadville stood his ground. "Leave'n go. If I didn't want it, I shouldn't ha' put it there. I'm cold."

For a man who wore the same clothes, winter and summer, who had never cared to possess an overcoat, this was a curious assertion. Sabina, observing that his hands shook, began to think he must be on the verge of an illness. If so, it would account for the general strangeness of his conduct.

"Please yourself," she said and rolled the trolly over to the table. "I couldn't find the butter anywhere, but Isolda has promised to send some down in the morning. Wud yer like a bit o' dripping?" She placed a small china dish heaped with pork dripping near her husband's plate. "Come on, make 'aste," she said, "supper's ready."

With his back to her and with those darkly stained hands still spread to the blaze, he muttered that he could not eat.

"You'll very soon be knocked up if you don't eat something," she said kindly. "Won't yer 'ave a bit o' this pork?"

"If I did I should bring me life up."

Concerned for his health she continued to press him. "Will 'ee 'av a drop of beer if I fetch it?"

"I don't want anything."

"Well, couldn't 'ee drink a cup of my cocoa?"

For a moment the world heaved dizzily about the man. He stumbled forward a space. "Of your—of your cocoa—I didn't—" he stammered, his spirit turning craven; but Sabina's innocent uncomprehending face, turned sideways from the table, arrested him on the brink; and he swung off into a wild, incoherent mutter, which presently resolved itself into oaths, such as he had not used since his seafaring days. He could not stop, the words poured from him like steam out of a safety-valve. Even Sabina, to whose common-sense point of view swearing was mere harmless breath, was taken aback. To surliness she was accustomed, cursing of a mild order was the male way of expressing gratitude for the gift of speech, but this? Turning in the wicker cone she looked at him searchingly and this look, puzzled and seeking to understand, brought him to his senses. He stammered, choked over his words and flinging himself into Old Squire's red-cushioned chair bade her 'leave him be.'

"Poor old sinner, 'e dunno what to do by 'isself," she thought excusingly. "Like a bear wi' a sore 'ead 'e is. Well, I better leave'n be."

She drew the pork towards her and cut it. She was reconsidering her decision to wait till morning before telling her husband that Gray was definitely beyond his reach. If his queerness and irritability were due to hope deferred it would be merciful to put him out of his misery, to give him the final blow. She glanced at the figure in the arm-chair. Leadville was sitting forward, his elbows on his knees, his head with its strongly growing black hair sunk between his hands. He looked unapproachable and the saying about 'sleeping dogs' occurred to her.

If she were to make an effort, were to tell him, she would certainly suffer for it. He would treat her to some sort of scene and she was tired. She could not remember when she had felt so tired. Her back ached and her head ached, she had even a whimsical feeling that her legs ached.

She would not tell him now. The news trembling on the tip of her tongue should wait till, strengthened by her night's rest, she were able to take his anger and disappointment for granted.

She found that she was hungry. What a blessing there was always to-morrow, with a fence of sleep shutting off one day and its troubles from the next. What she needed was a good supper and a long night's rest. Thank goodness, Richbell would be down before it was light. She, Sabina, could lie abed until the pains had gone out of her bones.

In the quiet room the only sounds were the slight movements of the figure at the table, the tinkle of a fork against china, the crackle of dry wood in the grate. Once a tiny explosion, a breaking of heated glass, was audible; but, at the same moment, Leadville rose with a loud scrape of his chair.

"You'm eatin' like a 'adger," he said, in a tone of suppressed irritability and, taking down his gun, began to clean it. The energy of his movements was almost violent. By this oiling and rubbing he was easing the strain on his nerves. Mould and rust grow in that damp climate like the Giant-killer's bean and Leadville rubbed and polished till the barrel was gleaming darkly in the dull light of the wall lamp, till it caught a red glint from the flaming driftwood.

"What be yer gwine to do with your gun?" asked Sabina taking quiet note of this outburst of energy. "Any wild fowl down?"

At Christmas stranger birds, sooty-plumaged, web-footed, delicate-fleshed, came in large numbers to the north coast and all men, hind and farmer alike, went out to 'get a duck for dinner.'

The relief of hearty movement seemed to have oiled Leadville's tongue for, staring down at the last specks of rust, he said dreamily, "I used to think as one day I should shet myself with'n."

"Whatever was 'ee gwine do that for?" She had the practical person's contempt for extravagant talk, moreover she had listened to this threat before, had even expressed her opinion that there 'was cleaner ways o' dying.' She began to stack plates and dishes on a tray.

"If you can't 'av what you wanted," said he, still speaking as if only half conscious of what he said, "what's the good of livin'?"

"If you can't 'av what you want," retorted Sabina, "you should make the best of a bad bargain."

"No," he said simply, "I bain't made that way."

She shook her head over his childishness. "You'm a very covechous man," she said. "If you wanted a farm so bad as that, why didn't you rent'n?"

The light of the fire was reflected in his dark eyes, a spark in the blackness. He had put the gun back over the door and was sitting forward, his gaze on the burning wood. "I didn't want nothing but my own," he said with unalterable conviction. "I'd a right to Wastralls and 'twas just your oogliness denyin' me of it."

Sabina smiled. How foolish he was, how unreasonable! Just a big child.

"Did you marry me," she inquired, thinking to clinch the matter and her voice was the voice of one who makes allowance for a boyish fancy— "did you marry me or the land?"

For a moment he did not answer, then the truth which he had lived for twenty years, forced its way out. "I married 'ee for the land," he said quietly.

But Sabina had her memories. Let him say what he would she could not doubt his young sincerity.

"And now," he added, "now I wish I 'adn't."

Ah, that was it—'now.' She had been loved. She could recall the days of courtship, the first years of their union, sweet words, little tender deeds, the potpourri of rose-leaves that a woman hoards. He had courted her for more than the land and, though he denied it, he could not shake her faith. The past was hers and, because it was dead, it would be always hers.

"You wish that I was gone?" she said. He had loved her once, now he fancied that he loved Gray. It was only a fancy and would pass. The past was hers and the future would be, but the present? Sabina had always lived in the present and it was the present which had betrayed her.

"I wish we was never married, I wish you," he hesitated for a word, "I wish you would let me go."

She had been clearing the table. Her hands worked in the familiar way. She collected cruet, knives, forks and put them in the appointed places, but without knowing that she had lifted a finger. "You wish I would let you go?" she said incredulously. "You don't mean what you say, Leadville. I'm sure you don't. You'm vexed now, you've 'ad things to try you to-day and you don't know what you'm sayin' of; you'll be better in the mornin'." She had not been able to let his words pass without a protest, the protest of a still hopeful heart. Surely he would deny them.

"I wish," he affirmed heavily, "you would let me go."

The difficult tears rose to her eyes and her chin trembled. "My dear," she said and her stable law-abiding spirit was behind the words, "you knaw we'm married. It's a funny thing after all these years you want to be let go."

But he persisted. "If I was to clear out of this..."

"Go—go away?" she stammered, as if his previous words had been a meaningless ejaculation. "Go right away? Whatever for?"

"I bin 'ere all these years and I 'aven't been 'appy. A man want a little 'appiness in's life."

"Oh, Leadville, don't say such things. I've done my best to make you 'appy and comfortable."

"You couldn't do it," he said and added with finality, "you wasn't the right one."

The tears were running down her face, her poor quivering face which to his eyes looked so old, so unattractive. "I've done my best—my best."

"If I was to clear out of this..." he said, returning to what occupied his mind. Why could she not believe him, realize that for her own sake, she must let him go? Even now it was not too late. He glanced at the brown jug on the stove—not too late yet.

"No," she cried, "no, don't 'ee go away."

"One of us got to go, then."

But she had found the answer, the word of power. "Not—not till death us do part," she responded.

"Aw," he said, "and that's it. Till death us do part," and he repeated the words as if they were the chorus of a song already sung, the refrain of a chant known long ago and until then forgotten. "Till death us do part."

He had spoken throughout as if hardly conscious of his words, but now a spurt of irritation, irritation at her folly, shook him. "You and your ways!" he cried harshly. "'Tis you that's responsible. You drove me to do things I wouldn't do."

Relieved by his return to this more ordinary mood Sabina's courage rose. "'Tis your own self that 'arnessed the 'arse," she said with greater confidence. "I've 'ad nothing to do with it. My 'ands is clean."

The man's inconsequent attention was caught by her last words. Glancing stupidly at his hands he saw to his surprise, and swiftly growing consternation, that they were dark with blood. The minor events of the afternoon—the slaughter of the seal, its skinning, the 'running out' of the oil, had been forgotten. He could see no reason, no reason but the one, for this significant stain. "Mine 'edn't," he cried shaking them as if he would shake it off. "Can't think whatever this is!"

"Looks as tho' you got blood on them."

His first shuddering dismay changed to fear. He glanced at her sidelong. "'Ow 'av I got blood on my 'ands, can yer tell me?"

"No, I can't." She also had forgotten the trifling incident of the seal. "But 'tis certainly blood."

To a man in Leadville's confusion of mind, a confusion shot with flashes of clear thought, the age of miracles was not past. That the dark intention of his spirit should have been made supernaturally visible, did not seem impossible, not even improbable.

"Get out—blood?" he cried furiously. "'Tis only dirt. I'll go and wash them."

Hurrying into the linhay he began to pump water over his hands, washing and re-washing them till they were red with cold, till not a speck of the betraying colour remained. The flow of the water, bright and unbroken, had a soothing effect on him. He watched it falling from the round mouth of the pump on to the grating, listened dreamily to it running out by the conduit under the flags; and with it his horror drained away, leaving him at peace. As the flow thinned to a trickle, like a child at innocent but mischievous play, he raised the green handle and brought another rush. The winter rains had filled the well and Mrs. Byron, though she wondered mildly what he might be doing, was too much occupied with her griefs to pay much attention.

However stout a woman's common sense it crumbles before such simplicity as that of Leadville. Alleging a long unhappiness, he had begged for the freedom which should straighten out the tangle of his life. "If I was to clear out of this—" he had said.

To accord it, was not in her. If their marriage was a mistake as he averred, and she could not grant that it was, the mistake once made must be accepted. They must, as she had said, 'make the best of a bad bargain.' Gray married and out of reach, Leadville would surely remember that when he had wandered into Trevorrick, like some flying creature into a garden, she had been the one, of all those rooted there who, opening her heart, had given him shelter. She could not take seriously that desire of his to spread his wings and lift himself once more into the blue. What was there for him, now that he was no longer young, but the security of the garden, the sheltering walls of that one heart?

Sabina, hungry for an old age of peace and affection, turned in thought to a couple well known in Tregols, the Henwoods of Curyarnon. Married after a long courtship and the father of boys and girls, Mr. Henwood had yet had two sons by a woman of the village. Though the scandal was open the wife had chosen to ignore it and, in the end, he had gone back to her. Now, an example of senile devotion, they were tottering hand in hand down the gradual hill. Sabina envied them. Like Mrs. Henwood she felt that she could wait and, when the time came, forgive.

The kitchen was always tidy, but some of the parcels that had been brought from Stowe still lay on the side-table and, rolling herself, in tired fashion, across the room she began to sort them. Cottons, needles, a roll of flannel, unbleached calico for the hams and a new account-book, they were speedily drafted into drawers and work-box; but behind the parcel of drapery lay an object, the purchase of which she had forgotten. For a moment she looked at it in sadness and uncertainty; then, with the faint dawnings of a smile. Gray had executed the commission with which she had been charged. She had bought the pipe, a good one with an amber mouthpiece, and it lay before Sabina on the blue and red table-cloth. Leadville smoked by fits and starts and, for some days, his foul and blackened pipe had lain untouched on the mantelshelf. With the thought of the man's material welfare she put the new pipe by the old. Let him go? Go where? He had no trade, no money and he was getting 'up in years.' Her kind heart saw him drifting on the tides of poverty, saw him submerged and she shook her head. For this reason and for every other, she must not let him have the freedom that he asked—it was too late.

For a moment the oppression that was clouding her mind lifted on a sunset thought. She could imagine his surprise when he found the new pipe by the old, his pleasure and the word of thanks she would be accorded. By then he would know Gray was out of reach and though his vanity might suffer—not even now could the wife believe it was more than vanity—the pipe smoked and smoking sweetly, must remind him of the tried companion who for so many years had looked after his creature comforts, and given him with one exception, everything he asked.

She must have patience.

She was so tired that if she did not go to bed she felt she would sink away through cone and trolly, sink into nothingness. Lifting the jug of cocoa from the stove and carrying it with her, she went out of the kitchen and down the long passage to her room.

"Good night!" she called.

# CHAPTER XIV

Sabina's voice, not having been modified by the habit of rooms, had a resonant, carrying note. "Good night!" she had said and the sound, travelling out to the linhay, fell on Leadville's ears.

Through the skylight in the high sloping roof, the moon was dimly sketching shelves and barrels, and the absorbed figure of the man. He stood, his eyes fixed on the swelling and diminishing flow of the water, his hand on the pump. The bell-like voice calling Good night, a good night to new days and the following years, broke the spell. The two short sounds did not, however, reach his mind as a word with a certain meaning. They were to him the beginning of a familiar sequence of sound. Tap, tap, tap, the hammer was at work again. A puzzled look came into his eyes and he drew his black brows together in the effort to understand who was knocking in—not nails, no, but large-headed brass tacks. He became aware, in some inward manner which yet was convincing, of a polished surface of light wood on which were two curving rows of round brass heads, two complete rows. The shaped board with the rows of cut clasps was oddly familiar. He had seen it before, but where? He struggled to retain the vision, to see more, but it broke into innumerable yellow points, specks of dancing light. He shook his rough head as if the lights were dazzling him and, turning away, began to dry his hands. From time to time he had had glimpses of wood and even of brass nails, but never so clear a vision. He wondered whether, now that the rows were complete to the last round head, the knocking would cease, this knocking which had haunted him for so long.

In order to husband the lamp-oil Sabina, before going to bed, had lowered the wick, but Byron had a dislike of shadows and obscurity. Before he turned up the light, however, a furtive glance assured him the brown jug was gone from the stove.

Its disappearance, though expected, gave him a shock. While he, in the linhay, had been oddly forgetful of the event he had prepared, the moment had come and passed, that moment so heavily charged with possibilities, the moment of the last chance. It was as if, having laid the train, another had touched off the fuse. The matter had been taken out of his hands and, though startled, he was conscious of relief. The thing was done.

Old Squire's chair, which stood during the day to the right of the hearth, had been pushed against the wall. Sabina, tidying the room, had supposed that her husband would soon go to bed; he, however, was no more conscious of a desire for rest than if it had been morning. Replenishing the fire he sat down, but though the maker of the chair had shaped it cunningly, Byron neither leaned back in it nor relaxed his limbs.

The catch of the door opening into the house was weak and, suddenly, the long passage that began at the kitchen and ended at the justice-room, was filled with whispering sounds. A breeze, wandering in, had lost itself in the darkness. It pulled at the handle until Leadville, sitting forward, his head sunk between his shoulders in the attitude of a bird of prey, his mind concentrated on the approaching and dreadful and longed-for end, looked up. For him the breeze was winged with fear. He fancied that the handle moved. Could Sabina be coming back for something she had forgotten? She had a fancy that she suffered from cold feet, that she must have a flagon of hot water in the bed. To Leadville this fancy had seemed part of her general unreasonableness.

"Yer laigs are gone," he had said irritably.

"As long as they're above ground-'they bain't gone."

"Any'ow you can't 'av cold feet."

"I tell yer, I can't sleep for 'em."

"Well, what's the good of a 'ot jar at the bottom of the bed when you'm to the top?"

"I put the bottle," she had said obstinately, "where I feel my feet's to. That's where I feel cold."

He remembered to have seen on the linhay shelf the old Hollands jar which was used as a hot-water bottle. Was she returning to fetch it? Was it her fingers that were moving the little brass door-knob? His fear grew until it mastered him. He had done with Sabina and she must not come back. He could not stand it. If she swung in on that loathly trolly and began to potter about, heating water, looking for the flagon, he felt that some containing wall would bulge and give and what was held up by it fall into the open.

"I should 'av to tell her," he said, staring at the handle. "Shouldn't be able to keep it in. 'Twould be out of me mouth before I knawed."

On that coast a gale may be blowing great guns one moment and the next drop into silence. The land wind which had piled cove and bay with the welcome oreweed had died down during the day and, out of the north, had come a flock of small white clouds. They trailed on their unknown errand across the sky and behind them, like a sheep-dog, ran a fitful wind. It sang in the ears of the old house and Leadville, made aware of it, turned his eyes contemptuously from the spasmodically moving door-knob. "That's only the wind," he muttered.

The rocky shelf on which Wastralls was built, lying behind Dark Head and lower than the ridges of the valley, lay also below the wind. A thickness on the turning earth it lay in an unnatural hush. On the beaches the tides roared and thundered. Above, but divided from the homestead by wide, clean, moonlighted space, the winds shrieked a warning; but the house, except for that one breath of disturbed and whispering sound, was very still. It kept a vigil. Byron, motionless in Old Squire's chair, knew that he too was waiting.

A board, in which were bolt-holes, which had indeed been part of a ship wrecked long ago, creaked loudly, startling the watcher. With whirring note the old clock had told the hour, once, twice, but he had not marked it. He had been like one turned to stone. In him only one tract of consciousness had burned with life and this glow, fierce and steady, burned in the innermost place, in the darkness and silence that are beyond thought. Recalled to the surface, the man became conscious of numb limbs and an aching back. He stretched himself, a little and very cautiously. He was not anxious to draw attention to himself. With the same caution he put another log on the sinking fire. He had been waiting, for what he hardly knew; but the dream, the old secret dream to which his clumsy hands had given form and substance, was rising through the blackness and the silence, changing into a fact. As he leaned back in the Windsor chair, he was being shown a picture, a picture from which, if he could, he would have turned his eyes. He was looking into the big shadowy justice-room at the end of the passage, the room in which Sabina lay.

He saw the grey walls, the little old windows curtained with white dimity and the four-poster which, for so long, had been the bed of bridal and of birth, the death-bed of a family. In it Old Squire had lain him down to sleep and then to die. In it his childless descendant was drawing her last breaths. Her last breaths! Byron saw them coming slowly, a mist on the cold air, more slowly and then no mist. Sabina was about to die. Die? He said the word softly to himself. His wife, the woman at whose side he had lived for so many years, was about to die. He shook his head over the word as something of which the meaning escaped him, which was portentous, which stirred him in a dim elemental way, but which he could not grasp. Sleep he could understand. Sabina asleep was something he had often seen. A healthy creature, once she had shut her eyes, she did not stir till morning. He was different, found it difficult to lose himself, slept lightly as a cat and dreamed. Day-dreams and night-dreams, he had lived in dreams; but Sabina...

She was asleep now. She was sleeping dreamlessly and from this empty sleep she would not rouse. Daylight would broaden in the east, the farmyard stir with life, and feet would come and go in the house. Do what they might, however, she would not waken. He frowned, knitting his brows over the to-morrow which was about to dawn, the to-morrow in which Sabina had no part. That she who was so vigorously alive should thus have been wiped out, that she should have gone, not for a little time but for ever, was unthinkable and yet...

A nerve vibrated with relief, with a slow thick satisfaction. Gone was she? In their long struggle then, he was the victor? He had come into the open, fought for the woman that he loved, the bit of land that was his 'by rights.' He had always had it in him to fight but not until driven to extremities had he shown his mettle. At long last he had proved that he and not Sabina was the one who counted, that fundamentally he was the stronger.

And yet...

The shallows of his mind were alive with darting thoughts. The long long contest had been declared in his favour, the adversary was not so much beaten as destroyed and yet, on the heels of his rejoicing, crept little yapping doubts.

The vision of the justice-room, of that quiet figure in the quiet chamber, was for him repellently interesting. As long as he could imagine the fine mist of her breath, the rising and falling of her breast, he was only conscious of his approaching triumph. Time, however, brought a change, for now Sabina was more than quiet, she was still. Her blue eyes were frozen, she rested in a peace deeper than that of sleep and, whereas the sleeper is harmless...

Though he did not yet understand, his satisfaction began to dwindle. He drew nearer to the hearth, to the warm living fire. The wind still shrieked a warning overhead but on the house, especially the part beyond the kitchen, a hush had fallen. Byron found the silence oppressive. If a mouse had come out of the wainscot and flitted bright-eyed about the floor, he would have welcomed it, but the place was empty even of minute and furtive life. The thick walls leaned together, brooding over stagnant space, over the dust of dead hopes, the smell and the suspicion of mould, of more than mould. They shut the man in with his dry husk of satisfaction, bade him observe it shrivelling before a new growth, a growth at which he dared not look, it seemed so closely to resemble fear.

Yet—fear?

In the unhappy past he had borne himself stoutly on the assumption that he was the stronger, that he had only to rise and assert himself. That very day he had put this contention to the proof and now Sabina, in her new stillness, was threatening—what was she threatening?

If he were to smoke a pipe he would be more at ease! Pipes were associated in his mind with long dreams of Gray, when he had wandered over the springy turf of the headland, seen her hair in the brown weed of the pools, the curve of her brow in the gull's wing; when he had sat by the fire and his vision had been broken, like water, by the light passing of her feet. Smoking, he might be able to banish the stark figure in the great four-poster and the crowding thoughts connected with it, might be able to replace them with Gray. He rose to fetch the tobacco-jar. It stood among the bottles on the cupboard shelf and to get it he must turn his back upon the door into the passage, upon that door behind which lay a something against which, though he could put no name to it, he must be on his guard. For a moment he hung irresolute on one foot, then sank back in the chair. He could not go. Though such a brave fellow and so strong, he did not dare.

During his intermittent labours he had slaughtered, as part of his work, every sort of farm creature. Sheep, pigs, bullocks, old and diseased animals, the wild-fowl that came over Trevorrick in the winter, the seals that haunted Morwen Cove. He had slaughtered as a duty. The creatures were, to him, food or refuse and he had killed them. He had also killed Sabina.

He tried to think of her as so much dead flesh, an old animal, maimed, useless, and perverse; but though the distorted trunk of Sabina might be dead, the dominant spirit with which he had been for so many years in conflict, that he had not killed. The vision of Sabina's dead body and frozen eyes began to fade. Worse things were about than bodies and glazed sightless eyes.

His wife had shown her affection for him by a cheery liking for his society, by an occasional shy caress. Although she used round terms she had been easy-tempered and if it had not been for Wastralls, that bone of contention, he would have had a good life with her. Sharp with the hinds, direct of speech, he had never seen her roused to wrath. She had told him once "It was not worth while being angry."

"I don't believe as you could, not to say, lose yer temper."

"Oh couldn't I, there's them that know; but it would be fulish to lose it for a trifle."

From the respect with which the labourers treated her, Byron had realized that her cheeriness must cover depths. She had impressed the men with a sense of power that had been limited, comfortably, by the flesh.

He found that he was trembling, that it needed all his strength to prevent his teeth from chattering. The fire had sunk to a heap of glowing ash and the December night was cold. With wary eye upon the door, he piled the grate high with logs, the last logs in the box.

In the past he had often taken sly and secret advantage of Sabina's trust. With a word here, a gesture there, he had tried to undermine her authority, turn local feeling in his favour. He had not dared an open break for that would have meant, or he believed it would, the severance of their relations. At last, however, his furtive tentatives had been laid aside and the accumulated unhappiness of the years had found vent in one soul-satisfying dastard blow.

In her blithe confidence Sabina had shut her eyes to the small disloyalties of the past. If she were aware of them she had, in her large-hearted way, forgiven. Now, in that grey and white room at the end of the passage, the parting of spirit from body must unroll before her the sordid past. She must learn that, after eating and drinking in domestic trust the food she had prepared, he had dropped poison in her cup.

Once more he found that he was trembling. He glanced at the fire but blue and purple flames were licking round the logs; the dank air was shot with an increasing warmth and, in the centre of each little window-pane, was a star of gold light. He had shivered, not because he was cold, not because the wind out of the north was mourning as it fleeted with cloud and moonshine overhead; but because he realized that having slain the body he was afraid of the spirit he had released.

Byron had not lived in the West without absorbing the beliefs of the countryside. He knew who in the hamlet had been 'piskie-led'n,' whose best horse had been inexplicably found dead, which bit of woodland was haunted. He had listened to the little feet that patter behind the wayfarer yet leave no prints on the soft sand and he had watched for the white rabbit that leaps and gambols on the bit of clear road by the graveyard, the rabbit that can be neither shot nor snared. With other of his neighbours, he did not care to pass sombre low-lying Treglyn after dark. The little ghost of an inconvenient child was said to rise out of the garden earth and Byron, at least, never caught sight of the house—a lurking house, set round with tamarisks—without remembering what of crime and horror had happened there, what still happened when the moon was at the full.

Such a man was at the mercy of superstitious fear. The quietude in which at first he had waited had been due to weariness, to a reaction from the intense emotion which had preceded his act. This expectant calm, however, had gradually become shot with doubt. His mind had wakened to a new aspect of the matter. Attempting to wrest Wastralls from a hand of flesh and blood, he found in its place the clasp of spectral fingers.

Byron, looking into the future saw a ghostly presence in the ancient house, saw it gliding on the old errands, pervading the rooms and passages. Would others see it too; would they, perhaps, perceive without seeing? He wondered whether Gray...?

Would that dim ghost avenge itself on him by trying to come between him and Gray, by intruding on their tender *tête-à-tête*, by filling the maid's mind with foul suspicion?

No tie is so close as that of blood and the women were of one family. Would Gray be sensitive to that flitting shadow? Behind the veils of the flesh, would spirit be able to communicate with spirit? Would the truth, whispered in every corner of the house, grow into a following fate? In time, when the maid had come to love him, she would glory in his having stopped at nothing to win her. But a first flicker is easily extinguished.

The hour was late and, in his growing discomfort, his growing fear, Byron thought of his chill room at the top of the house. He went there for sleep and sleep meant the laying by of dread, it meant escape. He glanced at the door which hung, quivering now and again under the uncertain onslaught of the wind, between his lighted shelter and the dark. He was thinking of another door, the one that shut Sabina into the justice-room. If ne tried to make for his burrow, for that safe place he knew of, he must pass it. Could he? His mind answered the challenge with a quick defiance. Could he? Of course he could..

He put his hands on the arms of the chair and sought to rise. He swayed his body forward, big head and broad deep-chested bulk; but under him his limbs failed. They hung leaden, lifeless. Not only had it become impossible for him to pass that farther door which stood sentinel by the foot of the stairs, but even to move. Escape through the gates of sleep? No, not by any gate.

She, to whom the injury had been done, was become his judge. She knew, at last, that she had been married for her inheritance; endured as a man endures the mole on his face and finally, for the sake of another woman, pushed into the grave. Events, stripped of life's concealing leafage, would be bare to her informed considering eye. Sabina had been wronged from the first day of their meeting to the last. Always a swift clear creature, he thought of her as running through the midnight passage, intent on vengeance, merciless.

The latch rattled suddenly, increasing the man's dread. He forgot the fitful wind, the faulty lock. His vivid imagination showed him, instead, a hand upon the door-knob, outlined for him in the night of the passage, a dim and bodiless greyness, told him the frail barrier of wood was all that stood between him and a just but awful vengeance. No wonder that mere flesh and blood shrank cowering, that to the guilty creature it was as if his parts were falling away from him, as if he were sinking into the thin unprotected shell of himself.

A gust of wind tore across the wide peace of the sky; and a loose tile slipped to fall crashing on the roof of the porch. The sharp smash of glass let in the night, let in the wind and the heavy roar of the sea. Byron, drowning in superstitious terror strained his ears to catch, among the many sounds, that which should fulfil his dread anticipation; and as he waited, as he listened, the latch of the door slipped over the catch.

Slowly the green door swayed to an impulse from the farther side. Cold air poured into the room from all the unwarmed chambers beyond the kitchen, from that great room at the end. The narrow strip of black began to widen ominously and, in Byron's guilty breast, it was as if his heart had ceased to beat. Between his lips, his dry tongue made a hoarse feeble sound, neither a cry nor a groan, but the utterance of a man in his extremity. The door swung creaking on its hinges and the flame in the ill-fed lamp leapt up and died. Above the other sounds, above that distant roar and the creaks and murmurs of an old draughty house, rose a heavy stumbling, the crash of a fall. The outer edge of fear, the limit of endurance had been passed and Byron had fallen in a swoon across the hearth.

# CHAPTER XV

Behind the hurrying clouds the moon had risen into a clear space of sky and now hung low, her chill yet faithful breast towards her mate. The light fell on the yard of Wastralls, on the still pond in the corner and the geese sleeping beside it, on the irregular outline of the houses and courts, and on the windows of the farmstead.

At one corner a little casement, that looked towards the morning sun, was swinging open, its white curtain flowing in the stream of air; and on the porch, through the black aperture of a broken pane, the light poured over winter-nipped geraniums. It poured too, through the diamonds of the kitchen window and lay in bright squares on table and floor. The ill-fed lamp, expiring in the sudden draught from the porch, had tainted the air and time had drawn over the face of the fire a veil of ash.

What looked like a heap of rags had been flung across the desecrated hearth. It lay beyond the square of moonlight and below the faint glow of the smouldering logs and, but for its density, might have been a companion shadow to those whispering in the corners of the wide low room.

With a clash of metal upon metal a door swung to, failed to catch and banged again. The huddle of clothes, as if recalled to life by the broken irritating sounds moved a little, and presently dragged itself with evident difficulty into a sitting posture. Byron, falling across the fender, had bruised himself against the steel edge; and he came out of nothingness into dull but growing discomfort. His shoulder, having struck the boss of the oven door, pained him; his head, having hit the stone floor, ached. What had happened? How had he hurt himself? Why was he lying on the kitchen floor? His heavy head swung round till his gaze was caught by the fitful movement of the door. He knitted his dark brows but the memories connected with it escaped him. A current of air was passing through some open window into Wastralls and, in obedience to its impulse, the door was swinging. The man's mind, alive to the practical, went from window to window on the ground-floor, until it found the one of which the fastening was insecure. He settled on it with a feeling of satisfaction and, making a further effort, dragged himself to his feet.

In spite of the low fire and the thin current of wintry air flowing in from the passage, the atmosphere of the kitchen was warm and pleasant. The moonlight made the few pieces of furniture, the high glazed china cupboard, the press, the tables, dimly visible. Byron, his hand to an aching back, was conscious of the homely comfortable nature of his surroundings.

He had forgotten the extremity of terror out of which he had slipped into a merciful unconsciousness, but he was still confused, still sore and, in the familiar aspect of the room, he found a certain solace. This was his home, his place, his for as long as he should live. He had a feeling that something had happened which made the place more indubitably, absolutely, his, than hitherto and, balancing himself first on one foot then on the other, he stared about him, heavily content. The thick walls, the many-paned windows, the plain familiar black of the rafters and white-wash of the walls! His! His till the end of time! He smiled to himself and the smile on that haggard, blood-stained face, was that of a child who after long waiting has been given the plaything it desires.

The arms of the big chair wooed him to comfort, but out of the void Byron had brought the conviction that his work was not yet finished. In a dull bemused way, the way of a man conscious of little but physical weariness, he pondered the effort which was required of him. What was it he had to do, before he could slouch away to bed?

His glance swung from side to side, questioning the friendly faces of the furniture, pausing eventually on the still swinging door. That door, yes. He considered its dark oblong and shining handle. The round brass knob, bright in the general dimness, a tiny moon against the blackness of the door, drew him; yet, deep in himself, was a stiff reluctance. He groped in the confusion of his mind for understanding, until suddenly, like an Icelandic geyser, memory tore its way out.

He remembered! They—a vague they of several personalities—had goaded him to desperation. He saw himself crossing a room, taking a bottle out of the cupboard, pouring the contents into a jug. One moment he had been innocent of this tremendous act, in the next it was accomplished. He stood amazed at this new vision of himself, the doer of deeds. The lack of hesitation, the steadiness, the decision surprised him. He had not known of what he was capable and, for a moment, he was wholly pleased.

Further recollections showed a falling off. He had become gradually conscious of guilt, he had grovelled in superstitious terror. Guilt? He shook his head, like a dog shaking drops of water from its coat. A man may do what he can. His deeds are between him and his soul; and the fear of punishment is a survival from the times when he was subservient to the will of another.

Whatever the quality of a man's deeds, the doing of them proves him. Byron, his back to the dying fire, his dark head rising above the mantelshelf, drew himself up. He had been humiliated and he resented it. Living by faith, he had long cherished the difficult belief that of the two personalities, his and Sabina's, his was the stronger. True, he had wasted his energies in a daydream while she ordered their lives; but he had known that this must come to an end and, behold, when the crucial moment arrived, he had played a man's part. If she were able to see the past in true perspective she must acknowledge the provocation given; must see that he had been driven, that no other course was open to him. A longer endurance on his part would have been weakness and would have justified her in withholding the land. She must, at long last, see how wrongly she had acted.

If, on the contrary, she were to resent his snatching from her that poor fag-end of life, if she were incapable to seeing his point of view, if in unsaintly rancour she decided to haunt her old home, he decided that he would not care. A spirit hand cannot strike, nor a ghostly whisper vex. She might wander through Wastralls, wail in the keyholes and the chimneys, but it should make no difference. She would be but a fancy of the dusk, a shade flitting from room to room, a presence. If Gray became conscious of it, she would only voice a regret which had already lost its poignancy. Sabina could not interfere with their possession of her house and property. She might 'walk' but, as he did not believe she could divulge the secret of her death, 'walk' she might.

Moreover, if she haunted Wastralls, it would only be to see come to pass what she least desired. Another would farm the land, another take her place indoors. For her to haunt them would only bring her additional pain. She, not they, would suffer. Byron laughed hoarsely, for by killing her he had indeed avenged her treatment of him; but, in that contented laughter, was still a note of surprise. He had known that he could act with decision, yet was surprised to find that he had done so. A thin wave of self-gratulation flowed over his weary mind. He had justified himself; yet—had he—altogether?

A man is not looked on as a 'foreigner' by his neighbours without knowing and resenting it. Only by an assumption of superiority can he equalize matters. For many years Byron had been contemptuous of the opinions held by the community. At last his contempt had found concrete expression. He had dared and he knew that no man of that community, no Rosevear, Brenton or Old would dare as much. Yes, he had shown a courage such as they, if they knew of it, must secretly envy and yet... He had not been altogether brave. Though he had taken life he had been abjectly afraid. Unable to recapture the ecstasy of that anguish he looked back in shame and doubt. Unseemly terror had given shape to a black nothing and that nothing had been stronger than he. Before he could be at peace with himself he must rise above this humiliation, prove it to have been momentary, a lapse.

Stiffening himself, he gazed at the door which had now swung wide, uncovering the black mouth of the passage. What a fool he had been to think that Sabina had come in search of him. And even if she had? Afraid of a dead woman? He set his teeth yet felt his heart leaping and the blood singing in his ears. Afraid? He would show—himself—that nothing, neither apparition nor invisible presence, could daunt him. Let Sabina have her will, she was only Sabina. He grasped eagerly at the new thought. Only Sabina! Not some unknown unimaginable terror, but the tame convenient Sabina with whom he had lived in domestic intimacy for so long. How could he have fancied that by dying she had become invested with horrific power? He cursed his folly; and the words that came to his tongue were big-sounding foreign words that he had already uttered once that night, words which had come to him out of the days when he had sailed with strange men in strange waters. The curses were echoed back to him out of the passage and, for a moment, the sound once more stirred his blood with the cold finger of fear. This time he only swore more loudly, and the old words, evoking the atmosphere of daredevilry with which he had been once familiar, gave him courage. Memories that lay at the back of his mind, memories of lands where human life is of less importance than that of a sheep, of dangers and adventures, recurred to him. His voice was no longer a hoarse threat. It filled the kitchen with a round full sound, dominating the seen and the unseen, stiffening him until he knew there was nothing he would not dare. He would even walk down the passage between the kitchen and the justice-room and open that green door at the end.

Those roistering nights in South American cities had been a reaction from the pent life on shipboard, had been spiced with hot dangers, mad loves and sudden death; but this last adventure was one on which no man would willingly embark. Byron, with his heart cold and middle age in his limbs, would go as a man goes on direful errand. He would go because he must prove his courage, his right to take Sabina's place, to own Wastralls, to play the lover. This was his hour and, if he avoided the issue, he must admit that those—he said 'those' but he meant one only—who had held him of no account were right. Byron's outer life had for many years been eventless; but his dreams had been a shifting drama full of colour, a play enacted for one spectator, himself. Now that dissatisfied one was insisting on reality instead of dreams and, in his state of dull-reaction from the terrors of the supernatural, he was willing. He saw, however, that what was to do, should be done at once. The courage of flesh and blood is a poor thing at best and, if he stayed upon his going, likely to run out at the finger-tips.

His hands, as he took a candle from the linhay shelf and lighted it, were cold. Drawing water, he braced himself by drinking great gulps of the icy fluid; and, thus invigorated, returned to the kitchen with his head up. Nor, indeed, until he reached the door did he hesitate and then it seemed to him that the room was a snug place and quite peculiarly safe. In leaving it he was courting danger, leaving himself without a wall to set his back against!

The candle flame leaping in a cross-current of air, revealed the door at the end of the passage, and Byron saw with relief that it was shut. This to his mind proved the hollowness of his late fears. A spirit should be able to pass through the wood of a shut door, to slip through crack or keyhole; but the contrary is maintained by those who claim to know. Doors, they say, may be burst open, handles may turn without visible agency; but, once the bolt is shot or the key turned, the haunt must remain on the other side. That closed green door proved to Byron that the disembodied Sabina had not left her room, that his terrors had been without foundation. With his lips twisted in a contemptuous grin he stepped into the passage.

His nailed boots struck the stones with a clash that echoed up the staircase. Wastralls was so resoundingly empty that the brave sound was heard whispering away in the attics, whispering as do the monuments of extinct families in the week-day quiet of a church. Step by step, for the air seemed to him of the consistency of mud, the man pushed his way. To left of him were doors, doors without significance, doors which opened upon innocent and commonplace parlours. He passed these without seeing them and came at last to the heavy door of the old justice-room.

This door had a strong lock and was of stout wood. Nevertheless, it was being shaken from within and, for a moment, Byron's courage failed. Remembering the draught in which his candle had flared, however, the cold air which had poured into the kitchen, he understood. A wind was tearing at the door, a draught from some window which had been blown open. He suspected the little Gothic casement in the eastern wall, the wood of which he knew to be worm-eaten and the fastening worn. It occurred to him, that, if for no other reason, he must have come in to close that window. As he pushed open the door, the waiting wind swooped on the candle flame and left him in darkness. A noise of banging and howling assailed his ears; but the countryman, his superstitious fears held at arm's length for the nonce, recognized it. He had been right. The Gothic window, which a sun-lover had set in the three-foot wall, was open and knocking against the plaster. Byron, forcing himself to walk with deliberate steps, crossed the room and shut it. At once the old stillness fell over the place, the silence that is more alarming than any sound. Byron, his back to the window, listened but the hush was unbroken. Nothing moved, nothing even breathed. He relighted the candle and a host of shadows darted away. The room, which had been a mere cavern of the winds, showed an accustomed face, the shining features of old furniture, the outline of a monumental bed. He looked about, anxious to establish a feeling of friendly relationship. These objects, giving service for house-room, had shared the place with him. They were older than he, so old they seemed to him part of Wastralls. The familiar shapes were pleasing to him. He raised the candle but, as he did so, became vaguely aware of change. The furniture wore a new look. The faint life that dwelt behind its wooden surfaces seemed, suddenly, to have grown less remote. He felt that the pieces were watchful and no longer friendly. He had lived with them in a long peace but, on that night, a pact had been broken. They knew and from being household goods had changed to household gods, the guardians of the home. No longer fitting obscurely into their appointed places, they had an air of purpose. They seemed on the verge of movement. Byron, startled by their covert hostility, yet drew his brows together. "Pack o' nonsense for me to think like that," he muttered, and thereby sealed their doom. When he brought Gray home he would send this old stuff to the dealer and buy new furniture, light woods, mirrors, bamboo. In spite of his stout heart, however, he stepped away rather hastily from the tall-boy. It appeared, in the uncertain light, to be leaning treacherously forward, to be about to fall and, with its weight of mahogany, to crush whatever was within reach.

The covert malignancy of these shining and familiar faces impressed Byron, but a man can conquer the inanimate, he can rend and smash and burn; at least he can if, aware of hostility, he were careful to strike first.

With an effort, he steadied himself. Before him, vast and shadowy, the great bed of 'Old Squire' stood out from the wall and Byron turned towards it with a tread that shook the ancient floor. Sabina had taken a housewifely pride in this bed. Every spring it had been stripped of curtains and valances, of ceiling and headcloths and of padded foot-cover. These when washed had been restretched, backaching job, to retain that stiff spotlessness for a twelvemonth. Sabina had never omitted an iota of this ritual. As the bed had been handed down to her, so it should be kept. The spring cleansing and restretching were part of the mysterious rhythm of life.

Beside the curtain stood that piece of mechanism which had enabled Sabina to move about the house and from which every night she swung herself into bed. On the other side was a small table on which lay a candlestick and the brown cocoa-jug.

As he approached the bed, the man forgot the dim hostility by which he was surrounded, in a practical doubt. How if the poison had proved insufficient and she should open her eyes, those ice-blue eyes and ask what had brought him thither? For a moment he stood humbly at the foot of her bed. He dared not look.

The candle-light fell on a quiet face, on closed eyes, on shut lips. She had said—"Good night."

Sabina lay on her back, a squat figure, occupying in that great bed but a little space. The bright silk quilt had been folded neatly back over the mahogany foot and her covering was as white as the hangings. It swept in a generous curve over her breast, this breast which no longer rose and fell.

The man ventured, at last, to look and his heart leapt with relief, with more than relief, with a primitive and savage joy. In the long struggle between them he had won.

The rose had faded from Sabina's cheek, but her lips were curving as if over a pleasant thought. She had taken with her into the dark the hope that she and her husband might soon be reconciled, that years of concord lay before them and this sweet expectation had given her a look of unfathomable peace. The serenity of her dead face was that of the blue night, the night that is beyond the clouds of earth. She was no longer the successful farmer, the stoutest heart in Tregols, but something infinitely remote. In dying she had proved that if life is transitory and insignificant, death hides behind closed lips, an intriguing mystery. Byron, vaunting the folly of a mad moment, of a dark dream interpretated in terms of earth, became slowly conscious of it. Drop by drop, the passion of his exultation fell. This was not the workaday woman he had known, the woman whose obstinacy and unreasonableness had so angered him, but a creature spiritually changed. He could not feel that she would bear any resentment against the instrument of what was, undoubtedly, a release. Life had chained and prevented her, now she was free and he no longer counted with her in any way. She was afar off. Human interests had dwindled to the humming of a hive and he, whom she had cherished, was become one among many. The conviction of this was not only humbling, it brought a sense of loss. The place where he had been wont to sit at ease had been shut against him and the door locked and bolted. He was outside and unimportant and forgotten.

The last dregs of his excitement ran out leaving him with a sense of emptiness. Sabina was dead and death had raised a barrier between them which should have given him a sense of security. But from such a one as the woman, folded in ineffable peace, who lay before him, was no need of escape. This Sabina was a development of the other, the generous large-souled creature for whom the mean and the sordid had no existence. Byron had come to face Sabina and prove himself the stronger, but he stood before her like a child that had lost its way. For some minutes he waited in desolate silence, his heart sinking, his sense of inexorable loss growing more poignant. Sabina was dead, she had set out upon a journey from which she was never to return and he was left. The great chest heaved suddenly and a sob burst from him. Stumbling, and with the hardly wept tears of manhood rolling over his cheeks, he turned away. The door slammed behind him as he made for the shallow stairs that led to his room. Once in his refuge he flung himself on the bed, muffling his tempestuous weeping in the pillow — as he had done, when, as a boy, he had fled the fatherly corrections of the elder Leadville.

On the morrow he would awaken to the old life of narrow interests and lusts and scheming; but that night he mourned with exceeding grief, mourned that golden bowl which had been his and which he had cast down and broken. The bed shook under his sobs and the little hours before the dawn scurried up, dragging after them a new and reluctant day. Byron was a weary man, overwrought both in body and mind; and by degrees the noisy gulps, the long shudders, the groans grew less frequent. He sank into broken sleep, started from it with a catch of the breath and a sudden desolate cry, but fell back again. His slumbers deepened until he lay quiescent, his heavy frame thrown across the bed, his arms outstretched. At intervals a quiver passed over his body, but he had drifted out upon quiet seas and was — poor miserable wight — at rest.

# CHAPTER XVI

In the bright moonlight Mrs. Tom stood at her garden gate to watch Mrs. Constantine Rosevear—or Mrs. Conny, as she was called—walk up the road. A big strong woman was Bessie Rosevear but full of nervous fears; and she had professed herself unable to go back to the mill unless some one 'put 'er 'ome.' The revelry of the evening, though sober and moderate, had carried the party into the small hours. Tom had gone off to bed and it fell, therefore, to one of the five maidens to accompany her aunt.

"Aw poor sawl, I'm pretty and sorry for 'er bein' so nervous," thought Mrs. Tom, making kindly allowance. "One of 'er boys should 'av come down to put 'er 'ome. They are always rangin' about in the evenings after the maidens, but any'ow Richbell was glad of a mouthful of fresh air."

The breath of the night, though tempered by the sea, was cool and she had thrown round her an old blue cloak lined with home-cured skins. They crackled slightly as she leaned against the low stone wall, thinking the warm and wandering thoughts of motherhood.

The voices of aunt and niece were blown back to her on that cool breath. Bessie was a slatternly creature and her house the untidiest in the parish, but she had bred tall sons, sons who, as long as she fed them well, seemed indifferent to the discomfort of their home. Mrs. Tom, listening contentedly to Richbell's voice with its clear laugh, found her thoughts straying from the handsome creature whose fortune was to seek to that one of the brood whose choice was made. As the mother of 'a long tail,' she was well pleased her eldest should be marrying so early and so well. Jim's 'auntie' would leave him what she had, 'while, whatever happened to Wastralls, S'bina would see they didn't want for nothing while she was livin'. The young couple would have every chance of gettin' on in the world; and the mother who had been a fish-seller's daughter, living from hand to mouth, took stock of their future with a grateful heart. She had done well for herself and Gray, 'with a good-livin' 'ard-workin' feller like Jim, might do even better.' She hoped the other maidens would follow their sister's example; but with the hope, a doubt, a doubt of Richbell, threaded itself darkly through the loose gold of her meditations. Richbell, the pretty madcap, was just the one to leap before she looked and, of the lads who wanted her, to take the least promising. Mrs. Tom shook her own still pretty head. The world would be a happier, more comfortable place, if parents had the arranging of their children's future, at least in matrimony.

From where she stood, a stretch of bright water was visible. The sea was calling in a hoarse undertone, a sort of thunderous roar which yet did not deaden other sounds and, looking down, Mrs. Tom's glance rested on the courts and outhouses of Wastralls. If Sabina had her way, Gray and her young husband would live there. Again the wise woman shook her head. 'Leadville might prove a snake in the grass. S'bina was a good sort but she wasn't sensible. If she 'ad been she would 'av left the farmin' to 'er man.' Mrs. Tom was sorry for Leadville 'mumpin' round like an ole dog and 'e wi' the finest farm in the valley and just longin' to put 'is strength into the workin' of it. A woman's place was in the house, making the butter and feeding the fowls and no good ever came of she takin' on a man's work. 'Twas bad for both of 'em and worse'n ever now she'd lost her laigs, poor sawl. It must make the man feel mad, 'er 'oldin' to the reins when 'e ought to 'av 'em!' Mrs. Tom, her time fully occupied with housewifely and maternal duties, could see the mistakes her neighbours were making and the proper remedy; but, as she could not hope to alter circumstances which had made those mistakes inevitable, she preserved the indulgent kindliness of her attitude.

The wind, sweeping round by the gate, made her fold herself more closely in the blue cloak. She thought of Gray in her new happiness and shivered a little as if conscious of a creeping chill. Her work was pretty near done. One by one each little bird would spread its young wings and fly away until, in the end, only the empty nest would remain to her. She would have been glad if Tom, sleeping deeply, had been at hand with his comfortable "Well, mother, tired be 'ee? Take and come on in and talk to me a bit."

The moonlight revealed the empty stretch of road, the sharp shadows of the hedges and, at the top, the rounded tower of the mill. A patch of moving blackness could presently be descried. Through the windy stir came the light patter of running feet and, in a minute, Richbell, breathless and gay, almost fell into her mother's arms.

"Now, Wild-e-go, where you gwine in such a hurry?" protested Mrs. Tom.

"Oh, mammy, I dunno. I'm so delighted I dunno what to do wi' meself."

"Av 'ee enjoyed yourself this evening then?"

"Ah, I should think I had!" With two lads glowering at each other across the harmonium, Richbell had been entirely happy.

"You'm a proper flirt."

"I can't help it. I don't ask the boys to come."

The mother passed a rough hand over the girl's curly mop. She was proud of Richbell's ''ead of 'air,' bronze hair with warm lights. "Did I hear you sayin' you was goin' to Percy 'Olman's place to tea?"

"Well, I'd nothing to do to keep me home."

"I'd sooner it was Will Brenton."

"Well, mammy, if I don't like him, what's the good for you to talk?"

Mrs. Rosevear sighed, for Will was heir to a good farm while Percy was a sailor, dependent for his prospects on an uncle who had other nephews. "My dear, you can't live with the man alone, you must 'av something to live on."

"I don't care. If I don't have grand things I must have others."

"As you make your bed, my dear, so you must lie. I 'ad to fight my way in the world and so must you, that's all; but—Will Brenton's a steady decent chap."

"Well, so he is, but I don't want to get married yet. Half the young girls that's married now, don't see no young life but I mean to."

Mrs. Tom was not to be turned from the point she was making. "An' Percy's always after the maidens."

Richbell laughed. She knew her power over the lads.

Mrs. Tom understood the laugh. "'E bain't always 'ome," she said, answering its young complacency. "Percy's a sailor and they say sailors 'av a wife in every port."

But Richbell's self-confidence was not to be shaken. "Oh, it's only a bit of chaff. Why, mammy, I like a bit of chaff myself."

"Yes, but you'll find, my dear, that what's good for the goose bain't always good for the gander. Maidens see a thing one way and wives another."

But the girl was not one to take advice. "I shall only be young once," she said, "and I shall travel me own road. You talk about me, didn't you have chaps after you? You haven't got the first man you went with, have you?"

She had carried the war into the enemy's country. From sage maturity Mrs. Tom fell back a score of years, fell back to the days when she too must make her choice.

"Did you now, mammy?" insisted the girl.

"My dear," Mrs. Tom was groping for her mislaid dignity, "your father was my first sweetheart!"

"Well, then," youth had caught a word here and a glance there, enough lime for her mortar, "well, then, he wasn't always your sweetheart."

"I was to Plymouth in service and he was 'ere. We didn't care for letter-writin'."

"Who was that chap in Plymouth, then?"

Mrs. Tom gave way. "Oh, a sailor, like they all are. 'E've done very well for 'isself. 'E's a captain now."

"Mammy!" Out of two hints Richbell had evolved a fact. "'Twasn't that man that left the impudent message for daddy last summer, was it?"

"Take and 'old yer tongue, do!" But recollection had lighted Mrs. Tom's eyes with laughter.

"Well, was it?"

"Iss. 'E said, 'Is ole Tom livin' yet? I'm waitin' for 'e to die. I want 'is shoes.'"

"He isn't married yet?"

"'E say 'e's waitin' for me."

"Why didn't you have him?"

"Because I liked your father best." Remembering the lesson she had been trying to inculcate, she added more soberly, "'E 'ad the promise of a good farm."

"That had nothing to do with it," said youth shrewdly. "You liked him."

"Well, I did." And she continued happily, "I 'eard 'e was goin' wi' Nina Old and I came 'ome to see."

"And was he?"

"I run right against them up to Four Turnin's and I gived 'im a look."

"I know," laughed Richbell delightedly. "I know how you looked."

"'An 'e lifted 'is 'at to me." She paused meditatively. "'Good evening,' he says and come straight over to me."

"Left her?"

"There and then."

"Iss, mammy?"

"We was married in a month from that day; but come, my dear, 'tis blowin' up for a storm and we better go in now. You got to go down to Wastralls early to-morrow mornin'."

They glanced along the road and, from Hember standing boldly out from the hillside, it was as if Wastralls lay in a hollow.

"Why," said Richbell, with suddenly awakened interest, "look, mammy, some one's still up down there. There's a light in the kitchen window."

"'Tis late, too."

The girl shivered and drew nearer to her mother. "I expect it's Uncle Leadville cleaning that old gun of his. I can't abide to see him rubbing away at it. That's all he do, all day long."

"Poor old sawl, that's all 'e 'av got to do."

"Mammy," her voice had lost its gaiety and self-confidence. She was a young creature, obscurely frightened. "I wish I wasn't going down there."

Mrs. Tom spoke sharply. "Why? 'Av Gray been talkin' to yer?"

"No, Gray's close as anything, but what is it?"

"Oh, my dear, 'tis nothing but 'er fancy. There, go along, I bain't going to tell 'ee."

"I don't need for Gray to tell me Wastralls is a whisht old house for young maidens."

"My dear," said Mrs. Tom reasonably, "you'll be able to run 'ome any time to see us and yer auntie is goin' to give yer twenty pound; good money, 'edn't it?"

"Iss, well, I know that's all right," returned Richbell soberly. Sabina's open-handedness had put many a pleasure in her way, nevertheless instinct warned her against the place and she was Mrs. Tom's own child.

"Well, why don't you like goin' there?"

"I don't feel I like," she hesitated, lowering her voice, "I don't feel I like Uncle Leadville."

"There's no 'arm in 'im," encouraged the mother, "although 'e do look downy. Any'ow 'e's nothing to do with you. You'll be with yer auntie."

"Iss." The girl could not put into words her feeling that Leadville being fundamentally different from the easy-going folk among whom she had hitherto lived was vaguely alarming. "Well, he never look yer straight in the face."

"My dear, that's the way of'n. 'E 'edn't goin' to take no notice of you."

"Mammy!" She put her young arms round her mother's neck, so proving herself the taller by a couple of inches, "I wish you would go down with me to-morrow morning—I don't feel I like goin' by myself."

Who could resist Richbell, when Richbell changed from gay defiance to entreaty? Not Mrs. Tom! "Well, I'll go down with you. I shall be able to see your auntie the same time. I'll light up the fire before I go and the kettle'll be boiling by the time I get back. Come, my dear," she turned and walked up the trim path of sea-gravel edged with quartz, "let's be goin' in, else we shan't get up early in the mornin'."

December dawns are late and though, as Mrs. Tom had feared, the tired family slept until after cockcrow, morning had not broken when she and Richbell hurried down between the tamarisks, silver-grey with frost, and in at the yard gate of Wastralls. George Biddick, crossing from the shed to the stables nodded a greeting, but otherwise the yard was deserted.

Mrs. Tom called after him. "Pretty rough wind last night."

"Iss," he said with a gesture towards the roof. "I see it's blawed off one of the tiles and broke a pane of glass."

"You won't be able to get it mended now till after Christmas," said Mrs. Tom sympathetically. She pressed her face against the window, peering in. "No one up yet?"

"Well, they didn't go to bed till late last night," Richbell reminded her.

"Dessay they've overslept theirself!" Mrs. Tom took the door key from under a stone where Sabina had hidden it in readiness. During the night, with one of the rapid changes to which that coast is liable, the wind had dropped. Frost had stilled the thousand voices of the earth and, in the house, doors hung without creak or movement and the chimneys were hushed. As she crossed the threshold Mrs. Tom shivered.

"'Tis a whisht old place," she said, "and cold."

Her voice came back to her, echoed from the passage. "Cold!"

"There always seems some one in the passage," she said whimsically, "some one who wants to talk and can only say what we do say."

Richbell tried the echo. "Mammy!" she said and "Mammy" was whispered back to her.

Mrs. Tom hung her cloak behind the door and turned upon the world a business face. "Here's the matches," she said, taking them from the mantelshelf, "and you'll find a candle in the linhay there. Now light up

"Leadville! Leadville!" cried the voice and he found its unhappiness irritating. "Are 'ee dead up there, too?"

"Dead? No. Can't 'ee wait a minute, man must dress."

He had slept on the outside of the bed and, though the yielding feathers marked where he had lain, the clothes were undisturbed. He knew, though without as yet understanding why, that he must be careful. Everything must be as usual. Hastily pulling the clothes from the bed he threw the room into disorder.

He had taken off his boots and his feet in their grey woollen wear fell noiselessly on the drugget. Upon the group at the foot of the stairs he came unexpectedly and, so coming, waited for a moment in fear and trembling. Mrs. Tom, lifting her voice to send yet another summons echoing aloft, presently caught sight of him. In the justice-room a dim light showed. She did not speak but pointed over her shoulder.

"Well," he quavered, aware of the dim light, "whatever's all this fuss about?"

"I dunno' ow to tell yer," returned Mrs. Tom. "'Tis awful thing. Poor S'bina's gone."

"Gone?" His voice rang out full of incredulity and, pushing past, he walked quickly into the bedroom. "What d'yer mean?"

The man's concern, if not his surprise, was genuine. Sabina's death assured, he could think of her as a tried and loyal comrade, dwell on her many virtues, mourn her as, whatever her shortcomings, she had deserved. Memories, kind and gay and casual, crowded into his mind. Though he might be glad that she was gone, he would miss her. Mrs. Tom, jealous for her friend and, with the accumulated knowledge of years to breed suspicion, weighed his words and considered his manner. Bitterly would she resent any failure on his part to render unto Sabina the conventional marks of grief. But Leadville did more. He showed real feeling, a sorrow that was unmistakably sincere.

She followed him into the dead woman's presence and together they went up to the bed. As the man, stooping towards Sabina, gathered the meaning of her immobility, of her sculptured calm, his voice rang out in a cry of grief and longing, a cry which lightened Mrs. Tom's heart of its suspicion.

"S'bina! Oh, my dear, speak to me. Whatever shall I do, whatever shall I do without yer?" He turned with an appeal to the other's womanly knowledge. "Be yer sure she's gone? Titch 'er 'ands and see whether they'm cold or not."

Mrs. Tom laid her hand on fingers already growing rigid. "Iss, my dear, she's gone right enough, I'm afraid."

He covered his face, breaking suddenly into gulping and ugly grief. The last doubt that had harboured in Mrs. Tom's mind blew out to sea. After all, Leadville 'wasn't a bad feller, 'e 'ad 'is feelin's!'

"Terrible job to be took away like this," he gasped after a few minutes, "and she all by 'erself too."

"Aw, poor sawl, iss," agreed Mrs. Tom, "but she's lookin' 'appy and peaceful. I believe she must 'ave died in 'er sleep and didn't know nothin' about it."

Leadville looked at her anxiously and his heart was in the question: "You don't think she suffered any pain, do you?"

"Why, look at 'er. You can see she didn't. If she 'ad suffered 'er face 'ud 'av been quite drawn. But there she is, lookin' so peaceful as a lamb." Her tears flowed again. "We shall all miss her. She was a good sawl."

"I dunno whatever I shall do without 'er."

"My dear life, 'tis nothing but right you should feel it so."

"Well, nobody knew what a good wife she's been to me. I 'adn't 'ad a penny to bless myself when she married me, but since then I 'aven't wanted for nothing. Never an angry word between us."

"Poor sawl, too."

"'Twas 'ard on the missis losin' 'er laigs but after that she never complained. She made the best of everything."

From the world beyond the justice-room, the world of living people and the everyday, came sounds of movement. Richbell, left in the passage, had returned to the kitchen and, once there, had mechanically resumed her work. Come life, come death, breakfast must be prepared.

"Come out now," said Mrs. Tom, the odour of 'fry' being wafted to her nostrils, "and 'av a bit of breakfast, Leadville. I'm sure you'll be wantin' it."

The man shook his head. "I don't feel I want any. I'd rather go out on the cliff by myself. Tidn't like she's dead to me and I must get used to it." He followed Mrs. Tom out of the room but his eyes were so dim he stumbled as he went.

"Well, she's dead right enough. 'Ow it 'appened I dunno. She seemed quite all right yesterday. She might 'av been a bit tired but what was that? I'm afraid," she looked at him thoughtfully, "I'm afraid, as she died suddint, we shall 'av to 'av an inquest."

Byron was on his way to the porch but at the word 'inquest' he stopped and, though Mrs. Tom dismissed the thought indignantly, her heart had said to her, "'E don't want no inquest."

"What do we want an inquest for, after doctor been tendin' 'er so long?"

"Did doctor say that she might die off quick like this?"

"'E was 'ere yesterday and seen 'er." Leadville was trying to remember. "I can't call to mind 'zactly what 'e said but 'e didn't give me a word of encouragement."

"'E knaw better than we do," said Mrs. Tom, musingly. "Did S'bina seem poorly after I went 'ome last night?"

Leadville constrained himself to answer as if the elucidation of the mystery were of as much moment to him as to her. "I don't think I took much notice of 'er but she wadn't very special. After you went she got the supper and, as soon as she'd eat it, went off to bed."

Mrs. Tom nodded with, however, an irrepressible doubt. "Wonder what made 'er go so early?"

"I dunno I'm sure." He spoke without considering whether what he asserted was in accordance with the facts. Mrs. Tom's questions were irritating him, they were like the buzz of flies on a hot day. "I didn't stay up very late. In fact we was both to bed by ten."

Mrs. Tom was careful not to look at him. She and Richbell, standing at their gate in the small hours, had seen a light in Wastralls. If the Byrons were abed who then was up? Perhaps Sabina, feeling unwell, had gone in search of a remedy. That was possible, of course, indeed quite likely. Not until later did Mrs. Tom remember that the light had been stationary. If Sabina had been seeking medicine or a hot-water bottle she would have been carrying a candle.

"Well, there's a lot of things to be done," she said, non-committally. "Can you tend to 'em?"

He shook his heavy shoulders, as if he would have shaken off something unwelcome. He would like to have told her he had not slept much the previous night but that was out of the question. "Oh well, you must leave me go out and think it over first," he said, making for the door, "I'll tell yer when I come back."

Death in a household, particularly sudden death, brings a rush of work. Mrs. Tom, realizing that the brunt of this must fall on her, as the wife of Sabina's nearest relative, was thankful to see that Richbell had made the tea and fried some bacon. She drew her chair to the table and sat down, sat down with the quick lamentable thought that here Sabina would never sit again. The thought flashed up into poignancy and passed. She must not think of it now, for there was work to be done.

"Now, my dear," she said, when they had eaten and the little breathing-space, between the knowledge of calamity and the girding up of loins, was at an end, "Now, my dear, you must go 'ome. 'Tis no place for you 'ere."

"Iss, mammy." The lively self-assertive girl was become pliant to her mother's hand.

Mrs. Tom made her dispositions. "'Tis a pity that Gray went to Gentle Jane, but Leonora must run over and bring 'er back—better be all together now. After you've gived the children their breakfast, Rhoda better run up to Cottages and ask Mrs. Bate to come down and set your auntie forth; and tell Aunt Louisa Blewett to come down and bring 'er machine with 'er to do the mournin's. Let Loveday go to St. Cadic and tell your Aunt Bessie to come down to 'elp us; and now I'll go and get the room straight."

"Is there anything else you'd like for me to do?" Richbell spoke in tones so subdued they hardly rose above a whisper.

"You can take my black things out of the box and ask your father to bring 'em down and if there's anything else I want, when 'e comes back 'e'll tell yer."

"Aren't you coming home?" Hember without mother would be unspeakably dreary.

The girl's tone, resigned yet unhappy, touched Mrs. Tom's heart. For a moment practical matters were put aside. "Now you mustn't go worryin' yerself," she said, her glance warm and motherly. "Yer auntie's 'ad a 'ard struggle, so it's a 'appy release she's gone. She's taken out of a world of trouble."

"Well, mammy, I can't help grievin'," protested the girl, her tears rising. "It seems so sudden."

"'Twas one good thing she died off in her sleep and didn't know nothing about it. It's our loss but her gain."

"But mammy, I think 'tis awful to be dead. Makes me creep."

"Dead? You mustn't think she's dead. I feel she's livin'. She's up there tellin' them everything about we down 'ere. She's 'appy and busy. No more tears. She've 'ad 'er share."

The girl was only anxious to be comforted. "Well, if that's what's she's doing, we didn't ought to grieve, we ought to be glad she's gone." Her little face lost its pinched expression and she moved more briskly. Nevertheless when, the breakfast dishes being cleared away, she was free to go, she went as if glad to leave this house to which she had come so unwillingly and which had at once proved itself the 'whisht' place of her imagination.

As she went up the road she looked back once or twice and each time she quickened her steps. The promise of dawn was brightening the east and in the bay some big sooty-plumaged birds could be dimly discerned, their web-feet set firmly on the very edge of the tide. A light was twinkling in the many panes of Wastralls kitchen, tiny glimmers that, affecting only the one spot, made the sombre outlines more darkly impressive. A part of the haunted night, what had happened there so lately gave it to the young girl's imagination an extra touch of gloom. With a quick shudder she set her face towards the lights of home.

# CHAPTER XVII

Leadville left the house with a hasty but heavy step. He had slept but little and his fall the previous evening had jarred and bruised him. Carrying his head even more forward than was his wont, he went along the shaly path which led, a little circuitously, up Dark Head. At another time he would have made the ascent without realizing he was not on level ground but, that morning, he stubbed his feet against the grey rock and stumbled over the cushions of sea-thrift. He was so tired, so stiff, that he, who had the sure-footedness of the mountain sheep, slipped on the smoother surfaces and came near to falling. When, at a turn in the path, a lew corner presented itself, an angle of rock about a few hardy plants, he uttered a grunt of satisfaction. Why should he go farther? Here was a refuge from the questioning of the women, a spot where he could rest. The cliff wall rose between him and the north and, when the southerly sun rose, its first beams would fall on that high but sheltered rock. He flung himself down and, as he lay on the tussocks of colourless grass, seemed in his weather-worn clothes as much a bit of natural waste as the oreweed drying on the rocks below.

The day was mild, one of those we owe to what we are told is not the Gulf Stream but something which has a similar effect. In the growing light the sea shone dimly, a pale expanse of quiet water. On the man's harassed mind the peace of the scene had, as ever, a soothing effect. His glance roved over the treeless country, the rare farmsteads with each a group of grey outbuildings, the Cornish moors and the far range of rounded hills. What he saw was dear to him as it was familiar. Those well-known slopes, swelling softly till they reached Rowtor and Brown Willy, sinking to the abrupt black rocks that edged the sea! Byron seemed to himself a part of that on which he looked. Wastralls had made ham. He was, as he had said in his youth, a clod of Wastralls earth, dust which at the appointed time would fertilize the land to a fresh harvest. To be of it and, at the last, to go back to it, was what he had asked of life. He had been obsessed by one large and simple idea and, in his extreme weariness, he returned to it, looking across the land he loved, lifting his eyes to the good sun. He was outwearied and he longed for warmth and comfort. The shelter of his corner promised forgetfulness. The land lay green about him, the sea sang its thunderous lullaby and sleep was in the soft touch of the air, the thin warmth of the December sun. Pillowing his shaggy head upon his arm, the man drifted from the manifold irritations, the aches and pains of life, into that state which doth so mysteriously resemble death.

For at least two hours, Leadville, warmed through by sunbeams and the sea-scented air, lay deeply asleep. When he stirred the red was in his cheek and his eyes were clear. He looked about him and remembered. He had killed Sabina and now must bear himself so that none should know or even suspect. It would, he thought, be easy enough. She had been a good wife to him and, as she was actually dead, he might show, without tempting Providence, a natural grief. His walk as he went down the hill was brisk and purposeful. To the dead their hour, a sob and a black coat; when they were underground it would be the turn of the living. From the future opening before him, Leadville turned his eyes. Sabina should have her due!

Before Rhoda, full of the importance of her message, reached Cottages, its inhabitants were agog. A little bird had carried the news of Mrs. Byron's death and those whom it least concerned were discussing it. Mrs. Bate, who lived in the end cottage of the hamlet, a tiny two-roomed place, had for many years been Stripper, or, as some call the woman who prepares the dead for their last journey, 'Nurse' to the community. As soon as a death occurred, she was sent for and her duty it was not only to strip the clothes from the corpse and array it in fine linen, but to receive the many visitors and conduct them, in turn, to the death-chamber. On the day of the funeral her position was one of some importance. She was the undertaker's right hand. Indeed, the responsibility for the smooth working of the arrangements rested on her rather than on him.

When the news reached Mrs. Bate, therefore, that Mrs. Byron of Wastralls had died during the night, she knew that she would be wanted. Though the possessor of a handsome jolly face she was given to timid fears and, after raking out her fire, she went across to Mrs. Blewett, the seamstress, better known as 'Aunt Louisa,' to have one of these resolved.

"Mrs. Rosevear sure to be there," she said anxiously, "and she could set Mrs. Byron forth if her liked; but she wouldn't do anybody out of a job, would she?"

'Aunt Louisa,' slim and, in spite of the wear and tear of life still graceful, was fitting the cover to her machine. "She bin poor 'erself," she said encouragingly. The two old bodies had lived in the same parish for seventy years, and as next-door neighbours, for thirty. She knew that Fanny Bate, in spite of her large well-covered frame and square face, found it difficult to stand alone.

"I wouldn't miss doing this," said Mrs. Bate, her old blue eyes still anxious, "for all the golden sovereigns in Trevorrick. When Judgment Day come, there won't be many from 'ere but what will look up and thank me for settin' 'em forth."

"If you set 'em forth," said Aunt Louisa, remembering the many shrouds her fingers had fashioned, "I've made the things for 'm."

"Iss, but I've nursed and tended them as well as set them forth," she would not admit the other's claim to a share in the work of preparing the neighbourhood for burial. "And I think of their souls, too, poor things. 'Tis better to look after their souls than their bodies. 'Tis an awful thing to die not being prepared to meet God. I sing hymns till they'm happy and not afraid to die. I 'ope 'tis all right with poor Mrs. Byron's soul," she paused, a little troubled by Sabina's eminent unpreparedness, "but she was always a good-livin' woman and God is merciful to the last."

Aunt Louisa turned her quiet grey eyes on the other woman and in them was a suggestion from, which Mrs. Bate shrank in pretended ignorance. "Must 'av died pretty and suddent!" said the seamstress.

"Well, I think she has been ailing for some time, she 'aven't been vitty since her accident!" Louisa was so 'forth-y,' but it didn't pay to say all you thought. She, herself, daring enough before the event, knew that 'a still tongue make a wise 'ead.'

"Mrs. Bate!" cried a voice from the road, where old Hawken, rather staggery about the feet, was making shift to carry an armful of fodder to his donkey. "Rhoda's comin' up the lane. I believe she want you."

"Thank you, Mr. 'Awken," said the old woman modestly, "but there's more'n me'll be wanted at Wastralls."

"You're the Stripper, bain't you? and you'll be wanted first. Iss, first and last."

The child, a sensible as well as pretty little girl of ten, came quickly from the direction of the sea. She was shocked to think that kind Auntie S'bina was dead. She was also impressed with the importance of her errand. Seeing Mrs. Bate at Aunt Louisa's door, she ran to her across the little green. "Mammy says, please will you come down to Wastralls at once and will Aunt Louisa come too and bring her machine."

"I'll be prettily glad to do anything for Mrs. Byron and your mammy," responded the latter, a little anxiously, "but I can't carr' the machine, my dear."

Old Hawken who had lingered, curious to hear what passed, seized the opportunity. "If you will wait a minute," he volunteered, "I'll put the ole dunkey in and drave 'ee down."

"Well, 'tis braäve and kind of 'ee, Mr. 'Awken."

"Time like this, everybody must do all they can to 'elp," and, as Mrs. Bate saw her neighbour drive off in the donkey-cart, she regretted that laying out the dead did not necessitate the transport of large and heavy parcels; but it was like Louisa, so it was, she got the best of everything and always had since she was born wrong side of the blanket and everybody allowed it was the right!

Meanwhile Mrs. Tom, her heart heavier than it had been for many a year, had set Sabina's room in order and removed the evidences of humble use. She took up the cocoa-jug, looked into it, then carried it away and put it on the upper shelf in the linhay. With the certainty of knowledge, she went to the bottom drawer of the tall-boy for the clothes in which Mrs. Bate was to 'set her forth'—'no need to stream up anything, S'bina 'ad 'er clothes ready, stockings, night-cap and all!' As Mrs. Tom hung them over the back of a chair, a belated tear ran down her cheek and she glanced from their smooth white folds to the still figure on the bed. A lifetime of friendship! She caught her breath in a sob but, because she had so much to do, tried to check her grief. Yet when, a little later, Tom brought the black dress for which she had asked, he found her sitting on the floor, her head against the chair and her tears falling unheeded on the hem of her friend's shroud.

"Why, mother, dear!" he cried with a quick rush of tenderness. "I shouldn't take on like that. You know we've all got to die sometime."

She put out her arms to him like a forlorn and sorrowful child. "I can't 'elp feeling of it. You know we was schoolgirls together."

"Well, well, my dear, she's gone. I'm pretty and sorry but still she's better off. We 'av got each other still and we need to be thankful for't."

Mrs. Tom clung to him. "I knaw. I've got a lot to be thankful for. I've got you and the childern, but to-day I can't 'elp thinkin' about 'er. What 'appy times we've 'ad together."

"I knaw, my dear." He held her close, closer than was his wont in prosperous times and, with her head on that middle-aged shoulder, Mrs. Tom wept till the rush of grief was spent.

When the women whom she had summoned made their appearance, however, though red-eyed, she had herself in hand. She and Mrs. Con Rosevear being the nearest relatives, the family, only too well aware of the latter's slatternly ways, would look to Mrs. Tom for direction. And she was ready for them. Experience had instructed her in the routine to be followed and, before long, Mrs. Bate with a bowl of hot water, with flannel, soap and scissors, had shut herself into the justice-room: Mrs. Con with the bustling help of a sister-in-law, Mrs. William Brenton of Cumean, was turning out the big parlour; and Aunt Louisa, like an embodied shadow, was slipping from room to room in search of mourning apparel. Mrs. Byron had stores of black material, in the piece and made up, and to the old woman was deputed the congenial work of looking for it. Her sewing machine had been given pride of place on the side-table in the kitchen and, already, the other was growing dark with the first results of her search, with crape, black ribbon, cottons, buttons, etc., a heterogeneous assortment. When Leadville returned from Dark Head, the work of preparation was so far forward, that the women, calling a halt, had gathered for a mid-morning cup of tea.

When life has passed the adventurous stage—if it ever does—it turns to the doings of others for its spice; and, in that homely room, about which were scattered so many black garments that the place looked as if draped for some funereal occasion, the five women discussed the dead.

"'Tis very good of 'ee, Aunt Louisa, to come at once to 'elp wi' the blacks, when I knaw you be always slagged wi' work," said Mrs. Tom, with the usual sweet civility of the Cornishwoman.

"Well, my dear," returned Mrs. Blewett, "at a time like this anybody 'ud do anything. I'd go on me 'ands and knees for Mrs. Byron. I've knawed 'er ever since she was a child and 'ave always done 'er sewin' for 'er. Why, some time back, I made the clothes to set 'er forth with! But I thought she was worth a hundred dead ones. Never thought, as I should live to make up 'er mournin's."

"She's lookin' so natural now," said Mrs. Bate, who had brought from the death-chamber the night-cap which had been put in readiness. The lacy frills of it were limp with the sea-damp and Mrs. Tom had offered to iron and goffer it. She was glad to do for her friend this last of many kindnesses.

"Aw, poor soul, she's at rest now. Gone out of a world of trouble. She's best off where she's to," said Aunt Louisa, in tones of conventional grief.

"I wonder," began Mrs. William Brenton, who being in Trevorrick on a week-end visit to her sister-in-law, had accompanied her and was delighted to find herself in the midst of such interesting occurrences. Living at Polscore, and that only since her marriage, for she was a woman from up-country, she was not deeply versed in local gossip. She endeavoured to remedy this by asking questions but, as she was not noted for discretion, her gleanings were apt to be scanty. "I wonder if she've left any will?"

Neither Mrs. Tom nor Mrs. Constantine looked up. The latter felt that after Leadville's death the farm should come to one of her tall sons, to Freathy, Ern or Tremain; while Mrs. Tom was sure that her girls, being Mrs. Byron's favourites, had the prior claim.

"You ought to know if anybody do," said Aunt Louisa, snipping the thread of a finished hem and turning her grey eyes on Mrs. Tom. The neat precise old woman gave a general impression, in colourless face, smooth scanty braids and capable hands, of greyness. She was like water overhung by trees, a limpid stillness in which shadows moved.

"Well," said Mrs. Tom carefully, "I don't know. S'bina was very close wi' money matters. She never let on to any one what she intend doin'."

Aunt Louisa's clear eyes moved thoughtfully from face to face. With the exception of Mrs. Tom she was far and away the cleverest woman in Trevorrick and she applied her wits—as do all of us, from scholar to ale-house gossip—to gathering stores of useless information. "Never 'eard tell of any will," she said, beginning to tack the seams of a skirt for little Rhoda, "and I never knawed of any lawyer comin' 'ere to do anything about a will."

"What you don't knaw, my dear," said. Mrs. Bate, tactless but admiring, "is good for sore eyes;" and in this statement she voiced so conclusively the opinions of all present that the hopes of both Mrs. Con and Mrs. Tom sank. If there were no will Leadville would inherit and there was no reason he should leave it to a Rosevear. In all probability he would marry again and rear a family. Mrs. Tom thought fleetingly of his infatuation for Gray and what might have been.

"Goodness!" said Mrs. Brenton cheerfully. "There'll be pretty ole capers if everything's left to Mr. Byron. 'E'll be turnin' the place upside down. 'E'll be tellin' us all 'ow to farm. Continuous croppin' 'e call it, but my maister say 'better leave things as they be and not make work when there's no need for it.' 'E don't believe in these new-fangled ways."

"I think," said Mrs. Con uneasily, "'e'll teel all those new things 'e's craikin' about and I wonder what Old Squire would say if 'is 'ead was above the earth."

"Some do say 'is 'ead's up now." Mrs. Tom's smile was faint, a twitch of the lips, a recognition of Mrs. Con's tremulous outlook. "I think if Leadville was to start 'is sugar-beet and terbacker teelin' 'e 'ud 'av a 'ot time wi' Old Squire!"

"Mrs. Byron," began Aunt Louisa and stopped to re-thread her needle. She spoke as if her mouth were full of pins. Use had made her able to speak through a bristling *chevaux de frise* while age made her forget whether the pins were there or not. "Mrs. Byron is the livin' image of Old Squire as I remember'n." She glanced at his elbow-chair, wide and built with a cunning hand. Pushed against the wall, its red cushions were hidden under billows of black material, but this drapery only made its outlines the more regal. None of those who looked but thought of the man for whom it had been made as still dimly occupying it. More than one had a glimpse of silver hair above a masterful face and caught the faint sound of an imperious voice. "I seed'n when 'e was in 'is coffin," continued Louisa, recalling further a mountainous bulk. "I warn't higher than the table when 'e died but I can remember mother takin' me in."

"'E was a great big man, wasn't 'e?" asked Mrs. Brenton.

"A lickin' great feller!" Aunt Louisa basted as she talked and the other women, most of them younger by a generation, listened with interest. With the exception of Mrs. Brenton they knew why the old woman's mother had been anxious to imprint the features of Freathy Rosevear on her child's plastic memory. "When he was dead," continued Aunt Louisa, who in her neatness, her precision, was as unlike her sire as any child might be, "they couldn't get his coffin overstairs. They had to take it up in pieces and put'n together in's bedroom. And then they couldn't get'n out. They 'ad to take out the big winder in the end of the 'ouse and slide'n down over the boords. I can remember as if 'twere yesterday. 'E was so 'eavy they had the bier out from Stowe to carr'n; for 'twas more'n the bearers could manage."

"And S'bina was like 'im," said Mrs. Con curiously. She had heard the tale of Old Squire's funeral before but that his granddaughter resembled him so closely was new to her.

"The spit of 'n. 'E was a great big red-faced feller with flamin' 'air which was always stickin' up on end and 'is voice, it was like it was going to wake the dead."

"I wonder at your mother takin' you to see 'im, an old dead man. It don't 'ardly seem the thing, do it?" said Mrs. Brenton looking round at the others but finding them, to her surprise, dull and unresponsive.

"She wanted for me to remember what 'e was like," said the old woman placidly and Mrs. Bate, who had received the night-cap from Mrs. Tom and was absent-mindedly smoothing the strings, smiled to herself a little wistfully. She was old now, but she had been a handsome maid. If only she had been alive when Old Squire was in his prime!

"I shouldn't think," said Mrs. Con, putting down her empty cup and leaning both elbows comfortably on the table, "that S'bina's coffin would cost so much, now, without laigs? Twill be all that the shorter and 'twont be so 'cavy for the men to carry. I should think one set of bearers 'd do."

"Surely," urged Mrs. Brenton, "they'll make it the right size? Twill look funny to 'av a dumpy coffin."

"'Ere, Betsy, you can tack this seam," said Mrs. Tom, who, seeing no reason for any one to be idle, was apportioning the sewing. This done she spoke with authority. "They must make S'bina's coffin the right length; for when 'er laigs was cut off she wouldn't 'av them throwed away. 'When I'm buried up,' she say, 'I'll 'av me laigs with me. Anybody can't rise up on the Last Day without laigs!'"

The others showed surprise. "Very thoughtful of 'er, I'm sure," said Mrs. Brenton.

"No," said Aunt Louisa in her pin-muted voice, "'twouldn't be decent to go before 'er Maker wi'out laigs. But I didn't know she 'ad 'em. Wherever's she kept 'em to?"

"Well, she got 'em in a box, salted away. She brought 'em 'ome from the 'orspital and they'm in the li'l parlour in the cupboard. I think we'd better get'n out against Mr. 'Enwood come to measure 'er."

"She'll make a vitty corpse, after all," said Mrs. Con, who had been haunted by the thought of that legless body and who would now be able to think of her cousin as made whole by the restoration of the carefully preserved limbs. Her person, large and soft, the person of a big eater and small doer, heaved in a gusty sigh of satisfaction. "Nights I've lied thinkin' when she die there'd 'av to be something put in the coffin to keep 'er from boompin' up and down."

Mrs. Bate got up. "I'll just put on 'er cap and then you can all come in and see 'er. She's the fines' body I've set forth for many a day. Some fat body, too, she be, some 'andsome body, fat as butter."

Before the others could take advantage of this invitation which, with the exception of Mrs. Con they were naturally eager to do, Leadville's step was heard on the linhay flags and he at once became the centre of interest. The corpse could wait but this was their first glimpse of the bereaved. Curiosity was veiled by industry and politeness and like the fates they snipped and stitched.

Fresh from his sleep in the sunshine and ready to do his part, he paused, on his way in, to break his fast. As he ate, the whirr of the sewing-machine caught his ear and at once some of his briskness passed.

"Well, Mrs. Tom, I'm come back," he cried, pulling open the little door. To him, the room, always dark, seemed full of soberly clad women and, between them, he made out masses of black material which, overflowing chairs and tables, lay in discreet heaps on the clean blue floor. The women glanced up with conventional murmurs and he perceived that, for the nonce, it was they who were at home there and not he. "What is there for me to do?"

Isolda put down the child's frock on which she was at work. "I think you better go into Stowe and see Mr. Henwood and tell'n to come out and measure 'er for 'er coffin."

Leadville viewed the task set him with disfavour. "I can't abide that job."

"It bain't a bit of good for 'ee to talk like that, my dear," said Mrs. Tom, as to a fractious child, "you know it's got to be done. As well 'av it done first as last."

"I know that." Traffic in the gruesome ceremonial of death was repugnant to him and he would have liked to take a broom and sweep these women and their blacks out of Wastralls, to clear the place of them and have it once more sweet and clean. "Still 'tis 'ard lines on a poor feller."

"Of course it be but, there, it can't be 'elped. I don't want to bother you more'n I can 'elp; but still there's things as must be seen to."

He stood before her, balancing first on one foot, then on the other.

"Well?" he said.

"There's the funeral and what about the food?"

"Tedn't a bit of good for 'ee to ask me. You must do zactly as you like. You knaw best, better than I do."

"I thought," she pursued, bent on getting his assent to the arrangements she considered should be made, "about 'avin' a 'am and a couple of chicken and a piece of beef and then I thought we'd better 'ave a couple of tarts and white cake and yeller cake: and tea. That will be enough."

"Iss," he said, longing to get away, "well, you know what to do."

"And you'll 'av to go and see doctor to get a certificate before you go down to Mr. 'Enwood. As 'e was 'ere yesterday, 'e may not want an inquest—still you never know."

"Well, I'll see'n."

"What day be yer thinkin' to 'av the funeral?"

Leadville was anxious to have it as soon as possible, but knew that this desire was not one to which he could give utterance. "I can't abear to think of 't," he said, conscious of his audience. "I feel as if I'm waitin' for 'er to come in. 'Tidn't like she's dead, to me."

The women glanced at him kindly. They were sorry for him, a poor forlorn creature, a widow man. "I'm afraid," said Mrs. Tom, regretfully, "we shall 'av to bury 'er up pretty quick. Mrs. Bate think she oughtn't to be kep' longer'n Monday."

"Monday?" cried the man and, for a moment, lifted his heavy lids and stared at her. "You don't mean it? Why it's now Saturday?"

"Well, my dear, she died on a full stomach and you know you can't keep her very long. Still I should be the last to 'urry 'er into 'er grave. We'll see what Mr. 'Enwood say."

Mrs. Con, glad of a moment's respite from the sewing, had been watching the speakers. "What 'av 'ee got on yer face there?" she asked peering, with short-sighted eyes, at a brown smear on the man's forehead, the smear his seal-blooded hand had made the previous evening when wiping away the drops of his fear.

"'E 'aven't washed yet," interposed Mrs. Tom and turned back to Byron. "I've put yer black clothes upstairs on yer bed and there's plenty of 'ot water you can 'av."

"Look like you've got blood there," persisted Mrs. Con, "'av you cut yerself?"

Byron swung over to the little mirror by the range. Across his forehead lay a broad smear, dark brown in hue. Though he recognized it instantly as blood, his forgetfulness of the unimportant past prevented his being able to account for it and superstitious dread swooped on him out of a clear sky.

"I dunno what that is," he stammered, already shaken out of his reasonableness and with a vague recollection of a similar episode on the previous evening. "It do look like blood! 'Owever did it get there?"

"Don't 'ee worry, Leadville," soothed Mrs. Tom and who knows whether her words were accidental or chosen. "There's no mark o' Cain on 'ee, Lorrd be praised."

"Mark o' Cain!" he muttered and Mrs. Tom saw leap into his eyes a questioning terror.

"I expect you've scratched yourself somewhere," she said easily. "Take'n go and wash it off." Pouring hot water into a dipper she offered it to him and Leadville, treading delicately among the heaps of black material, went out. He had brought from Dark Head a clear simplicity of purpose, but now his mind was like a ruffled pool. "Mark o' Cain?" he muttered to himself as he went upstairs. "What do they knaw about it? It's all tommy-rot, they can't knaw anything, 'tis only what they'm surmisin'. Can't trust they women, their tongues is always waggin'. They'll ferret out the last rat that's in the mow."

As he put his hands into the dipper he noticed they were trembling and, with this, his caution began to reassert itself. The women must not be allowed to suspect that there was anything concealed. "If I don't take care," he admonished himself, "I shall find meself in a box. Pretty feller me, to take so much notice o' they. I've done more'n they'll ever bear to think on and 'ere I'm all twitchy because of their silly talk."

After washing his face he examined it in the toilet-glass for any sign of a hurt, but the skin was unbroken.

"I 'aven't cut meself," he said perplexedly, and suddenly the episode of the seal occurred to him. He laughed aloud. "Mark o' Cain indeed! And me, what don't believe in they old ideas! Iss, they'm too fanciful for our day o' livin'." He shook his heavy shoulders. "I mus' pull meself together. I must remember, only thing that's 'appened is that I've lost the missus— poor sawl."

In the room below the women had returned to their work of 'makin' up the mournin's.'

"'E seem rather cut up about it, not like 'e belong to be," commented Aunt Louisa.

"Well, what can 'ee expect," said Mrs. Brenton, "only lostin' 'is wife this mornin'? Can't expect for'm to be bright and cheerful!"

"I don't expect anything," said the old woman, "still you can't 'elp noticin' things."

# CHAPTER XVIII

As Leadville on his black stallion turned the corner below Church Town, he met the Wastralls wagon coming back from Stowe with a load of coal and oil. The sight of the teamster, leading his horse as it zigzagged across the sharp ascent, brought the other a sudden tingling realization of power. Yesterday Rosevear had been a hind on his wife's farm and Byron, though ostensibly, blusteringly master, had not been able to dismiss him. Now, opportunity, spruce and debonair, was walking towards him up the wide curve of the road.

Reining in his horse—a gift from Sabina, who liked him to be well mounted—he waited till Jim, this 'proper jump-the-country' was abreast of him.

"The missus is gone!" He was not thinking of Sabina but of the alteration in their relative position.

Jim's face had been as cheerful as his thoughts. Though in workaday clothes he wore them with a holiday air and had adorned his cap with the iridescent wing-feather of a drake. He was in pairing mood and had seen in Stowe 'a lickin' great wardrobe' that he would like for Gray 'if she'd a mind to't.' His nest-building thoughts were scattered by Byron's untimely news and his face lengthened. "Gone?" he repeated. "'E don't say so? Poor sawl! I'm awful sorry. Was it a fit or what was it?"

Byron, impatient to assert himself, ignored the question. Sitting his horse with a touch of swagger he said truculently: "I'll leave yer know I'm maister now."

Jim believed that he had a reason to dislike the speaker and none whatever to avoid a quarrel. Better bad blood between them than that Byron, under the cloak of kinship, should be able to come worrying Gray.

"Iss," he said, accepting the challenge, "missus is 'ardly cold, but still I s'pose you think you'm maister now."

In Byron's fierce eyes was the longing to begin the inevitable fight. The youth, blithe and with his handsome face upturned, was incarnate provocation. One hearty blow and Byron saw the contour of that admirable nose for ever changed.

"When you finish up to-night you can come in," he growled, "and I'll pay you your wages. I don't want you 'ere, on the place, any longer."

Jim did not seem impressed. "I can clear now if you like." It would serve the 'ole hunks' right if he were left with the horse and wagon on his hands.

"An' if yer don't want to 'av yer bones broken," continued the other, pausing on a darkling thought that the sea did not always give up its dead, "you'll clear out of this part altogether."

In Jim's eyes was a little dancing light. "Shen't clear out for the likes of you."

"Well, now, you take this for a warning. If you don't you'll wish you 'ad."

"We'll see about that," and being of those whose spirits rise at the prospect of a fight he smiled. "We'll see who is the best man of the two, me or you."

A grimmer smile was on Byron's face. Knowing his strength he could look forward, past the irritating unpropitious moment, to the happy hour when they should come to grips. "Oo d'yer think's afraid of you, yer banty cock?" he cried, contemptuously, and prepared to ride on.

"If you was as big as a church and tower I ain't afraid," cried the youth after him. As the affair seemed to be hanging fire, he tried a rousing word. "An' if I'm in yer way I shall stay where I'm to."

Byron flashed him a look full of sinister possibilities, the look of one who had taken into consideration that cliffs are sheer and nights dark. "I'll see about that, then."

The prospect of a fight was dwindling into nothingness. "There's people," said Jim, on a last hope, "'ud rather see me than you."

"Any more of your cheek, young sprat, and I'll wring your neck."

But he had realized the countryside would cry shame if he were seen brawling in public while his wife lay dead at home. They would not be blinded to the reason and such knowledge might breed suspicion. He must wait. Grinding his heel into the stallion's side he started at a gallop, leaving Jim disappointed but smiling, for with him, too, it was a case of 'Gay go the Gordons.'

A little annoyance was enough to upset Byron for hours. In a fume of exasperation and bitter feeling he now urged his horse to a speed which drew on him the attention of other wayfarers.

"If 'e ride that rate 'e must be goin' after a doctor. I should think man's missis was goin' to straw—first child, too," said a man from Little Petherick to whom Leadville was a stranger.

"Thiccy feller's Mr. Byron to Wastralls," corrected his companion, "and I know there's no chick nor child there, nor any comin'. 'E do always ride as if Old Nick was after 'un. 'E'll break 'is neck one of these odd days."

The short interview with Rosevear had been unsatisfactory in more ways than one, for the youth's last words had planted a thorn. Not only had he smiled at Byron's threats but his smile, had been of a quality which made the other's blood run cold. Behind it lay assurance, a knowledge he might not divulge but which, like a hidden weapon, was for use at need. The other's jealousy, temporarily in abeyance, stirred and he sought a reason, other than the simple love of fighting inherent in the male, for Jim's smile. Not many cared to try conclusions with the strongest man in the parish. Byron had browbeaten the few who crossed his path, but Jim was game. What had happened to give him confidence? How were matters between him and Gray? That drive into Stowe! The farmer ground his teeth at the thought of it. Was she promised and did Rosevear feel sure of her? A fool for his pains! Such promises were of cobweb stuff. She might promise—his little umuntz—for she did not know, but the end would be the same.

The black stallion was damp with sweat when Byron pulled up at Dr. Derek's freshly painted gate—which in its brightness, its specklessness, was the outward and visible sign of the doctor's tastes! A pathway, gravelled with small white stones and edged with scarlet tiles, led directly to a cream-coloured house, the wide windows of which were brilliantly clean but uncurtained. On the door a highly polished knocker twinkled above a discreetly closed brass letter-flap. Dr. Derek was just returned from his morning round and, though the midday meal was on the table, his constant curiosity with regard to Mrs. Byron, would not allow him to keep her husband waiting. The farmer was, therefore, shown at once into the consulting-room.

The little doctor, round and rosy, was seated before a table of light polished wood. Byron, as he went up the room, gathered an impression of bright glass and metal surfaces, in a well-lighted sunshiny place. So bright was everything, the glass cupboards full of silver implements, the polished woods, the glazed bookcases, that the man, used to low tones within doors, blinked. The high lights of innumerable small objects, the sharply defined pattern of carpet and upholstered chair, confused him and for a moment he stood tongue-tied. At last the difficult words came.

"I've bad news for 'ee, sir."

If that well-regulated organ, which Dr. Derek called his heart, ever varied in its beat this was one of the occasions. He had been convinced that with such injuries as had been inflicted by her accident Mrs. Byron could not recover and, by doing so, she had proved him mistaken. Was it possible that after all...

"Sorry to hear it, Byron. The missus isn't worse, I hope?"

The man breathed heavily. "I'm sorry to tell 'ee, sir, she's gone."

Dr. Derek sat back in his cane elbow-chair. It was a sign, with him, of elation but his face was decorously long. "Dear, dear, you don't say so? How did it happen?"

Byron twisted his hat in his hands. In the meticulously clean room he showed clumsy, weather-browned and out of place. "She wasn't like herself all day, yesterday," he volunteered after a pause, during which Dr. Derek, waiting and knowing he must wait, had occupied himself with a retrospect. No woman could survive such injuries. If it had been one leg or if the head had not been hurt! Her partial recovery had been the effort of a healthy organism, a fine effort but foredoomed. The event had justified his prognosis. "She went to bed early," continued Byron, dragging out his words as if they were creatures with a will opposed to his, "she thought if she did she might be better by the mornin'."

"Did she take her food?"

"She was eatin' like a 'adger last night. I couldn't 'elp noticing it. I thought 'twas a poor sign."

"What did she have for supper?"

Byron recalled, not the articles of food but, the look of the table. "Well, I believe as she 'ad a piece of cold pork."

"Ah!" said the doctor and, behind his gold-rimmed glasses, his eyes gleamed with the satisfaction of the investigator who has run a fact to earth. "And I said she was to be careful about her food. If you remember I recommended a light diet?"

Byron, without understanding it, had noted the satisfaction. "Iss, doctor, but 'er mind was runnin' on pork." He did not know what a light diet was nor that fat pork, when indulged in freely and late at night, was unwholesome.

"A hearty meal," mused the doctor, "and a heart suffering from overstrain. Well—what happened?"

"Since 'er accident, she've been sleepin' downstairs and I never 'eard nothin' of 'er till Mrs. Rosevear come over early this mornin' and found 'er dead in bed." He shook his head. "It frightened all the lot of us."

The doctor, turning to a brass dish, picked up an agate penholder. "Very sad, Byron, very sad; but I'm afraid only what was to be expected."

It was the countryman's turn to experience surprise. The doctor had taken Sabina's death as a matter of course. Very satisfactory, but on what grounds? "You don't say so, sir," he began cautiously. "I'd no idea!"

"If people in a weak state of health will eat pork late at night, in other words give their stomach more work than it is capable of doing," explained Dr. Derek and, behind his twinkling spectacles, his cold and keen eyes emitted a friendly gleam, "the heart is apt to stop work. It's not a bad death, Byron. She didn't suffer."

"I'm pretty and thankful to hear that, sir. We was rather afraid, poor sawl, there by 'erself, might 'av 'ad a 'ard death."

"You can put that fear out of your mind. In all probability she passed in her sleep, just—" he snapped his fingers—"snuffed out. Now, let's see, do you want me to come over?"

So far, matters had gone better than Byron had dared to hope; but now his heart sank. If Dr. Derek were to see Sabina he might realize—Byron accredited him with miraculous powers—on what a fairy superstructure his diagnosis was built. "Well, sir," he said, "just as you like. If you think you ought to come, do so. I shouldn't like for people to talk after she were buried up and say we didn't do what we ought to 'ave done; but she's dead and stiff."

"You don't make a point of it, then?"

"I want you to zactly please yerself, sir."

"Humph!" The doctor considered. "I saw her yesterday and I'm pretty busy. Yes, yes, it isn't necessary." His gold nib in its cool agate holder began to run in smooth flowing style over a sheet of partly printed paper. "Show that to the undertaker," he said, passing the certificate to Byron.

"Thank you, doctor, and for all the trouble you've took of 'er." He placed the paper carefully in his pocketbook and prepared to go. "Seems rather hard that after all you couldn't pull 'er through!"

In Dr. Derek's bosom the professional man was often at war with the scientific. "The fact is, Byron," he said honestly, "I didn't expect to save her. I've never thought she would live so long." His experienced glance dwelt fleetingly on the other's face. "You look pretty seedy, yourself. If you don't take care we shall have you on the sick list."

"Well, sir, 'twas awful sudden, 'twas. I don't feel to believe she's really gone. I'm like I'm in a dream." But, in his hidden mind, he was wondering why the man who saw so much could not pierce to the little more.

"Must have been a terrible shock to you. When is the funeral to be?"

"Monday, I believe, sir."

"Walking, I suppose?"

The man looked surprised. "What else would we 'av, sir?"

"No, of course, I was forgetting. Well, I'll try to come to it. I had the greatest possible respect for your wife as a farmer. She should have been a man."

"'Tis great respect you're payin' her, sir."

The doctor smiled enigmatically. "That's as may be," he said and, indeed, for him to say a woman resembled a man was the reverse of complimentary. In his experience the sterile female frequently approximated to the male in type and habits; and he thought such approximation a sign of degeneracy. He had been interested from a scientific point of view in Mrs. Byron. She had led a man's life and she was childless. Was the latter a consequence, or had the childlessness determined her way of life? He could find arguments in support of both theories.

Byron had brought to the interview a mind filled with misgiving. Dr. Derek had a reputation for ability and the other had hardly ventured to hope his tale would pass muster. He had told the truth because he dared not do other and behold it had stood him in good stead, that and the fact that Dr. Derek, for the sake of his professional reputation, had not been altogether sorry to hear of Mrs. Byron's death. As he rode at a walking pace down the hilly street the farmer could congratulate himself on the outcome.

The streets of Stowe, like spokes of a wheel, converge on the quay; and back from it, but near at hand, lie the huddle of warehouses, shops and inns, which supply the needs of sailormen. The quayside itself is, at low tide, a sheer drop of many feet; but the children play on its unprotected verge and the drunken man rolls gaily home from the waterside pubs and there is no tale of casualties. In one of the less frequented streets, opposite the Farmer's Arms, stood the undertaker's shop with, in the window, by way of advertisement, a baby's coffin and a hollow mortuary urn. Henwood, the undertaker, a little chattery man, fond of society and overfond of his glass, was generally to be found on his neighbour's premises; and, when Byron rode up, was fetched therefrom by the wife whose tongue was supposed to drive him thither. As Dr. Derek would have said, however, it was a moot point whether Mrs. Henwood's temper was the cause of his going, or his going the cause of her temper.

He came in, wiping his mouth with the back of his hand and, the subject of beer being to him the most congenial in the world, opened the proceedings by asking Byron if he would have a glass. The latter, preoccupied and anxious, had not known he was thirsty.

"I don't mind if I do 'av one," he said, with that increase of cordiality which an offer of hospitality induces.

"Wait a moment, then." Little Henwood, who was a man of girth rather than height, rolled himself down the shop. When he reached the door at the end, he opened the upper half and called to some one within. "Sandra! would you mind running in for a jug of beer?"

A clatter of tin pans reached Byron's ears, then a voice the reverse of amiable. "Do you think I'm going to run my foot in and out for you—yer walkin' beer-barr'l? Fetch it yerself."

"'Tidn't fer me, my dear," twittered the little man.

"Mr. Byron don't want beer when he's come for yer to make a coffin. 'Tis for yerself I reckon and quench yer thirst in this world you can but Lorrd knows yer throat will be dry enough in the next."

"Well, 'av it your own way then, my dear, but Mr. Byron's thirsty as a gull. He's comed all the way from Trevorrick. Perhaps," he added disarmingly, "you'll 'and me out a jug—a jug of water, my dear."

"And 'ave you empt that water away and go after beer? Do you think, Mr. Henwood; you've married a fool?"

"I wish I 'ad, I wish I 'ad," muttered Henwood and shaking a head on which a rim of grey curls surrounded an unreverend tonsure he came slowly back. "Don't you take no notice of 'er," he said, lifting the mortuary urn out of the window.

"I don't," said the other simply. "I've 'ad enough of that."

"Where there's a will there's a way," said the little undertaker making for the door, "and thiccy urn 'olds just about a pint. I'll be back in a jiffy."

Left to himself, Byron glanced down the shop. He felt curiously at home in it; and this was strange because he could not remember ever to have been there before. At the end was a shed lighted from above and furnished with a carpenter's bench, trestles and some newly planed boards. A sack of shavings stood in a corner and the air carried a scent of wood. Byron sniffed it appreciatively. It wakened in him a dim memory, a memory so elusive that, try as he might, he could not capture it. The place was familiar, the boards, the smell of wood, but something was lacking, some sound. As he stood, puzzling over the circumstance, Henwood returned with the brimming urn.

Setting it carefully on a small black stool or cricket, he turned to the window and, lifting the lid of the baby's coffin, took from within two rather smeary glasses. "The Lorrd 'elps them as 'elps 'emselves," he said cheerfully. "Missus 'ud never think of looking in thiccy coffin and many a drink I've 'ad from'n."

The other drank in silent appreciation of the undertaker's mother-wit. He found it pleasant after the annoyances, the secret fears and elations of the morning, to be in contact with this simple soul, whose one idea was beer and yet more beer.

"Not much doing," said Henwood, conversationally, as he returned the glasses to their hiding-place, "but what's my loss is other people's gain and, after all, though I do my duty by the dead the livin' 'as always been more to my taste. What can I do for you, Mr. Byron?"

"I want for 'ee to come over to measure my wife for 'er coffin."

"My dear life, you don't mean to say she's dead?"

"Iss, the poor sawl, she died off in her sleep last night and we want for you to come and do the business."

The little man considered, his head on one side. "You want 'er buried decent, I s'pose?"

So that Sabina was hurried into the grave, Byron was indifferent as to the furnishings of her journey but he knew better than to let this appear. "Of course I do—although I don't believe in wastin' so much money to be put'n under the turf, when it could be used for something better. The missus used to think same as I do, she was never one for grandeur."

"Well, you got to study other people's tongues, you know."

"If it wasn't for that," said the countryman with his grim smile, "you'd cut a poor shine, I reckon. Well, what sort of wood be yer goin' to put in?"

"I've a good piece of oak here, seasoned wood, what about that? I cut a coffin for Colonel Pendarves out of it, but there's enough for another."

Bargaining was second nature to these men and Henwood, in suggesting what he knew would not be acceptable, was only observing the rules of the game.

Byron made the expected answer. "Oak 'edn't for the likes o' we, it's for the gentry folk. What other 'av you got?"

"There's ellum. It's good hard wood and lastin'."

"Don't matter 'ow long it last when 'tis once in under the earth."

Henwood led the way into the shed and pointed to some timber.

"Why don't you 'av a polished pitch pine wi' brass fittin's? Thiccy stuff was only landed last week." He touched the wood with spatulate hands, the hands of the craftsman. Next to his beer he loved 'a bit o' seasoned wood.' "You wouldn't wish for a handsomer coffin than that 'uld make."

"Pitch pine is more like it," agreed the buyer. "What would it cost?"

"I dunno as I could tell 'ee to a pound or two. There's a lot o' things to consider. There's the linin's and the fittin's; and then there's the gloves for the bearers and their 'arf crowns. Was you thinkin' to 'av one set of bearers or two?"

"'Tis a braäve way to Church Town and the missus was a big woman, I think we better 'av the two."

"Sixteen half-crowns is a good bit. That'll make two pound. You see that tally up."

"Well, 'av it done decent, but she wouldn't like no show nor fuss. I know she wouldn't."

"We'll 'ave it plain as possible then." He made a note on the wood itself and then stood thoughtful. "When would you like to 'av it?"

"Mrs. Rosevear said I'd better leave it to you."

Henwood tapped his teeth with the broad wood pencil. "Weather's braäve and cold," he said meditatively, "but if she died off sudden — —"

"She done 'er day's work as usual and ate a good supper but doctor said 'twas 'er 'eart. Accident must 'av strained it. 'E didn't think she'd live so long as she 'av."

"She must 'er died on a full stomach, so I should bury her up as soon as we can. To-day's Saturday, but I can be ready by Monday."

"We must 'av it that way."

"Very well, then, tell Mrs. Rosevear we shall leave the 'ouse at 'arf-past one."

As Byron went out, the little man's glance travelled beyond him on an errand in no way connected with the business in hand. Life was 'terrible short' and he must make the most of his time, get down as many 'cups o' beer' as he could before his journeymen were set to make that coffin which must be put together without his help.

The Farmer's Arms beckoned and he went.

# CHAPTER XIX

That afternoon, having snatched a moment from her work of setting Wastralls in the pious order which a death and consequent funeral demand, to run home, Mrs. Tom found Hember kitchen deserted by all but Gray. The range was open and on a stool by the dull fire—a stool usually appropriated by Smut the old black and white cat—sat the young girl. She was, of course, in black; but the dress, not having been worn for some time, was a little tight. The promise of Gray's frame was womanly and as she sat, huddled on the low stool, she looked not only unhappy, but uncomfortable. The mother, appraising the woe-begone face and uneasy figure, saw that here also was work for her. Aunt Louisa could alter the dress but it was for Mrs. Tom to comfort this little heart which in all its eighteen years had had no greater grief than the loss of Smut's frequent kittens.

"My dear," she said and hung her purple knitted bonnet behind the door, thereby giving a pleasant air of permanency to her visit. "Where's the childern to?"

"They'm with dad."

"And Richbell?"

"Gone up to Shoppe for some black ribbon."

"She needn't have troubled to do that," said Mrs. Tom, with a lack of her usual perspicacity, "there's plenty down to Wastralls."

Gray's little tear-blurred face showed a faint lightening, as of a thinning in the rain-cloud. "I heard them telling," she said tentatively, "that Art Brenton is home."

"Art?" said Mrs. Tom severely. "'Im an' Percy 'Olman's a pretty pair. I should think the maid 'ud 'av somethin' else to do 'stead of gaddin' round the lanes!"

Gray knew her mother's opinion of Richbell's various admirers. "I wouldn't worry my head about her," she said, a touch of sympathy in her voice. "I don't believe she means to have any one of them. She's only just amusing herself and, when the time comes, she'll know better."

"Let's 'ope she will." Mrs. Tom had not found that young people showed a greater wisdom than their forbears with regard to matrimony. "Please God she won't do so silly as yer auntie did, turn up 'er nose on all the chaps round 'ere and marry a stranger that she don't know nothing 'tall about."

"Poor auntie after all!" The tears welled up till Gray's dark eyes were shining stars.

Mrs. Tom changed the subject. "I'm pretty and glad you're back, my dear. 'Ow did Mrs. Andrew treat yer?"

"Oh, she treated me as if I was one of 'er own," but Gray's tones were flat. With Aunt Sabina newly dead what did it matter how old Mrs. Andrew had treated her? "She'd have liked for us to stop altogether."

"Well," said the mother, but with a little knit of perplexity between the brows, "you might do worse'n that. Still—I wish Gentle Jane was a little farther away from Wastralls."

Gray had no difficulty in following the trend of her mother's thoughts. "I don't think Uncle Leadville 'ud bother to come over there," she said, adding, as if struck by a fresh idea, "I suppose he knows?"

"Dunno whether he do or no. Everything's been upside down to-day and that reminds me— —" she turned to the cupboard in the wall and took from the top shelf a box of stationery. "My dear, if you 'aven't got nothing else to do, I think you'd better write some letters for me."

Gray rose from the stool. "I shall be glad to have the job." Her lip quivered, her whole soft face crumpled into childish lines. "Oh, mammy," she said, looking forlornly across the gulf of the generations, "I do keep on thinking and thinking."

Middle age accepted the further burthen. "Iss, I know you must be!" Mrs. Tom, putting comforting arms about her, drew the young head to rest against her shoulder and, at ease after what had seemed a long loneliness, Gray sobbed out the thought that had been troubling her.

"'Tis the first night since auntie's accident that she've been left by herself." The circumstances of this death, seeming to reflect on her conduct, had added a poignancy to what would otherwise have been endurable.

"We can't pick nor choose our hour," said Mrs. Tom gravely; "'cos, when 'tis the Lorrd's time, it must be ours whether we'm ready or no."

"Yes, mammy, but I've got the feeling that if I hadn't gone away it wouldn't have happened."

But Mrs. Tom could comfort her daughter with the larger outlook that proves our insignificance. We are less important than we feared. We are of no importance at all. "My dear, you mustn't look at the black side. Her time was come and she'd be sorry for you to grieve yerself so. I knaw you've been like a daughter to 'er all these months and she did dearly love yer; but when it come to the end she wouldn't be wantin' you nor me. She had other things to think about."

"Supposing she was suff'rin', mammy?"

"She couldn't 'av suffered anything, my dear, and that you'll say when you see 'er face. 'Tis lovely, just like an angel. She must 'a passed away in 'er sleep."

Mrs. Tom's words, turning mortal death into the visitation of God, had the effect she wished. Gray, forgetting the personal equation, had a quieting vision of powers at once superhuman and beneficent. The Unknown, that was God and Good, had blossomed about her homely aunt and, through those dead eyes, all might look for a little moment into the Beyond.

"You'm a better 'and for writin' letters than I be," said Mrs. Tom, returning after a time to the simple needs of the hour. "And there is people who must know that yer auntie is gone." She turned to the table, rummaging in the box of stationery. "I always keep some mournin' letters in the bottom of this. Ah, 'ere 'tis," and she extracted some black-edged paper.

Gray, with death at once simplified and exalted, was able to follow her lead. She had been to a school in Stowe kept by two Welsh ladies and was passably instructed, that is to say, knew how to cast accounts and phrase a simple letter. "Who must I write to, mammy?"

"Well, my dear, there's the Rosevears of St. Issy and St. Minver and there's the Trudgians to Wadebridge and the Jackas and Sowdens and Trebilcocks. They'm all relations, you knaw. Tell 'em your poor auntie died in 'er sleep and the funeral's goin' to be—" she paused, remembering day and hour had been left for the undertaker to fix. "Well, now you must leave a place for that and put it in after we know." She glanced about the kitchen, which for Hember looked cheerless, being indeed dusty and unswept. "And when you've finished the writing, you better try and clean up a bit."

"Why—you aren't goin' back, are you?"

"Yes, I must for a bit, but I shan't be long. You'll find there's plenty for yer to do. Time quickly goes when you're busy."

She nodded briskly and, refusing to be moved by her daughter's unwillingness, set off down the lane. She had left the cleaning of Wastralls well begun. Above stairs and below, the rooms had to be turned out, scrubbed and set in order; and, no doubt, this washing and polishing, though applied to an already clean house, had its useful side. It affected not only the walls and furniture but the emotions of the workers and was a panacea for inconvenient feelings. Grief expended itself in hard conscientious rubbings and nerves were turned, to the benefit of their owners, into elbow-grease. Mrs. Tom, having set every one to work, had thought she might slip away without being missed but, on her return, heard her name being called about the house. The undertaker had come to measure the body for its wooden dress and she was required to bring him into the room where Sabina, her hands folded over the Bible on her chest, lay sleeping. Mrs. Bate, in her capacity of Stripper, had already conducted thither a number of admiring visitors but they had been without exception of her own sex. The old woman was by no means shy, nevertheless when Henwood drove up behind a black long-tailed horse, which seemed surprised at being required to move at other than a walking pace, she hurried in search of Mrs. Tom.

"If you don't mind, my dear," she said with something as near a blush as her old cheeks could show, "I'd rather for you to take'n in."

Mrs. Tom agreed. "I don't mind. I'll do it if you want for me to."

The other emphasized her feelings by a tap on Mrs. Tom's arm. "The truth is, I was always a bit shy and I don't like tellin' about they laigs. Laigs is laigs and I can 'ardly explain them to a man."

Which shows that Mrs. Bate, in spite of the illegitimacy of Janey and Jenifer, had a modest mind.

"Why, my dear life, 'e's used to laigs. Been measurin' bodies all 'is lifetime. 'E wouldn't take any notice of 'em, or you, uther."

"Well, other bodies got laigs but this one 'aven't got any. Don't seem hardly decent to talk about 'em."

Little Henwood, however, when the matter of the legs was explained to him, behaved with propriety; showing only a calm satisfaction that the coffin he was about to make, should be of the usual length and shape. He said nothing that could bring a blush to spinster cheeks—if Mrs. Bate who, in spite of the matronly title, had never been married, could be called a spinster—but demeaned himself with a practical common sense which won him some tolerable opinions.

"The coffin will be 'ere to-morrow early, I'll bring it meself and put 'er in."

"'E knaw 'is business, that one do," said Mrs. Tom, as she watched him drive off behind the surprised-looking horse. "Got a good 'ead on his shoulders."

Mrs. William Brenton, however, happened to be his wife's cousin. She sniffed disparagingly. "Proper l'il tubby. When Sandra was ill, 'e was such a glutton 'e drank up all the brandy that Passon sent down for 'er 'e did."

"Iss," said her sister-in-law who if not 'gifted wi' good looks' was easy-natured, "but 'twas because she said she wouldn't drink that 'ell-brew, not even to please the Passon. She's get better wi'out it. Iss and from that time she started to cheat the craws."

"Undertakin'," said Aunt Louisa, "is a drinkin' job. Never seem to got enough work to full up a man's time and what can 'ee expect?"

"Expect?" cried Mrs. Brenton virtuously. "I expect for'm to 'av self-respect and not make pigs of theirself."

"Then, my dear, you expect more'n you'll get. We do all knaw what men is. If they bain't out drinkin' they're out courtin' somebody's li'l maid." She began to fold the dress she had been altering and, as she did so, looked towards Mrs. Tom. "Well, now, I've done that. Is there anything else I can do?"

"No, I think you've done enough to-night." The mistress of the ceremonies knew better than to over-tax her assistants. "But I hope you'll try and come to-morrow as there's a good bit more to do yet." With a glance she included the other occupants of the room.

"Oh, my dear, I bain't goin' to leave 'ee till it's all finished now, what next?" said Aunt Louisa, taking the pins from the crumples of her old lips. "I was goin' to Mrs. Martyn because she got two children now where she only expected one, but she must wait. I'm sure she won't mind."

"Iss, my dear," murmured Mrs. Bate, "livin' can wait, but the dead must be tended to."

The little band left in a body, 'almost' thought Mrs. Tom, 'as if they was afraid of meeting some of the Little People.' Though she herself had never seen so much as a Jack-in-the-box—as Will-o'-the-wisps are called in the West—she knew that where death is, other less familiar, even less desirable appearances may be gathered; and she did not wonder that the women clung to the companionship of the living. Long after the dusk had rendered the speakers invisible, she could hear the rise and fall of their voices. A sudden shower dashed its raindrops into her face and with a sigh she turned back into the kitchen.

"Awful catchy weather," she said: she would give Leadville his supper, light the candles in Sabina's room and then she, too, would go home.

A step in the porch made her look up and she found that Jim Rosevear, his day's work done, had followed her into the house.

"Why, Jim?" She noted the raindrops on his hair and coat and that for some reason he was looking dissatisfied.

"'E've give me my walkin' ticket, to-day," said the young man and his eyes, on either side of that delicately bridged nose, had the hard look of a hawk's, "so I've come for me wages."

Mrs. Tom's brows went up but, if she simulated surprise, she did not feel it. "Well, I shouldn't trouble," she comforted, "you could not stop 'ere very well."

That, he did not dispute. "But there's means and ways of doin' a thing."

"'E don't mean all 'e say, poor old villain."

"'E mean this all right." He went to the heart of the matter. "'Tisn't best 'e come meddlin' after Gray no more, or I'll bash 'is oogly face for'n."

"Oh, I shouldn't go quarrellin'. With 'im quietness is the best noise. Let's 'ope 'e'll be more sensible when 'e knows 'ow things is." She looked kindly at the man and continued to drop balm. "I'm sorry for the poor chap. 'Twas nothing but natural 'e should want to work the farm, anybody would and now 'e'll 'av 'is chance."

"Fine 'and 'e'll make of it," said implacable youth.

"Well, that'll be 'is look-out." She headed him in another direction. "What be yer thinkin' to do?"

"I'll talk it over with Gray to-night and, if she's agreeable, I think I'll take on Aunt Urs'la's offer."

The fact that Gentle Jane was just over the ridge from Trevorrick, gave Mrs. Tom a sense of impending trouble. "There's no 'urry for that yet," she said thoughtfully, "and Gray's terribly upset over 'er auntie's death. Why don't 'ee take 'er up to Plymouth for a week or two? I'm sure mv sister Ellen would be pretty and glad to 'av yer."

"Well, I dunno," but his face, brightening at the suggestion, lost its hardness. Ellen Warne's husband was in process of evolving from a carpenter into a builder and they were thriving hospitable folk. "I'll see what Gray got to say about it."

"As funeral's on Monday I think as you could go on the Tuesday." She looked as simple as a sheep but, under the kind suggestion, lay an anxious hope that it might prove acceptable. In Plymouth, Gray would be out of Leadville's reach.

"I haven't travelled very much. Never been further'n Bodmin," said the young man and already the note of holiday was in his voice.

"No, Gray 'aven't nuther," smiled the mother. "I'm sure you'll be delighted. Plymouth is a lickin' great place, nothin' but streets and 'ouses and bobbing up against people all day long. Ah, now," as the door of the porch was kicked open, "'ere's Leadville comin'. Now, my dear, I shouldn't say anything to'n if I was you, a still tongue make a wise 'ead. 'E've had quite enough to-day to upset'n."

Byron, coming out of the dark yard into the lamplit kitchen, did not at first perceive the second occupant of the room. He was in a good humour, for the men he had met in Stowe had been more friendly than usual and, in the attitude of the Wastralls hinds, he had gauged a new respect. The latter had come to him for orders and their manner had been conciliatory. If, in the past, they had given unwilling service, from henceforth he was their employer; and, in their submission, he, strangely enough, saw himself justified.

As he caught sight of Rosevear, however, his brows came together in the familiar line and Mrs. Tom, watching, felt her heart sink. A brawl in the house, where his wife lay dead but as yet uncoffined, would be unseemly and she cast about in her mind for means to prevent it.

"'Enwood 'av been 'ere," she said, thrusting the thought of Sabina between the men. "You ought to leave the 'inds knaw as the funeral's on Monday. I thought p'raps Jim could go around and tell'n?"

Leadville, obliged to consider the suggestion, tossed it aside on the gale of his dislike. It is customary for the hinds belonging to a farm—not only the men working there at the moment, but all who have done so in the past—to carry the coffin of their employer from the home to the graveyard. In payment of their services they receive a meal, a pair of gloves and half a crown; and, at a time when wages ranged between eleven and fifteen shillings a week, this custom was honoured with a careful observance.

"Old George can do that. 'E been 'ere longest, longer than 'e 'av and 'e'll know 'oo to tell." The appeal to him for direction had, however, the effect Mrs. Tom had anticipated. Turning to the cupboard he took out his cashbox and counted down the teamster's wages.

"That's right, 'edn't it?"

The other glanced perfunctorily at the coins. "No, 'edn' right. There's another week owing. You gave me no notice."

Byron looked up with a scowl. He wanted to deny that the extra payment was customary, to precipitate a quarrel; but Mrs. Tom, looking on, was ready. She stepped up to the table.

"Iss, my dear," she said, in her sweet and placid tones, tones which denied the possibility of ill-feeling on either side. "That is the way of it 'ere. You 'aven't worked a farm and wouldn't know; but 'ere we do give a week's notice or a week's pay."

The farmer turned towards her, conscious of the need for caution, yet longing to persist.

"Iss, my dear," she said again, "'tis a week's notice or a week's pay."

At length, with a contemptuous flinging down of extra coins, Byron completed the transaction. Without a word Jim swept up the money and turned to go. As he swung out of the room, his head up, his nailed hoots ringing on the flags, Leadville, in a sudden access of irritation, flung after him a few hot words. "And mind what I've told yer. You pick yer bones off from 'ere."

The young man, pausing on the threshold, looked back. In his eye was a defiant sparkle and his smile was blithe. He would welcome trouble. "I've told yer before, I don't take no more notice of 'ee than that!" and he snapped his fingers in derision.

With a furious oath Byron sprang forward but Mrs. Tom was before him. From where she stood it was easy to push the door to and she did so, nimbly and with a will. By the time the raging farmer had opened it again, Jim had disappeared into the mirk of the, as yet, moonless night. Mrs. Tom, at his back, smiled her relief. For the moment the quarrel, hanging over them like a rain-filled cloud, had been averted and, if her plan of 'land between' were carried out, they would not meet again for some time.

"Now, my dear," she said in kindly wise, "don't 'ee go takin' no notice of'n, 'tis naught but a young chap and cockerils do craw loud. Take and set down by the fire now. I'm sure you must be tired."

Byron paid little heed to her but, in the end, her deft and quiet movements as she laid the supper, her familiar voice relating the small events of the day, talking of Sabina and the respect shown her by the neighbourhood, had the desired effect. He threw himself into Old Squire's chair and, pulling off his mud-caked boots, stretched his feet to the glow. The black garments upon which the women had been employed were piled beside Aunt Louisa's machine on the side-table; but otherwise the place was as usual, austerely tidy and yet comfortable, the plain dignified living-room of a thriving farmer. Byron, tired after his day at Stowe, glad to have taken the first step towards getting rid of Rosevear, leaned back. He was happy in that this space between four thick walls was now, at last, actually his.

"'Av yer thought it over," said Mrs. Tom, breaking eggs into a pan and proceeding to fry them, "'oo you'll 'av 'ere to stay wi' yer? 'Cos you can't live by yerself and I shan't be able to come always, so I should settle it up if I was you."

"What d'yer mean?

"Must 'av somebody to cook for yer and do the work."

Byron, preoccupied, had yet a feeling, dim but friendly, for Mrs. Tom. Her essential motherliness appealed to one whose reality was masculine. He recognized in her a deep knowledge which made subterfuges and insincerity of no avail and, if he had not hitherto spoken freely to her, it was because there had been no need of speech. Mrs. Tom knew all the things of which Sabina had been so amazingly ignorant; and now Sabina, with what had seemed to him her wilful misinterpretation of facts, was gone. He saw no reason to conceal his immediate hope.

"I shall be 'aving a wife soon," he said and, in saying it, showed that although he might have gauged correctly Mrs. Tom's insight he had altogether missed her attitude. She turned sharply, staring at him. Accustomed to have her facts dressed in the clothing which obtained among her neighbours, his honesty repelled, even alienated, her. To know was one thing, to admit your knowledge was another and, in Mrs. Tom's eyes, Byron's candour was shocking and indecent. She stopped him with a hasty, "A wife? My dear, yer poor wife ain't 'ardly cold yet?"

But Byron's perceptions had been dulled by the vividness of a secret hope. "Iss," he persisted, unable to realize his companion's point of view, "but I'm gwine marry again."

"Do-an 'ee say that then," implored Mrs. Tom, whose words were a loose robe under which her thoughts could move at ease, "it don't sound vitty."

Her earnestness, penetrating the mist of his illusions, reached the man. He looked up, puzzled and anxious. Had he gone too far? Had he said anything to arouse suspicion? Surely not, nevertheless he would be careful, he would even affect a show of grief.

"I shall prettily miss S'bina," he began tractably, and Mrs. Tom nodded. If the words were uttered perfunctorily the phrasing was correct. "I do miss her," he continued, warming to the task. "I'm grievin' now." With his feet stretched luxuriously, his body niched in the comfort of the big chair, he looked woebegone indeed. "Nobody knows what a day I've 'ad and she only just gone. Everybody I met stopped me and wanted to know a parcel of questions and me keep on tellin' till I was muddled up. I didn't knaw no more'n Adam what I were tellin' of'm." Having offered his oblation he relapsed into a pleading sincerity. Not for years had he spoken of his affairs, but the change in them, the hope of a belated happiness, had unlocked his lips. "But still I can't live wi' that and soon I'm gwine marry—no stranger to you."

Mrs. Tom put her annoyance into a shake of the frying-pan. "Now, my dear feller," she said, "hain't a bit o' good for 'ee to think anything about that. 'Tis so well to put it out of yer mind for ever. One thing I don't want to knaw anything about it, bain't right as I should and, another thing, I know she 'edn't for you." Obliged to admit a knowledge she would have denied, she spoke with warning emphasis. "She never did think anything about yer, nor never will."

Though Byron's belief that his good star was in the ascendant was unshakeable, her conviction, expressed so firmly, troubled and irritated him. He sprang out of the chair and, in his stocking feet, began to walk up and down. Mrs. Tom, as she took knives and forks from the kitchen drawer, looked at him uneasily. To her mind he suggested a bull. He had the close-curled hair, the thick body and the gaze alternately fierce and brooding. He was like a bull too in his ways, rushing here, rushing there, a head-strong creature using force when subtlety would have proved the better weapon. The uneasiness she felt, being for her child, was like a smouldering fire, a very little fanning and it would burst into flame.

"You may say what you like!" Now that Sabina was dead he could see no reason for Mrs. Tom to oppose his suit. With the freehold of Wastralls and his late wife's savings he would be the richest farmer in the district. "She'm too young to knaw her own mind. I can make her care and I will." His face grew bleak with the intensity of his emotion. "I'll 'av 'er if I go through fire and water."

Only dread of what he might do, a dread impersonal and foreboding, could have kept Mrs. Tom to her purpose. "Well," she said, rallying her forces, for after all, poor soul, she had only one woman's share of courage. "'Tis as well to tell yer, first as last—she's Jim Rosevear's."

Byron had paused in his uneasy walk. He heard but he was unable to believe, indeed he took this simple statement for a malicious invention. Not for a moment did he credit it; but he was wrath with Mrs. Tom. If for reasons he could not fathom she wanted Gray to marry Rosevear, she must be made to realize that she was dealing with some one who, in this matter, would not stand any nonsense. His eye grew menacing. "I dare you to say such a thing to me," he cried, "to me what's mad in love with her."

Mrs. Tom put down the frying-pan. Her fear for her child was momentarily pushed aside by outraged affection. After twenty years of married life and before his dead wife had been carried out of the house, Leadville could proclaim his love for another woman! True or not he should not say it, not to her. Taking the purple bonnet from behind the door she tied it on. Leadville, however, was still too much obsessed by passion to realize the effect he had produced; indeed, not until she was walking out of the house did the breeze of her going reach him.

"What's the matter with yer?" he cried, shaken out of his absorption.

"I'm done wi' yer and I'm goin' 'ome."

"Goin' 'ome? Whatever be goin' 'ome for?"

"And what's more I 'ope I shall never come inside the door no more."

"What 'av I done?"

"Done?" she cried explosively.

He looked at her in a bewilderment, the genuineness of which angered her the more.

"You talkin' like that and poor S'bina lying there. I'm fairly ashamed of yer. A dog'd knaw better than that. I don't knaw 'ow she 'ad so much patience, puttin' up wi' you all these years. Thank 'Eaven, I've no need to."

He understood that she was annoyed on his late wife's account. To him it was as if Sabina had been dead a year and he marvelled that she should still exert an influence over others.

"Oh, come now," he said hurriedly, "I didn't mean to vex you, but when people's dead and gone— —"

"'Twould serve yer right," cried Mrs. Tom still indignant, "if she should haunt yer."

"Haunt me?" stammered Byron with a quick change of mood. "She wouldn't do that? You don't think she'd do that, do yer?"

"You knaw best whether she should or no," and she perceived without understanding why, that this random shot had hit the target.

"Well, why should she?" The man relapsed into his ordinary manner. "I don't like that kind of talk. Take an' come in now like a good sawl and take no more notice of't."

Though Mrs. Tom yielded, she preserved a certain stiffness of manner. The eggs were cold and leathery but she declined to fry others. "'Tis your own fault yer supper's spoilt. S'bina was always studyin' you but you'll 'av no one now to wait on you like she did, I bet a crown."

She looked over the supper-table to see that nothing had been forgotten. "You 'av a cup o' cocoa at night, don't yer?"

Again that baffling glimpse of something hidden. "Cocoa?" said he. "'Twas S'bina that drinked the cocoa. I—I 'ate it."

"Very well, then, I'll get yer a cup o' beer," and as she drew it from a cask in the linhay her glance rested for a moment on the high-girdled brown jug, the jug which Sabina had always used for her cocoa. Mrs. Tom regarded it thoughtfully. Many a time she had seen it standing on the stove, waiting till Sabina should be ready to carry it to her room. It was a part of the nightly ritual of locking up, undressing, sleep-wooing, a part of the old order which, with Sabina, had passed away.

In spite of his bulk Byron was a moderate eater. The quality of his food was, as he said, a matter of indifference and he swallowed the leathery eggs as contentedly as if they had been worthy examples of Mrs. Tom's skill.

"I think I should like to 'av a pipe," he said as soon as his hunger was appeased. "I 'aven't smoked much lately, 'aven't felt like it." Crossing the room he put a hand on the high mantelshelf in search of his pipe. The restlessness of the past months had ebbed, leaving him at peace. He craved the dreamy satisfaction of tobacco. "Why, what's this? 'Ere's a new pipe! 'Owever did it get 'ere?"

Mrs. Tom, glancing up from her work of clearing the table, saw that he held in his hand the pipe with an amber mouthpiece which she had brought from Stowe.

"Why, that's the one poor S'bina bought for yer!"

The unexpected was to Byron the threatening and the presence of the pipe disturbed his new serenity. His mind began to bubble with suspicion, with wild extravagant surmise. It did not occur to him that the purchase of the pipe was a sign of Sabina's persistently kindly thought, a survival from the disowned discredited past. "She did?" he muttered, turning on it a look of mingled fear and aversion. "I didn't know that. You don't mean to say she put it there?" It was as if she had crept from her bed of death, had stolen in, shrouded but invisible and set the mysterious pipe where his hand would chance on it.

Mrs. Tom, observant and wondering, filled the wooden wash-up bowl with water and set it on the table. "I dare say she did."

"Did she put it there," he hesitated, calculating, "did she put it there, last night?"

Last night when he was planning her death, had she too had her thoughts, her plans? It was a disconcerting, to a guilty man, even an alarming thought.

"It don't seem only last night, it seem ages since," said Mrs. Tom, beginning to wash the cloam. "We bought it into Stowe and gived it to S'bina and what she did with it then, I dunno. I s'pose she put it on the chimley-piece."

It fell from his fingers and, hitting the steel fender, broke in two. "I won't 'av it," he cried, violently. His face was grey. He was beside himself with superstitious dread. Sabina, who should have been dead, still lived. The old belief in her, as strong and incalculable, had revived. He was like one expecting a blow and not knowing from what quarter it would come. "I won't 'av it, I don't want'n. 'Ow do I know? It might be poisoned!"

Mrs. Tom continued tranquilly to cleanse plates and dishes, but her mind was busy. "A pipe poisoned? Get away man, you'm mad. What do yer mean? Why, she bought it for a present for yer."

Byron looked from the pipe to Mrs. Tom and a glimmer of common sense returned. He broke into an uneasy laugh. "Don't know what's come over me," he said, picking up the pieces. "I'm all twitchy to-night. I dunno what I'm sayin'. I'm carried off."

"Want a good night's rest," said she comfortably. "That's what's the matter with 'ee. I shall be finished in a minute, then you'll be able to lock up after me and go away to bed."

"Lock up after you?"

"I'll light the candles in S'bina's room—they're thick an' long and I think they'll burn all the night—and then I must be goin' 'ome."

"You bain't goin' 'ome to-night, be yer?" Fear, scarcely driven out, had returned.

"Why, of course I be. Surely you bain't afraid to stay 'ere?

"Well—there'll be no one in the 'ouse but me."

"Why, S'bina won't 'urt 'ee! Poor sawl, she's gone past 'urtin'."

He would be left alone with this strange incalculable Sabina who sprang surprises on him, from whom not even his most private belongings were safe and who had been wronged. The shadow of past horrors, the horrors of the preceding night, fell on him.

"I can't stay 'ere alone," he said. "I can't. No, I can't."

"Well, my dear, there's the children to see to, and the 'ouse and everything. Besides there's no bed for me to sleep in if I do stay 'ere and I'm tired as a dog."

He was unable to offer a suggestion but his anxiety was written so plainly on his face that Mrs. Tom would not deny him. If he were afraid to be left, she must stay.

"I'll see what Tom got to say," she began uncertainly, and the trouble died off Leadville's face. He looked about him and said in an excusing tone:

"'Tis a whisht old house, so it is."

"Well now," said Mrs. Tom who, after a little thought, had seen how she would manage, "I'll be off 'ome and whiles I'm gone you bring the li'l bed from the top room and I'll make it up when I come down."

"I want for 'ee to 'av a decent bed." He was for once considerate.

"Search out a blanket or two for me and I shall be all right."

Her manner was matter of fact, but more than once that evening Leadville had given her food for thought. Why should he be so uneasy, so irritable and why, oh why, should he be frightened of the one creature on earth who had held him dear? "When I've time," said Mrs. Tom to herself as she went up the road, "I'll ponder it in my mind."

"'Twas Aunt Sabina's wish for us to be married then, she made the arrangements." Gray was glad to make this known. She would not have people think that she had married without the countenance of her family and, in particular, of the aunt who had been so good to her. So much had happened since the morning of her wedding-day, she was so different a person from the shy and frightened girl who had driven out of Wastralls yard, that she had almost forgotten the menace of Byron's love. Uncle Leadville had been the ogre of her story but her marriage had changed the ogre back into a man and she could speak frankly to him of Aunt Sabina's part in what had been done. She was far from guessing that her simple words would take from him a last delusion; yet, as she spoke, she saw his face change and she wondered.

The people, too, were uneasily conscious that he had not taken the announcement of his niece's marriage as they would have expected. What was wrong? No whisper had ever linked her name with his, moreover, Sabina was but three days dead. They wondered over his grey strained face, his eyes which saw what was withheld from them and, into their wonder, crept a tinge of apprehension.

While they hesitated Byron flung into the silence—as a bomb is flung into a crowd—his bitter thought.

"I took 'er life and she've served me out for it."

A thrill ran through the listeners. With their Celtic perception they had been aware of half-seen forces and thoughts, of shadows moving remotely, of a background from which unforeseen events might issue. Not for a moment did they believe Byron's wild statement, they only realized he was, in some way unknown to them and beyond their guessing, a guilty man; and upon them began to press the feeling that a spirit was abroad, a spirit which, like clouds swept up from the rim of the sea, might be winged with unknown and ruinous possibility.

"She knawed," he said; and in his voice was awe and an emotion more poignant, more personal. Piercing the many veils he had found the ultimate, that ultimate which mercy hides. He understood at last that he had been living in a world of illusions and that Sabina, kindly, tolerant, had left him there. She had not taken them seriously, had not perhaps realized they were heady stuff which might give off the vapour of death. From start to cruel finish she had preserved her careless superiority, and now when he thought her bested had turned in her grave and laughed. By a word, scribbled in haste at an odd moment, she had made a mock of his pretensions, put him in his place. Secret humiliation is the black and bitter bread of which all shall eat but to be set at naught before his fellows breaks a man. "Like a twig in 'er 'ands I was," and he snapped his big fingers, like one snapping a stick in two. From the beginning Sabina had been the better man and his revolt had been as hopeless as that of a child.

"A life for a life," he muttered, using a phrase with which he was familiar, twisting a little its plain meaning. Sabina was taking from him, not his life but the fullness thereof, she was leaving him the vessel but leaving it irreparably damaged, like an old bucket through the holes of which the grass may grow.

Byron's eye rose to the gun suspended over the door. The feel of it would be comforting. It was his only possession. Sabina's money was nothing to him, let it go with the rest but the old gun...

It seemed to him far away. Between him and it rose, like an insuperable obstacle, the faces of the relatives. He saw in these faces always the eyes, the eyes that had witnessed his humiliation. Behind them were the brains that knew him now for what he was, a poor thing, futile, impotent. If he could but reach the old gun he would take it and he would go.

What an intolerable burden were the eyes!

Mrs. Tom, seeing Byron glance at the gun, hanging in its thongs over the lintel, misread his mind. She had been anxiously on the watch but by degrees had lost her fear that he was dangerous. To himself, perhaps, but no longer to others. Gray's marriage, presented as an accomplished fact, had done its work. No longer a wild desire, she was only a loss among others; but the sum total of these had been sufficient, Mrs. Tom thought, to bring home to the unhappy man his sin. Conscious of guilt, he might be driven to a further recklessness, might feel that, for such as he, was only the one way out. Knowledge is responsibility and Mrs. Tom was moved by her sense of justice to intervene. Byron should know the truth, that truth which she had kept even from Tom, which she had hidden in a fold of her mind, wrapping it up and putting it out of sight.

"Leadville," she said, leaning forward between her husband and his cousin and speaking without any premonition of the event she was precipitating, "rest yer 'eart content. She never drinked that cocoa that you meant for 'er to."

For a moment the burden of those intent eyes was lifted from Byron. The people turned towards Mrs. Tom. What was she saying? What lay between Byron and the woman whom only that afternoon they had committed to the earth? "I took 'er life," the man had said, flinging their curiosity a bone of fact. They were learning now that the bone had had meat on it.

"Never drinked it?" Byron did not evince any surprise at Mrs. Tom's knowledge, did not feel any. He was only conscious of his overwhelming need to escape—to escape from the eyes. His mind seized on this new fact, examining it with an anxious care. What was it to him? Would it show him the way out?

"No, 'twas that 'eavy supper. Doctor said so and it was. I saved the cocoa and 'tis out there in the jug."

On finding the drink untouched when tidying the room on the morning of Sabina's death, she had set it aside. Cocoa can be warmed up. Putting it on the linhay shelf she had not thought of it again until Leadville, walking in his sleep, had revealed the nature of the draught. Even then she had not thrown it away. It was evidence which might be needed. "'Tis out there still," and with a slight movement of the head she indicated the linhay. If she could convince Byron that he was not guilty of his wife's death, she might lessen for him his sense of overwhelming disaster, wring the black drop out of his remorse.

To the broken man only the irony of it came home and it came home so overwhelmingly that, in the bitterness of his spirit, he laughed. He had had a vision of Sabina hanging the sword of fate over his head, hanging it on the thread of her life, a thread which he, in a moment of amazing folly, had cut. But nothing of the sort had happened. Her dying was no tragedy of stealthy murder but the scrapping by nature of a worn-out organism. The memory of past emotion, of grizzly fears, of things tremendous and dire and sinister, passed before him—a procession of wraiths! They had had no foundation in fact, they had risen out of his mind, preposterous things, as preposterous as he. For what had he done? Nothing! Like a puppet, a creature of wire and paste-board, he had pranced and waved his arms. Never—not at the beginning, not during the long years of his servitude, not even when he had tried to burst his bonds, had he been anything but impotent. He had loved Wastralls—to no purpose! He had loved Gray and, while he dreamed, another had been at the wooing; even the crime he would have committed was fallen like a spent arrow at his feet. He had set out to prove himself the man of blood and iron who would force his way, through demon hosts and the flaming swords of heaven, to gain his ends; he who was destined to fight with shadows for a dream.

Sabina's death from heart-weakness after hard work and a heavy supper, was fate's last jest at his expense. Life had justified his wife's light estimate of his powers and he, who had believed himself able to control circumstance, had been proved harmless as a tame ranter in a booth. Futile, impotent! The tides of darkness were rising in the wide low room, were rising about the people, hiding all but the watching eyes. Leadville was conscious of coldness. A dark world and cold. Had he ever thought that he was young, that he was strong, that there was no man in Trevorrick who could 'put it across him'? That must have been long ago.

What a thing was this impotence! Like a brown shrivel in place of a nut-kernel it was rottenness but not dissolution. To live day after day through interminable time and see the spread of the black mould, to long for that last mercy of the mould! Life, the pricking life of kisses, the ecstasy of the first-born, the content of ripening, can become leprous, a thing to escape from at any cost. Damnation? Ay, a threat, the threat of ignorance. No hell that any future life may hold can equal what we know and, if the gate be open...

Isolda Rosevear had said, "I saved the cocoa, 'tis out there still," and, in the chambers of the man's distraught mind, the words echoed helpfully.

"Sabina left the cocoa a-purpose," he said and saw the way clear. "She left it——" For him too, as for all living creatures was hope, the hope of deliverance. In sudden haste, he turned and went out. Delay had been his curse but the need he was about to satisfy was so imperative that he did not stay even to complete his sentence.

On the linhay shelf, apart from other cloam, stood the brown high-girdled jug. Though the place was in darkness Byron's hand went out to it as unerringly as when he sought the blue phial in the wall cupboard: and, as he lifted it down, he heard with an eager thankfulness the sound of liquid swishing against the earthenware.

Sabina, knowing how much he could stand, had made ready for him a way of escape. "She left it for me," he said and, with a sob of relief, lifted the brown jug to his lips.

# CHAPTER XX

A death in the family brings to some members of it unwelcome holiday. Tom Rosevear, though not particularly fond of his cousin, would not have thought it 'decent' to do more work than was necessary on the day 'poor S'bina 'ad gone 'ome'; and when he had shot 'a wild duck or two,' counted the seventy-three red-brown bullocks of his herd and arranged for the death of a nineteen-score pig, he found time hang heavy on his hands. Without his wife, Tom was like a whip-handle without a lash. Once or twice during the afternoon he put his head in at the door, but finding only Gray, went off again. He was as dissatisfied as a dog with a sore toe and, though when evening darkened he sat down with the children and took his tea, he ate without relish. The room which Gray, ashamed of previous slackness, had set in order, was homelike and snug; but in his thoughts Tom found vague fault with it. The old sofa was shabby and the oilcloth worn, the place too was small, too small for so large a family. When the meal was over he fetched the last number of the *Cornishman* from the parlour table and set himself, unhappily, to read the paragraphs that bore on matters agricultural: and it seemed to him—the lack of one being the lack of all—that even the *Cornishman* was dull.

The hum of good-natured clack, of bubbling irrepressible life, that note which is peculiarly the note of a growing family and which was characteristic of Hember, had sunk to the merest suggestion of a sound. The younger girls, having stayed away from school, showed by an inclination to bicker that they missed their regular routine of work. Gray, absorbed in her own affairs, was silent; while Richbell, who had been trimming a hat and found her mother's fingers were needed to give the smartening touch, sat staring at the unsatisfactory result of her industry. As the evening wore on, one by one, the children slipped cheerlessly away to bed. Gray, who had lighted a fire in the parlour, went to sit there with her sweetheart and, upon the usually pleasant kitchen, settled an unsatisfactory hush.

"'Tis time mammy was home," said Richbell as the rain of a sudden shower beat on the window and went singing on across the shelterless land.

Tom, who had been nodding over the newspaper, looked at his feet. "If I 'adn't took off me boots, I'd go down and fetch 'er." He was a man of

medium height who spoke slowly, fetching up his words like water from a well, fetching them, too, with considerable creaking of the machinery. In appearance he was spare and hard, with a Viking moustache and close dark hair which fitted to his skull like a cap. His wisdom being only of the heart he was likely to remain in that state of life to which it had pleased God to call him. His wife could rely on him for counsels of moderation, she could rely also on an affection which, like home-brewed, was good from the froth to the dregs.

"I can hear steps," cried Richbell, her discontented face brightening and, as she spoke, Mrs. Tom, the raindrops shining on the wool of her bonnet, her cheeks flushed by the quick walk uphill, came in. "Oh, mammy," said the girl in tones that were themselves a welcome, "we thought you was lost."

Tom laid aside the *Cornishman*. "Just thinking you was pisky-laid'n," he said, with the smile on which she had rested her heart content for many a year. So glad was she of it after the discomfort, the hinted mystery of the evening that, as she passed his chair, she pressed her cheek for a moment against his. He responded by catching and pulling her down upon his knee.

"Take and sit down 'ere a minute," he said, in his most cheerful tone. Mrs. Tom was a busy creature, strong to work and to manage and it was not often that her spirit flagged, that she showed the need of a stay. "Now tell us all what you bin doing."

From the room beyond, Gray and Jim, their love-dreams shattered by the sound of an arrival, came to round out the circle. They had been sitting in the firelight, discussing the projected journey to Plymouth and the disagreeable ways of Uncle Leadville. It did not surprise them to find Mrs. Tom throned on her Jim's knee, for they believed in the permanency of 'sweet-hearting.' What were twenty years?

In the home atmosphere—the atmosphere created by her return—Mrs. Tom was able to dismiss the dim but ugly suspicions Leadville's manner had engendered and take a simple, more prosaic view of his state. The man was, as he had said, 'carried off' and the strangeness of his looks and words were due in all probability to the shock he had received. He had not loved Sabina but, to lose her thus suddenly, had unnerved him. Let him have a good night's rest and he would be his usual brusque and sombre self. She turned from the thought of him to give her attentive hearers a recital of the day's events. They would like to know who had called and what had been said, would like to take part at second hand in the stir caused by Sabina's death. Tom had a further interest. His mind had grasp. Unable to originate, he could adapt and improve, and he was anxious to hear what arrangements were being made for the funeral.

"I think," said Mrs. Tom, at last, and there was a question, perhaps even a glint of unkindly hope in her tone, "I think Leadville, poor old chap, want for me to sleep down there to-night for company. What d'yer think about it, Tom?"

Rumblingly, out of the depths, came his considered fiat. "I don't see why you can't."

"No—o."

"The maidens 'ere," he glanced at his pretty daughters, "the maidens 'ere are big enough to look after the childer and me. I don't think I should care to be left by meself if I was in 'is place."

"I don't s'pose you would." And with the ghost of a sigh she got up. "Well, to-morrow I shall make arrangements with Mrs. Bate. Might 'ave done it to-day, but I forgot. Now I'll go. 'Tis no good putting off the evil hour; still, you do all seem pretty and comfortable in here." Never had the little room, the close quarters, seemed so attractive; and Tom too, looking round, found his discontent had evaporated. It was a jolly snug little place, so it was.

He went with her to the door and they found that, between scudding clouds, the moon was showing a bright face. The lane lay white between the stone hedges with their crown of tamarisk and, at its foot, the Trevorrick River ran with faint occasional sparkle across the sands. Mrs. Tom had warmed her heart at the domestic fire. What was one night away? She could look back at Tom, standing on the doorstep, and send him an affectionate good night. After all, in keeping Leadville company, she was doing what Sabina would have wished.

When she reached Wastralls she found an empty kitchen. Leadville, following her directions, had brought down a small bed, set it in the angle of the wall, between table and linhay door and, that done, had gone to his own. The lamp was burning brightly, the fire glowed red between the bars, the cushions of Old Squire's chair, the cloth on the side-table, made notes of cheerful colour and the room, dark-raftered, whitewashed, had an encouraging homeliness of aspect. A pang of loss stabbed Mrs. Tom, for this had been her friend's home—had been! Only yesterday those brave blue eyes of hers had rested contentedly on objects made familiar by a lifetime of careful use. Sabina, to Mrs. Tom, was not dead. She had gone away, exchanged this known and comfortable world for things new and strange. The other was bound to believe the change was for the better; but after all a change is a change. She wished the veil that now hung between herself and Sabina were not so thick, so deadening; she wished, with a sad heart, that

she might have been permitted to draw it aside. There must be much Sabina would like to tell her.

The candles in the justice-room were burning steadily. Before arranging the pile of pillows and blankets Leadville had left ready, Mrs. Tom stole down the passage and went in. She must say good night to Sabina, this Sabina who could not hear. She looked to see that no draught was filtering through blind and curtain to set the lights guttering, then turned to her friend; but, as her glance fell on the set cold face, she had a sense of disappointment. Sabina was so remote. No word of hers could carry so far, nor could the eager seeking of her spirit find this other which for so long had been in touch with hers. The figure in the bed was not Sabina. It was the cloak she had worn and, taking off, had thrown away. It had been shaped to her uses, it had been hers, but that was all.

Turning away, she closed the door on it and went back to the kitchen. The ache of her loss, realized in this quiet hour, was a gnawing pain but she had been at work from before dawn and her limbs were heavy. Extinguishing the lamp, she settled herself between the blankets. As her eyes accustomed themselves to the change of light she saw that the room was not in darkness. Pale diamonds of moonlight lay on floor and table, filling the space with a soft greyness in which the few articles of furniture, the tables, the big chair and the glazed cupboard, loomed darkly clear. In spite of grief, Mrs. Tom was too tired to be wakeful. Her eyelids closed on the familiar objects which spoke so loudly of Sabina and she fell asleep.

A little later, but while the moon was still a mild radiance lighting the low warm room, she was roused—and being the mother of young children she slept lightly—by a distant but regular sound, the sound of approaching steps. Sick or sleepless or frightened little ones often stole to her bedside and she awoke therefore, not to fear but a kind readiness. As she opened her eyes she realized that she was not in her sea-scented upper chamber at Hember, but this did not alarm her. Too unself-conscious for small timidities, her mind leaped to the surmise that Leadville, having been 'twitchy-like' all day, was worse. Before he thrust back the kitchen door she was considering which of the simple remedies at her command would prove most beneficial.

"Why Leadville, whatever's the matter..." she was beginning when something about him, some departure from the normal, checked her words; and she perceived that, though he had come into the room with head thrust forward in everyday fashion, his aspect was unusual. His features were set and his eyes had an inward look. It was as if something behind his eyes and not they themselves, were looking out. He was staring across the room and his glance had focused itself on the wall behind Mrs. Tom. She had thought

he saw her but, in a moment, she realized her mistake. He was not aware of her, in fact was looking through her. To him she was unsubstantial as the sea-mist, nay as the warm air of the kitchen. His was the illumination of a dream. The objects he saw were not the actual furnishings of the kitchen but the figments of a mind asleep.

Mrs. Tom, who had seen children walking in their sleep, recognized the look. It was as if an intelligence, banished to some remote cell of being, had seized the opportunity of slumber to assert itself. The body moved, but unconsciously and as if under a spell. It obeyed, but clumsily and as if it had a difficulty in interpreting the wishes of this new master.

She was not alarmed but at a loss. The children 'walked' when they had eaten too many raw blackberries or had sat overlong at their lessons or been frightened; and Leadville, 'poor sawl too,' was only a big child. He had had a shock and this was the result. She wondered what she had better do? A little maid could be led back to bed and tucked in again and left, but Leadville? She decided to wait and see. Perhaps, in a minute or two, he would go of himself.

Meanwhile the sleep-walker, after standing by the door for some moments, had crossed the room and seated himself on the window-bench. Mrs. Tom was tired and very drowsy. Reassured as to his needs and purpose, she found it difficult to remain awake. Her lids were closing, her mind was drifting from the contemplation of his dark and motionless figure and she was nodding off again, when the elbow on which she was leaning, slipped. Jarred into wakefulness she glanced hastily at Leadville. For a moment she had been oblivious of him. She hoped to find that he had gone quietly back to bed, but no, he was still sitting in the moonlight.

To Mrs. Tom it seemed either that the moonlight was particularly bright or that she saw by it more clearly than usual, for not only was Byron's figure clear and sharp but his features were darkly visible. She could see that he was interested in something which was taking place on the other side of the room, that his eyes moved as if watching some one who, to Mrs. Tom, was invisible.

"Old chap see something," she thought and, looking at the blank space about the hearth, felt her flesh creep. Of a folk who accept the supernatural, the unusual, without doubt or question, she took it for granted that Leadville in his sleep-walking condition would have powers to which she could not pretend. That what he saw he had first created, did not occur to her. What moved about the hearth was, she believed, actually there; and she was intensely, tremulously interested. Who could it be? Sabina?

She had at first supposed that, unnerved by his wife's sudden and unexpected death and with his self-control relaxed by sleep, he had not been able to resist the inclination to wander restlessly about the house. She had had to admit, however, that there was more in this sleep-walking than mere shock and restlessness. Byron was conscious in a peculiar way, conscious of things and events. He saw something and this something or somebody, was moving about as if engaged on a domestic task. Could Sabina, having put off mortality, be here in the spirit; was her wraith haunting the rooms familiar to her, viewlessly busy in the old way? Mrs. Tom strained her eyes in a pathetic attempt to catch a glimpse of the dear long-known features and full figure, but no spectral greyness lightened the heavy obscurity of that part of the room and nothing moved, nothing that is, that she could see. She turned back presently to Leadville and it seemed to her that either the moonlight was brighter or she more observant, for now his face had grown so clear to her, its very expression could be seen. She looked at him and then began hurriedly to hope she had been mistaken and that the unseen form he was watching was not Sabina's for, if it were, how should his gaze be at once so furtive and so menacing? What did it mean?

If, at the suggestion of an unseen companion her flesh had crept, what was her state when in Leadville's eye she read a threat? Under her the little bed shook until she feared lest she might attract his attention.

She did not know that to him she was the invisible occupant of the room. His subconscious mind was reconstructing a scene out of the past in which she had no part and he was therefore entirely unaware of her. For some time he continued to follow the movements of the unseen person by the fireplace and, gradually, his intent look changed to a smile, a smile of satisfaction. He had learned what he would know and he was smiling to himself over it, smiling after such a fashion that the watcher shrank back and back until she was against the wall. This was a 'whisht' old house and she was alone in it with a dead woman and with this man.

Her thoughts, hitherto vague as mist, distilled a clear drop ... 'a dead woman and why dead?'

The question frightened her and, for a moment, she shut her eyes. If only she could have shut the eyes of her mind, for suspicion was one thing, actual knowledge another. But no, a word was being whispered in her unwilling ear and already, although she refused to admit it she knew what lay behind Leadville's terrifying smile.

That time last night a light had been burning in the kitchen, yet he had told her he was in bed by ten. She had doubted then and, during the day, had found a hundred reasons for continuing to doubt. If her mind had

swung uncertain, anxious to think generously, to discredit its own acumen, uncertainty was now over. The blood was drumming in her ears but, suddenly, above it rose the soft padding sound of a stockinged foot. Mrs. Tom opened her eyes quickly and from that moment forgot herself and her reluctance in an absorbed attention. For her the time was come when what was still hidden would be made clear. Leadville had got up from his seat and was crossing the room. He went directly to the wall cupboard, opened the green door and took something from the shelf. There was no groping, his hand fell at once on what was required and he turned away with it to the range. As if expecting to find a vessel of some kind on the top, he passed his hand slowly across the cavernous space. As it did not meet with an obstacle he paused and, for a moment, stood balancing in his habitual way from one foot to the other. Mrs. Tom saw that he was at a loss, that the directing impulse was no longer clear. In her curiosity, her distress, she had risen and followed him; and now stood by the table watching his face, his face which though the eyes were open was yet blind. On it trouble was depicted, trouble and anxiety. The onlooker had more than a suspicion of his purpose, knew indeed as well as if she had seen it what he held in his hand. Had he not cried out that the pipe Sabina had bought for him was poisoned?

She wondered what he had thought to find on the oven-top, what saucepan, kettle, pan. She had no doubt as to what he would do, but the actual means?

Leadville swayed from side to side in a long uncertainty and it was evident that his trouble grew. His face twitched, those unseeing eyes of his stared anxiously; and at last in a voice, hoarse and smothered, he uttered with immense effort two words:

"The ... jug..."

Startled by this desolate and abominable sound, Mrs. Tom shrank back from him. The words had come from those depths in which was lurking the guilty spirit of the man, they had come in spite of the swaddling bands of sleep, they had come laden and heavy laden. He wanted—a jug; and her thoughts flew to the jug that had stood on the table by Sabina's bed, the brown high-girdled jug which, after supper, was always placed on the oven-top that the contents might be kept warm until she was ready to drink them. Mrs. Tom remembered his expression when she had offered to brew cocoa for his supper—"Twas S'bina that drinked the cocoa.'

Byron had torn the veil from his deed. Mrs. Tom knew what was kept in the wall cupboard and where. She knew upon what bottle his hand had fallen. Presently she would make sure but she already knew. The measure meted to the old and damaged and useless of the farm animals had been

meted to Sabina; and the hand that poured the poison had been the one which owed her everything.

After that exclamation which seemed to have been torn from some remote corner of his being, Leadville's agitation began to pass. His disappointment, even his purpose was forgotten and, for some time, he stood quietly by the range, his face wearing a fixed but no longer an intent look. The impulse that had driven him remorselessly, which had reconstructed for him the scene of the preceding night, which had shown that, like Zimri, there was for him no peace, was fading.

The chill of the night had begun to invade the kitchen and the sleep-walker seemed to be dully conscious of discomfort. He shivered slightly, stirred and then slowly, heavily, turned away. During the last few minutes he had lost vitality, grown older; and it was a man shouldering the full burthen of his years who went out of the kitchen and up the shallow treads of the stair.

# CHAPTER XXI

The day following Sabina's death had been to Byron as a tract of hilly and dangerous country. He had traversed it, as he believed, without more than an occasional stumble and, at the day's end, had seen from the mountain-tops of sleep a vision of rich lands under the suns of fair to-morrows, a vision not altogether dispersed when he awoke. Springing out of bed he surveyed with eager hope the yellowing dawn. Mrs. Tom, being in no mind to trouble herself about him, he had been allowed to sleep on and, exhausted by the emotions, by the mental gymnastics of the previous day, he had done so until the eastern horizon was afire. From his upper window he looked up Trevorrick River, now December-full and purring over a wide bed of slates and quartz. The day was mild and still. A girl, in a blue coat and carrying a can, was crossing the stepping-stones and he recognized her as Jenifer Bate. The cloak hung in straight lines about her swelling figure and on her head was a gooky bonnet—a sort of winter sun-bonnet—which had belonged to her dead mother. She had brought Mrs. Bate down to Wastralls and was returning with milk for the people at Cottages. "She think weather'll be catchy," he said to himself with the joyous feeling that she was mistaken. The wind had dropped till not a breath stirred the beaded tamarisk but, far overhead, clouds were drifting lazily from the north. As long as they sailed the sky in that direction there would be no rain.

Below stairs the women were busy roasting chickens and otherwise preparing for the morrow. Sunday in the West is a time of rest from labour; of gathering in the chapels for friendly intercourse; but death, with a high hand, substitutes for local custom a universal law and not one of Mrs. Tom's helpers had failed her. In a corner of the kitchen a meal had been prepared for Byron and he slipped quietly into the chair set in readiness. For the first time since his wife's death he was conscious of flavour in the food. Breakfast was the good beginning of a good day and he ate and drank with relish. His mind had been like the sands at low water, a place of quags and pools and unsuspected rocks but now the tide of life had risen and he had forgotten what lay below. Yesterday was wholly gone and before him lay long hours— hours of realization, of happiness such as he had never before known. The women moved quietly about and in the midst of that orderly bustle Byron sat, speaking now and then in answer to some remark but always as if his

mind were preoccupied. The meal ended, he made perfunctory offer of his services but was relieved to find the work had been so arranged that his room was more desired by the women than his help.

"That one's glad to be gone out of it," said Mrs. Con as his heavy figure passed the window on its way to the waste lands; and all could see that Byron was no longer slouching along in the mooning and indifferent manner to which they were accustomed.

"He'm like Parson's Fool, like everything that's good, but don't want to work for't," remarked Aunt Louisa, her big scissors going 'crusp, crusp' through some black material that was spread over the table.

Mrs. Tom repeated in an indifferent voice, the old tag:

"'s'E 'av got fever o' lurk
Two minds to eat and none to work.'"

She was looking ill and, when the women commented on her appearance, had spoken of a sleepless night. She was in fact oppressed by the horror of her late experience. As she went about the tasks of the moment she was as if in a cloud, a cloud on which the scene of the previous night was reflected, now from one point of view, now from another.

Unable to forget it she threw herself into the work with an energy which aroused the admiration of the other women and made Aunt Louisa wonder. "She don't work 'ome like that," mumbled the old woman over her mouthful of pins, "nor I don't believe 'tis cos she was so fond of S'bina. That one know more'n we think she do," and throughout the day which, for Mrs. Tom, was unbearably long, a haunted miserable day, Aunt Louisa kept a thoughtful eye upon her.

Byron, striding out of the yard, struck across the wide spread of shallow water and up the natural rock embankment which, on that side of Trevorrick valley, prevented the sea from overrunning the 'wastralls.' The turf, cropped closely by his bullocks, clipping into the bright yellow green of marsh, breaking into grey spire-grass towards the west, stretched before him up the coast. With his happy feet he meant to beat the boundaries of the farm, of the goodly acres which, after a time of waiting longer than that of Jacob, were his. A tamarisk hedge ran north and south between the commons—which a century ago had been arid sand—and Hember fields. Byron, walking by this, looked across the undulating ground to the sandy ramparts on the sea-edge. Piled by forgotten tides they resembled in their tiny crests and hollows, their unexpectedness, their general conformation, the huddle of a mountain range. By them the plain behind was protected from the worst rigours of the Atlantic and Byron saw them as a useful factor

in his plan for the development of the commons. At present cattle pastured on the turf, rabbits flickered through the spire-grass and the wide space was quiet and at rest. It lay, peacefully, under the eye of day and that which moved on its green bosom moved as if time did not exist. But Byron meant to alter this, to change the face of the dunes. He would tear up the turf which fitted to the land as curling hair fits to a man's head and he would plant the seaward side with a sea-plant, with asparagus. Farther in, he would have strawberries. He knew they did well on the south coast, on the sandy strip beyond Southampton; and he planned a journey which should enable him to observe the methods of other men, which should teach him how to turn the sand beneath his feet into gold. As he walked by a clump of hawthorn and bramble he touched a rabbit gin and, with a sinister snap, the teeth came together. Byron pulled it out and reset it. He meant to rid the land of its rabbits and it pleased him to mark his intention; but gins and guns were ridiculously inadequate, his trapping would be of a more efficacious kind. It should exterminate.

Returning to the house for a midday meal he once more made perfunctory offer of his services.

"Funeral being to-morrow," said Mrs. Tom, and her glance gave him a momentary, quickly banished qualm, "of course there's things to be arranged out-of-doors as well as in. You'll 'av to clear the yard to make room for all the carts; and 'tis a pity there hain't time to give front door a coat of paint. 'Tis looking terrible grimy."

"I know the paint's rubbed off but there 'edn't time to do't now," said Byron and, lest she should have other suggestions to make, hurried through his meal and went out. A glance round the yard showed that old George was at work preparing the place for the influx expected on the morrow, an influx which would be welcome to Byron when it came but the thought of which was momentarily disturbing. Sufficient unto the hour the emotion thereof. This was the day of anticipation, the day between the end of the old order and the beginning of the new. He would not have it broken in upon by claims from either side. Shaking off thoughts of yesterday and to-morrow, as a man shakes raindrops from his coat, Byron turned out of the yard. This time he went uphill. Dark Head lay before him to the south and from its crest he could survey the good lands that sloped from the ridge—the cornfields and the cider orchard, the meadows between which Trevorrick River wound its way and above which St. Cadic Mill lifted a grey tower. Byron's heart sang to the rhythm of his striding feet and his mind busied itself with schemes. If the hinds would not work the land as he wished he would advertise for strangers, experienced men. He would find them cottages, there were some on the farm, Hindoo Cottage, Hesselwood,

Towan Veals. The men would keep each other in countenance. For all he was himself a 'foreigner,' he knew how the country people would look on these strangers. But in the end, when he was reaping his fat harvests, when one field was bringing in what would cover the rent of a farm, the folks about would change their note. He saw himself on the crest of the wave, a man who had fought his way to the top, who had deserved what he had won. And how much more than the material award would that winning be!

From where he stood on the landward slope of Dark Head, the slope that was washed by the morning and the midday sun, his glance fell naturally on the square outstanding block of Hember, the cheery ugly house, grey but with its many bright windows set in white cement, the house which had some far-off look of a hive and about which was always the murmur of life. A sunny garden, sunk between stone walls, between black wind-bent firs, ran down to the road and in it a girl was moving from patch to patch of earth. His heart leapt for, as her hair gave out no dazzle of light beneath the sun, he knew it must be Gray. He would have known without that indication, without any; his blood would have recognized her in the dark. His 'little umuntz!' The significant black gown gave her an unfamiliar look but, in his eager pleasure at the sight of her, he missed the difference, missed too another difference, that change that comes to fruit when, after hanging green upon the bough, the sun has warmed it to ripeness and a hand, a desirous hand, has gone out to it. From time to time Gray stooped over the garden beds. She was picking the flowers that yet lingered in sheltered nooks, the flowers of the dying year and those that were burgeoning to greet the new. A rosebud that would never open hung on the brier, a few snowdrops had pushed up from their bulbs. Gray was binding her treasure-trove with a long dark hair. Flowers from Hember garden should lie between Sabina's dead fingers and go down with her into the grave; and, as the girl moved from one lew corner to another, her tears fell on the old roots and on the blossoms in her hand. Leadville watching, wondered what she was about. His mind being wholly occupied with the future, he had forgotten that past for which Sabina stood.

Until the flowers were gathered to the last bud he stood looking on and in his eyes was a kindliness strange to them. Gray, moving hither and thither on her loving task, showed young and helpless. Once she was his, once he had overcome her faint reluctance—and, thinking of it, his face hardened with resolution. He would take any measure he esteemed necessary to gain his end. But, once he had overcome the reluctance which he must admit, he would be good to her. He would live for her—for her and Wastralls. She should have no wishes that he would not gratify. She should be rich, looked up to and beloved; and what more could a woman want? The thought of

what he would do when Gray was his and Wastralls his, quickened his steps and he walked on, in a warm content, walked until he, even he, felt a weariness in his bones. A scarlet sun was setting in splendour over a milky sea as he made his way home. In the kitchen Mrs. Bate, now installed as housekeeper, had prepared a meal. He ate of it in happy silence, not missing Mrs. Tom, if anything pleased to have only a servant in the room. The place, with only the old women present, seemed more utterly his.

For a little he sat on by the hearth, his shirt open at the neck to the agreeable warmth of the fire, his eyes on the leaping blue and purple flames. It had been a 'borrowed' day, it had been full of happy anticipation, of planning no longer vague. To-morrow would be even better for, with its dawning, the countryside would gather to Sabina's funeral and all must recognize him as owner of the place. His heart sang a wild measure of triumph. He was no longer a man in the forties, moving with unimpaired strength yet with a growing stiffness, but one who had renewed his youth. That day had been the beginning. He was dreaming great dreams, passionate hot dreams, the dreams of a man with immense capacities for emotion. Mrs. Bate, shutting up for the night, broke in at long last on a vision of himself teaching a little son—his son and Gray's—to ride the black stallion; and, getting up, he stretched himself with a laugh, a laugh the old woman thought indecorous.

"You'm for overstairs? Well, so be I."

"Do I rake out the ashes, maister?" she asked timidly.

"Oh, leave'n be." He had no more use for petty economies than he had for petty spite. The day of small things was at an end.

To Mrs. Tom the revelation of the previous night had been as the rolling away of a mist from the face of a landscape already dimly familiar. Its horrific nature had banished sleep and darkened a natural grief but had not startled her by its unexpectedness. Subconsciously she had expected something of the sort to happen. She did not dwell on Sabina's stubborn withholding of the land, on her failure to understand the more emotional more desperate nature of her husband. She accepted it as a fact. Sabina had been like a person riding out to sea, who had believed fondly that she was only fording a river and, with patience and management, must presently find her horse's hoofs on the shingle of the opposite bank. Tragedy had been the outcome and this Mrs. Tom, with her sure instinct for life, had known would come to pass. Not even the form it had taken had seemed other than natural. A man's weapons are those to his hand, the things he has handled from his youth up, not something strange and foreign. Byron had poisoned his wife, as he had poisoned old Shep and many another used-up creature.

With the means to hand the only wonder was that he had not done it before. He had been married twenty years and every day must to him have been more unhappy and more disappointing than the last. Mrs. Tom was aware of the provocation he had received but accepted it as a cause, not an excuse. Because she saw it with the imagination of the country-woman who, having never been to a theatre is yet able to stage for her own pleasure the dramas being enacted within her reach, saw it with a deadly clarity from faint beginnings to the culmination, her moral sense was not the less outraged. Her attitude towards animals used for food had not affected her belief that human life was sacred; and Byron's crime, though easy to understand, was to her mind unpardonable.

But Mrs. Tom's attitude was not one of mere condemnation. That warm and pitiful heart had agonized through the dark hours over her friend's fate, over the snatching away of that fag-end which was all Sabina had of life. Sabina who had been so trusting, so simple! Well, she had not known. She was saved that. She had carried her optimism with her, her fond belief that all would come right, that discomforts were only of the moment and that peace must follow, peace and affection. Good, she would have said, must prevail. Mrs. Tom, reviewing that sunny faith, that placid acceptance of weather conditions, both in life and with regard to the land, that wholesome jovial point of view, felt her gorge rise against the man who had lived with Sabina without loving her who, for his own ends, had done her to death.

How had he dared? To that question Mrs. Tom could fit the answer. With Sabina living he could not hope to win Gray. Not because of Wastralls had he been moved to do this thing. Mrs. Tom, accustomed to the facile passions of the West, shrank from contemplation of an emotion so devastating. In a land where sexual lightness is looked on, not as sinful but inconvenient, where the village light-o'-love lives to a respected old age and the love-child has as many chances of success in life as he who bears his father's name, such a passion as that of Byron for Gray is rare. Mrs. Tom, although she knew, could hardly believe. She was thankful there could be nothing in it, that Gray had made her choice; yet with that thankfulness went the pricking of a further doubt. If Byron had done so dire a deed in order to clear his path, how would he act when it was brought home to him that his deed was to make no difference, that the path was blocked for him beyond all clearing? Mrs. Tom was angry for Sabina, but for Gray she was afraid. Would Jim be able to protect her? He was, after all, only a young chap. Between her anger and her fear she hung in sore trouble until the hour struck that ushered in another workaday morning.

Mrs. Tom was glad to leave the blankets. She had tossed among them till they seemed all hair and hardness, and it was a relief to fold them away

and begin the labours of the day. 'Great Thomas,' the other hind, so called because he gave promise in limb and shoulder of unusual strength, came in with the milk. 'Uncle George' brought the tale of his requisitions among the farm-labourers of the vicinity and, by the time the kitchen was ready and the sewing-machine in place, Mrs. Tom's helpers were beginning to arrive. Never had their familiar faces been so welcome to her. By companionable talk they were to banish the haunting terror of the night and it seemed at first as if this might be. Before long, however, Mrs. Tom found that the effect on her mind of Leadville's revelation was darker, more insistent than she had believed. Between her and the everyday talk came the sleep-walker and she saw again Leadville's smile. At times during the morning she could, so great was the tension, have cried out.

That smile ...

It had been a writing on the wall, the interpretation of which was death and, though she carried this ghastly knowledge in her breast, she must behave as usual, or Aunt Louisa— — She knew instinctively it would be Aunt Louisa, always taking soundings, who would guess. Perhaps even now ...

She glanced up suddenly and met that cool grey eye fixed on her consideringly. Yes, Aunt Louisa was awake to every scent and sound. Marvellous old creature! She must be seventy, yet age had not impaired her faculties, had not taken from her the power of scenting out a mystery, of satisfying her avid curiosity. The feeling that she was already suspicious had a stimulating effect on Mrs. Tom. She pulled herself together and, plunging into the work, was successful for a time in banishing a too-persistent memory.

Nevertheless, when in the late afternoon the house was adjudged ready for the morrow and the women, all but Mrs. Bate, prepared to go, Mrs. Tom's relief was unspeakable. The dead woman lay in her coffin, legs in place; the leaves had been fitted into the parlour table and the best damask spread upon it. Floors, windows, paint, every corner was meticulously clean and on the linhay shelves were stacked cold meats in generous provision. Everything must be as Sabina would have wished and it was in the minds of all that, at this her funeral feast, Sabina was still hostess. Byron's claim to be owner had by them been tacitly ignored. As long as Sabina was above ground Wastralls was hers, and it was from her dead and silent lips that they had taken their orders.

Driven by Mrs. Tom's example they had worked hard and as they went together up the lane, after the manner of tired bodies, they spoke but little. She herself, unable to stave off any longer her troubled thoughts, walked

quickly and, as she turned in at her own gate, bade them a good night she had some ado to keep from being tremulous. She was overwrought. She wanted to get back to Tom, to his affection and his good counsel; and her heart, running before, whispered that a certain shoulder in an old coat was the one safe and comfortable pillow for a tired head.

As she crossed the threshold, intent on pouring out her troubles and finding heartease, she heard the sound of voices. It being Sunday, Gray, who played the harmonium at the little chapel, had gone thither; but the other maidens uncertain what, in the circumstances, was expected of them, had not ventured to accompany her. They were gathered in the kitchen where Tom, too, was sitting. Mrs. Tom, controlling herself to a last effort, told them she was sure their auntie would not have wished them to stay home from chapel on her account. Better for them the sight of kindly faces, the familiar routine of the service, than this brooding quiet.

"An' yer mournin's is all made up ready. 'Tis wonderful that they have been done so smart. Aunt Louisa is the quickest 'and for 'er needle I ever seen in my life."

While, with the dilatoriness natural to young people, they fastened strings and hooks Tom, from his seat on the old sofa, asked her concerning the funeral. A burial, like a birth or a marriage, was part to him of the pageant of life; and each part brought its particular and pleasurable emotion.

"I expect the people from all around'll be 'ere," he said in measured tones and to each syllable he gave its due volume of sound. He spoke with effort but the sounds he produced were strong and full of substance, rough sounds and not in the least mellow but satisfying to the ear as home-made bread is to the inner man. "You've provided a plenty of food for them 'aven't yer?"

"Plenty of everything, I believe," said his wife and there was a note in her voice, a note of tension, which he recognized but did not understand. What had upset her? Was she still grieving or was she overtired? "We shall 'av tea in the kitchen for the bearers and a table laid in the Big Parlour for the mourners. Now Rhoda, make haste or the others'll be to Church Town before you'm started."

"'Twill be a pretty grand sight," pursued Tom, "with so much people. I bet 'twill be the finest funeral that 'av been for many a year."

Mrs. Tom saw the last loiterer on her way and, returning, sat down on the cushioned stool which was generally occupied by Smut. The old cat, thus dispossessed, sprang into her lap and pushed its little pointed face

against her hand. But Mrs. Tom put it down. "No, Smutty, I 'aven't got the 'eart to take yer up to-night."

"Ah, mother," said Tom, fancying he had found the key to her haggard looks, "I'm afraid you're missin' poor S'bina. 'Tis a sad thing for yer. I don't believe there's a day gone but you've seen one another."

"Iss, I do miss 'er and I shall miss 'er." But her acquiescence, lacking fullness, showed him he had not reached the heart of the matter.

"Well and what is it?" he asked and in his rough full tones and his eyes, was the kind comprehension of which she stood in need.

"Tidn't 'er dyin' I'm thinkin' about, 'tis 'ow she did die."

"'Er goin' so suddint?" said Tom, cautiously.

"No, nor 'tidn't that uther but—well, it do look very funny and there's things I've seen—" she paused, gazing anxiously at her husband. "Old chap surely done something—between you and I."

"Old chap 'av?" Tom's face, expressive as was natural to one who helped out his words with gesture, showed a deepening interest. "You don't mean it? Why do 'ee think so?"

Thus encouraged she plunged into her tale and, though she told it in rambling fashion, with discursions and superabundant detail, it was convincing. The interpretation Isolda put on Byron's sleep-walking was one Tom could accept. Simple and primitive, such a deed did not seem to him impossible. It was wrong, it was wicked, but it might happen and his wife told him that it had. Poor Sabina, and she had had no idea what sort of a man she was marrying and what she was bringing on herself! A black heart if ever there was one, but what could you expect? Tom was visibly moved. He punctuated his wife's tale with exclamations of ruth and horror but he did not feel it as deeply, as emotionally, as she. Mrs. Tom thought of Byron vindictively and with a personal animus. She would have been glad to see him taken to gaol, to have had him hanged; but to Tom he was still what he had always been—an intruder. The willingness to "eave 'alf a brick' at his head had been there from the beginning and Tom was of those who wait and do not trouble but who, if the opportunity occurs, will seize it.

"Well, do seem funny, sure, mother," he said as his wife made an end. "Nothin' 'scapes your eyes, I knaw."

But Mrs. Tom wanted more than generalities. "What should you do?"

"If 'e done it, 'twas tarr'ble wicked of'n."

"Tarr'ble, sure."

"But 'tis done now," he said slowly. "Poor S'bina can't be fetched back."

She caught at the suggestion. "I only wish she could then. 'Twould be a great blow for'n."

"Iss, 'twould, and any'ow if 'e've done what you think 'e 'av, she'll surely haunt'n."

"I don't believe 'e'll care even if 'e is haunted." In her desire for tangible punishment she showed a waning faith in other influences.

"No, p'raps 'e won't. But 'e knaw 'e've done it and the Lorrd knaw and 'e'll be brought to judgment."

"You think it'll come to light some day?" she asked eagerly.

"I dunno about that, God's ways bain't our ways."

"Well, what should you do about it?"

He considered. "I should 'old me tongue and say nothing about it, if I was you. 'Cos if't got to policeman's ears you'd be 'ad up for your words."

His caution, that of a law-ignoring folk who manage their own affairs and keep silence concerning them, did not satisfy her.

"But if he did do't," she persisted, "'e ought to be punished."

"You knaw, mother, there's no proof so 'tedn't no good to say anything about it."

"Well," she said sharply, "there's this—bottle's gone out of cupboard! What's become of it? I s'pose that won't be any proof? And Leadville seem to be very uneasy, but that won't be any proof uther? And I feel sure in me bones and veins 'e wanted for 'er to die, but that's no proof?"

Tom was not to be moved. "A still tongue," said he, "make a wise 'ead and anyway a craikin' tongue do often mean a sore one."

She gave up the attempt to influence him. "I s'pose then, I shall 'av to rest me 'eart content, but you've no idea 'ow desperate towards 'im I feel. Knowin', too, that 'e owes 'er everything, for what was 'e, nothing but a come-by-chance? And for 'im to serve 'er like 'e 'av!"

"I reckon 'e's like one of they cuckoos. They do say cuckoo hi-ists the other li'l birds out o' the nest."

She was paying but scant attention. "I don't feel I can bear to speak 'im civil. Tidn't," she added mysteriously, "for what 'e've done but for what 'e've tried to do. Doctor, 'e said she died of 'eart failure and I s'pose doctor ought to know."

Tom could not follow his wife's flying thought. "Well," he said in those rough full tones which contained the very body of sound, "I don't believe doctors knaw everything. If they did 'twould make a fine newspaper. Nobody told Dr. Derek about the cocoa. He thought she 'ad 'er supper as usual and then died off suddint in 'er sleep."

"Iss," said Mrs. Tom thoughtfully and passed a hand over Smut who, accepting the fact that her mistress was too much engrossed in making mouth-noises—the main occupation of human beings—to pet her, had climbed quietly back into her lap and gone to sleep. "Iss—doctor didn't know anything about the cocoa."

She, herself, knew more than any one but was disinclined to impart the knowledge. After all it was not the act that damned a man but the intention; and she did not want Tom to think Leadville less guilty than he seemed to her. She remained silent going back over their talk and, on the whole, she found it comforting. Tom, deprecating the idea of human interference, had given utterance to one pregnant sentence: "'E knaw 'e've done it and the Lorrd knaw and 'e'll be brought to judgment."

"Iss, the Lorrd knaw," she told herself, "and I can see as old chap won't 'av everything 'is own way; but I wanted more'n that, I—I wanted S'bina to git 'er own back." She hushed her vindictive longings with a common-sense reflection. "Well, don't s'pose she'd be any 'appier if she did."

# CHAPTER XXII

As the funeral procession was to leave Wastralls at 1.30 P.M., by eleven that morning the road from Four Turnings was black with farmers' carts, with people from the hamlets of Church Town, of Shoppe and of Cottages, with people who had come from the distant towns of St. Columb and Wadebridge. For three generations Mrs. Byron's family had taken a leading part in the affairs of the district. The memory of man went back to Old Squire—a personality so pronounced that it had obliterated the more shadowy figures of its ancestry. From Old Squire, who had added acre to acre, to Sabina Byron the bold yet conservative farmer, was but a life and imagination had leaped it. Like her grandfather she was an outstanding figure, a woman of whom the countryside had been half proud, half envious. The lamentable tragedy of her accident, setting her apart from struggling humanity, had affected the popular opinion. Successful beyond the ordinary she had in a twinkling been reduced to helplessness and, before interest in her—the tenacious interest of the agricultural mind—had had time to wane, the last misfortune had overtaken her. The people would follow her to her grave, not only out of respect for the Rosevears, but as a protest against fate which, not content with the inevitable, the building up or the breaking down, must introduce into the affairs of man, a harsh caprice.

On ordinary occasions people approached Wastralls by way of the yard but this being one of ceremonial the visitors went past the blind wall at the end and up the weed-grown avenue of 'grubby elms.' The double-leaved door, studded with iron heads, stood hospitably open and, on the hearth, a hearth which had not been modernized, a pile of seasoned wood was burning. On the stone chequers of the floor lay some faded rugs, the colours of which were yet bright enough to throw the sombre figures of the mourners into relief. The dull Oriental reds made a strange setting for these men and women from whom work and time had stolen the young comeliness and who, in their harsh ill-fitting black, appeared so awkward and ill at ease. The proportions of the hall were good but man, who had dreamed it and set it up, seemed unworthy of it, a poorer thing than that which he had made.

Beyond the entrance hall the parlours, giving on the passage, showed also an inviting face. These rooms, owing to the thickness of their walls, the smallness and eastern aspect of the many-paned casements, were gloomy. They smelt, not of the sea but its pervading damp and of the mould which crept like leprosy over boot and book and furniture. In both, fires had been lighted but the smoke showed little liking for the damp chimneys and, in the grates, the sea-coal smouldered without flame. In the Big Parlour the best china, silver and glass had been set out and a meal laid; and the gleam of polished surface, the white glow of the freshly laundered damask, the colour of the plates and dishes made a pleasant impression. Mrs. Tom and Richbell, rising early, had helped to carry from the linhay the food piled on its shelves. Fowls were at one end of the table, beef and ham at the other and between stood mountains of splits, bowls of Cornish cream, junkets and cake and pastry. The mourners as they came in would help themselves and plates, with darkly bright knives and shining forks, were stacked in readiness. The Little Parlour had, as far as possible, been denuded of furniture; for the mourners after they had eaten, would form up there in couples, ready when the coffin should have been brought forth, to follow it.

Tom Rosevear had prophesied a large gathering and the event justified him. The many who could 'call cousin' with Sabina Byron came through the deep winding lanes to take part in her funeral and besides these persons— literally 'the mourners'—were a number who did not go up to the house but stood about on Trevorrick Sands, waiting. Though lacking the right conferred by kinship—and in the West you are not invited to a funeral, you go, if a relative, as a matter of course—they, too, would follow her and see her committed 'earth to earth'; and so numerous were they that it was said afterwards that the only person in Tregols parish who did not attend Mrs. Byron's funeral was an old 'bedlier' of the name of Hawken and she, poor soul, had been bedridden up 'in the teens of years.'

Byron had carried with him overstairs a mood of serenity and content; but when he awoke in the morning his mental weather had changed from Set Fair to an uncertain condition of the mercury which expressed itself in a heavy dull sensation at the pit of his stomach. Waves of excitement were flowing through him. This would be a great day. Before a crowd of witnesses—and already they were leaving their distant homes, crossing in the ferry from Rock, coming by train from Wadebridge, driving in from Treremborne and Trerumpford and Treginnegar—Sabina would be finally dispossessed of Wastralls. He who, for so long, had taken second place would come into his own. It was he who would receive them. They would eat his bread, follow him in the long procession, acknowledge him as a neighbour, as a kinsman and, above all, as the owner of the farm. To

him, Sabina's funeral was a public ceremony. All men would see her laid to rest, or as he put it 'turned out'; all men would allow his right to enter into possession.

Wastralls! The thought of it was like wine running warmly through his body. Wastralls, his! His mind turned for a moment to the dreary waste of the past, he saw it stretching like the shifting sands of the coast-line to a grey horizon and, with a shudder, he came back. That was over. Thank God he had left those years behind; them and all that had to do with them. He acknowledged to himself, as he drew on his black clothes, that hitherto he had made no attempt to stand well with his neighbours. They had had hearts at ease while he had been gnawing his fingers in despite. It was his fault, nay not his but the fault of embittering circumstance, that he had no friends; but now that Wastralls was his, all this would be changed.

In spite of the warmth about his heart, in spite of his happy anticipations, when at last he found himself in the hall ready to receive the mourners, his courage began to ebb. The adventure was too crucial, meant too much to him. The sensation at the pit of his stomach which had been obliterated by those hot thrills of excitement, returned and in a more acute form. His feet grew cold and the occasion became an ordeal he could have wished were over.

The individuals, converging by train, by road, by ferry on Trevorrick were each an unknown quantity and he found that he was afraid of them and that, as the moments passed, he grew more and more afraid. As he stood by the hearth, listening for the sound of wheels which should announce the first arrival, his unstable nerves, working on his body, gave him a sensation of actual physical sickness. He turned to the chimney-piece and leaned his elbows on it, wondering how much longer he would be able to stand there.

Not far from him, her expressive face set in sober lines, Mrs. Tom Rosevear stood beside Mrs. Con. Their duty it was to receive the wives of the mourners and pass them on to Mrs. Bate who, as Stripper, would take them to pay the dead woman a last visit.

"I don't believe as you've been in to see poor S'bina," said Mrs. Tom to her companion. Byron's presence was disturbing to her and she spoke more by way of distracting her thoughts, than because she thought Betsy would care to pay the customary visit. "Why don't you go now before the rest come? There'll be plenty to do, directly."

Mrs. Con's stout body quivered a negative. "My dear life, I couldn't bear to see 'er. I should be picturin' of 'er everywhere if I did."

"Don't 'ee be so silly," encouraged the other. "I don't believe there's 'ardly any funeral in the parish but what I've seen them."

Mrs. Con sank her voice to a mysterious whisper. "'Av you never seed anything after, Isolda?"

"I never seed nothing worse then meself. More need to be afraid of the livin' than the dead."

"Well, my dear, you'm different to me. I'm that narvous if I was to see a body, I knaw I should ever after be fancying I seed its dead face."

A cart drove up to the open door and the Sowdens of Trerumpford, a childless couple who, even in that land of fat stockings were accounted well-to-do, came towards Byron. He had been for a moment in conversation with the undertaker who, the sixteen pairs of black gloves for the bearers in a parcel under his arm, was asking how soon it would be convenient for him to screw down the coffin.

"Mrs. Bate'll let you know," said Byron hastily and turned to shake old Sowden by the hand. Pleased that this important farmer should be the first to cross his threshold be showed it by his greeting; but to Beulah Sowden it made little difference how he was received. He was a little tight silent man, with glassy eyes and an unresponsive manner. Accepting Byron's cordiality with his usual reserve he left his wife, a faded person in a gooky bonnet, to offer their condolences. The Sowdens were come because Sabina Byron's mother had been cousin to Beulah and, as soon as the civilities incumbent on them had been duly observed, they stood aside to make room for others. Not a spark had Byron been able to strike from either. He glanced at them a little doubtfully as they went down the room. Was their reserve natural or assumed? They had uttered the customary phrases, in the customary way and their manner had been sufficiently friendly if a trifle, the least bit in the world, patronizing. It was difficult for him to grasp that, to the Sowdens and their like, the situation was in no way altered. He, though he had spent his life among them, must remain a 'foreigner.' Byrons they knew but he was no Byron, only a waif of the sea, who out of charity had been given the name.

In attending Sabina's funeral they were certainly accepting her husband as their host but they had the topsy-turvy feeling that her death had cancelled the connexion and that he, rather than she, had become the 'late lamented.' Under the politeness of their words had lurked a feeling that they were meeting him for the last time, that it would not be necessary to conceal much longer the faint hostility with which he inspired them. A fat inheritance had fallen to him, an inheritance which had belonged to men of their blood, and which they begrudged. The inheritance was land and

they loved land, loved it more than money or any other possession. This man, who so civilly bade them welcome, was one who, pushing his way in by the gate of marriage, had seized what was more theirs than his. Unable to dispossess him they were yet wholly unable to reconcile themselves. The Sowdens had made way for the Bennett Trudgians of Wadebridge, cock-eyed father and a daughter so vivid that, though in black, she made a rainbow impression. They were followed by a voluminous widow, Mrs. Andrew of Gentle Jane. She had called at Hember for Gray and with Gray had come Jim Rosevear. Byron, when his glance fell on the three, forgot his fancy that he was on trial as a new neighbour. He shook hands with Mrs. Andrew and he looked at Gray; and, as he looked, instinct told him that, in some subtle way, the spirit those soft contours shrined had expanded. He shook the thought away. This was Gray and he had not seen her for a weary while but she was not changed. How could she be? His hand closed eagerly over hers and he searched her face for a response—the old response of answering blood; but her eyes were downcast resting, as it happened, on her own gloved hand. It was as if that little hand were part of a mystery which had all her attention.

The intriguing thought persisted. Gray, secret and pale, yet with a suggestion of unfolding petals, woke in Byron a curiosity as intense as it was anxious. What had happened to her? What experience, in which he had had no part, was she cherishing behind that veil of civil words and smiles? His jealousy, never long quiescent, woke.

Already, however, new arrivals were surging in over the threshold. The moment was unpropitious and already Gray had withdrawn her hand. He could not hope for any words with her till the funeral was over. He must rest his heart on the fact that at least she was there under his roof and must remain till he was free to go to her.

The hour was one of conflicting feelings, as numerous as the stones in Trevorrick River which, in summer, is all stones and in winter brings down yet more of them. Behind Gray stood Jim Rosevear and Byron turned on him the old lowering scowl. There was a score to settle! The dark colour purpled in his swarthy cheek but, though he clenched his fists, it was in order to keep the peace, not break it. The insult conveyed by Jim's accompanying Gray in the sight of everybody could not be immediately avenged.

"My 'ands is tied," he thought, "and 'e knaws 'e can come 'ere to-day. Wants a lesson, that one do."

"The bearers are in the kitchen," he said, pitching his voice on a loud note and pointing to the passage. If he could he would humiliate Jim, show the countryside this was a labourer who had come to the wrong door, who

had not come as a mourner but for his half-crown, his meal, his pair of black gloves.

But in Rosevear he had met his match. "I'm 'ere as a mourner, not a bearer."

"Iss, my dear!" began Mrs. Andrew in a softly flowing voice and launched herself on a vague explanation in which the words 'Rosevear of Treketh and Dusha Rosevear who you know married Freathy Rosevear' and 'sister of Cap'n Josiah Rosevear of Fraddon,' occurred. Byron knew little about the ramifications of his wife's family but, remembering Jim was a Rosevear, came to the conclusion he must be some sort of cousin.

"Mourner?" he said but less confidently, "well — —"

For all his wrath he must go gently. If he insulted Jim, if he uttered the words in his mind, "Well, relation or no, get out of my sight," he would offend Mrs. Andrew and who knew how many more.

Mrs. Tom, having disengaged herself from the Sowdens, came to the rescue. She had had no suspicion that Jim would stand on his rights and come to the funeral. These young people, the folly of them!

"Why, Gray, my dear, I've been expectin' you this long time. I'm so glad you're 'ere," and, placing herself between man and maid, she walked away with them.

When they reached the Big Parlour, however, she turned on the young man. "You ought not to 'ave come."

In Jim's eye was a dancing light. "Why couldn't I come? I 'bain't afraid of'n!"

"No," she retorted, "but this 'edn't a time for stirrin' up strife. You knaw 'e won't touch yer to-day."

"I'll give 'im the chance when they'm all gone if 'e like."

"Don't 'ee talk so fulish," and she thought with satisfaction that the young people would soon be on the road to Plymouth, out of harm's way. "You must think of Gray now. You men are so pig-'eaded as a cock in a fowls' pen."

Gray, who had fallen behind her mother, came up.

"You can settle with Uncle Leadville when we're back home," she said, with a little air of matronly authority which sat sweetly on her young face and which changed to a softer emotion the challenge in Jim's eyes.

"Must I now?" he said, bending over her.

"I don't want to go to Plymouth with no black eyes then," she answered poutingly.

"I'll leave old chap till after we've 'ad our..." his voice sank to a murmur and he led her away up the room, to a corner which the light from the deep-set windows hardly reached. For all the help that either would be, Mrs. Tom might as well have been without them. She smiled the realization of this to Richbell and the two, understanding that it rested with them to make good the deficiency, fell to work. The room was filling quickly and they were needed to cut beef and ham, fill cups from the big old-fashioned teapots and hand plates. Busy though she was, however, Mrs. Tom had a thought to spare for individual needs. Constantine Rosevear had entered in the wake of his three sons and was sitting under the window, staring into his hat. She thought he looked far from well. The little network of red in his cheeks had a purplish tinge and the light blue eyes had lost colour.

"'E's takin' it 'ard," she thought and went up to him.

"You'll 'av a bit o' dinner, Conny, won't yer?"

He shook his head. "'Twould choke me if I did."

"Oh, do 'ee try to eat a little bit." Con's feelings towards his cousin had always been for her an open book. After Sabina's accident, the miller had ceased coming to Wastralls; and Mrs. Tom had understood that this was not due to indifference but oversensitiveness. He could not endure to see the woman, whose strength and vitality he had all his life admired, reduced to helplessness.

"'Tis a long time," said Mrs. Tom sadly, "since you 'ad anything ter eat in this 'ouse."

He sighed. "It's been a very sad 'ouse since 'er accident."

"I'm sure 'twould be 'er wish for yer to 'av something."

"I knaw. She was very kind." Many a piece of well-paid work had come to him through Sabina but he was thinking of the woman herself. He was not an introspective man. He could not have explained even to himself, why the death of a person whom he rarely saw, should make so great a difference. "She was very kind," he repeated heavily, "but I don't want anything."

His three tall sons were at the table helping themselves; his wife, almost tidy for once in her new black—trust Betsy to have nothing put away for an occasion like the present—was talking to her brother, Mr. John Brenton of St. Eval. They looked pleased with themselves and fate; but the big miller, for all his comfortable girth and good broadcloth, was as one who had lost his grip.

Mrs. Tom, obliged by her hospitable duties to leave him for a little, carved and served and talked with the thought of him foremost in her mind. She was listening for a certain expected sound and, though her hearing was a little dulled, she did not miss it. The bearers, waiting in the kitchen, had been fed on simpler fare than that provided for the mourners. They were ready now and the irregular tramp of feet along the passage told her that they were coming to take up their burden. She went back to Con, for she could no longer trust herself to speak. The back of her throat ached with the tears she was trying to restrain. Sabina had been born in Wastralls, she had lived there all her days and now she was to be carried out. Con, too, felt the full poignancy of the moment. His eye met Mrs. Tom's a little wildly and he pulled at his neckcloth to loosen it. Sabina's place would know her no more. She was going and never would she come back to them. His heart was a wordless protest. He rose unsteadily and the two, the man who loved her, the woman who had been her friend, went into the hall.

At a Cornish funeral it is customary for the relatives to follow the coffin — which is carried on poles by eight bearers — in a certain order. Precedence is regulated by the degree of kinship and, to a certain extent, by age. With the exception of old folks who, unable to walk so far, follow in their gigs and carts, the mourners traverse the distance from house to graveyard on foot. The arrangement of these couples, with due regard to their individual claims, is a work requiring knowledge of the family ramifications and in this Tom Rosevear shone.

When his wife, followed by Con, came out she found the work of assigning their positions to the mourners was nearly finished. Couples lined one side of the hall and yet others were waiting in the Little Parlour. An air of sombre readiness pervaded the gathering. Henwood, carrying the black crickets on which the coffin was to stand, hurried out of the door. He planted them on a level space, the space which had been used for that purpose since death first recognized that Wastralls had become a human habitation. At a sign from her husband, Mrs. Tom went to the head of the procession. As Sabina's nearest relative it was her place to walk with Byron.

The door of the justice-room opened and the hinds, in dark suits and black ties, came out. The poles, which they held against their breasts, were slanted to allow for the narrowness of the opening and their faces wore a look of purpose. They were anxious to get the varnished and glittering coffin out of the room, round corners and through the hall, without hitch or stumble and the task seemed to them bristling with difficulties. They were thinking, not of what this long brightly decorated box contained but of the trust reposed in them.

Mrs. Tom pulled down her veil and, for a moment, leaned her weight on Constantine. To see Sabina carried feet foremost over the threshold of her home was too much for her powers of self-control and, behind the veil, her tears were flowing. Con, understanding but inarticulate, pressed her arm. They two were the real mourners; of all that concourse they alone would miss Sabina out of their daily lives. As the coffin was earned past, a shiver ran through the man's large body. With Sabina gone he, too, was in sight of the end. A week ago the thought would have troubled him but to it he was now indifferent. So does life, taking one by one the things we value, make us ready for its own putting off.

The bearers—and the sexton, once bullockman at Wastralls, was of their number—set the coffin down on the black crickets. Behind them the queue of mourners was receiving belated additions. Leadville had taken his place beside Mrs. Tom, her husband was behind him with Betsy, Constantine with Gray.

The day was calm with a tang of cold, a day when the gulls gathered in the new-ploughed fields and, the sea being still, the murmur of other waters could be heard. As the coffin was carried down the avenue under the low wind-bent branches, the sexton started a hymn. Many present being choir members, it was taken up at once and a volume of tuneful sound went before the procession up the lane.

Sleep on beloved, sleep and take thy rest,
Lay down thy head upon thy Saviour's breast;
I love thee well, but Jesus loves thee best—
Good night, good night, good night.

Mrs. Tom had walked in many a similar procession. Only that summer she had followed a brother to the grave and now, in obedience to Henwood's signal, she moved forward after the bearers. She was at the moment too much occupied with herself to realize that the long line was actually on its way. Once in the open air, however, and the chill freshness of the morning had its usual effect and, by the time the head of the black serpent was pushing past St. Cadic, she was sufficiently recovered to spare glance and thought—neither at all kindly—for the man keeping step with her.

For Byron the morning had been chequered. Some of the mourners, in particular those from a distance, had met him with an assumption of friendliness. Though a stranger he was now the owner of Wastralls and, in that capacity, they would meet him in the market-place and on public business. One or two of the wives expressed the hope that he would look in when passing. He was not only a substantial farmer but a widower and, on the whole, a man who filled the eye. Even Mrs. Tom, embittered and

grudging, could not deny that at the head of the procession he looked well. By no means the tallest man present, his heavy dignified carriage made him appear bigger than he actually was. He walked, too, with a certain arrogance. The men who followed him were mentally lesser men and he was conscious of it. He was leading the way, was for the first time in his proper place. The errand on which he was bound did not occupy his attention. The coffin, when it passed him in the hall, had roused in him a queer inexplicable emotion, a fleeting sense of association, but not because of what it contained. Of Sabina he scarcely thought. She belonged to the past, that past on which he had definitely and thankfully turned his back. His face was towards the future, his mind was crowded with the brick and scaffolding of the edifice he hoped to rear; and he found in his breast such a consciousness of power that he was fain to give it expression by joining in the hymn.

"I love thee well, but Jesus loves thee best," he rumbled in his deep voice and Mrs. Tom, hearing him, stared. To her it was as if he were uttering blasphemies.

"The shirkin' old villain," she thought indignantly, "walkin' there as 'e belong to walk. I dunno 'ow 'e dare. Actually singin' in the hymn too, the two-faced dragon. 'Tis enough to bring a judgment on 'im, so it is."

Winding out of the valley between hedges which, though it was December, were still green, the procession came at last to Hilltop. Here the road made a wide bend. The grey tower of the church was in sight and the sexton, in order to toll the bell, took a short cut across the fields. Mrs. Byron, though a chapel-goer would be buried by the parson of the parish, laid beside Old Squire in the shadow of the church. To the people this ritual, which for them had lost its potency, was still part of the established order. The rector was appointed by powers outside their knowledge and had his place. They neither welcomed nor objected to him. He served his purpose.

Seen from above, the churchyard must have looked like a shallow vessel filling with ink. So numerous were the mourners that, after crowding the little old edifice to overflowing, they poured down the paths and over the grassy mounds. About the Rosevear graves the couples and groups had solidified into a mass. Their faces, like pink disks in a dark setting, were shadowed by their veils and their black headgear. They had turned towards the pit which had been digged; and the minds of all were occupied with thoughts, not of the resurrection but of the dampness and coldness of the body's last resting-place. Down in the earth, pressed down by a weight of mould and stones, shut away for ever from the fires and talk! During the night rain had fallen and the water had not yet soaked away through the

stiff clay of the grave. It lay, covering the bottom, an inexpressibly dreary adjunct to the grey sides and crumbling verge. The mourners' hearts vibrated with pity for the woman who had looked her last on friendly faces, who was on her way to lie, rain-water below, saturated clods above, in the chill unfriendly bosom of the earth. When the coffin was brought out and 'Peace, Perfect Peace' was raised, they joined in with a sense of relief. It could not be that the Mrs. Byron, whom they all knew, was to lie there in the wet and the dark. With an optimism as indestructible, as logical, as hers had been, they promised themselves and her, not death but life.

As the signal was given to lower the coffin into the grave, out of the clouded sky fell a quavering dazzle of sunlight, omen to these heavy anxious hearts of better times in store. It fell on the brass handles, the name-plate, and the two curving rows of cut clasps, scintillating from the bright surfaces in a myriad tiny glints. Byron, standing between Tom and Constantine Rosevear at the head of the grave, noticed it, as did the others; and to him it was not only sunshine falling unexpectedly on a coffin but something personal to himself.

He had gone mechanically through the service, had glanced with disfavour at the wreaths and harps and other floral sacrifices, had even in his heart made ribald comment on 'Peace, Perfect Peace, with loved ones far away.' The mood of exultation in which he had left Wastralls had changed to one of slowly mounting irritation. This burying was after all a tedious business. The creak and strain of the ropes which indicated that the coffin was being let down drew from him a sigh of relief. In another minute he would be able to turn his back on this place of sepulture.

The flash of sunlight, however, had caught his eye and had done more than that. Its transient gleam had linked the fleeting sense of familiarity he had felt, when the coffin had been carried past him out of Wastralls, with other moments strung bead-like on the past. This was the shape, those the infinitesimal glimmers, which he had seen in visions. Again and again he had heard the hammer at work, seen the glint of polished wood, the curve of the cut clasps. The lid of Sabina's coffin! For years his dim familiar, it was now actual and present. He shivered as if a breath laden with the odours, the dank chill of the grave, had risen from its depths. That hammering—but it was not he who had knocked in nail after nail.

Byron forgot, in sudden curiosity, that curiosity with which the vision always inspired him, where he was and what he was doing. He must find out whether the lines had been completed to the last nail. Something of peculiar importance hung on this fact.

Con Rosevear, having moved a little, was now between him and the grave and, in the dark oblong, the coffin was sinking out of sight. A moment more and it would be too late. With one of the movements which, in a man of his age and bulk were so surprisingly quick, Byron thrust the other aside. The sun gleam had faded, the shadows of the wintry afternoon, the shadows of the pit were closing over the coffin. Byron, on the grassy verge, leaned forward in a perilous attempt to see and, to the bystanders, it seemed as if the man, driven crazy by grief, were about to throw himself into the grave. An emotional race, they were prepared for such manifestations but, even as they closed with Leadville, to pull him back into safety, they were conscious of surprise, of a new almost grudged respect. They had not thought him fond of his wife.

The sudden jerking of his arms, under the clutch of well-meaning but mistaken fingers, prevented Byron from satisfying himself as to whether the nails were all in place. This matter of the last nail had on a sudden assumed a terrible importance. If it had been hammered home he would be delivered from the obsession of this coffin which for so long he had seen in preparation. In the making of it he had had no part—and that was strange! Yes, all things considered it was very strange. He had never been able to think of his vision as an illusion. It was real and tangible but in some curious way out of reach. Now he had chanced upon it. Chance? He had been walking towards it all the time! He must know, however, whether the circles were complete, whether that last nail...

He flung off the arresting hands and made a further effort to see, but those busy with the ropes were using greater dispatch and others were thrusting themselves between the graveside and the man. His strength not being as the strength of ten he was forced to desist. Panting and wild-eyed, he stood debating with himself whether he would not make one more effort when Mrs. Tom, calling to him from behind, caught his attention.

"Come now," she said, thinking he must have been moved to this exhibition of feeling by a late remorse. "S'bina's gone and all the cryin' and grievin' in the world'll never get 'er back."

"S'bina?" he echoed and the eagerness faded from his face, leaving it curiously grey. "I wanted to see——"

He had turned his back on the grave and she noticed that his manner was preoccupied. "I wanted to make sure. Was..." he scanned her face with eyes which, as she said afterwards, should have warned her, "was the nails all drived in?"

"The nails?" repeated Mrs. Tom, wondering what he meant but anxious to humour him. "What be tellin' about? Of course they was drived in?" Did he think Sabina had not been properly screwed down?

Drawing her out of the wondering group he bent to her ear. "They never was all drived in before," he confided and looked at her inquiringly. He had failed to see but she, yes, she might have been more fortunate.

"Well, they are now, I knaw."

She spoke so confidently that he was convinced. "'Tis a good job then."

"Iss."

"If they'm drived in to the last one I shall never 'ear that 'ammerin' again."

"No," she said, "of course you won't."

He gave her a sidelong considering glance. "Did you 'ear it?"

She was still thinking of the screws. "No," she said with a shiver of distress. "I wasn't near enough. I—I was in the Big Parlour. But come on now, 'tis time for us to be goin' 'ome. They're fullin' in the grave."

He turned for a last longing look. "I should like to 'av seen for myself," he said grudgingly. He had forgotten why he was in the churchyard by an open grave, forgotten who lay in its depths, forgotten everything but the question as to whether the curving rows of cut clasps were complete to the last nail. The stones and clods were being shovelled on to the coffin, obliterating for ever the trifling handiwork of man, surrendering what could not be withheld. With a sigh of dissatisfaction, Leadville turned and, walking out of the churchyard, took the homeward road.

# CHAPTER XXIII

On the opposite side of the road through Church Town was a little tavern, the only one in the parish at which spirits could be obtained. By this, drawn up and waiting, were a number of conveyances and, among them, the Wastralls cart. 'Uncle George,' more familiar than Byron with the routine of a funeral, had driven to meet him. The farmer, striding by, would have passed unseeing, but the old man stepped into the road.

"I be come for 'ee, maister."

For a moment, Byron gazed at the figure confronting him as if it were that of a stranger, then the mists cleared. He glanced round as if awakening from a dream and, climbing into the cart, took the reins. The experiences of the day, the unwonted crowd, the publicity, the return of the old obsession, had been fatiguing, and he was glad to ride. As he jogged along, letting Lady go as she pleased, his thoughts ran before him and he saw the evening as a time of blessed peace. These gigs and carts with which the road was thronged, these black-clad people, would then be gone and he would have the place to himself. Many of the mourners had, indeed, turned in the direction of their distant homes and, when he reached Towan Lane, yet others shouted a Good night but a goodly number were returning to Wastralls.

Those on foot had horses to 'tackle up' and men were waiting in the yard to help them. When Byron reached the gate, he remembered that he had a last duty to perform. He was tired of the people, he wished they would go home but he must not spoil the good impression he hoped he had made.

"You'd better come in, all of 'ee," he said in a tone of would-be heartiness, "and 'av a cup of tea."

A few refused, alleging the distance they had to go, but others and, among them, Sabina's nearest relatives, accepted the invitation. Between the hedges the afternoon air had been stagnantly warm but a sea-breeze was sweeping through the leafless boughs of the elms and its breath was cold. Gray Rosevear, walking demurely at her father's side, drew the open sides of her coat together and, with her little gloved hands, began to fasten them. She, too, wished the day over. For her it had been a long dreariness shot with unpleasant imaginings. Simple and devoted, caring for little but

her home and the home-circle, her aunt's death was the first trouble she had known. Jim and her relationship to him, though they had unsealed a fount of deep emotion, though they possessed her to the exclusion of most other interests, had not influenced Sabina's claim. The last rosebud, the first snowdrops of Hember, had been laid by the weeping girl in her aunt's dead hand and, every year, faithful affection would place a similar offering on the mould that covered her. Gray would not forget and, when her children came, she would plant in their young memories the tradition of the splendid woman. She, herself, was of those who build a fire on the domestic altar, who keep it burning for the warmth and comfort and betterment of all who come within reach of its beams but who find no historian.

Let in over the door of Wastralls was a brown stone. On this had been cut a shield bearing the Rosevear arms. The winds of over a hundred years had breathed on this stone, crumbling the edges, smoothing the sharp surfaces. The charges were now nearly obliterated and Gray, glancing up as she walked towards the door, felt a twinge of regret. Wastralls, more than either Hember or St. Cadic, was the Rosevear home and now it would belong to Uncle Leadville. She did not, being so tender a little soul, actually grudge him the inheritance; but she felt sorry some arrangement could not have been made which would have left a Rosevear in possession. Jim, of course, if any relation, was a very distant one but there were her Uncle Con's boys. Tremain, the youngest, had thoughts of Canada. It would have been better if he could have remained at home and Uncle Leadville gone, oh, very much better.

Byron, leading the way up the drive, wondered whether Mrs. Bate would have the tea in readiness. He wanted to see the back of his guests, to be alone; and it was with a feeling of annoyance that he caught sight of an individual in parley at the open door. The stranger wore town clothes and was a tall thin man with reddish hair. Byron, supposing him to be a relative who, by mischance of travelling, had arrived too late, held out his hand. "'Oo be you?" said he, downright but friendly.

"Mr. Criddle," answered the stranger in a matter-of-fact tone, "of Messrs. Criddle and Nancarrow, of Wadebridge."

The name left Byron unenlightened. The ground was thick with Criddles but he had never heard they were related to the Rosevears. He began to think the man must have come on business, must be a traveller for machinery, or patent medicine, or manures.

"We've 'ad rather a busy day," he said, determining to get rid of him as soon as possible.

"So I understand," returned Mr. Criddle. "The news only reached me this morning, or I should have been over earlier; but there were arrangements to be made before I could leave."

Behind Byron, the mourners had been dragging wearily up the slope. To some of them, however, Criddle of Messrs. Criddle and Nancarrow, was a familiar figure; and his presence, promising fresh developments on a day which had been tame for lack of them, proved stimulating. Bent backs straightened and men quickened their steps, those who recognized Criddle giving whispered information to those with whom they walked. Byron, more mystified than ever, spoke with a touch of impatience. "Well, I'm sorry, but you must excuse me to-day."

Mr. Criddle's smile was reflected on the faces about. "I have brought the late Mrs. Byron's will," he explained.

Leadville could not have been more taken aback. For years, afraid lest his wife might make a will—not inimical to him, she loved him too well for that—but with provisions of which he might not altogether approve, he had kept a watch on her movements and, more particularly, on the trend of her thoughts. Once or twice, sounding her, he had said they ought to put their wishes into writing but she had shaken her bright head with "Time enough yet." He could have sworn he knew her simple mind from end to end and that, living from day to day, she had not troubled about the future.

"Her will?" he cried, bluffly incredulous. "She never made none."

"While Mrs. Byron was at the hospital she sent for me and had her will drawn up."

"She was too ill to 'tend to any wills."

"At first, yes."

Byron's incredulity was shaken. Believing Sabina too far on her way to the next world to have a thought for this, he had relaxed his watch. Had she taken advantage of his absence? He hesitated and, in smooth tones, the lawyer explained. "When she was getting better she sent for me, made her will and"—he tapped his pocket—"left it in my care."

The statement carried conviction. Byron could not but admit that, with regard to this will-making, Sabina had acted after her usual fashion. Once she saw the necessity for action she lost no time and, with her, 'eaten meat' was soon forgotten. Had her husband been at hand she would as a matter of course have told him of her intentions. He cursed the folly that had kept him away. "I think she ought to have let me knaw," he said uneasily. In her weak state of health, how was it likely she would be able to frame a sensible will?

Mr. Criddle was in a hurry. The train service between Wadebridge and Stowe was inadequate and, unless he used dispatch he might lose the last train. Drawing from his pocket a long blue-grey paper he glanced at the people waiting about. "No doubt the relatives of the late Mrs. Byron will wish to hear the will read."

On the document in plain black print was "Will of Mrs. Sabina Byron," and these words, pregnant with unknown far-reaching possibilities, sent a thrill through those present. Of all who had attended the funeral, these were the privileged, they were to have a first-hand knowledge of the provisions of Sabina's will and, if there should be dramatic developments, they would be on the spot. Leadville, looking to them for sympathy with him in his uneasiness, saw on their faces only curiosity and realized that they were indeed 'the relatives of the late Mrs. Byron.'

"You better come in 'ere," he said and led the way through the house. In the Big Parlour Sabina's most cherished possessions, porcelain painted by a Chinese hand which had long since lost its cunning, lacquer which has accompanied it overseas, old Georgian silver, dark above fine damask, had been set out; but Byron ignored the invitation of the open door. "There'll be more room out here in the kitchen," he said.

In placing themselves about the wide low room, it was noticeable that the mourners seated themselves in accordance with their standing and expectations. Byron, with a sharp assumption of ownership, placed Old Squire's chair at the head of the table and sat in it. Tom and Constantine Rosevear took the chairs on each side of him and Mr. Criddle sat at the end. Between them were the substantial farmers who had married Rosevear connexions or were themselves cousins, such men as old Sowden, John Jacka of Forth Dennis, Solomon Old, Tom Trebilcock. A group of young people. Con's three sons, the Hember girls and Hilda Trudgian, were clustered about the window-bench; while the older women, veils up and cloaks unfastened, sat by the fire.

In the hush of strained attention, the unfolding of the blue-grey paper made a sharp whisper of sound. "This is the last Will and Testament of me, Sabina Byron of Wastralls, Tregols Parish, in the Duchy of Cornwall, the wife of Leadville Byron."

After a few words of preamble came the first bequest. "I give, devise and bequeath to my dear husband, the said Leadville Byron, my property in trust securities, the income thereof to be paid to him during his life and, after his decease, to be divided between the children then living of my cousins Thomas Freathy Rosevear of Hember and Sydney Constantine Rosevear of St. Cadic in equal shares.

"The money on deposit at the bank and the balance standing in my name, I leave to the said Leadville Byron."

As he gathered the sense of these provisions, Leadville nodded a qualified approval. He and his wife, having lived well within their income, it was only right he should be left the money he had helped to save. He should, he thought, have been left the capital too but his main concern was with the ready money lying at the bank. He would need it to initiate the changes of which for so long he had dreamed and, while one tract of his mind was attending closely to the reading, another beheld the vision of an accomplished hope, the fields of Wastralls under intensive culture, the motors carrying produce to Truro, to Plymouth and yet farther afield, the steamers bearing it up the coast to Cardiff and other hungry towns. A dock could be blasted out of Morwen Cove, a stone quay built and, behind it, a row of up-to-date cottages. In a few years, with his energy, his ideas, he would have amassed capital—all the capital he needed.

"What money 'as she left then, sir?"

When Mr. Criddle moved, his linen made a rustling sound which was suggestive of withered leaves and this suggestion was carried further by his dry appearance and wooden gesture. Laying down the will, he looked over the top of his glasses at the inquirer and embarked on a statement.

"The late Mr. Freathy Rosevear, Mrs. Byron's grandfather, invested money in mines. For a time this investment was shaky and unsaleable but it recovered and is now paying a good dividend. As you are already aware, her father did not leave her much beyond the house and land. Since the property has been in her hands it has increased in value and the savings have been considerable. Altogether the income of about twelve thousand pounds, well invested, will come to you."

"And the money in the bank?"

"I inquired this morning." He consulted a notebook in which various sets of figures were entered. "Ah, yes, here it is. The late Mrs. Byron had three hundred pounds on deposit and a balance of a hundred and ninety pounds, eighteen shillings and tenpence."

Again Byron nodded but this time his satisfaction was unalloyed. Though his wife had always given him what he required he had not had any considerable sums at his disposal; and to find himself in possession of nearly five hundred pounds, to spend as he chose, also a regular income of about the same amount, gave him a feeling of opulence. Sabina, generous with her pence, had been reserved as to the sum total of her property. He had not guessed her savings to be so large.

The lawyer read on. A few small legacies were left to relatives—to Mrs. Isolda Rosevear, the linen in the big chest: to Constantine, the horse Sabina had been wont to ride about her fields: to the men who had been in her employment ten years, the sum of fifty pounds each; to those more newly come, a pound for each year of their service. Byron listened without heeding. With hands thrust deeply into his trousers pockets, with head sunk between his shoulders, he was awaiting the moment when the land— Wastralls itself—should be declared his and he could face this concourse of alien faintly hostile people with the accomplished fact. What did it matter who had the big strawberry roan that was eating his head off in the stable, or what became of a few sheets and table-cloths? He cared for nothing but the land, the five hundred acres which had been his, yet not his, for so long. The will would set all doubt as to its ownership at rest. Sabina had, after all, been wise to set her wishes down in black and white.

"The land, house and hereditaments of Wastralls," began the lawyer in his dry voice, each word clipped of sound and the whole giving the effect of a well-kept but withered hedge.

In his big chair at the head of the table Leadville stirred slightly, clenching his hands. At last!

"I will devise and bequeath the land house and hereditaments of Wastralls to my cousin, Gray Rosevear."

The up-turned attentive faces about the table, expressed for a moment only intense surprise. Leadville, leaning forward, made a husky hesitating sound—"What?"

In his precise voice, the lawyer re-read the bequest and about his words, as the information sank into people's minds, rose a little whisper of astonished comment.

"Gray?"

"Did 'ee ever 'ear the like?"

"Some's born lucky!"

"Well, Gray now."

A chair went over with a sudden crash and Leadville was on his feet. Before the slower-witted men had realized his purpose he had crossed the room, snatched the will out of Criddle's hand and, scattering the women, was at the fire. He meant to destroy it, to press it down among the logs, to hold it until it was burned to ashes. Flinging it on the wood, he glanced round for the poker but the Rosevears had begun to recover from the stupefaction into which his reckless action had thrown them. Tom had the lean strength

of whipcord and Con that of a bull. As they closed with Byron, bearing him away from the fire, Mrs. Tom snatched up the paper and, pressing out the flame, ran back with it out of harm's way.

"I'm afeared 'tis a good bit burned," she said as she returned it to the lawyer but that individual looked at her calmly over the tops of his glasses.

"This is only a copy, Mrs. Rosevear. The will is in my safe at home."

His voice carried, and in spite of the general confusion, men smiled to themselves. Cunning chaps, these lawyers, up to snuff. Tom Rosevear, wiping a heated face, picked up Old Squire's chair and put it back at the head of the table. For the moment, with devils tearing at his heart, Byron stood in their midst, then, sullenly, he resumed his seat. Two heads could be knocked together but there were a dozen men in the room. Except for the relief to his feelings what would a fight advantage him? Moreover, as he had failed to burn the will, as in fact the will was not there to be burnt, he must take other measures. "She've left the land to me," he asserted violently.

At the time he drew up the will, Mr. Criddle had pointed out to his client that her husband might feel aggrieved at being passed over and she had given him her reasons for leaving Wastralls to a Rosevear. He had them in readiness.

"She made what she considered a proper provision for you, Mr. Byron, when she left you the money."

"Provision? Don't want none o' that. 'Tis the land I want."

"I understood from my client that you had never done any farming."

"Never 'ad the chance."

Mr. Criddle's sandy brows went up in expostulation. "Mrs. Byron told me you had been a sailor and that, after her marriage with you, she had suggested your renting land but that you had refused. I understood her to say she had even been willing to sink capital in buying some but you impressed her as not wishing to take the responsibility."

"She told you so?" began Byron and choked over the words. His tongue was not glib, he could not explain that he had been misrepresented and this inability, giving him a feeling of helplessness before this man of words, abated the violence of his mood. "A damned lie," he muttered, "a damned lie!"

From the group of women about the hearth, a voice cut into the discussion. "She thought," said Mrs. Tom, moved by her secret knowledge to a bitter word, "as she'd maybe live as long as 'er 'usband."

Mr. Criddle accepted this contribution with a little bend of the head. "She did. She said as much. She thought if she should predecease Mr. Byron he would, by that time, be too old to start farming on his own account."

Byron brushed this aside as irrelevant. He was becoming gradually conscious of meshes about his feet—meshes from which, however, he still thought he could escape. "But," he said and he believed it, "she can't leave the land to any one else, what's 'ers is mine."

"The law gives women the right to dispose of their property," returned the lawyer patiently. His mind was divided between Byron and the clock. A few minutes more and, if he were not to miss the train, he must start on the drive back.

"You don't mean," Byron was aghast but incredulous, "that the law gives 'er the right to leave the land away from me?"

"It does."

"The missus could do as she liked with the land?" began the unhappy man and there was such poignant anxiety in his tones that, even Mrs. Tom, angry and embittered, felt a qualm of pity. 'Poor old toad, too, he was taking it hard!'

"Yes!"

Sabina had had the power and she had used it, used it simply and without heart-searchings or artifice. The world was turning round with him, but he still had his hands on that which he had taken. In spite of will and lawyer he would hold to it. He felt that nothing could relax his grip, that the land was his from now on until time should make him more intimately a part of it, yet something was slipping from him—slipping——

He looked from face to face along the sides of the table, from Con, heavy and ruminative, to Beulah Sowden, whose glassy eyes stared unresponsive as ever and so to Tom Rosevear. The day was being driven out by the shadow hosts of evening but the faces were still distinct. The unhappy man searched them with the old, desperate, 'Who is on my side, who?'

"What good," said he in an urgent troubling voice, "what good would Wastralls be to Gray—a young maid?"

Being farmers all, their prejudices, their outlook, would put them against the will. They could not approve of land being left to a woman. Anything else but not land. Byron thought that with them to back him he might force the lawyer-fellow to see reason. After all, it was the men of the community who made the law and, if these would give it as their opinion that the will was unjust, was unnatural, it might be upset.

To a man, those to whom he made his appeal, were kind of heart. They were sorry for Byron. They would have been sorry for any one who stood to lose a fair farm, for any one whose hopes had been disappointed. They agreed, too, that it was a pity the land should have been left to a maid. Where they joined issue with Byron was in the universal feeling that the land belonged to Rosevears. Anything was better than that it should go out of the family. They would not help him to get the will upset. On the contrary.

The failure of his appeal sent a gust of fury through Byron. They would see him wronged and not lift a hand to prevent it? What matter? He would have it in spite of them. "The land's mine," he blazed and brought his fist down on the table, with a thump that jarred from every loose surface a protesting sound and threatened to split the thick wood. "'Tis mine and by 'itch or by crook I'll 'av it. A mistake's been made and—" he flung down the gage, "you do all knaw it 'as, but we'll 'av it put right."

The other men looked to Mr. Criddle for direction.

"I'm sorry," the lawyer said in his unimpassioned way, "that you should be disappointed, but the intention was clear and the will is properly executed. You will be only wasting time and money if you try to upset it."

Byron's mind was moving quickly. "The missus thought I should be old by the time she was taken," he argued. "I bain't old, I'm so young as any. There isn't a man 'ere can put it across me."

Into this atmosphere, already full of conflicting thought, of possibilities more ominous than any there suspected, Mrs. Tom threw a barbed and poisoned phrase. "S'bina 'ad no thought of dyin' and you knaw, Leadville, that she 'adn't."

He turned at the words. The corner by the hearth was growing dark but the firelight revealed a face here and another there. Mrs. Tom was on the outskirts of the group and in her accusing eyes and on her pale features was a writing Byron could and, for all his unwillingness, must read. Mrs. Tom was telling him that his secret was known to her and that in the provisions of the will she recognized the truth of her Tom's words. That for which Leadville had schemed and done evil, that was what, to the upholding of righteousness, he was to lose.

But the man was not yet broken to the acceptance of his fate. Mrs. Tom might suspect, she could not know. He turned to the lawyer with a movement that suggested the flicking off of a troublesome fly.

"I don't believe," he said, "that missus would leave it to Gray. She wouldn't do such a thing. How could she take Wastralls from me when I bin 'ere all me life? You've made the will out wrong."

As far as Mr. Criddle's experience went, a last will and testament never satisfied the survivors. It was unfortunate that Mrs. Byron's should have come into operation while her husband was still a comparatively young man; but, after all, he had the money and there were more farms than those in Trevorrick. To the poignant aspect of the matter he was blind.

"Mrs. Byron was quite clear on the point, in fact though she did not insist on it she told me she hoped that, when Miss Gray married, she would not change her name. Being Rosevear land, Mrs. Byron felt that Wastralls should belong to a Rosevear."

The younger people, grouped on and about the bench, whispered among themselves but Byron's voice overrode their murmurs. "I could call myself Rosevear," he offered eagerly, "the name's nothing."

"You 'aven't a name of your own, Mr. Byron," said Con in his slow heavy fashion, "and one name's so well as another to you."

"Iss," agreed the other impatiently, "a man's the same, whether 'e got one name as another."

"Those are the provisions of the will," continued Mr. Criddle, ignoring the suggestion. In his clipped voice he read to the end. Gray was left residuary legatee and Thomas Freathy Rosevear and Sydney Constantine Rosevear were to be the executors. "And lastly I revoke all former wills made by me, in witness whereof I have hereunto set my hand."

# CHAPTER XXIV

The lawyer, pressed for time, hurried over his farewells and, going out, pulled the door to behind him. The faulty latch failing to hold, the door swung back to fall with a little jingling clash against the post and this irritating sound, metallic and irregular, alone broke the hush of expectation that, with Mr. Criddle's departure, had fallen on the room.

His withdrawal, freeing this large family from the observation of a stranger, took from the members of it any self-consciousness they may have felt; and enabled them to give their whole attention to what was passing, to centre it, in fact, on Byron, on this man who, like a widow, was not to inherit the property but to be pensioned off with an annuity! The women about the hearth, the young people on the window-bench, the men at the table, all were wondering what Byron would say and do, whether, indeed, he quite understood.

He sat before them, with his broad shoulders hunched and a hand over his eyes, withdrawn and, though one of a crowd, solitary. Behind him rose the polished back of the old chair. He had placed it at the head of the table. He had sat in it to emphasize the fact of his ownership and there were those present who thought he had, by so doing, brought ill-luck on himself. He had stretched covetous hands to what Old Squire had set apart for his descendants and in his own way, at his own time, Old Squire, dead yet very much alive, had taken action. In the disposition of the property the people recognized his hand. Sabina had been the instrument of an older more imperious will. Rosevear land was for Rosevears. Those who had had it before this nameless wight came up out of the sea should keep it. Their grip was fixed on it, their roots went down to its rock foundations, they were of it, sprung from it, the living manifestations of it, while he—he who would have taken it from them—he was 'a foreigner.' He had no right, no part among them. As he was come, so would he go. The sea had spewed him up and in due time the earth would swallow him and the memory of him would perish.

The door banged at will, the latch catching and slipping like a nerveless hand. In the old chimneys of the old house, the drear December wind

whined and entreated; and first one person then another began to stir and whisper.

In their cramped quarters under the window, the young people were responding to the faint calls of everyday life. Conscious of tension, of a something in the atmosphere that threatened and insisted, they glanced anxiously at the door. Its foolish rattling indecision suggested to them that it was open, that they had only to get up, take a quick step or two and it would provide a way of escape. Something, perhaps an appeal to their emotions, more likely a dull discussion was pending; and they were impatient to breathe fresh air, indulge in a little chaff and sweethearting, get back to the normal. The troubles of their seniors, the dark incomprehensible tragedy of Byron, were beyond their understanding. They were glad when their mothers and aunts began to move, to speak in restrained tones, to whisper of Isolda's linen, of Con's red roan and of the fifty pounds that would fall to high-shouldered George Biddick, the good old hind who had been on the farm for so many years, all the working years of a life. As they talked they fastened cloaks and pulled down veils, beginning as it were to move and so setting an example the young folks would be glad to follow.

The miller had been sitting, solid and motionless, at Byron's right hand. As the women began their tentative movements, he rose, drew a deep breath of relief and drifted in Mrs. Tom's direction. She gave him a pleasant word. "The 'awse, that S'bina give you, Con, 'll 'av a good 'ome with you."

"She knawed I liked Prince," the other said heavily. His eyes had been resting on his three sons and he now uttered a plain thought.

"Pity Gray wadn't a boy, seems a pity for the farm to go to a maid, still S'bina bin fair enough." Tom was S'bina's next of kin, and in choosing his eldest child to inherit Wastralls she had acknowledged his claim. Con, thinking of his hearty lads, regretted, while accepting, her decision.

Mrs. Tom did not take offence. "Iss!" she sighed, voicing her one grievance against fate, "I only wished I 'ad a boy..."

The young folk were frankly a little envious of Gray's good fortune and Jim Rosevear who, having taken to heart Mrs. Tom's mild scolding was standing a little behind the St. Cadic men, stooped to the girl's ear with a congratulatory word. Her eyes, as she answered him, were full of tears.

"Dear auntie! I had no idea she was goin' to give me the farm. I feel I ought to have done more for her."

"My tender dear, you done all you could do."

Upon this simple talk, born of a general willingness to be accommodating, to live and let live, broke an arresting voice. The sense of

disaster, irremediable and dire, was slowly closing down on Byron; but, until he had done his utmost to escape, he would not admit he was in straits.

"I been thinkin'," he said, looking from Tom Rosevear to his cousin, "I been thinkin' if Gray 'as Wastralls p'raps she would like for me to stay on an' teel it for 'er. I've wanted the farm all along. I think 'tis very cruel to 'av it took away now; but—" he did not attempt to disguise his anxiety—"you can make it right for me if you like."

Tom had joined Constantine and, into the bearing of the two, though only so lately made executors, was crept a faint consciousness of their position. They had been placed in authority and they were used to wielding it. They stood together, listening gravely to the man's appeal, giving it, as far as appearances went, their consideration. In reality they were wondering how to avoid a direct refusal. That Byron should have set his heart on Wastralls seemed to them mere perversity. As well cry for the moon.

"I dunno," said Tom evasively. He did not want to hurt the man's feelings but he and Con had been put in charge of the property and were responsible to Sabina for its administration. "I dunno 'bout that. We shall 'av to think it over. What do you say, Constantine?"

"I think," said his more direct coadjutor, "I think the best way is to do as S'bina wished."

But Byron was unable to take a wrapped-up 'No' for an answer. "I was 'er 'usband," he pleaded and if he had addressed his words to the nether stone in St. Cadic Mill, they would have had as much effect. "I was 'er 'usband and I think she meant for me to 'av it, only there been a mistake made in the will."

Mrs. Tom who had been standing behind the two men took a step forward. "I know S'bina trusted you in everything——"

He caught at the words, turning eagerly, triumphantly on the executors. "There—I knaw she did."

"In everything else," pursued Mrs. Tom steadily, "besides Wastralls."

"Besides Wastralls?" he stammered.

"But that," and there was a note in her voice, a note of mingled grief and satisfaction which only Tom understood, "that, she said, you would never 'av."

Byron threw up his-hands in a wild gesture. "My good God! She must 'av been maäze or she wouldn't 'av done it. Surely you bain't goin' to let 'er fulish fancies take it away from me?"

Working adjacent farms, Sabina's cousins could not be blind to the fact that she and her husband had been at odds as to the management of Wastralls. They were, too, as averse to the changes he would have introduced as she could be. She had appointed them her executors. They would see her wishes were carried out. The disappointment to Byron, the crumbling of his hope, of something more intimate than hope, did not weigh with men intent on a plain duty.

Realizing that his appeal had as much effect on them as wind beating on a boulder, the other shifted his ground. As reasonable beings they must see he could be of use to them. "I'm here and I knaw every hitch and stitch of the place. Who'll take it on and work it for Gray? For certain she can't. She don't know a mangold from a turmit. She can't manage it by 'erself and 'er father can't do it. 'E got 'is own work to do."

The shadows had been encroaching and already it was growing difficult to distinguish one pale disk among the many faces from another. As Byron paused there was a movement among the young people and Jim Rosevear, bearing himself modestly, stepped up to the table.

"I reckon," he said, and the claim was put forward quietly and in a matter-of-fact voice, "I reckon I got the right now to work the land!"

Turning from the executors, Byron stared, speechlessly and in bewilderment, at the young man. To him, Jim was a hind whom he had lately dismissed and that he could be in any way concerned with Wastralls was impossible. Byron felt much as if a strange dog had found its way in at the door. "You?" he said. "What right 'av you to be 'ere? Didn't I tell yer, other day, to never put foot inside this 'ouse again?"

"Now then, now then!" interposed Constantine, big and authoritative as a London policeman. Those present felt he had the right to impose his will on them, that the ownership of Wastralls had passed from the one man to the other, that never more would Byron be in the position to drive out even a dog. "We'll 'av none of this, no quarrellin' 'ere."

Byron felt it, too, and his spirit revolted in a last frenzy of protest. He cursed Jim with a bitter concentrated curse but there was acceptance of his lot, of the calamity which had overtaken him, in the final, sullen, "Let'n clear out of this."

To Jim, as to the others, Byron was merely an angry, disappointed man. "The shoe's on the other foot," he cried, his spirits rising, the ready but provocative smile on his lips. "Come to that, 'tis for you to go, not me."

Byron swept out an annihilating arm. This gadfly, he would brush him off, silence him. "Cuss yer, get out of me sight."

But Jim, wheeling lightly, appealed to the executors. "I've a right to be 'ere?"

To Byron's confused surprise, Tom nodded briefly and Constantine, with a grunt of assent, admitted the claim. "What right 'av yer got then?" He realized that Jim must be settled with, before they could get back to the matter in hand—the farming of Wastralls. Byron still nursed a flicker of hope that he might be left as manager or bailiff, that this fate which was hovering would not be allowed to swoop.

Before Jim's light tongue could reel off the ready answer, Constantine interposed. "Let Gray speak," said he, probing among the shadows for his niece. "'Tis 'er land."

"Iss, come now, Gray," said her father encouragingly. "'Tis for you to say."

Never had Gray disputed her father's seldom-imposed will and now, though so reluctant that it seemed to her, her feet were leaden, she came to the table. Her heart was beating fast. The publicity, even this modified publicity of the family, was, to one of her retiring nature, very unwelcome; nevertheless she carried herself with a modest dignity. She had even a little air of confidence, as if in her bosom was a store of courage on which she could draw at will; and this confidence in one so timid, so unassuming, appeared as a grace. That day as, with colour in her cheeks and a steady light in her midnight eyes, Gray faced her redoubtable relative, she was at her finest and most desirable.

"Uncle Leadville," she began simply and the man shrank with a gesture of repudiation from the wounding title; but all her life he had been 'Uncle' to her and he would be so to the end. "Uncle Leadville, I'm sorry if what Aunt S'bina done is against your wish, but the land was hers and she could do what she liked with it. You know it has always belonged to her family and been worked, in the way that we are used to down here. I'm very sorry to go against you in anything but—" she paused and her serious steady gaze shifted from the dark face, watching her as a condemned man watches the sinking sun the night before he is shot, to Jim's blithe countenance; and, as it shifted, her eyes softened, filling with an expression no one in the room, not even Byron himself, could mistake, "but I think it's only right my husband should work the farm for me."

"My husband," Gray had said and when her voice ceased the words were still echoing through the room. They had fallen on Byron's ears, on his passionate craving heart as fall words of doom against which there is no appeal.

"Your 'usband?" he ejaculated but not because he had any doubt. We walk in twilight until light falls through a window and in that moment of revelation it did not need Gray's further words to enlighten him.

"We was married last Friday into Stowe."

To the Hember and St. Cadic Rosevears this was no news; but Mrs. Byron's death on the night of the wedding, the subsequent rush of work, the funeral, had prevented it from being bruited abroad. The more distant relatives looked at each other and at the young couple, surprised yet, on the whole, pleased. So Gray, sly puss, had picked her man and married him on the quiet. And who was he? Rosevear of Treketh's son. Not much money there but Mrs. Andrew of Gentle Jane was his auntie and very fond of him. Likely looking chap too! The maid had had her wits about her when she chose him; though, as things had turned out, she was more of a catch than he. And Sabina had probably known! She would be glad the maid was wedding a Rosevear, even though it was one of a different family. Well! well! They sent a sigh after vanished youth and prepared themselves to utter the kind commonplaces of congratulation. The connexion would be a satisfactory one. The young people would live in the old home and the Rosevear tradition be maintained. The hearts of the elders, accepting them as members of the family, blessed them to increase, a long line of stout descendants. The erratic genius, the Lucifer of a later day, was to be driven out that the old order might be continued, world without end. Amen.

Instinctively, though the words of congratulation were on their lips the people waited for Byron to take the initiative. They did not know what Gray's simple statement meant to him, had no suspicion that a dream-castle had been tumbled about his ears, the dream in which he had shrined hope and desire. Destroy these figments and you destroy the purpose of a life and, as a consequence, the will to live. Byron's dream had not been only of Gray, though she had been at the heart of it—the reddest hottest coal of the fire. He had dreamed too of his strength, that strength through which all else should be added unto him; and he was being gradually forced to see it as an illusion. Some one had been strong, but not he. Some one had given and withheld, had ordained what he should have, what he should go without, but it was not he. He thrust at the young people a question which seemed to them irrelevant.

"Did 'er knaw? Did S'bina knaw?"

That was the crucial point, the point by which his self-respect must stand or fall. Had Sabina done this thing or was it merely an unforeseen event?